THE BOOK OF SPIES

THE BOOK OF SPIES

AN ANTHOLOGY OF LITERARY ESPIONAGE

*Edited and with an Introduction
by Alan Furst*

THE MODERN LIBRARY

NEW YORK

LIBRARY OF CONGRESS CATALOGING-IN-PUBLICATION DATA
The book of spies : an anthology of literary espionage / edited and with an
introduction by Alan Furst.
p.   cm.
Contents: Eric Ambler, from A coffin for Dimitrios—Anthony Burgess, from
Tremor of intent—Joseph Conrad, from Under western eyes—Maxim Gorky,
from The spy—Graham Greene, from The quiet American—John le Carré,
from The Russia house—W. Somerset Maugham, from Ashenden—
Charles McCarry, from The tears of autumn—Baroness Orczy,
from The scarlet pimpernel—John Steinbeck, from The moon
is down—Rebecca West, from The birds fall down.
ISBN 0-679-64251-X
1. Spy stories, English.   I. Furst, Alan.
PR1309.S7 B66 2002
813'.54—dc21
2002067070

Modern Library website address: www.modernlibrary.com

2 4 6 8 9 7 5 3 1

Contents

2

Introduction

Alan Furst

"That is when this business was really amusing. After the War is over, we'll do some amusing secret service work together. It's capital sport!"

The speaker is Captain Sir Mansfield Smith-Cumming, known only as "C," head of the British Secret Intelligence Service. His potential partner in the capital sport is Compton Mackenzie, soon to be director of Britain's Aegean Intelligence Service. The war is the First World War, and the time he refers to was the era of the Great Game, played by secret agents of the British and Russian empires as they struggled for dominance in Afghanistan and central Asia.

Ian Fleming took Mansfield Smith-Cumming's "C" and, tongue in cheek, made it "M" in his James Bond novels. Compton Mackenzie repeated the above quote in a book called *Greek Memories,* ran afoul of the Official Secrets Act—the book was withdrawn, then reissued with material deleted—and was so angry he wrote a furious satire of the Secret Intelligence Service called *Water on the Brain.* And the Great Game, with tales of heroes and scoundrels and dark deeds, gave birth to the contemporary spy novel.

Spying went on long before the Great Game, of course—Moses, in the Old Testament, famously sent men "to spy out the land of Canaan," to "see what the land is like, and whether the people who live in it are strong or weak," and the trade has long been called "the second-oldest profession." But I've chosen to represent the origins of the genre with Baroness Orczy's *The Scarlet Pimpernel*—staged as a play in 1905, and published as a novel the same year. There are, certainly, other candidates—John Buchan; Erskine Childers, especially *The Riddle of the Sands*, published in 1903; E. Phillips Oppenheim; P. G. Wodehouse, who summoned up a "Mad Mullah" as one of his villains; William Le Queux; all the way back to Rudyard Kipling's *Kim* in 1901. Really, there's no single starting point; the form grows out of the literary shadows, but then, in a genre that depends on obliquity and deception and distorted mirrors, what else?

Ambiguity everywhere, in this neighborhood, even in the genre's unsteady title—*spy novel*. The word *spy* is more or less understood as a noun or a verb, but it's a lousy adjective. If the so-called spy novel had to include actual spying—individuals obtaining secret information without being known to have done so—there'd be damn few spy novels. But, as with many other phenomena in our slippery world, you have to call it *something*, and the book business long ago settled on *spy novel*, or its elevated cousin, *espionage fiction*, as the more-or-less official name.

For a collective description of the selections in *The Book of Spies*, the best phrase I could wrestle out of the language was *the literature of clandestine political conflict*. You wouldn't want to pin that on a shelf in your bookstore, but it's accurate, for it may then include intelligence officers, secret agents, diplomats, secret police, special operations personnel, terrorists, interior ministers, detectives, political assassins, guerrillas, members of a national resistance, the eternally popular amateurs-caught-up-in-a-game-far-more-dangerous-than-they-can-understand, and, even, a few spies. This is harsh reality. But becomes exciting and interesting, with the proper alchemy, in the hands of the novelist.

The potential is magnetic. The characters in the above paragraph—all of whom appear in the following pages—work at the blurred edge

of the Manichean universe, where Good struggles with Evil for the destiny of humankind. Work, often enough, plagued by moral uncertainty, and always in secrecy—thus always in danger, in foreign lands, living the sort of independent and adventurous existence that may lead to love or lechery or both.

There were two standards for the selections in *The Book of Spies:* good writing—we are here in the literary end of the spectrum, thus no James Bond—and the pursuit of authenticity. At least four of our authors—Maugham, le Carré, and Greene having served with British, and Charles McCarry with American, intelligence services—write from practical, firsthand experience. Maxim Gorky was deeply involved in clandestine life both during and after the Russian Revolution. Joseph Conrad came from a Polish family of aristocrats living under, and engaged in conspiracy opposed to, Russian domination. Rebecca West, Eric Ambler, and John Steinbeck took part in World War II propaganda efforts. Baroness Orczy came from a Hungarian émigré family, and Anthony Burgess, early in life, worked as a teacher in Malaysia during a period of communist insurgency and guerrilla war. Thus all our authors have some contact, shading from actual intelligence work to life in a particular political climate, with the world as a theater of deception.

Taken as a subgroup, the former intelligence officers share a certain literary perspective: sophisticated, cynical, and mordant. Greene, le Carré, Maugham, and McCarry, and a number of novelists influenced by them, write with a kind of cloaked anger, a belief that the world is a place where political power is maintained by means of treachery and betrayal, and, worse, that this gloomy fact of life has as much to do with elemental human nature as it does with the ambitions of states. It's a bad world, where bad people do bad things, so let us begin Chapter One and put a good person—at least one who's trying—into this hell and watch him do even worse. By the final paragraph, it's evident that victory is not moral triumph, and, with a few turns of the globe and changes in politics, no longer victory. Not good.

But not always. Clandestine conspiracy is always good when the opposition is evil. Thus Steinbeck's resistance fighters are heroes, as are Baroness Orczy's British aristocrats, because they are fighting murder-

ous Nazis, in the first case, and murderous French revolutionaries, in the second. Clandestine conspiracy is always bad, on the other hand, when initiated by the secret police. Told from the perspective of Conrad and Gorky, who knew what they were writing about, this kind of secret work is not at all sophisticated and cynical, it's vicious and brutal, period. Equally so Rebecca West's Bolshevik operatives—many of whom would join the secret police once their side took power. Conrad, whose family was destroyed by exile to Siberia, writes with passionate sorrow of a student, Razumov, ensnared, almost against his will, in the sort of conspiracy that guarantees the attention of the czarist secret police. They are, like the operatives in West's *The Birds Fall Down,* omnipotent, and merciless. Gorky's treatment of the police agent in *The Spy,* however, is tempered by an anguished Russian pity—Klimkov cannot help himself, the world happens to him, and his sad fate is, by the forces of political evolution, preordained.

For humor in espionage fiction—certainly one of literature's leaner subgenres—I've included the magnificent *Tremor of Intent,* by Anthony Burgess. Burgess may well have started out with the idea of writing a send-up of spy novels, not spying, but what seems to have happened next is extraordinary. He appears to have become fascinated by the genre, and thereby produced a fruity and seductive spy fiction where passages meant to skewer the conventions of the form—the physical confrontation between secret agents, the honey trap—don't so much satirize them as do them better, a *lot* better.

Something always to be kept in mind when reading spy novels is that, whether they admit it or not, they are of necessity political novels, so it's useful to note the date, better the *era,* of publication. *Tremor of Intent* was published in the mid-sixties, so its war was the cold war, a war that novelists were allowed to dislike. For comparison see Charles McCarry's point of view in *The Tears of Autumn* (1974), where the war is Vietnam, and the driving emotion is close to regret—for bravery betrayed, and for politics ascendant.

Neither of those books could have been written, like Eric Ambler's *A Coffin for Dimitrios,* in the late 1930s, when the Great Game was no game at all, because its final score meant the survival or collapse of nations. Ambler's plot is woven in and around political gangsterism in the

service of fascism—and crime—in the Balkan Europe of the period between the wars. The mild-mannered and mildly puzzled Charles Latimer, writer of murder mysteries, and his recruiter, Colonel Haki of the Turkish secret police, are serious characters. Latimer is a hesitant hero, with more persistence than courage, who nonetheless confronts evil and defeats it.

Best for last, Somerset Maugham's *Ashenden,* which is a serious contender for the best novel ever written in the genre. This may not be immediately apparent: the narrative is quite cold, and quite simple, and the spy Ashenden is not at all ambivalent about what he must do—you might wish he were, but he is not. Maugham is quite explicit in a preface to the 1941—note the date—edition: "But there will always be espionage and there will always be counter-espionage. Though conditions may have altered, though difficulties may be greater, when war is raging, there will always be secrets which one side jealously guards and which the other will use every means to discover; there will always be men who from malice or for money will betray their kith and kin and there will always be men who, from love of adventure or a sense of duty, will risk a shameful death to secure information valuable to their country."

Thus Maugham the spy. But Maugham the novelist can't quite let him have the last word, now that he is to "offer to the public a new edition of these stories. They purpose only to offer entertainment, which I still think, impenitently, is the main object of a work of fiction."

The writers in the pages that follow are, we like to think, equally impenitient and have come, each in his or her own very individual way, to the same conclusion.

THE BOOK OF SPIES

FROM *A COFFIN FOR DIMITRIOS* (1939)

Eric Ambler (1909–1998)

*Where the line of geopolitical sophistication crosses the line of literary en-
tertainment, there stands Eric Ambler. Born in London, Ambler wrote six
novels of European intrigue—built on the politics of conflict that led up to
World War II—before 1940. Ambler's instinct for plot dynamics and character production is close to perfect—he is perhaps the most entertaining of
all espionage novelists. Having grown up in a theatrical family, he wrote
many screenplays, including training and propaganda films during the
war, and his novels, sophisticated and authentic as they are, work hard at
holding the audience. Along with* A Coffin for Dimitrios, *his best would
include* Journey into Fear, The Levanter, Judgment on Deltchev,
and The Light of Day—*which was made into the film* Topkapi.

———

CHAPTER I
ORIGINS OF AN OBSESSION

A Frenchman named Chamfort, who should have known better, once
said that chance was a nickname for Providence.

It is one of those convenient, question-begging aphorisms coined to discredit the unpleasant truth that chance plays an important, if not predominant, part in human affairs. Yet it was not entirely inexcusable. Inevitably, chance does occasionally operate with a sort of fumbling coherence readily mistakable for the workings of a self-conscious Providence.

The story of Dimitrios Makropoulos is an example of this.

The fact that a man like Latimer should so much as learn of the existence of a man like Dimitrios is alone grotesque. That he should actually see the dead body of Dimitrios, that he should spend weeks that he could ill afford probing into the man's shadowy history, and that he should ultimately find himself in the position of owing his life to a criminal's odd taste in interior decoration are breath-taking in their absurdity.

Yet, when these facts are seen side by side with the other facts in the case, it is difficult not to become lost in superstitious awe. Their very absurdity seems to prohibit the use of the words "chance" and "coincidence." For the sceptic there remains only one consolation: if there should be such a thing as a superhuman Law, it is administered with sub-human inefficiency. The choice of Latimer as its instrument could have been made only by an idiot.

During the first fifteen years of his adult life, Charles Latimer became a lecturer in political economy at a minor English university. By the time he was thirty-five he had, in addition, written three books. The first was a study of the influence of Proudhon on nineteenth-century Italian political thought. The second was entitled: *The Gotha Programme of 1875.* The third was an assessment of the economic implications of Rosenberg's *Der Mythus des zwanzigsten Jahrhunderts.*

It was soon after he had finished correcting the bulky proofs of the last work, and in the hope of dispelling the black depression which was the aftermath of his temporary association with the philosophy of National Socialism and its prophet, Dr. Rosenberg, that he wrote his first detective story.

A Bloody Shovel was an immediate success. It was followed by *"I," said the Fly* and *Murder's Arms.* From the great army of university professors who write detective stories in their spare time, Latimer

soon emerged as one of the shamefaced few who could make money at the sport. It was, perhaps, inevitable that, sooner or later, he would become a professional writer in name as well as in fact. Three things hastened the transition. The first was a disagreement with the university authorities over what he held to be a matter of principle. The second was an illness. The third was the fact that he happened to be unmarried. Not long after the publication of *No Doornail This* and following the illness, which had made inroads on his constitutional reserves, he wrote, with only mild reluctance, a letter of resignation and went abroad to complete his fifth detective story in the sun.

It was the week after he had finished that book's successor that he went to Turkey. He had spent a year in and near Athens and was longing for a change of scene. His health was much improved but the prospect of an English autumn was uninviting. At the suggestion of a Greek friend he took the steamer from the Piræus to Istanbul.

It was in Istanbul and from Colonel Haki that he first heard of Dimitrios.

A letter of introduction is an uneasy document. More often than not, the bearer of it is only casually acquainted with the giver who, in turn, may know the person to whom it is addressed even less well. The chances of its presentation having a satisfactory outcome for all three are slender.

Among the letters of introduction which Latimer carried with him to Istanbul was one to a Madame Chávez, who lived, he had been told, in a villa on the Bosphorus. Three days after he arrived, he wrote to her and received in reply an invitation to join a four-day party at the villa. A trifle apprehensively, he accepted.

For Madame Chávez, the road from Buenos Ayres had been as liberally paved with gold as the road to it. A very handsome Turkish woman, she had successfully married and divorced a wealthy Argentine meat broker and, with a fraction of her gains from these transactions, had purchased a small palace which had once housed a minor Turkish royalty. It stood, remote and inconvenient of access, overlooking a bay of fantastic beauty and, apart from the fact that

the supplies of fresh water were insufficient to serve even one of its nine bathrooms, was exquisitely appointed. But for the other guests and his hostess's Turkish habit of striking her servants violently in the face when they displeased her (which was often), Latimer, for whom such grandiose discomfort was a novelty, would have enjoyed himself.

The other guests were a very noisy pair of Marseillais, three Italians, two young Turkish naval officers and their "fiancées" of the moment and an assortment of Istanbul business men with their wives. The greater part of the time they spent in drinking Madame Chávez's seemingly inexhaustible supplies of Dutch gin and dancing to a gramophone attended by a servant who went on steadily playing records whether the guests happened to be dancing at the moment or not. On the pretext of ill-health, Latimer excused himself from much of the drinking and most of the dancing. He was generally ignored.

It was in the late afternoon of his last day there and he was sitting at the end of the vine-covered terrace out of earshot of the gramophone, when he saw a large chauffeur-driven touring car lurching up the long, dusty road to the villa. As it roared into the courtyard below, the occupant of the rear seat flung the door open and vaulted out before the car came to a standstill.

He was a tall man with lean, muscular cheeks whose pale tan contrasted well with a head of grey hair cropped Prussian fashion. A narrow frontal bone, a long beak of a nose and thin lips gave him a somewhat predatory air. He could not be less than fifty, Latimer thought, and studied the waist below the beautifully cut officer's uniform in the hope of detecting the corsets.

He watched the tall officer whip a silk handkerchief from his sleeve, flick some invisible dust from his immaculate patent-leather riding boots, tilt his cap raffishly and stride out of sight. Somewhere in the villa, a bell pealed.

Colonel Haki, for this was the officer's name, was an immediate success with the party. A quarter of an hour after his arrival, Madame Chávez, with an air of shy confusion clearly intended to inform her guests that she regarded herself as hopelessly compromised by the

Colonel's unexpected appearance, led him on to the terrace and introduced him. All smiles and gallantry, he clicked heels, kissed hands, bowed, acknowledged the salutes of the naval officers and ogled the business men's wives. The performance so fascinated Latimer that, when his turn came to be introduced, the sound of his own name made him jump. The Colonel pump-handled his arm warmly.

"Damned pleased indeed to meet you, old boy," he said.

"Monsieur le Colonel parle bien anglais," explained Madame Chávez.

"Quelques mots," said Colonel Haki.

Latimer looked amiably into a pair of pale grey eyes. "How do you do?"

"Cheerio—all—the—best," replied the Colonel with grave courtesy, and passed on to kiss the hand of, and to run an appraising eye over, a stout girl in a bathing costume.

It was not until late in the evening that Latimer spoke to the Colonel again. The Colonel had injected a good deal of boisterous vitality into the party; cracking jokes, laughing loudly, making humorously brazen advances to the wives and rather more surreptitious ones to the unmarried women. From time to time his eye caught Latimer's and he grinned deprecatingly. "I've got to play the fool like this—it's expected of me," said the grin; "but don't think I like it." Then, long after dinner, when the guests had begun to take less interest in the dancing and more in the progress of a game of mixed strip poker, the Colonel took him by the arm and walked him on to the terrace.

"You must excuse me, Mr. Latimer," he said in French, "but I should very much like to talk with you. Those women—phew!" He slid a cigarette case under Latimer's nose. "A cigarette?"

"Thank you."

Colonel Haki glanced over his shoulder. "The other end of the terrace is more secluded," he said; and then, as they began to walk: "you know, I came up here to-day specially to see you. Madame told me you were here and really I could not resist the temptation of talking with the writer whose works I so much admire."

Latimer murmured a non-committal appreciation of the compliment. He was in a difficulty, for he had no means of knowing whether

the Colonel was thinking in terms of political economy or detection. He had once startled and irritated a kindly old don who had professed interest in his "last book," by asking the old man whether he preferred his corpses shot or bludgeoned. It sounded affected to ask which set of books was under discussion.

Colonel Haki, however, did not wait to be questioned. "I get all the latest *romans policiers* sent to me from Paris," he went on. "I read nothing but *romans policiers.* I would like you to see my collection. Especially I like the English and American ones. All the best of them are translated into French. French writers themselves, I do not find sympathetic. French culture is not such as can produce a *roman policier* of the first order. I have just added your *Une Pelle Ensanglantée* to my library. Formidable! But I cannot quite understand the significance of the title."

Latimer spent some time trying to explain in French the meaning of "to call a spade a bloody shovel" and to translate the play on words which had given (to those readers with suitable minds) the essential clue to the murderer's identity in the very title.

Colonel Haki listened intently, nodding his head and saying: "Yes, I see, I see it clearly now," before Latimer had reached the point of explanation.

"Monsieur," he said when Latimer had given up in despair, "I wonder whether you would do me the honour of lunching with me one day this week. I think," he added mysteriously, "that I may be able to help you."

Latimer did not see in what way he could be helped by Colonel Haki but said that he would be glad to lunch with him. They arranged to meet at the Pera Palace Hotel three days later.

It was not until the evening before it that Latimer thought very much more about the luncheon appointment. He was sitting in the lounge of his hotel with the manager of his bankers' Istanbul branch.

Collinson, he thought, was a pleasant fellow but a monotonous companion. His conversation consisted almost entirely of gossip about the doings of the English and American colonies in Istanbul. "Do you know the Fitzwilliams," he would say. "No? A pity, you'd like them.

Well, the other day . . ." As a source of information about Kemal Ataturk's economic reforms he had proved a failure.

"By the way," said Latimer after listening to an account of the goings-on of the Turkish-born wife of an American car salesman, "do you know of a man named Colonel Haki?"

"Haki? What made you think of him?"

"I'm lunching with him to-morrow."

Collinson's eyebrows went up. "*Are* you, by Jove!" He scratched his chin. "Well, I know *of* him." He hesitated. "Haki's one of those people you hear a lot about in this place but never seem to get a line on. One of the people behind the scenes, if you get me. He's got more influence than a good many of the men who are supposed to be at the top at Ankara. He was one of the Gazi's own particular men in Anatolia in nineteen-nineteen, a deputy in the Provisional Government. I've heard stories about him then. Bloodthirsty devil by all accounts. There was something about torturing prisoners. But then both sides did that and I dare say it was the Sultan's boys that started it. I heard, too, that he can drink a couple of bottles of Scotch at a sitting and stay stone cold sober. Don't believe that though. How did you get on to him?"

Latimer explained. "What does he do for a living?" he added. "I don't understand these uniforms."

Collinson shrugged. "Well, I've *heard* on good authority that he's the head of the secret police, but that's probably just another story. That's the worst of this place. Can't believe a word they say in the Club. Why, only the other day . . ."

It was with rather more enthusiasm than before that Latimer went to his luncheon appointment the following day. He had judged Colonel Haki to be something of a ruffian and Collinson's vague information had tended to confirm that view.

The Colonel arrived, bursting with apologies, twenty minutes late, and hurried his guest straight into the restaurant. "We must have a whisky-soda immediately," he said and called loudly for a bottle of "Johnnie."

During most of the meal he talked about the detective stories he had read, his reactions to them, his opinions of the characters and his

preference for murderers who shot their victims. At last, with an almost empty bottle of whisky at his elbow and a strawberry ice in front of him, he leaned forward across the table.

"I think, Mr. Latimer," he said again, "that I can help you."

For one wild moment Latimer wondered if he were going to be offered a job in the Turkish secret service; but he said: "That's very kind of you."

"It was my ambition," continued Colonel Haki, "to write a good *roman policier* of my own. I have often thought that I could do so if I had the time. That is the trouble—the time. I have found that out. But . . ." He paused impressively.

Latimer waited. He was always meeting people who felt that they could write detective stories if they had the time.

"But," repeated the Colonel, "I have the plot prepared; I would like to make you a present of it."

Latimer said that it was very good indeed of him.

The Colonel waved away his thanks. "Your books have given me so much pleasure, Mr. Latimer. I am glad to make you a present of an idea for a new one. I have not the time to use it myself, and, in any case," he added magnanimously, "you would make better use of it than I should."

Latimer mumbled incoherently.

"The scene of the story," pursued his host, his grey eyes fixed on Latimer's, "is an English country house belonging to the rich Lord Robinson. There is a party for the English week-end. In the middle of the party, Lord Robinson is discovered in the library sitting at his desk—shot through the temple. The wound is singed. A pool of blood has formed on the desk and it has soaked into a paper. The paper is a new Will which the Lord was about to sign. The old Will divided his money equally between six persons, his relations, who are at the party. The new Will, which he has been prevented from signing by the murderer's bullet, leaves all to one of those relations. Therefore"—he pointed his ice cream spoon accusingly—"one of the five other relations is the guilty one. That is logical, is it not?"

Latimer opened his mouth, then shut it again and nodded.

Colonel Haki grinned triumphantly. "That is the trick."

"The trick?"

"The Lord was murdered by none of the suspects, but by the butler, whose wife had been seduced by this Lord! What do you think of that, eh?"

"Very ingenious."

His host leaned back contentedly and smoothed out his tunic. "It is only a trick, but I am glad you like it. Of course, I have the whole plot worked out in detail. The *flic* is a High Commissioner of Scotland Yard. He seduces one of the suspects, a very pretty woman, and it is for her sake that he solves the mystery. It is quite artistic. But, as I say, I have the whole thing written out."

"I should be very interested," said Latimer with sincerity, "to read your notes."

"That is what I hoped you would say. Are you pressed for time?"

"Not a bit."

"Then let us go back to my office and I will show you what I have done. It is written in French."

Latimer hesitated only momentarily. He had nothing better to do, and it might be interesting to see Colonel Haki's office.

"I should like to go back with you," he said.

The Colonel's office was situated at the top of what might once have been a cheap hotel, but which, from the inside, was unmistakably a government building, in Galata. It was a large room at the end of a corridor. When they went in a uniformed clerk was bending over the desk. He straightened his back, clicked his heels and said something in Turkish. The Colonel answered him and nodded a dismissal.

The Colonel waved Latimer to a chair, gave him a cigarette and began rummaging in a drawer. At last he drew out a sheet or two of typewritten paper and held it out.

"There you are, Mr. Latimer. *The Clue of the Bloodstained Will,* I have called it, but I am not convinced that that is the best title. All the best titles have been used, I find. But I will think of some alternatives. Read it, and do not be afraid to say frankly what you think of it. If there are any details which you think should be altered, I will alter them."

Latimer took the sheets and read while the Colonel sat on the corner of his desk and swung a long, gleaming leg.

Latimer read through the sheets twice and then put them down. He was feeling ashamed of himself because he had wanted several times to laugh. He should not have come. Now that he *had* come, the best thing he could do was to leave as quickly as possible.

"I cannot suggest any improvements at the moment," he said slowly; "of course, it all wants thinking over; it is so easy to make mistakes with problems of this sort. There is so much to be thought of. Questions of British legal procedure, for instance . . ."

"Yes, yes, of course." Colonel Haki slid off the desk and sat down in his chair. "But you think you can use it, eh?"

"I am very grateful indeed for your generosity," said Latimer evasively.

"It is nothing. You shall send me a free copy of the book when it appears." He swung round in his chair and picked up the telephone. "I will have a copy made for you to take away."

Latimer sat back. Well, that was that! It could not take long to make a copy. He listened to the Colonel talking to someone over the telephone and saw him frown. The Colonel put the telephone down and turned to him.

"You will excuse me if I deal with a small matter?"

"Of course."

The Colonel drew a bulky manila file towards him and began to go through the papers inside it. Then he selected one and glanced down it. There was silence in the room.

Latimer, affecting preoccupation with his cigarette, glanced across the desk. Colonel Haki was slowly turning the pages inside the folder, and on his face was a look that Latimer had not seen there before. It was the look of the expert attending to the business he understood perfectly. There was a sort of watchful repose in his face that reminded Latimer of a very old and experienced cat contemplating a very young and inexperienced mouse. In that moment he revised his ideas about Colonel Haki. He had been feeling a little sorry for him as one feels sorry for anyone who has unconsciously made a fool of himself. He saw now that the Colonel stood in need of no such consideration. As his long, yellowish fingers turned the pages of the folder, Latimer remembered a sentence of Collinson's: "There was something about tor-

turing prisoners." He knew suddenly that he was seeing the real Colonel Haki for the first time. Then the Colonel looked up and his pale eyes rested thoughtfully on Latimer's tie.

For a moment Latimer had an uncomfortable suspicion that although the man across the desk appeared to be looking at his tie, he was actually looking into his mind. Then the Colonel's eyes moved upwards and he grinned slightly in a way that made Latimer feel as if he had been caught stealing something.

He said: "I wonder if you are interested in *real* murderers, Mr. Latimer."

CHAPTER II
THE DOSSIER OF DIMITRIOS

Latimer felt himself redden. From the condescending professional he had been changed suddenly into the ridiculous amateur. It was a little disconcerting.

"Well, yes," he said slowly. "I suppose I am."

Colonel Haki pursed his lips. "You know, Mr. Latimer," he said, "I find the murderer in a *roman policier* much more sympathetic than a real murderer. In a *roman policier* there is a corpse, a number of suspects, a detective and a gallows. That is artistic. The real murderer is not artistic. I, who am a sort of policeman, tell you that squarely." He tapped the folder on his desk. "Here is a real murderer. We have known of his existence for nearly twenty years. This is his dossier. We know of one murder he may have committed. There are doubtless others of which we, at any rate, know nothing. This man is typical. A dirty type, common, cowardly, scum. Murder, espionage, drugs—that is the history. There were also two affairs of assassination."

"Assassination! that argues a certain courage, surely?"

The Colonel laughed unpleasantly. "My dear friend, Dimitrios would have nothing to do with the actual shooting. No! His kind never risk their skins like that. They stay on the fringe of the plot. They are the professionals, the *entrepreneurs*, the links between the business men, the politicians who desire the end but are afraid of the means, and the

fanatics, the idealists who are prepared to die for their convictions. The important thing to know about an assassination or an attempted assassination is not who fired the shot, but who paid for the bullet. It is the rats like Dimitrios who can best tell you that. They are always ready to talk to save themselves the inconvenience of a prison cell. Dimitrios would have been the same as any other. Courage!" He laughed again. "Dimitrios was a little cleverer than some of them. I'll grant you that. As far as I know, no government has ever caught him and there is no photograph in his dossier. But we knew him all right and so did Sofia and Belgrade and Paris and Athens. He was a great traveller, was Dimitrios."

"That sounds as though he's dead."

"Yes, he is dead." Colonel Haki turned the corners of his thin mouth down contemptuously. "A fisherman pulled his body out of the Bosphorus last night. It is believed that he had been knifed and thrown overboard from a ship. Like the scum he was, he was floating."

"At least," said Latimer, "he died by violence. That is something very like justice."

"Ah!" The Colonel leaned forward. "There is the writer speaking. Everything must be tidy, artistic, like a *roman policier*. Very well!" He pulled the dossier towards him and opened it. "Just listen, Mr. Latimer, to this. Then you shall tell me if it is artistic."

He began to read.

"Dimitrios Makropoulos." He stopped and looked up. "We have never been able to find out whether that was the surname of the family that adopted him or an alias. He was known usually as Dimitrios." He turned to the dossier again. "Dimitrios Makropoulos. Born eighteen eighty-nine in Larissa, Greece. Found abandoned. Parents unknown. Mother believed Roumanian. Registered as Greek subject and adopted by Greek family. Criminal record with Greek authorities. Details unobtainable." He looked up at Latimer. "That was before he came to our notice. We first heard of him at Izmir in nineteen twenty-two, a few days after our troops occupied the town. A *Deunme* named Sholem was found in his room with his throat cut. He was a moneylender and kept his money under the floorboards. These were ripped up and the money had been taken. There was much violence in Izmir at that time and little notice would have been taken by the military authorities.

The thing might have been done by one of our soldiers. Then, another Jew, a relation of Sholem's, drew the attention of the military to a negro named Dhris Mohammed, who had been spending money in the cafés and boasting that a Jew had lent him the money without interest. Inquiries were made and Dhris was arrested. His replies to the court-martial were unsatisfactory and he was condemned to death. Then he made a confession. He was a fig-packer and he said that one of his fellow workmen, whom he called Dimitrios, had told him of Sholem's wealth hidden under the floorboards of his room. They had planned the robbery together and had entered Sholem's room by night. It had been Dimitrios, he said, who had killed the Jew. He thought that Dimitrios, being registered as a Greek, had escaped and bought a passage on one of the refugee ships that waited at secret places along the coast."

He shrugged. "The authorities did not believe his story. We were at war with Greece, and it was the sort of story a guilty man might invent to save his neck. They found that there had been a fig-packer named Dimitrios, that his fellow workmen had disliked him and that he had disappeared." He grinned. "Quite a lot of Greeks named Dimitrios disappeared at that time. You could see their bodies in the streets and floating in the harbour. This negro's story was unprovable. He was hanged."

He paused. During this recital he had not once referred to the dossier.

"You have a very good memory for facts," commented Latimer.

The Colonel grinned again. "I was the President of the court-martial. It was through that that I was able to mark down Dimitrios later on. I was transferred a year later to the secret police. In nineteen twenty-four a plot to assassinate the Gazi was discovered. It was the year he abolished the Caliphate and the plot was outwardly the work of a group of religious fanatics. Actually the men behind it were agents of some people in the good graces of a neighbouring friendly government. They had good reasons for wishing the Gazi out of the way. The plot was discovered. The details are unimportant. But one of the agents who escaped was a man known as Dimitrios." He pushed the cigarettes towards Latimer. "Please smoke."

Latimer shook his head. "Was it the same Dimitrios?"

"It was. Now, tell me frankly, Mr. Latimer. Do you find anything artistic there? Could you make a good *roman policier* out of that? Is there anything there that could be of the slightest interest to a writer?"

"Police work interests me a great deal—naturally. But what happened to Dimitrios? How did the story end?"

Colonel Haki snapped his fingers. "Ah! I was waiting for you to ask that. I knew you would ask it. And my answer is this: it *didn't* end!"

"Then what happened?"

"I will tell you. The first problem was to identify Dimitrios of Izmir with Dimitrios of Edirné. Accordingly we revived the affair of Sholem, issued a warrant for the arrest of a Greek fig-packer named Dimitrios on a charge of murder and, with that excuse, asked foreign police authorities for assistance. We did not learn much, but what we did learn was sufficient. Dimitrios had been concerned with the attempted assassination of Stambulisky in Bulgaria which had preceded the Macedonian officers' *putsch* in nineteen twenty-three. The Sofia police knew very little but that he was known there to be a Greek from Izmir. A woman with whom he had associated in Sofia was questioned. She stated that she had had a letter from him a short time before. He had given no address, but as she had had very urgent reasons for wishing to get in touch with him she had looked at the postmark. It was from Edirné. The Sofia police obtained a rough description of him that agreed with that given by the negro in Izmir. The Greek police stated that he had had a criminal record prior to nineteen twenty-two and gave those particulars of his origin. The warrant is probably still in existence; but we did not find Dimitrios with it.

"It was not until two years later that we heard of him again. We received an inquiry from the Yugoslav Government concerning a Turkish subject named Dimitrios Talat. He was wanted, they said, for robbery; but an agent of ours in Belgrade reported that the robbery was the theft of some secret naval documents and that the charge the Yugoslavs hoped to bring against him was one of espionage on behalf of France. By the first name and the description issued by the Belgrade police we guessed that Talat was probably Dimitrios of Izmir. About the same time our Consul in Switzerland renewed the passport, issued apparently at Ankara, of a man named Talat. It is a common Turkish

name; but when it came to entering the record of the renewal it was found from the number that no such passport had been issued. The passport had been forged." He spread out his hands. "You see, Mr. Latimer? There is your story. Incomplete. Inartistic. No detection, no suspects, no hidden motives, merely sordid."

"But interesting, nevertheless," objected Latimer. "What happened over the Talat business?"

"Still looking for the end of your story, Mr. Latimer? All right, then. Nothing happened about Talat. It is just a name. We never heard it again. If he used the passport we don't know. It does not matter. We have Dimitrios. A corpse, it is true, but we have him. We shall probably never know who killed him. The ordinary police will doubtless make their inquiries and report to us that they have no hope of discovering the murderer. This dossier will go into the archives. It is just one of many similar cases."

"You said something about drugs."

Colonel Haki began to look bored. "Oh, yes. Dimitrios made a lot of money once I should think. Another unfinished story. About three years after the Belgrade affair we heard of him again. Nothing to do with us but the available information was added to the dossier as a routine matter." He referred to the dossier. "In nineteen twenty-nine, the League of Nations Advisory Committee on the illicit drug traffic received a report from the French Government concerning the seizure of a large quantity of heroin at the Swiss frontier. It was concealed in a mattress in a sleeping car coming from Sofia. One of the car attendants was found to be responsible for the smuggling but all he could or would tell the police was that the drug was to have been collected in Paris by a man who worked at the rail terminus. He did not know the man's name and had never spoken to him; but he described him. The man in question was later arrested. Questioned, he admitted the charge but claimed that he knew nothing of the destination of the drug. He received one consignment a month which was collected by a third man. The police set a trap for this third man and caught him only to find that there was a fourth intermediary. They arrested six men in all in connection with that affair and only obtained one real clue. It was that the man at the head of this peddling organi-

sation was a man known as Dimitrios. Through the medium of the Committee, the Bulgarian Government then revealed that they had found a clandestine heroin laboratory at Radomir and had seized two hundred and thirty kilos of heroin ready for delivery. The consignee's name was Dimitrios. During the next year the French succeeded in discovering one or two other large heroin consignments bound for Dimitrios. But they did not get very much nearer to Dimitrios himself. There were difficulties. The stuff never seemed to come in the same way twice and by the end of that year, nineteen thirty, all they had to show in the way of arrests were a number of smugglers and some insignificant peddlars. Judging by the amounts of heroin they did find, Dimitrios must have been making huge sums for himself. Then, quite suddenly, about a year after that, Dimitrios went out of the drug business. The first news the police had of this was an anonymous letter which gave the names of all the principal members of the gang, their life histories and details of how evidence against every one of them might be obtained. The French police had a theory at the time. They said that Dimitrios himself had become a heroin addict. Whether that is true or not, the fact is that by December, the gang was rounded up. One of them, a woman, was already wanted for fraud. Some of them threatened to kill Dimitrios when they were released from prison but the most any of them could tell the police about him was that his surname was Makropoulos and that he had a flat in the seventeenth *arrondissement*. They never found the flat and they never found Dimitrios."

The clerk had come in and was standing by the desk.

"Ah," said the Colonel, "here is your copy."

Latimer took it and thanked him rather absently.

"And that was the last you heard of Dimitrios?" he added.

"Oh, no. The last we heard of him was about a year later. A Croat attempted to assassinate a Yugoslav politician in Zagreb. In the confession he made to the police, he said that friends had obtained the pistol he used from a man named Dimitrios in Rome. If it was Dimitrios of Izmir he must have returned to his old profession. A dirty type. There are a few more like him who should float in the Bosphorus."

"You say you never had a photograph of him. How did you identify him?"

"There was a French *carte d'identité* sewn inside the lining of his coat. It was issued about a year ago at Lyons to Dimitrios Makropoulos. It is a visitor's *carte* and he is described as being without occupation. That might mean anything. There was, of course, a photograph in it. We've turned it over to the French. They say that it is quite genuine." He pushed the dossier aside and stood up. "There's an inquest to-morrow. I have to go and have a look at the body in the police mortuary. That is a thing you do not have to contend with in books, Mr. Latimer—a list of regulations. A man is found floating in the Bosphorus. A police matter, clearly. But because this man happens to be on my files, my organisation has to deal with it also. I have my car waiting. Can I take you anywhere?"

"If my hotel isn't too much out of your way, I should like to be taken there."

"Of course. You have the plot of your new book safely? Good. Then we are ready."

In the car, the Colonel elaborated on the virtues of *The Clue of the Bloodstained Will*. Latimer promised to keep in touch with him and let him know how the book progressed. The car pulled up outside his hotel. They had exchanged farewells and Latimer was about to get out when he hesitated and then dropped back into his seat.

"Look here, Colonel," he said, "I want to make what will seem to you a rather strange request."

The Colonel gestured expansively. "Anything."

"I have a fancy to see the body of this man Dimitrios. I wonder if it would be impossible for you to take me with you."

The Colonel frowned and then shrugged. "If you wish to come, by all means do so. But I do not see . . ."

"I have never," lied Latimer quickly, "seen either a dead man or a mortuary. I think that every detective story writer should see those things."

The Colonel's face cleared. "My dear fellow, of course he should. One cannot write about that which one has never seen." He signalled the chauffeur on. "Perhaps," he added as they drove off again, "we can incorporate a scene in a mortuary in your new book. I will think about it."

The mortuary was a small corrugated iron building in the precincts

of a police station near the mosque of Nouri Osmanieh. A police official, collected *en route* by the Colonel, led them across the yard which
separated it from the main building. The afternoon heat had set the air
above the concrete quivering and Latimer began to wish that he had
not come. It was not the weather for visiting corrugated iron mortuar-
ies.

The official unlocked the door and opened it. A blast of hot,
carbolic-laden air came out, as if from an oven, to meet them. Latimer
took off his hat and followed the Colonel in.

There were no windows and light was supplied by a single high-
powered electric lamp in an enamel reflector. On each side of a gangway which ran down the centre, there were four high, wooden trestle
tables. All but three were bare. The three were draped with stiff, heavy
tarpaulins which bulged slightly above the level of the other trestles.
The heat was overpowering and Latimer felt the sweat begin to soak
into his shirt and trickle down his legs.

"It's very hot," he said.

The Colonel shrugged and nodded towards the trestles. "They
don't complain."

The official went to the nearest of the three trestles, leaned over it
and dragged the tarpaulin back. The Colonel walked over and looked
down. Latimer forced himself to follow.

The body lying on the trestle was that of a short, broad-shouldered
man of about fifty. From where he stood near the foot of the table,
Latimer could see very little of the face, only a section of putty-
coloured flesh and a fringe of tousled grey hair. The body was wrapped
in a mackintosh sheet. By the feet was a neat pile of crumpled clothing: some underwear, a shirt, socks, a flowered tie and a blue serge suit
stained nearly grey by sea water. Beside this pile was a pair of narrow,
pointed shoes, the soles of which had warped as they had dried.

Latimer took a step nearer so that he could see the face.

No one had troubled to close the eyes and the whites of them stared
upwards at the light. The lower jaw had dropped slightly. It was not
quite the face that Latimer had pictured; rather rounder and with
thick lips instead of thin, a face that would work and quiver under the
stress of emotion. The cheeks were loose and deeply lined. But it was

too late now to form any judgment of the mind that had once been behind the face. The mind had gone.

The official had been speaking to the Colonel. Now he stopped.

"Killed by a knife wound in the stomach, according to the doctor," translated the Colonel. "Already dead when he got into the water."

"Where did the clothes come from?"

"Lyons, all except the suit and shoes which are Greek. Poor stuff."

He renewed his conversation with the official.

Latimer stared at the corpse. So this was Dimitrios. This was the man who had, perhaps, slit the throat of Sholem, the Jew turned Moslem. This was the man who had connived at assassinations, who had spied for France. This was the man who had trafficked in drugs, who had given a gun to a Croat terrorist and who, in the end, had himself died by violence. This putty-coloured bulk was the end of an Odyssey. Dimitrios had returned at last to the country whence he had set out so many years before.

So many years. Europe in labour had through its pain seen for an instant a new glory, and then had collapsed to welter again in the agonies of war and fear. Governments had risen and fallen; men and women had worked, had starved, had made speeches, had fought, had been tortured, had died. Hope had come and gone, a fugitive in the scented bosom of illusion. Men had learned to sniff the heady dreamstuff of the soul and wait impassively while the lathes turned the guns for their destruction. And through those years, Dimitrios had lived and breathed and come to terms with his strange gods. He had been a dangerous man. Now, in the loneliness of death, beside the squalid pile of clothes that was his estate, he was pitiable.

Latimer watched the two men as they discussed the filling-in of a printed form the official had produced. They turned to the clothes and began making an inventory of them.

Yet at some time Dimitrios had made money, much money. What had happened to it? Had he spent it or lost it? "Easy come, easy go," they said. But had Dimitrios been the sort of man to let money go easily, howsoever he had acquired it? They knew so little about him! A few odd facts about a few odd incidents in his life, that was all the dossier amounted to! No more. And for every one of the crimes

recorded in the dossier there must have been others, perhaps even more serious. What had happened in those two- and three-year intervals which the dossier bridged so casually? And what had happened since he had been in Lyons a year ago? By what route had he travelled to keep his appointment with Nemesis?

They were not questions that Colonel Haki would bother even to ask, much less to answer. He was the professional, concerned only with the unfanciful business of disposing of a decomposing body. But there must be people who knew and knew of Dimitrios, his friends (if he had had any), and his enemies, people in Smyrna, people in Sofia, people in Belgrade, in Adrianople, in Paris, in Lyons, people all over Europe, who *could* answer them. If you could find those people and get the answers you would have the material for what would surely be the strangest of biographies.

Latimer's heart missed a beat. It would be an absurd thing to attempt, of course. Unthinkably foolish. If one did it one would begin with, say, Smyrna and try to follow one's man step by step from there, using the dossier as a rough guide. It would be an experiment in detection really. One would, no doubt, fail to discover anything new; but there would be valuable data to be gained even from failure. All the routine inquiries over which one skated so easily in one's novels one would have to make oneself. Not that any man in his senses would dream of going on such a wild goose chase—heavens no! But it was amusing to play with the idea and if one were a little tired of Istanbul . . .

He looked up and caught the Colonel's eye.

The Colonel grimaced a reference to the heat of the place. He had finished his business with the official. "Have you seen all you wanted to see?"

Latimer nodded.

Colonel Haki turned and looked at the body as if it were a piece of his own handiwork of which he was taking leave. For a moment or two he remained motionless. Then his right arm went out, and, grasping the dead man's hair, he lifted the head so that the sightless eyes stared into his.

"Ugly devil, isn't he?" he said. "Life is very strange. I've known

about him for nearly twenty years and this is the first time I've met him face to face. Those eyes have seen some things I should like to see. It is a pity that the mouth can never speak about them."

He let the head go and it dropped back with a thud on to the table. Then, he drew out his silk handkerchief and wiped his fingers carefully. "The sooner he's in a coffin the better," he added as they walked away. . . .

CHAPTER IV
MR. PETERS

Two days later, Latimer left Smyrna. He did not see Muishkin again.

The situation in which a person, imagining fondly that he is in charge of his own destiny, is, in fact, the sport of circumstances beyond his control, is always fascinating. It is the essential element in most good theatre from the *Œdipus* of Sophocles to *East Lynne*. When, however, that person is oneself and one is examining the situation in retrospect, the fascination becomes a trifle morbid. Thus, when Latimer used afterwards to look back upon those two days in Smyrna, it was not so much his ignorance of the part he was playing but the bliss which accompanied the ignorance that so appalled him. He had gone into the business believing his eyes to be wide open, whereas, actually, they had been tightly shut. That, no doubt, could not have been helped. The galling part was that he had failed for so long to perceive the fact. Of course, he did himself less than justice; but his self-esteem had been punctured; he had been transferred without his knowledge from the role of sophisticated, impersonal weigher of facts to that of active participator in a melodrama.

Of the imminence of that humiliation, however, he had no inkling when, on the morning after his dinner with Muishkin, he sat down with a pencil and a notebook to arrange the material for his experiment in detection.

Some time early in October nineteen twenty-two, Dimitrios had left Smyrna. He had had money and had probably purchased a passage on a Greek steamer. The next time Colonel Haki had heard of him he

had been in Adrianople two years later. In that interim, however, the Bulgarian police had had trouble with him in Sofia in connection with the attempted assassination of Stambulisky. Latimer was a little hazy as to the precise date of that attempt but he began to jot down a rough chronological table.

TIME	PLACE	REMARKS	SOURCE OF INFORMATION
1922 (October)	—Smyrna	Sholem	Police Archives
1923 (early part)	—Sofia	Stambulisky	Colonel Haki
1924 — —	—Adrianople	Kemal attempt	Colonel Haki
1926 — —	—Belgrade	Espionage for France	Colonel Haki
1926 — —	—Switzerland	Talat passport	Colonel Haki
1929–31 (?) —	—Paris	Drugs	Colonel Haki
1932 — —	—Zagreb	Croat assassin	Colonel Haki
1937 — —	—Lyons	*Carte d'identité*	Colonel Haki
1938 — —	—Istanbul	Murdered	Colonel Haki

The immediate problem, then, was quite clear-cut. In the six months following the murder of Sholem, Dimitrios had escaped from Smyrna, made his way to Sofia and become involved in a plot to assassinate the Bulgarian Prime Minister. Latimer found it a trifle difficult to form any estimate of the time required to become involved in a plot to kill a Prime Minister; but it was fairly certain that Dimitrios must have arrived in Sofia soon after his departure from Smyrna. If he had indeed escaped by Greek steamer he must have gone first to the Piræus and Athens. From Athens he could have reached Sofia overland, via Salonika, or by sea, via the Dardanelles and the Golden Horn to Bourgaz or Varna, Bulgaria's Black Sea port. Istanbul at that time was in Allied hands. He would have had nothing to fear from the Allies. The question was: what had induced him to go to Sofia?

However, the logical course now was to go to Athens and tackle the job of picking up the trail there. It would not be easy. Even if attempts had been made to record the presence of every refugee among the tens of thousands who had arrived, it was more than probable that what

records still existed, if any, were incomplete. There was no point, however, in anticipating failure. He had several valuable friends in Athens and if there was a record in existence it was fairly certain that he would be able to get access to it. He shut up his notebook.

When the weekly boat to the Piræus left Smyrna the following day, Latimer was among the passengers.

———

During the months following the Turkish occupation of Smyrna, more than eight hundred thousand Greeks returned to their country. They came, boatload after boatload of them, packed on the decks and in the holds. Many of them were naked and starving. Some still carried in their arms the dead children they had had no time to bury. With them came the germs of typhus and smallpox.

War-weary and ruined, gripped by a food shortage and starved of medical supplies, their motherland received them. In the hastily improvised refugee camps they died like flies. Outside Athens, on the Piræus, in Salonika, masses of humanity lay rotting in the cold of a Greek winter. Then, the Fourth Assembly of the League of Nations, in session in Geneva, voted one hundred thousand gold francs to the Nansen relief organisation for immediate use in Greece. The work of salvage began. Huge refugee settlements were organised. Food was brought and clothing and medical supplies. The epidemics were stopped. The survivors began to sort themselves into new communities. For the first time in history, large scale disaster had been halted by goodwill and reason. It seemed as if the human animal were at last discovering a conscience, as if it were at last becoming aware of its humanity.

All this and more, Latimer heard from a friend, one Siantos, in Athens. When, however, he came to the point of his inquiries, Siantos pursed his lips.

"A complete register of those who arrived from Smyrna? That is a tall order. If you had seen them come . . . So many and in such a state . . ." And then followed the inevitable question. "Why are you interested?"

It had occurred to Latimer that this question was going to crop up again and again. He had accordingly prepared his explanation. To

have told the truth, to have explained that he was trying, for purely academic reasons, to trace the history of a dead criminal named Dimitrios would have been a long and uneasy business. He was, in any case, not anxious to have a second opinion on his prospects of success. His own was depressing enough. What had seemed a fascinating idea in a Turkish mortuary might well, in the bright, warm light of a Greek autumn, appear merely absurd. Much simpler to avoid the issue altogether.

He answered: "It is in connection with a new book I am writing. A matter of detail that must be checked. I want to see if it is possible to trace an individual refugee after so long."

Siantos said that he understood and Latimer grinned ashamedly to himself. The fact that one was a writer could be relied upon to explain away the most curious extravagances.

He had gone to Siantos because he knew that the man had a Government post of some importance in Athens; but now his first disappointment was in store for him. A week went by and, at the end of it, Siantos was able to tell him only that a register was in existence, that it was in the custody of the municipal authorities and that it was not open to inspection by unauthorised persons. Permission would have to be obtained. It took another week, a week of waiting, of sitting in *kafenios*, of being introduced to thirsty gentlemen with connections in the municipal offices. At last, however, the permission was forthcoming and the following day Latimer presented himself at the bureau in which the records were housed.

The inquiry office was a bare tiled room with a counter at one end. Behind the counter sat the official in charge. He shrugged over the information Latimer had to give him. A fig-packer named Dimitrios? October nineteen twenty-two? It was impossible. The register had been compiled alphabetically by surname.

Latimer's heart sank. All his trouble, then, was to go for nothing. He had thanked the man and was turning away when he had an idea. There was just a remote chance . . .

He turned back to the official. "The surname," he said, "may have been Makropoulos."

He was dimly aware, as he said it, that behind him a man had entered the inquiry office through the door leading to the street. The sun

was streaming obliquely into the room and for an instant a long, distorted shadow twisted across the tiles as the new-comer passed the window.

"Dimitrios Makropoulos?" repeated the official. "That is better. If there was a person of that name on the register we will find him. It is a question of patience and organisation. Please come this way."

He raised the flap of the counter for Latimer to go through. As he did so he glanced over Latimer's shoulder.

"Gone!" he exclaimed. "I have no assistance in my work of organisation here. The whole burden falls upon my shoulders. Yet people have no patience. I am engaged for a moment. They cannot wait." He shrugged. "That is their affair. I do my duty. If you will follow me, please."

Latimer followed him down a flight of stone stairs into an extensive basement occupied by row upon row of steel cabinets.

"Organisation," commented the official; "that is the secret of modern statecraft. Organisation will make a greater Greece. A new empire. But patience is necessary." He led the way to a series of small cabinets in one corner of the basement, pulled open one of the drawers and began with his fingernail to flick over a series of cards. At last he stopped at a card and examined it carefully before closing the drawer. "Makropoulos. If there is a record of this man we shall find it in drawer number sixteen. That is organisation."

In drawer number sixteen, however, they drew a blank. The official threw up his hands in despair and searched again without success. Then inspiration came to Latimer.

"Try under the name of Talat," he said desperately.

"But that is a Turkish name."

"I know it. But try it."

The official shrugged. There was another reference to the main index. "Drawer twenty-seven," announced the official a little impatiently; "are you sure that this man came to Athens? Many went to Salonika. Why not this fig-packer?"

This was precisely the question that Latimer had been asking himself. He said nothing and watched the official's fingernail flicking over another series of cards. Suddenly it stopped.

"Have you found it?" said Latimer quickly.

The official pulled out a card. "Here is one," he said. "The man was a fig-packer, but the name is Dimitrios Tala*dis.*"

"Let me see." Latimer took the card. Dimitrios Taladis! There it was in black and white. He had found out something that Colonel Haki did not know. Dimitrios had used the name Talat before nineteen twenty-six. There could be no doubt that it *was* Dimitrios. He had merely tacked a Greek suffix on to the name. He stared at the card. And there were here some other things that Colonel Haki did not know.

He looked up at the beaming official. "Can I copy this?"

"Of course. Patience and organisation, you see. My organisation is for use. But I must not let the record out of my sight. That is the regulation."

Under the now somewhat mystified eyes of the apostle of organisation and patience Latimer began to copy the wording on the card into his notebook, translating it as he did so into English. He wrote:

NUMBER T.53462

NATIONAL RELIEF ORGANISATION

Refugee Section: ATHINAI

Sex: Male. *Name:* Dimitrios Taladis. *Born:* Salonika, 1889. *Occupation:* Fig-packer. *Parents:* Believed dead. *Identity Papers or Passport:* Identity card lost. Said to have been issued at Smyrna. *Nationality:* Greek. *Arrived:* October 1, 1922. *Coming from:* Smyrna. *On examination:* Able-bodied. No disease. Without money. Assigned to camp at Tabouria. Temporary identity paper issued. *Note:* Left Tabouria on own initiative, November 29th, 1922. Warrant for arrest, on charge of robbery and attempted murder, issued in Athinai, November 30, 1922. Believed to have escaped by sea.

Yes, that was Dimitrios all right. The date of his birth agreed with that supplied by the Greek police (and based on information gained prior to nineteen twenty-two) to Colonel Haki. The place of birth, however, was different. According to the Turkish dossier it had been Larissa. Why had Dimitrios bothered to change it? If he were giving a false name, he must have seen that the chances of its falsity being dis-

covered by reference to the registration records were as great for Salonika as for Larissa.

Salonika, eighteen eighty-nine! Why Salonika? Then Latimer remembered. Of course! It was quite simple. In eighteen eighty-nine Salonika had been in Turkish territory, a part of the Ottoman Empire. The registration records of that period would, in all probability, not be available to the Greek authorities. Dimitrios had certainly been no fool. But why had he picked on the name Taladis? Why had he not chosen a typical Greek name? The Turkish "Talat" must have had some special association for him. As for his identity card issued in Smyrna, that would naturally be "lost" since, presumably, it had been issued to him in the name of Makropoulos by which he was already known to the Greek police.

The date of his arrival fitted in with the vague allusions to time made in the court-martial. Unlike the majority of his fellow refugees, he had been able-bodied and free from disease when he had arrived. Naturally. Thanks to Sholem's Greek money, he had been able to buy a passage to the Piræus and travel in comparative comfort instead of being loaded on to a refugee ship with thousands of others. Dimitrios had known how to look after himself. The fig-packer had packed enough figs. Dimitrios the Man had been emerging from his chrysalis. No doubt he had had a substantial amount of Sholem's money left when he had arrived. Yet to the relief authorities he had been "without money." That had been sensible of him. He might otherwise have been forced to buy food and clothing for stupid fools who had failed to provide, as he had provided, for the future. His expenses had been heavy enough as it was; so heavy that another Sholem had been needed. No doubt he had regretted Dhris Mohammed's half share.

"Believed to have escaped by sea." With the proceeds of the second robbery added to the balance from the first, he had no doubt been able to pay for his passage to Bourgaz. It would obviously have been too risky for him to have gone overland. He had only temporary identity papers and might have been stopped at the frontier, whereas in Bourgaz, the same papers issued by an international relief commission with considerable prestige would have enabled him to get through.

The official's much-advertised patience was showing signs of wear-

ing thin. Latimer handed over the card, expressed his thanks in a suitable manner and returned thoughtfully to his hotel.

He was feeling pleased with himself. He had discovered some new information about Dimitrios and he had discovered it through his own efforts. It had been, it was true, an obvious piece of routine inquiry; but, in the best Scotland Yard tradition, it had called for patience and persistence. Besides, if he had not thought of trying the Talat name . . . He wished that he could have sent a report of his investigations to Colonel Haki, but that was out of the question. The Colonel would probably fail to understand the spirit in which the experiment in detection was being made. In any case, Dimitrios himself would by this time be mouldering below ground, his dossier sealed and forgotten in the archives of the Turkish secret police. The main thing was now to tackle the Sofia affair.

He tried to remember what he knew about postwar Bulgarian politics and speedily came to the conclusion that it was very little. In 1923 Stambulisky had, he knew, been head of a government of liberal tendencies, but of just how liberal those tendencies had been he had no idea. There had been an attempted assassination and later a military *coup d'état* carried out at the instigation, if not under the leadership of the IMRO; the International Macedonian Revolutionary Organisation. Stambulisky had fled from Sofia, tried to organise a counterrevolution and been killed. That was the gist of the affair, he thought. But of the rights and wrongs of it (if any such distinction were possible), of the nature of the political forces involved, he was quite ignorant. That state of affairs would have to be remedied, and the place in which to remedy it would be Sofia.

That evening he asked Siantos to dinner. Latimer knew him for a vain, generous soul who liked discussing his friends' problems and was flattered when, by making judicious use of his official position, he could help them. After giving thanks for the assistance in the matter of the municipal register, Latimer broached the subject of Sofia.

"I am going to trespass on your kindness still further, my dear Siantos."

"So much the better."

"Do you know anyone in Sofia? I want a letter of introduction to an

intelligent newspaperman there who could give me some inside information about Bulgarian politics in nineteen twenty-three."

Siantos smoothed his gleaming white hair and grinned admiringly. "You writers have bizarre tastes. Something might be done. Do you want a Greek or a Bulgar?"

"Greek for preference. I don't speak Bulgarian."

Siantos was thoughtful for a moment. "There is a man in Sofia named Marukakis," he said at last. "He is the Sofia correspondent of a French news agency. I do not know him myself, but I might be able to get a letter to him from a friend of mine." They were sitting in a restaurant, and now Siantos glanced round furtively and lowered his voice. "There is only one trouble about him from your point of view. I happen to know that he has . . ." The voice sunk still lower in tone. Latimer was prepared for nothing less horrible than leprosy. ". . . Communist tendencies," concluded Siantos in a whisper.

Latimer raised his eyebrows. "I don't regard that as a drawback. All the Communists I have ever met have been highly intelligent."

Siantos looked shocked. "How can that be? It is dangerous to say such things, my friend. Marxist thought is forbidden in Greece."

"When can I have that letter?"

Siantos sighed. "Bizarre!" he remarked. "I will get it for you tomorrow. You writers . . . !"

Within a week the letter of introduction had been obtained, and Latimer, having secured Greek exit and Bulgarian ingress visas, boarded a night train for Sofia.

The train was not crowded and he had hoped to have a sleeping car compartment to himself; but five minutes before the train was due to start, luggage was carried in and deposited above the empty berth. The owner of the luggage followed very soon after it.

"I must apologise for intruding on your privacy," he said to Latimer in English.

He was a fat, unhealthy-looking man of about fifty-five. He had turned to tip the porter before he spoke, and the first thing about him that impressed Latimer was that the seat of his trousers sagged absurdly, making his walk reminiscent of that of the hind legs of an elephant. Then Latimer saw his face and forgot about the trousers. There

was the sort of sallow shapelessness about it that derives from simultaneous over-eating and under-sleeping. From above two heavy satchels of flesh peered a pair of pale-blue, bloodshot eyes that seemed to be permanently weeping. The nose was rubbery and indeterminate. It was the mouth that gave the face expression. The lips were pallid and undefined, seeming thicker than they really were. Pressed together over unnaturally white and regular false teeth, they were set permanently in a saccharine smile. In conjunction with the weeping eyes above it, it created an impression of sweet patience in adversity, quite startling in its intensity. Here, it said, was a man who had suffered, who had been buffeted by fiendishly vindictive Fates as no other man had been buffeted, yet who had retained his humble faith in the essential goodness of Man: here, it said, was a martyr who smiled through the flames,—smiled yet who could not but weep for the misery of others as he did so. He reminded Latimer of a high church priest he had known in England who had been unfrocked for embezzling the altar fund.

"The berth was unoccupied," Latimer pointed out; "there is no question of your intruding." He noted with an inward sigh that the man breathed very heavily and noisily through congested nostrils. He would probably snore.

The new-comer sat down on his berth and shook his head slowly. "How good of you to put it that way! How little kindness there is in the world these days! How little thought for others!" The bloodshot eyes met Latimer's. "May I ask how far you are going?"

"Sofia."

"Sofia. So? A beautiful city, beautiful. I am continuing to Bucureşti. I do hope that we shall have a pleasant journey together."

Latimer said that he hoped so too. The fat man's English was very accurate, but he spoke it with an atrocious accent which Latimer could not place. It was thick and slightly guttural, as though he were speaking with his mouth full of cake. Occasionally, too, the accurate English would give out in the middle of a difficult sentence, which would be completed in very fluent French or German. Latimer gained the impression that the man had learned his English from books.

The fat man turned and began to unpack a small attaché-case con-

taining a pair of woollen pyjamas, some bed socks and a dog-eared paper-backed book. Latimer managed to see the title of the book. It was called *Pearls of Everyday Wisdom* and was in French. The fat man arranged these things carefully on the shelf and then produced a packet of thin Greek cheroots.

"Will you allow me to smoke, please?" he said, extending the packet.

"Please do. But I won't smoke just now myself, thank you."

The train had begun to gather speed and the attendant came in to make up their beds. When he had gone, Latimer partially undressed and lay down on his bed.

The fat man picked up the book and then put it down again.

"You know," he said, "the moment the attendant told me that there was an Englishman on the train, I knew that I should have a pleasant journey." The smile came into play, sweet and compassionate, a spiritual pat on the head.

"It's very good of you to say so."

"Oh, no, that is how I feel."

"You speak very good English."

"English is the most beautiful language, I think. Shakespeare, H. G. Wells—you have some great English writers. But I cannot yet express all my ideas in English. I am, as you will have noticed, more at ease with French."

"But your own language . . . ?"

The fat man spread out large, soft hands on one of which twinkled a rather grubby diamond ring. "I am a citizen of the world," he said. "To me, all countries, all languages are beautiful. If only men could live as brothers, without hatred, seeing only the beautiful things. But no! There are always Communists etcetera."

Latimer said: "I think I'll go to sleep now."

"Sleep!" apostrophized his companion raptly; "the great mercy vouchsafed to us poor humans. My name," he added inconsequentially, "is Mister Peters."

"It has been very pleasant to have met you, Mr. Peters," returned Latimer firmly. "We get into Sofia so early that I shan't trouble to undress."

He switched off the main light in the compartment leaving only the dark blue emergency light glowing and the small reading lights over the berths. Then he stripped a blanket off his bed and wrapped it round him.

Mr. Peters had watched these preparations in wistful silence. Now, he began to undress, balancing himself dexterously against the lurching of the train as he put on his pyjamas. At last he clambered into his bed and lay still for a moment, the breath whistling through his nostrils. Then he turned over on his side, groped for his book and began to read. Latimer switched off his own reading lamp. A few moments later he was asleep.

The train reached the frontier in the early hours of the morning and he was awakened by the attendant for his papers. Mr. Peters was still reading. His papers had already been examined by the Greek and Bulgarian officials in the corridor outside and Latimer did not have an opportunity of ascertaining the nationality of the citizen of the world. A Bulgarian customs official put his head in the compartment, frowned at their suitcases and then withdrew. Soon the train moved on over the frontier. Dozing fitfully, Latimer saw the thin strip of sky between the blinds turn blue-black and then grey. The train was due in Sofia at seven. When, at last, he rose to dress and collect his belongings, he saw that Mr. Peters had switched off his reading lamp and had his eyes closed. As the train began to rattle over the network of points outside Sofia, he gently slid the compartment door open.

Mr. Peters stirred and opened his eyes.

"I'm sorry," said Latimer, "I tried not to waken you."

In the semi-darkness of the compartment, the fat man's smile looked like a clown's grimace. "Please don't trouble yourself about me," he said. "I was not asleep. I meant to tell you that the best hotel for you to stay at would be the Slavianska Besseda."

"That's very kind of you; but I wired a reservation from Athens to the Grand Palace. It was recommended to me. Do you know it?"

"Yes. I think it is quite good." The train began to slow down. "Goodbye, Mr. Latimer."

"Good-bye."

In his eagerness to get to a bath and some breakfast it did not occur to Latimer to wonder how Mr. Peters had discovered his name.

CHAPTER V
NINETEEN TWENTY-THREE

Latimer had thought carefully about the problem which awaited him in Sofia.

In Smyrna and Athens it had been simply a matter of gaining access to written records. Any competent private inquiry agents could have found out as much. Now, however, things were different. Dimitrios had, to be sure, a police record in Sofia; but, according to Colonel Haki, the Bulgarian police had known very little about him. That they had, indeed, thought him of very little importance was shown by the fact that it was not until they had received the Colonel's inquiry that they had troubled to get a description of him from the woman with whom he was known to have associated. Obviously it was what the police had *not* got in their records, rather than what they had got, which would be interesting. As the Colonel had pointed out, the important thing to know about an assassination was not who had fired the shot but who had paid for the bullet. What information the ordinary police had would no doubt be helpful; but their business would have been with shot-firing rather than bullet-buying. The first thing he had to find out was who had or might have stood to gain by the death of Stambulisky. Until he had that basic information it was idle to speculate as to the part Dimitrios had played. That the information, even if he did obtain it, might turn out to be quite useless as a basis for anything but a Communist pamphlet, was a contingency that he was not for the moment prepared to consider. He was beginning to like his experiment and was unwilling to abandon it easily. If it were to die, he would see that it died hard.

On the afternoon of his arrival he sought out Marukakis at the office of the French news agency and presented his letter of introduction.

The Greek was a dark, lean man of middle age with intelligent, rather bulbous eyes and a way of bringing his lips together at the end of a sentence as though amazed at his own lack of discretion. He greeted Latimer with the watchful courtesy of a negotiator in an armed truce. He spoke in French.

"What information is it that you need, Monsieur?"

"As much as you can give me about the Stambulisky affair of nineteen twenty-three."

Marukakis raised his eyebrows. "So long ago? I shall have to refresh my memory. No, it is no trouble, I will gladly help you. Give me an hour."

"If you could have dinner with me at my hotel this evening, I should be delighted."

"Where are you staying?"

"The Grand Palace."

"We can get a better dinner than that at a fraction of the cost. If you like, I will call for you at eight o'clock and take you to the place. Agreed?"

"Certainly."

"Good. At eight o'clock then. *Au 'voir*."

He arrived punctually at eight o'clock and led the way in silence across the Boulevard Maria-Louise and up the Rue Alabinska to a small side-street. Half way along it there was a grocer's shop. Marukakis stopped. He looked suddenly self-conscious. "It does not look very much," he said doubtfully; "but the food is sometimes very good. Would you rather go to a better place?"

"Oh no, I'll leave it to you."

Marukakis looked relieved. "I thought that I had better ask you," he said and pushed open the door of the shop.

Two of the tables were occupied by a group of men and women noisily eating soup. They sat down at a third. A moustachioed man in shirt sleeves and a green baize apron lounged over and addressed them in voluble Bulgarian.

"I think you had better order," said Latimer.

Marukakis said something to the waiter who twirled his moustache and lounged away shouting at a dark opening in the wall that looked like the entrance to the cellar. A voice could be heard faintly acknowledging the order. The man returned with a bottle and three glasses.

"I have ordered vodka," said Marukakis. "I hope you like it."

"Very much."

"Good."

The waiter filled the three glasses, took one for himself, nodded to Latimer and, throwing back his head, poured the vodka down his throat. Then he walked away.

"A votre santé," said Marukakis politely. "Now," he went on as they set their glasses down, "that we have drunk together and that we are comrades, I will make a bargain with you. I will give you the information and then you shall tell me why you want it. Does that go?"

"It goes."

"Very well then."

Soup was put before them. It was thick and highly spiced and mixed with sour cream. As they ate it Marukakis began to talk.

———

In a dying civilisation, political prestige is the reward not of the shrewdest diagnostician but of the man with the best bedside manner. It is the decoration conferred on mediocrity by ignorance. Yet there remains one sort of political prestige that may still be worn with a certain pathetic dignity; it is that given to the liberal-minded leader of a party of conflicting doctrinaire extremists. His dignity is that of all doomed men: for, whether the two extremes proceed to mutual destruction or whether one of them prevails, doomed he is, either to suffer the hatred of the people or to die a martyr.

Thus it was with Monsieur Stambulisky, leader of the Bulgarian Peasant Agrarian Party, Prime Minister and Minister for Foreign Affairs. The Agrarian Party, faced by organised reaction, was immobilised, rendered powerless by its own internal conflicts. It died without firing a shot in its own defence.

The end began soon after Stambulisky returned to Sofia early in January nineteen twenty-three, from the Lausanne Conference.

On January the twenty-third, the Yugoslav (then Serbian) Government lodged an official protest in Sofia against a series of armed raids carried out by Bulgarian *comitadji* over the Yugoslav frontier. A few days later, on February the fifth, during a performance celebrating the foundation of the National Theatre in Sofia at which the King and Princesses were present, a bomb was thrown into a box in which sat several government ministers. The bomb exploded. Several persons were injured.

Both the authors and objects of these outrages were readily apparent.

From the start, Stambulisky's policy towards the Yugoslav Government had been one of appeasement and conciliation. Relations between the two countries had been improving rapidly. But an objection to this improvement came from the Macedonian Autonomists, represented by the notorious Macedonian Revolutionary Committee, which operated in both Yugoslavia and in Bulgaria. Fearing that friendly relations between the two countries might lead to joint action against them, the Macedonians set to work systematically to poison those relations and to destroy their enemy Stambulisky. The attacks of the *comitadji* and the theatre incident inaugurated a period of organised terrorism.

On March the eighth, Stambulisky played his trump card by announcing that the Narodno Sobranie would be dissolved on the thirteenth and that new elections would be held in April.

This was disaster for the reactionary parties. Bulgaria was prospering under the Agrarian Government. The peasants were solidly behind Stambulisky. An election would have established him even more securely. The funds of the Macedonian Revolutionary Committee increased suddenly.

Almost immediately an attempt was made to assassinate Stambulisky and his Minister of Railways, Atanassoff, at Haskovo on the Thracian frontier. It was frustrated only at the last moment. Several police officials responsible for suppressing the activities of the *comitadji*, including the Prefect of Petrich, were threatened with death. In the face of these menaces, the elections were postponed.

Then, on June the fourth, the Sofia police discovered a plot to assassinate not only Stambulisky but also Muravieff, the War Minister, and Stoyanoff, the Minister of the Interior. A young army officer, believed to have been given the job of killing Stoyanoff, was shot dead by the police in a gun fight. Other young officers, also under the orders of the terrorist Committee, were known to have arrived in Sofia, and a search for them was made. The police were beginning to lose control of the situation.

Now was the time for the Agrarian Party to have acted, to have

armed their peasant supporters. But they did not do so. Instead, they played politics among themselves. For them, the enemy was the Macedonian Revolutionary Committee, a terrorist gang, a small organisation quite incapable of ousting a government entrenched behind hundreds of thousands of peasant votes. They failed to perceive that the activities of the Committee had been merely the smokescreen behind which the reactionary parties had been steadily making their preparations for an offensive. They very soon paid for this lack of perception.

At midnight on 8 June all was calm. By four o'clock on the morning of the ninth, all the members of the Stambulisky Government, with the exception of Stambulisky himself, were in prison and martial law had been declared. The leaders of this *coup d'état* were the reactionaries Zankoff and Rouseff, neither of whom had ever been connected with the Macedonian Committee.

Too late, Stambulisky tried to rally his peasants to their own defence. Several weeks later he was surrounded with a few followers in a country house some hundreds of miles from Sofia and captured. Shortly afterwards and in circumstances which are still obscure, he was shot.

———

It was in this way that, as Marukakis talked, Latimer sorted out the facts in his own mind. The Greek was a fast talker but liable, if he saw the chance, to turn from fact to revolutionary theory. Latimer was drinking his third glass of tea when the recital ended.

For a moment or two he was silent. At last he said: "Do you know who put up the money for the Committee?"

Marukakis grinned. "Rumours began to circulate some time after. There were many explanations offered, but, in my opinion, the most reasonable and, incidentally, the only one I was able to find any evidence for, was that the money had been advanced by the bank which held the Committee's funds. It is called the Eurasian Credit Trust."

"You mean that this bank advanced the money on behalf of a third party?"

"No, I don't. The bank advanced the money on its own behalf. I happened to find out that it had been badly caught owing to the rise

in the value of the *Lev* under the Stambulisky administration. In the early part of nineteen twenty-three, before the trouble started in earnest, the *Lev* doubled its value in two months. It was about eight hundred to the pound sterling and it rose to about four hundred. I could look up the actual figures if you are interested. Anyone who had been selling the *Lev* for delivery in three months or more, counting on a fall, would face huge losses. The Eurasian Credit Trust was not, nor is for that matter, the sort of bank to accept a loss like that."

"What sort of a bank is it?"

"It is registered in Monaco which means not only that it pays no taxes in the countries in which it operates but also that its balance sheet is not published and that it is impossible to find out anything about it. There are lots more like that in Europe. Its head office is in Paris but it operates in the Balkans. Amongst other things it finances the clandestine manufacture of heroin in Bulgaria for illicit export."

"Do you think that it financed the Zankoff *coup d'état?*"

"Possibly. At any rate it financed the conditions that made the *coup d'état* possible. It was an open secret that the attempt on Stambulisky and Atanassoff at Haskovo was the work of foreign gunmen imported and paid by someone specially for the purpose. A lot of people said, too, that although there was a lot of talking and threatening, the trouble would have died down if it had not been for foreign *agents provocateurs.*"

This was better than Latimer had hoped.

"Is there any way in which I can get details of the Haskovo affair?"

Marukakis shrugged. "It is over fifteen years old. The police might tell you something but I doubt it. If I knew what you wanted to know . . ."

Latimer made up his mind. "Very well, I said I would tell you why I wanted this information and I will." He went on hurriedly. "When I was in Stambul some weeks ago I had lunch with a man who happened to be the chief of the Turkish Secret Police. He was interested in detective stories and wanted me to use a plot he had thought of. We were discussing the respective merits of real and fictional murderers when, to illustrate his point, he read me the dossier of a man named Dimitrios Makropoulos or Dimitrios Talat. The man had been a scoundrel

and a cut-throat of the worst sort. He had murdered a man in Smyrna and arranged to have another man hanged for it. He had been involved in three attempted assassinations including that of Stambulisky. He had been a French spy and he had organised a gang of drug pedlars in Paris. The day before I heard of him he had been found floating dead in the Bosphorus. He had been knifed in the stomach. For some reason or other I was curious to see him and persuaded this man to take me with him to the mortuary. Dimitrios was there on a table with his clothes piled up beside him.

"It may have been that I had had a good lunch and was feeling stupid but I suddenly had a curious desire to know more about Dimitrios. As you know, I write detective stories. I told myself that if, for once, I tried doing some detecting myself instead of merely writing about other people doing it, I might get some interesting results. My idea was to try to fill in some of the gaps in the dossier. But that was only an excuse. I did not care to admit to myself then that my interest was nothing to do with detection. It is difficult to explain but I see now that my curiosity about Dimitrios was that of the biographer rather than of the detective. There was an emotional element in it, too. I wanted to explain Dimitrios, to account for him, to understand his mind. Merely to label him with disapproval was not enough. I saw him not as a corpse in a mortuary but as a man, not as an isolate, a phenomenon, but as a unit in a disintegrating social system."

He paused. "Well, there you are, Marukakis! That is why I am in Sofia, why I am wasting your time with questions about things that happened fifteen years ago. I am gathering material for a biography that will never be written, when I ought to be producing a detective story. It sounds unlikely enough to me. To you it must sound fantastic. But it is my explanation."

He sat back feeling very foolish. It would have been better to have told a carefully thought out lie.

Marukakis had been staring at his tea. Now he looked up.

"What is your own private explanation of your interest in this Dimitrios?"

"I've just told you."

"No. I think not. You deceive yourself. You hope *au fond* that by

rationalizing Dimitrios, by explaining him, you will also explain that disintegrating social system you spoke about."

"That is very ingenious; but, if you will forgive my saying so, a little over-simplified. I don't think that I can accept it."

Marukakis shrugged. "It is my opinion."

"It is very good of you to believe me."

"Why should I not believe you? It is too absurd for disbelief. What do you know of Dimitrios in Bulgaria?"

"Very little. He was, I am told, an intermediary in an attempt to assassinate Stambulisky. That is to say there is no evidence to show that he was going to do any shooting himself. He left Athens, wanted by the police for robbery and attempted murder, towards the end of November nineteen twenty-two. I found that out myself. I also believe that he came to Bulgaria by sea. He was known to the Sofia police. I know that because in nineteen twenty-four the Turkish secret police made inquiries about him in connection with another matter. The police here questioned a woman with whom he was known to have associated."

"If she were still here and alive it would be interesting to talk to her."

"It would. I've traced Dimitrios in Smyrna and in Athens where he called himself Taladis, but so far I have not talked to anyone who ever saw him alive. Unfortunately, I do not even know the woman's name."

"The police records would contain it. If you like I will make inquiries."

"I cannot ask you to take the trouble. If I like to waste my time reading police records there is nothing to prevent my doing so, but there is no reason why I should waste your time too."

"There is plenty to prevent your wasting your time reading police records. In the first place, you cannot read Bulgarian and in the second place, the police would make difficulties. I am, God help me, an accredited journalist working for a French news agency. I have certain privileges. Besides"—he grinned—"absurd as it is, your detecting intrigues me. The baroque in human affairs is always interesting, don't you think?" He looked round. The restaurant had emptied. The waiter was sitting asleep with his feet on one of the tables. Marukakis sighed. "We shall have to wake the poor devil to pay him."

On his third day in Sofia, Latimer received a letter from Marukakis.

My dear Mr. Latimer, (he wrote in French)
Here, as I promised, is a précis of all the information about Dimitrios Makropoulos which I have been able to obtain from the police. It is not, as you will see, complete. That is interesting, don't you think! Whether the woman can be found or not, I cannot say until I have made friends with a few more policemen. Perhaps we could meet to-morrow.
Assuring you of my most distinguished sentiments.

N. *Marukakis*

Attached to this letter was the précis:

POLICE ARCHIVES, SOFIA 1922–24
Dimitrios Makropoulos. *Citizenship:* Greek. *Place of birth:* Salonika. *Date:* 1889. *Trade:* Described as fig-packer. *Entry:* Varna, December 22nd 1922, off Italian steamer *Isola Bella. Passport or Identity Card:* Relief Commission Identity Card No. T.53462.

At police inspection of papers in Café Spetzi, Rue Perotska, Sofia, June 6th 1923, was in company of woman named Irana Preveza, Greek-born Bulgar. D. M. known associate of foreign criminals. Proscribed for deportation, June 7th 1923. Released at request and on assurances of A. Vazoff, June 7th 1923.

In September 1924 request received from Turkish Government for information relating to a fig-packer named "Dimitrios" wanted on a charge of murder. Above information supplied a month later. Irana Preveza when questioned reported receiving letter from Makropoulos at Adrianople. She gave following description:

Height: 182 centimetres. *Eyes:* brown. *Complexion:* dark, cleanshaven. *Hair:* dark and straight. *Distinguishing marks:* none.

At the foot of this précis, Marukakis had added a handwritten note.

N.B. This is an ordinary police dossier only. Reference is made to a second dossier on the secret file but it is forbidden to inspect this.

Latimer sighed. The second dossier contained, no doubt, the details of the part played by Dimitrios in the events of nineteen twenty-three. The Bulgarian authorities had evidently known more about Dimitrios than they had been prepared to confide to the Turkish police. To know that the information was in existence, yet to be unable to get at it was really most irritating.

However, there was much food for thought in what information was available. The most obvious tit-bit was that on board the Italian steamer *Isola Bella* in December 1922, between the Piræus and Varna in the Black Sea, the Relief Commission Identity Card number T.53462 had suffered an alteration. "Dimitrios Taladis" had become "Dimitrios Makropoulos." Either Dimitrios had discovered a talent for forgery or he had met and employed someone with such a talent.

Irana Preveza! A real clue that and one that would have to be followed up very carefully. If she were still alive there must surely be some way of finding her. For the moment, however, that task would have to be left to Marukakis. Incidentally, the fact that she was of Greek extraction was suggestive, Dimitrios would probably not have spoken Bulgar.

"Known associate of foreign criminals," was distinctly vague. What sort of criminals? Of what foreign nationality? And to what extent had he associated with them? And why had attempts been made to deport him just two days before the Zankoff *coup d'état*? Had Dimitrios been one of the suspected assassins for whom the Sofia police had been searching during that critical week? Colonel Haki had pooh-poohed the idea of his being an assassin at all. "His kind never risk their skins like that." But Colonel Haki had not known everything about Dimitrios. And who on earth was the obliging A. Vazoff who had so promptly and effectively intervened on behalf of Dimitrios? The answers to those questions were, no doubt, in that secret second dossier. Most irritating!

He had sent a note to Marukakis, and on the following morning received a telephone call from him. They arranged to meet again for dinner that evening.

"Have you got any farther with the police?"

"Yes. I will tell you everything when we meet this evening. Good-bye."

By the time the evening came, Latimer was feeling very much as he had once used to feel while waiting for examination results: a little excited, a little apprehensive and very much irritated at the decorous delay in publishing information which had been in existence for several days. He smiled rather sourly at Marukakis.

"It is really very good of you to take so much trouble."

Marukakis flourished a hand. "Nonsense, my dear friend. I told you I was interested. Shall we go to the grocer's shop again? We can talk there quietly."

From then until the arrival of the tea he talked incessantly, about the position of the Scandinavian countries in the event of a major European war. Latimer began to feel as baleful as one of his own murderers.

"And now," said the Greek at last, "as to this question of your Dimitrios, we are going on a little trip to-night."

"What do you mean?"

"I said that I would make friends with some policeman and I have done so. As a result I have found out where Irana Preveza is now. It was not very difficult. She turns out to be very well known—to the police."

Latimer felt his heart begin to beat a little faster. "Where is she?" he demanded.

"About five minutes' walk away from here. She is the proprietress of a *Nachtlokal* called *La Vierge St. Marie.*"

"Nachtlokal?"

He grinned. "Well, you could call it a night club."

"I see."

"She has not always had her own place. For many years she worked either on her own or for other houses. But she grew too old. She had money saved, and so she started her own place. About fifty years of age, but looks younger. The police have quite an affection for her. She does not get up until ten in the evening, so we must wait a little before we try our luck at talking to her. Did you read her description of Dimitrios? No distinguishing marks! That made me laugh."

"Did it occur to you to wonder how she knew that his height was exactly one hundred and eighty-two centimetres?"

Marukakis frowned. "Why should it?"

"Very few people know even their own heights exactly."

"What is your idea?"

"I think that that description came from the second dossier you mentioned, and not from the woman."

"And so?"

"Just a moment. Do you know who A. Vazoff is?"

"I meant to tell you. I asked the same question. He was a lawyer."

"Was?"

"He died three years ago. He left much money. It was claimed by a nephew living in Bucureşti. He had no relations living here." Marukakis paused and then, with an elaborate air of simplicity, added: "He used to be on the board of directors of the Eurasian Credit Trust. I was keeping that as a little surprise for you later, but you may have it now. I found out from the files. Eurasian Credit Trust was not registered in Monaco until nineteen twenty-six. The list of directors prior to that date is still in existence and open to inspection if you know where to find it."

"But," spluttered Latimer, "this is most important. Don't you see what . . ."

Marukakis interrupted him by calling for the bill. Then he glanced at Latimer slyly. "You know," he said, "you English are sublime. You are the only nation in the world that believes that it has a monopoly of ordinary common sense."

FROM *TREMOR OF INTENT* (1966)

Anthony Burgess (1917–1993)

Anthony Burgess is best known for his worst book, A Clockwork Orange, *a mean-spirited novel that became a famous film. Burgess was a comic genius, delightful and amusing in the* Enderby *novels, in the neglected classic* Honey for the Bears, *and in* Tremor of Intent, *meant to be a comic play on the genre—its first page bearing obscure initials, obscure places, and references to unexplained operational history. Thus satire—but it is also on the first page that the narrator admits to his "two chronic diseases of gluttony and satyriasis which, anyway, continue to cancel each other out."* Tremor of Intent *begins on a gastronomic cruise of the Black Sea, on a ship called the* Polyolbion.

———

2

Going to the First Class bar, Hillier expected the last word in cushioned silk walls, a delicious shadowless twilight, bar-stools with arms and backs, a carpet like a fall of snow. What he found was a reproduction of the Fitzroy Tavern in Soho, London W.I, the Fitzroy as it used

to be before the modernisers ravaged it. The floor had cigarette-ends opening like flowers in spilt beer; a man with long hair and ear-rings was playing an upright piano that must have cost a few quid to untune; on the smoked ceiling there were tiny chalices made out of silver paper and thrown up to stick, mouth down, by their bases. The long wooden bar-counter was set with small opaque windows which swivelled on ornate Edwardian frames, obstacles to the ordering of drinks. A job-lot of horrid art-student daubs covered the walls. There even seemed to be a hidden tape-recording of Soho street sounds, the Adriatic brutally shut out. The Tourist bar, Hillier thought, must have a very luxurious décor, no fun to the decorators.

The passengers, though, were not dressed like touts, yobs, junkies and failed writers. They were dressed like First Class passengers, a dream of rich rippling textures, and some of the men had golden dinner-jackets, a new American fashion. The aroma of their smokes was heady, but some of them seemed to be drinking washy halves of mild beer. Hillier's professional nose at once divined that they were really disguised cocktails. He had not expected that he would have to fight his way to the bar, but this, to the rich, must be part of the holiday. There was, however, no paying with money and no handfuls of soaked change. That would be taking verisimilitude too far. Hillier signed for his large Gordon's and tonic. And the barman, who had got himself up to look dirty, would undoubtedly have liked to look clean.

Hillier was at once accosted by the forward youth called, he remembered, Alan Walters. He was dressed in a well-cut miniature dinner-jacket and he even had a yellow Banksia in his buttonhole. Hillier hoped, for the lad's own sake, that his glass of tomato-juice did not contain vodka. Master Walters said: "I've found out all about you."

"Oh, you have, have you?" said Hillier, with a pang of fear that perhaps the boy really had.

"That man Wriste told me. For thirty bob. A very mercenary type of man." His accent was not right, not rich enough. "Your name's Jagger and you're connected with typewriters. Tell me all about typewriters."

"Oh no," said Hillier, "this is meant to be a holiday."

"It's all nonsense about people not wanting to talk shop on holiday," said Alan. "Shop is all most people have to talk about."

"How old are you?"

"That's an irrelevant question, but I'll tell you. I'm thirteen."

"Oh, God," murmured Hillier. The nearest group of drinkers—fat men become, with subtle tailoring, merely plump; silk-swathed desirable women—looked at Hillier with malice and pity. They knew what he was going to suffer; why had he not been here before to suffer equally with them?

"Right," said the boy. "Who invented the typewriter?"

"Oh, it's so long ago," said Hillier. "I look to the future."

"It was in 1870. There were three men—Scholes, Glidden and Soule. It was in America. They were financed by a man named Densmore."

"You've just been reading this up," said Hillier, uneasy now.

"Not recently," said Alan. "It was when I was interested in firearms. Technically, I mean. I'm still interested practically." The neighbour drinkers would have liked to ignore Alan, but the boy was, after all, a kind of monster. They listened, drinks poised, mouths open. "It was the Remington Company, you see, who first took it up. A typewriter is a kind of gun."

"The Chicago typewriter," said a voice. "It ties up well enough." Hillier saw that the Indian girl, Miss Devi, had just joined the nearest group. She was holding a martini. She was very beautiful. She was dressed in a scarlet sari embossed with gold images of prancing, tongued, many-armed gods. A silver trinket embellished her nose. Her hair was traditionally arranged—middle parting, plaits on each side of it. But the remark about the Chicago typewriter had come from the man standing by her. This must be her boss, Mr. Theodorescu. He was of a noble fatness; the fat of his face was part of its essential structure, not a mean gross accretion, and the vast shapely nose needed those cheek-pads and firm jowls for a proper balance. The chin was very firm. The eyes were not currants in dough but huge and lustrous lamps whose whites seemed to have been polished. He was totally bald, but the smooth scalp—from which a discreet odour of violets breathed—

seemed less an affliction than an achievement, as though hair were a mere callow down to be shed in maturity. He was, Hillier thought, about fifty. His hands were richly ringed, but this did not seem vulgar: they were so big, strong and groomed that the crusting of winking stones was rather like adornment by transitory flowers of acknowledged God-given instruments of skill and power and beauty. His body was so huge that the white dinner-jacket was like a moulded expanse of royal sailcloth. He was drinking what Hillier took to be neat vodka, a whole gill of it. Hillier feared him; he also feared Miss Devi, whom he had seen nearly naked. There had been a man who had inadvertently spied a goddess bathing. Actaeon, was it? Was he the one who had been punished by being turned into a stag and then devoured by fifty dogs? This boy here would know.

This boy said: "It was Yost who was the real expert. He was an expert mechanic. But the Yost method of inking soon became obsolete. What," he coldly asked Hillier, "was the Yost method of inking?"

"I used to know," said Hillier. "I've been in this game a long time. One forgets. I look to the future." He'd said that already.

"Yost used an inked pad instead of a ribbon," said Alan sternly. Others looked sternly at Hillier too. "It's my opinion," said Alan, "that you know nothing about typewriters. You're an impostor."

"Look here," bullied Hillier, "I'm not having this, you know." The god whom Hillier took to be Mr. Theodorescu laughed in a gale that seemed to shake the bar. He said, in a voice like a sixteen-foot organ-stop:

"Apologise to the gentleman, boy. Because he does not wish to disclose his knowledge to you does not mean that he has no knowledge. Ask him questions of less purely academic interest. About the development of Chinese typewriters, for instance."

"Five thousand four hundred ideographic type faces," said Hillier with relief. "A three-grouped cylinder. Forty-three keys."

"I say he knows nothing about typewriters," said Alan staunchly. "I say he's an impostor. I shouldn't be surprised if he was a spy."

Hillier, like a violinist confidently down-bowing in with the rest of the section, started to laugh. But nobody else laughed. Hillier was playing from the wrong score.

"Where's your father?" cried Mr. Theodorescu. "If I were your father I would take you over my knee and spank you hard and then make you apologise to this gentleman. Abjectly."

"He's over there," said Alan. "He wouldn't do anything." At a table just by the Fitzroy Street entrance a dim swollen man was being adjured, by a frizz-haired woman much his junior, to down that and have another.

"Well, then," said Mr. Theodorescu, veering round massively as by silent hydraulic machinery, "let me apologise on the boy's behalf." He shone his great lamps on Hillier. "We know him, you see. You, I think, have just joined us. In a sense, he is all our responsibility. I believe he is sincerely sorry, Mr.—"

"Jagger."

"Mr. Jagger. Theodorescu myself, though I am not Rumanian. This is Miss Devi, my secretary."

"I regret to say," said Hillier, "that we have already met. It was very unfortunate. I feel like apologising, but it was not really my fault." It had not been Actaeon's fault.

"I always forget about the locking of bathroom doors," said Miss Devi. "It comes of having my own private suite on land. But we are surely above these foolish taboos."

"I hope so," said Hillier.

"Typewriters, typewriters," crooned Theodorescu. "I have always felt that our house should have a distinctive type-face, very large, a sort of variant of the old black-letter. Would it be possible to write in Roman and Arabic letters on the one instrument?" he asked Hillier.

"The difficulty there would be to arrange things so that one could type from both left to right and right to left. Not insuperable. It would be cheaper to use two typewriters, though."

"Very interesting," said Theodorescu, searching Hillier's face, it seemed, with one eye, two eyes not being necessary. Alan Walters was now standing alone at the bar, sulking over a new tomato-juice which Hillier this time hoped contained vodka, a large one.

"He knows nothing about it," he mumbled. It was recognised that he had been a rude boy; the grown-ups had turned their backs on him. "Yost and Soule," he muttered to his red glass. "He knows nothing

about them. Silly old Jagger is a Yost Soule, a lost soul, ha ha ha."
Hillier didn't like the sound of that. But Theodorescu was large
enough to be able to be kind to the lad, saying:

"We have not yet seen your beautiful sister this evening. Is she still
in her cabin?"

"She's a Yost Soule, like Jagger here. She reads about sex all the
time, but she knows nothing about it. Just like Jagger."

"You may have tested Mr. Jagger on the history of the typewriter,"
said Theodorescu urbanely, "but you have not tested him on sex. Nor,"
he added hurriedly, seeing Alan open his mouth on a deep breath, "are
you going to."

"Jagger is a sexless spy," said the boy. Hillier reminded himself that
he was not here to be a gentleman, above such matters as impertinent
and precocious brats. He went close to the not over-clean left ear of
Alan and said to it, "Look. Any more nonsense from you, you bloody
young horror, and I'll repeatedly jam a very pointed shoe up your
arse."

"Up my arse, eh?" said Alan very clearly. There were convention-
ally shocked looks at Hillier. At that moment a white-coated steward,
evidently Goanese, entered with a carillon tuned to a minor arpeggio.
He walked through the Soho pub like a visitor from a neighbouring
TV stageset, striking briskly the opening right-hand bars of Beethoven's
"Moonlight" Sonata.

"Ah, dinner," said Theodorescu with relief. "I'm starving."

"You had a large tea," said Miss Devi.

"I have a large frame."

Hillier remembered that he had asked for a place at Miss Devi's
table, which also would mean Theodorescu's. He was not sure now
whether it had really been a good idea. Sooner or later Theodorescu's
sheer weight, aided by Master Walters's shrill attrition from another
point, however distant, in the dining-saloon, would bruise and chip the
Jagger disguise. Besides, he knew he had made himself uglier than he
really was, and he couldn't help wanting to be handsome for Miss Devi.
Foolish taboos, eh? That's what she'd said.

3

"You think it good, the cuisine?" asked Theodorescu. The dining-saloon was very far from being like that fried-egg-on-horsesteak restaurant that, in Hillier's post-war London days, had stood just across the street from the Fitzroy. Conditioned air purred through the champagne light and, only a little louder, stringed instruments played slow and digestive music from a gallery above the gilded entrance. The musicians all seemed very old, servants of the Line near retirement, but they made a virtue of the slow finger movements that arthritis imposed on them: Richard Rodgers became noble, processional. The appointments of the dining-saloon were superb, the chairs accommodating the biggest bottom in comfort, the linen of the finest Dunfermline damask. Theodorescu's table was by a soft-lit aquarium; in this, fantastic fish—haired, armoured, haloed, spined, whiptailed—gravely visiting castles, grottos and gazebos, ever and anon delivered wide-mouthed silent reports to the human eaters. There were just Theodorescu, Miss Devi and Hillier at the table. The Walters family, Hillier was mainly glad to see, were seated well beyond a protective barrier of well-fleshed and rather loud-talking tycoons and their ladies. Mainly but not wholly glad: Miss Walters seemed to look very delightful in a shift dress of flame velvet with a long heavy gold medallion necklace. She was reading at table, and that was wrong, but her brother sulked and her father and stepmother ate silently and solidly, Mrs. Walters urging further helpings on her dim but gulous husband.

So far Hillier had joined Theodorescu in a dish of lobster medallions in a sauce cardinale. The lobster had, so the chief steward had informed them, been poached in white wine and a court-bouillon made with the shells, then set alight in warm pernod. The saloon was full of silent waiters, many Goanese, some British (one, Wriste's wingerpal, had come up to whisper "Ta for the Guinness"). There was no harassed banging and clattering through the kitchen doors; all was leisurely.

"I think," said Theodorescu, "you and I will now have some red mullet and artichoke hearts. The man who was sitting in that place be-

fore you was not a good trencherman. I tend to feel embarrassed when
my table companions eat very much less than I: I am made to feel
greedy." Hillier looked at Miss Devi's deft and busy long red talons.
She was eating a large and various curry with many side-dishes; it
should, if she ate it all, last her till about mid-night. "I think we had
better stay with this champagne, don't you?" said Theodorescu. It was
a 1953 Bollinger; they were already near the end of this first bottle.
"Harmless enough, not in the least spectacular, but I take wine to be a
kind of necessary bread, it must not intrude too much into the meal.
Wine-worshipping is the most vulgar of idolatries."

"You must," said Hillier, "allow me to have the next bottle on *my*
bill."

"Well now," said Theodorescu, "I will make a bargain with you.
Whoever eats the less shall pay for the wine. Are you agreeable?"

"I don't think I stand a chance," said Hillier.

"Oh, I think that nauseous boy has impaired your self-confidence.
At table I fear the thin man. The fat laugh and seem to cram themselves, but it is all so much wind and show. Are you at all a betting
man?"

"Well—" In Hillier's closed tank a sort of fermentation was taking
place; a coarse kind of *Schaumwein* of the spirit made him say: "What
do you have in mind?"

"Whatever sum you care to name. The Trencherman Stakes." Miss
Devi tinkled a giggle. "Shall we say a thousand pounds?"

Could that, should he lose, be charged to his expenses, wondered
Hillier. But, of course, it didn't apply. A cheque signed by Jagger was
only a piece of paper. "Done," he said. "We order the dishes alternately. All plates to be thoroughly cleaned."

"Splendid. We start now." And they worked away at the red mullet
and artichoke hearts. "Slowly," said Theodorescu. "We have all the
time in the world. Speaking of champagne, there was some serious talk—in 1918, I think it was, the second centenary of the first
use of the name to designate the sparkling wines of Hautvillers—some
talk, as I say, of seeking canonisation for Dom Pérignon, champagne's
inventor. Nothing came of it, and yet men have been canonised for
less."

"Very much less," said Hillier. "I would sooner seek intercession from Saint Pérignon than from Saint Paul."

"You're a praying man, then? A believer?"

"Not exactly that. Not any longer." Careful, careful. "I believe in man's capacity to choose. I accept free will, the basic Christian tenet."

"Excellent. And now, talking of choosing—" Theodorescu beckoned. The chief steward himself came across, a soft-looking ginger-moustached man. Hillier and Theodorescu ordered ahead alternately. Hillier: fillets of sole Queen Elizabeth, with sauce blonde; Theodorescu: shellfish tart with sauce Newburg; Hillier: *soufflé au foie gras* and to be generous with the Madeira; Theodorescu: avocado halves with caviar and a cold chiffon sauce. "And," said Theodorescu, "more champagne."

They ate. Some of the nearer diners, aware of what was going on, relaxed their own eating to watch the contest. Theodorescu praised the red caviar that had been heaped on the avocado, then he said:

"And where, Mr. Jagger, did you receive your Catholic education?"

Hillier needed to concentrate on his food. "Oh," he said, at random, "in France." He had given away too much already; he must maintain his disguise. "At a little place north of Bordeaux. Cantenac. I doubt if you'd know it."

"Cantenac? But who doesn't know Cantenac, or at any rate the Château Brane-Cantenac?"

"Of course," said Hillier. "But I'd understood that you weren't a wine man. The Baron de Brane who made Mouton-Rothschild great."

"A strange place, though, for a young Englishman to be brought up. Your father was concerned with viticulture?"

"My mother was French," lied Hillier.

"Indeed? What was her maiden name? It's possible that I know the family."

"I doubt it," said Hillier. "It was a very obscure family."

"But I take it that you received your technical education in England?"

"In Germany."

"Where in Germany?"

"Now," said Hillier, "I suggest *filet mignon à la romana,* and a little butterfly pasta and a few zucchini."

"Very well." The chief steward was busy with his pencil. "And after that some roast lamb *persillée* and onion and gruyère casserole with green beans and celery julienne."

"And more champagne?"

"I think we might change. Something heavier. '55 was a great year for clarets. A Lafite Rothschild?"

"I could ask for nothing better."

"And for you, my dear?" Miss Devi had eaten a great deal, though not all, of her curries. She wanted a simple crème brûlée and a glass of madeira to go with it. She had had her fill of champagne: her eyes were bright, a well-lighted New Delhi, no smouldering jungles. Hillier grew uneasy as, while they awaited their little fillets, Theodorescu bit hungrily at some stick-bread. It might be bluff: watch him. The dining-saloon was emptying at leisure: in the distance a dance-band was tuning up: the aged fiddlers had departed. The diners nearest the contestants were less interested than before: this was pure gorging, their full stomachs told them; the men were, behind blue smoke-screens, now satisfying hunger for the finest possible Cuban leaf. The Walters family was still there, the girl reading, the boy inhaling a balloon-glass, the wife smoking, the husband looking not very well.

"Whereabouts in Germany?" asked Theodorescu, cutting his fillet. "I know Germany. But, of course, I know most countries. My business takes me far and wide." I have been warned, thought Hillier. He said:

"What I meant was that I studied typewriters in Germany. After the war. In Wilhelmshaven."

"Of course. A great naval base reduced to a seaside centre of light industries. You will probably be acquainted with Herr Luttwitz of the Olympia Company."

Hillier took a chance, frowning. "I don't seem to remember a Herr Luttwitz."

"Of course, stupid of me. I was thinking of a quite different company altogether."

"And what," asked Hillier, when the roast lamb came—he could tell

it was delicious, but things would soon be ceasing to be delicious—"is your particular line of business?"

"Pure buying and selling," shrugged Theodorescu massively. Was it imagination, or was he having difficulty with that forkful of onion and gruyère casserole? "I produce nothing. I am a broken reed in the great world—your great world—of creativity."

"Pheasant," ordered Hillier, "with pecan stuffing. Bread sauce and game chips." Oh, God. "Broccoli blossoms."

"And then perhaps a poussin each with barley. And *sauce béchamel velouté*. Some spinach and minced mushrooms. A roast potato with sausage stuffing." He seemed to Hillier to order with a pinch of defiance. Was he at last feeling the strain? Was that sweat on his upper lip?

"That sounds admirable," said Hillier. "Another bottle of the same?"

"Why not some burgundy? A '49 Chambertin, I think."

The eating was growing grimmer. Miss Devi said: "I think, if you will excuse me, I shall go out on deck." Hillier rose at once, saying:

"Let me accompany you." And, to Theodorescu, "I'll be back directly."

"No!" cried Theodorescu. "Stay here, please. The ocean is a traditional vomitorium."

"Are you suggesting," said Hillier, sitting again, "that I would play so mean a trick?"

"I'm suggesting nothing." Miss Devi, turning before going through the vomitory of the dining-saloon, smiled rather sadly at Hillier. Hillier, without half-rising, gave her a little bow. She left. "Let us push on," frowned Theodorescu.

"I don't like this talk of pushing on. It's an insult to good food. I'm thoroughly enjoying this."

"Enjoy it, then, and stop talking."

Enjoying it doggedly but with a lilt of potential triumph, Hillier suddenly heard a crash, a flop, a groan, and little screams from, he now saw, the Walters table. The head of the head of the family had cracked down among the fruit-parings, upsetting cruet and coffee-cups. A stroke or something. A coronary. The stewards who, as the dining-saloon emptied, had been discreetly closing in to watch the eating con-

test, now converged, with the remaining diners, on to the Walters table, a sudden boil on the smooth skin of holiday. Both Hillier and Theodorescu looked down guiltily at their near-empty plates. A steward ran off for the ship's doctor. "Shall we," said Hillier, "call it a draw? We've both done pretty well."

"You yield?" said Theodorescu. "You resign?"

"Of course not. I was suggesting we be reasonable. Over there a horrible example has been presented to us." The ship's doctor, in evening dress of the mercantile marine, was shouting for the way to be cleared.

"It's time we moved on," said Theodorescu. He called the chief steward. "Bring," he said, "the cold sweet trolley."

"This gentleman's in a pretty bad way, sir. If you don't mind waiting a minute—"

"Nonsense. This isn't a hospital ward." It looked like it, though. A couple of orderlies had come in with a stretcher. While Mr. Walters, snoring desperately, was being placed upon it, a Goanese steward trundled the cold sweet trolley along. Mrs. Walters was weeping. The two children were nowhere to be seen. Mr. Walters, in cortège, was carried out. Theodorescu and Hillier very nearly had the dining-saloon to themselves. "Right," said Theodorescu. "Harlequin sherbet?"

"Harlequin sherbet." They served each other.

"I think," said Theodorescu, "a bottle of Blanquette de Limoux."

"What an excellent idea."

They got through their sweets sourly. Peach mousse with sirop framboise. Cream dessert ring Chantilly with zabaglione sauce. Poires Hélène with cold chocolate sauce. Cold Grand Marnier pudding. Strawberry marlow. Marrons panaché vicomte. "Look," gasped Hillier, "this sort of thing isn't my line at all."

"Isn't it? Isn't it, Mr. Jagger? What is your line then?"

"My teeth are on fire."

"Cool them with some of this nectarine flan."

"I think I shall be sick."

"That's not allowed. That is not in the rules."

"Who makes the rules?"

"I do." Theodorescu poured Hillier a wonderful chill tumbler of

frothing Blanquette. Hillier felt better after it. He was able to take some chocolate rum dessert, garnished with whipped cream and Kahlua, also some orange marmalade crème bavaroise, loud with Cointreau. "How about some apple tart normande with Calvados?" asked Theodorescu. But Hillier had an apocalyptical vision of his insides—all that churned mess of slop and fibre, cream sluggishly oozing along the pipes, the flavouring liqueurs ready to self-ignite, a frothing inner sea of souring wine. A small Indian township could have been nourished for a day on it all. This was the West that Roper had deserted. "I give up," he gasped. "You win."

"You owe me one thousand pounds," said Theodorescu. "I wish to be paid before we reach Yarylyuk. No. I may leave the cruise before then. I wish to be paid before noon tomorrow."

"You can't leave before Yarylyuk. It's our next port."

"There are such things as helicopters. Much depends on certain messages I may receive."

"You can have a cheque now."

"I know I can have a cheque now. But what I want is cash."

"But I haven't any cash. At least, not that amount."

"There's plenty in the purser's safe. You have, I take it, traveller's cheques or a letter of credit. Cash." He now lit a cigar as unshakily as if he'd merely dined on a couple of poached eggs. Then he walked out of the dining-saloon dead straight. Hillier ran, pushing against him. That traditional vomitorium.

4

"And how," asked Hillier somewhat guiltily, "is your husband?" He felt vaguely responsible for Mr. Walters's coronary; he had propagandised for gluttony instead of, after at latest the *filet mignon,* standing up to denounce it in a Father Byrne-type sermon. But he had thought he stood a good chance of winning a thousand pounds, a useful sum for his retirement. Now he had to pay out all that in cash and he couldn't do it. At any rate, the money had been demanded, with the grace of a brief moratorium. He felt, though, with a spy's intuition, that it might not

really come to that. The first thing was to find out more about Theodorescu. That was why he was here, on the touchline of the dance, drinking Cordon Bleu mixed with crème de menthe—a reef of crushed ice below—at the simple graceful metal bar of the open-air recreation deck. He was looking for Miss Devi. It was proper anyway, quite apart from pumping her for information, to want to see Miss Devi on this delicious Adriatic summer night with its expensive stellar and lunar show put on for the dancing tycoons and their women. He would, alternatively, have liked to see something of Miss Walters, but her father was very ill, there were questions of decency.

But Mrs. Walters seemed above such questions, knocking back large highballs while her husband snored desperately in the sickbay. Hillier was able to see her more closely now, even to glance with shamed favour into the deep cut of her midnight blue straight satin, a gauzy stole of evening blue loose on her shoulders. Her hair was a frizzed auburn, not too attractive; she had a mean heart-shaped face with eyes she narrowed in a habit of cunning; her ears were lobeless and jangled no rings. She was no more than thirty-eight. She said now, in a contralto surprisingly unresonant: "He brought this on himself. That's his third stroke. I warn him and warn him but he says he's de-termined to enjoy life. Look where enjoying life has put him."

"In a decently-run order of things," said Hillier sententiously, "the pleasures of wealthy age would be reserved for indigent youth."

"You kidding?" said Mrs. Walters. A vulgar woman perhaps at bot-tom. "He was brought up on bread and jam, he says. Weak tea out of a tin can. Now he's got the better of bread, he reckons, owning all these flour-mills. Those children of his, believe it or not, have not eaten one slice of bread since the day they were weaned. He won't have bread in the house." All the time she talked, she looked distractedly beyond Hillier, as though expecting someone.

"But," repeated Hillier, "how *is* your husband?"

"He'll recover," she said with indifference. "They've been injecting things into him." And now she flashed brilliantly, swaying her hips minimally, as a sort of paradigm of a fancy man approached—a man who, Hillier felt, must, beneath the green dinner-jacket, the pomade, talc, cologne, after-shave lotion, anti-sweat dabs in the oxters, have a

subtle and ineradicable odour of cooking-fat. They were both vulgar: let them get on with it.

Hillier strolled away from the bar, drink in one hand, one hand in side-pocket, pleased that the thought of cooking-fat did not make him feel queasy. He had given most of the monstrous dinner to the sea—quietly, in a quiet corner near some lifeboats. It had all tasted of nothing as it came up, one flavour cancelling out another. Now he felt well, though not hungry. Gazing benevolently at the dancers, who were performing some teen-age hip-shake, jowls shaking in a different rhythm, he was happy to see that Miss Devi was on the floor, partnered by a junior ship's officer. Good. He would ask her for the next dance. He hoped it would be something civilised, in which bodies were clasped firmly against each other. These new youngsters, who could have all the sex they wanted, were very sexless really. Their dances were narcissistic. They were trying to make themselves androgynous. Perhaps it was the first stage in a long process of evolution which should end in a human worm. Hillier had a vision of human worms and shuddered. Let us have plenty of sex while it is still there. I warn him and warn him but he says he's determined to enjoy life. Mrs. Walters and her fancy man had gone off somewhere, perhaps towards the lifeboats. Why were lifeboats aphrodisiacal? Perhaps something to do with urgency. Adam and Eve on a raft.

The hip-shaking stopped, dancers returned to their tables. Miss Devi was alone with the junior ship's officer. He, a mere servant, could easily be seen off. Hillier waited, watching the two suck up something long through straws. The band-leader, who seemed very drunk, said: "This next one would be for the oldsters, if there were any oldsters here." Everything laid on, even flattery. The band started to play a slow fox-trot.

Miss Devi seemed quite pleased to be asked to dance by Hillier. "I rather regret that silly wager now," said Hillier as they did feather-steps. "I don't mean because I lost—that's nothing—but because it was a sort of insult to India. I mean, look at it as a sort of tableau in a play by Brecht or somebody—two Western men gorging, a thousand pounds on it, and India watches, sad-eyed, aware of her starving millions."

Miss Devi laughed. Her slender body, strained back in the dance, was delicious in his arms. Hillier, as he often did when close to a desirable woman, began to feel hungry. "Starving millions," she repeated, with a sort of cool mockery. "I think that we all get what we want. Having too many children and not farming the land properly—that's as much as to say 'I want to starve.'"

"So you don't go in for compassion, pity, things of that sort?"

She thought about that, dancing. "I try not to. We should know the consequences of our acts."

"And if a mad stranger breaks into my house and knifes me?"

"It's pre-ordained, willed from the beginning. You can't fight God's will. To pity the victim is to resent the executioner. God should not be resented."

"It's strange to me to hear you talking about God." She looked coldly at him, stiffening. "I mean here, on a luxury cruise, dancing a slow fox-trot."

"Why? Everything's in God—slow fox-trot, saxophone, the salted peanuts on the bar. Why should it be strange? The universe is one thing."

Hillier groaned to himself: it was like Roper talking, except that Roper wouldn't have God. "And the universe has only one law?" he said.

"The laws are contained in it, not imposed. Whatever we do, we obey the law."

"What does Mr. Theodorescu say when you talk like that?"

"He tends to agree with me. He accepts the primacy of the will. We should do what we want to do. Never nurse unacted desires."

Good. "And if we desire a person, not just a thing?"

"There must be a harmony of wills. Sometimes this is predestined. Usually it has to be contrived out of one person's desire. It's the task of the desirer to bring about a reciprocal desire. That's perhaps the most Godlike function a human soul can take on. It's a kind of creation of destiny."

As logic this made little sense to Hillier, but he wasn't going to tell her that. Nor did he just yet propose to swoop down to the practical and personal application of her theory. Plenty of time, all the night be-

fore you. Switch on the oven and stack the dishes in the warming-drawer. "You yourself," he said, "whose desirability is not in question, must have had this reciprocity wished on you many times. And in many countries."

"Some countries more than others. But I have little time for social life."

"Mr. Theodorescu keeps you pretty busy?"

"Oh, what a terrible sour note that was." She screwed up her face delectably. "That saxophone-player seems to be drunk. What did you say? Oh, yes, pretty busy."

Hillier now saw the steward Wriste, smoking, watching the dancing from a far door. He had put on a shirt and spotted bow-tie for the evening. Catching sight of Hillier, he waved cheerily but discreetly, opening his mouth with a kind of toothless joy. Hillier said: "Typing and so on? I've been working on the design of a cheap lightweight electrical typewriter. You can carry it about and plug it into a lamp-socket."

"We're dancing," said Miss Devi, "under the starry Adriatic sky, and all you can think of to talk to me about is typewriters."

"The universe is one thing. God and typewriters and drunken saxophonists. What sort of business does Mr. Theodorescu do? Mr. Theodorescu is also part of the universe."

"He calls himself an entrepôt of industrial information. He buys and sells it."

"And is he always paid in cash?"

She didn't answer. But "Look," she said, "if you're trying to find out whether Mr. Theodorescu and I have a *personal* relationship, the answer is no. And if you're going to ask me to use my *personal* influence to get your debt rescinded, then the answer is again no. People shouldn't gamble with Mr. Theodorescu. He always wins."

"And supposing I refuse to pay him?"

"That would be most unwise. You might have an unfortunate accident. He's a very powerful man."

"You mean he'd harm me physically? Well then, perhaps I'd better get in first. I can fight as dirtily as the best of them. I think a gentleman ought to be willing to accept the cheque of another gentleman. Mr.

Theodorescu wants cash and is ready to engineer unfortunate accidents. I don't think Mr. Theodorescu is a gentleman."

"You'd better not let him hear you say that."

"Where is he? I'll say it to his face with pleasure. But I suppose he's flat out on his bunk or in his luxe suite or whatever it is."

"Ah, no. He's in the radio-room, busy with messages. Mr. Theodorescu is never ill. He can eat and drink anything. He is, I think, the most virile man I know."

"Sorry," said Hillier to a couple he'd nearly bumped into. And, to Miss dancing Devi, "Yet he's not virile enough to want to draw you into a reciprocal nexus of desire."

"You use very pompous words. Mr. Theodorescu is interested in a different kind of sex. He has exhausted, he says, the possibilities of women."

"Does that mean that the precocious Master Walters will have to watch out?"

"He is also the discreetest man I know. He is very discreet about everything."

"My tastes are normal. I don't need so much discretion."

"What do you mean?" But, before he could answer, she surveyed his face with cat's eyes. "It seems to me," she said, "that you are for some reason trying to make yourself ugly. The face I am looking at doesn't seem to be your face at all. You are perhaps a man of mystery. That young and forward boy doesn't believe you have anything to do with typewriters. A minute ago you were too quick to bring typewriters into our discourse, as though you were trying to convince yourself that typewriters are your professional concern. Why are you here? Why are you taking this voyage? Who are you?"

"My name is Sebastian Jagger. I'm a typewriter technician." Hillier sang those words gently in a free adaptation of Mimi's aria in the first act of *La Bohème*. This did not clash with the music of the fox-trot. The pianist, who seemed as drunk as his leader, was doing something atonal and aleatoric; meanwhile drummer and bassist assured the dancers that this was still the dance they had started off to dance. "I've been doing some work for Olivetti. I'm returning to England for a time, but I'm taking a holiday first."

"I would like to strip you," she said, her eyes deliciously malicious, "and see what sort of man you really are."

"Let us," said Hillier gallantly, "have some reciprocal stripping."

The music suddenly, except for the pianist, stopped. A glowingly healthy though tubby man with grey curls, evening dress and dog-collar was standing on the players' rostrum. "My friends," he intoned with easy loudness. The pianist came in with a recitative accompaniment but then was hushed. The congregation listened, arms still about each other as in a love feast. "It has been suggested to me that we end now. As most of you will know, one of our fellow-passengers is in the sickbay. Our revelry is, apparently, all too audible there. The worst is feared, I fear, for the poor man. It would be reverent and considerate to end the evening quietly, perhaps even in meditation. Thank you." He got down to some light applause. The band-leader called:

"You've had it, chums. Proceed quietly to your homes and do nothing naughty at street-corners."

"I think," said Miss Devi, her left arm still lightly about Hillier, "you're being insolent."

"You're a great one for the forms, aren't you?" said Hillier. "You admire discretion, you resent insolence. An indiscreet God had the insolence to make me what I am. What I am you are more than welcome to find out. At leisure. Stripping," he added, "was the process you had in mind."

"I shall lock my cabin door."

"You do that. You lock it." Hillier's stomach growled with hunger. Miss Devi's arm was still about him. He slowly dislodged it. "That silver ring-thing on your nose," he said. He tweaked it and she started back. "Keep it on," he said. "Don't, whatever else you do, take off that." She raised her head high as though with the intention of placing a water-vessel on it, sketched a small spitting gesture, and then, with Aryan dignity, made her way off through the dispersing crowd.

Wriste was still on the periphery. His friend the winger was with him, a lean, burnt, sardonic man in early middle age, still dressed as for the dining-saloon. "I thought you was doing all right there," said Wriste. "Ta for the Guinness," said the winger once more, leering. Hillier said:

"I want food brought to my cabin."

"You've got to hand it to him," nodded the winger. "Unless, of course, he's just showing off."

"All passengers' wishes must, providing they seem reasonable, be acceded to without question," said Wriste primly. "What can I get for you, sir?"

"Crustaceans, if you know what those are. No garnishings, but don't forget the red pepper. A painfully cold bottle of Sekt."

"Right, sir. And the number of the cabin you have in mind, if you don't know it already, is fifty-eight. Gorblimey," said Wriste old-fashionedly, "how the poor live."

5

It was not possible to proceed to that cabin with any degree of furtiveness, even though the hour was very late and the corridor-lights had been dimmed. The snores along the corridor were so loud that Hillier found it hard to believe them genuine; soon doors might fly open and outrage be registered from under curlers and out of mouths with their dentures removed. As an earnest of this, Wriste suddenly appeared at the end of the corridor to say "Good luck, sir" as though Hillier were going in to bat. And Master Walters, in endragoned Chinese brocade dressing-gown, was pacing like a prospective father, puffing a Black Russian in a Dunhill holder. Hillier, remembering that "father" was a relevant word here, asked kindly if there was any news.

"News?" The face, for all the precocity, was very young and blubbered. "What news would there be? As a man sows so shall he reap. Arteriosclerosis. He knew he was bringing it on." There seemed to be a flavour of Miss Devi's callous philosophy in all this.

"One can't always be blamed for the state of one's arteries," said Hillier. "Some people are just lucky."

"If he dies," said Alan, "what's going to happen to Clara and me?"

"Clara?"

"My sister. That other bitch can take care of herself, which is just what she's doing. My father wouldn't listen to reason. I told him not to

re-marry. We were doing very nicely on our own, the three of us. And everything will go to *her*, everything. She hates us, I know she does. What will happen to us then?"

Snores answered. "Modern medical science," said Hillier lamely. "It's amazing what they can do nowadays. He'll be right as rain in a day or two, you'll see."

"What do you know about it?" said Alan. "What do you know about anything? Spying up and down the corridor, as I can see, spy as you are. If he dies I'll get her. Or you can get her, being a spy. I'll pay you to get her."

"This is a lot of nonsense," said Hillier loudly. A voice from a cabin went shhhhhh. As he'd thought, there were people awake. "We'll talk about this in the morning. But in the morning everything will be all right. The sun will shine—it will all be a bad dream, soon forgotten. Now get to bed."

Alan looked at Hillier, who was naked under a bathrobe. "That's two baths in half a day," he said. Thank God, the boy still had some in-nocence in him. "At least you're a very clean spy."

"Look," said Hillier, "let's get this absolutely clear. I'm *not* a spy. Have you got that? There *are* spies, and I've actually met one or two. But I'm not one of them. If you could spot me as a spy, I can't very well be a spy, can I? The whole point of being a spy is that you don't seem to be one. Have you got that now?"

"I bet you've got a gun."

"I bet you've got one too. You seem to have everything else."

The boy shook his head. "Too young for a licence," he said. "That's my trouble—too young for everything. Too young to contest a will, for instance."

"Too young to be up at this hour. Get to bed. Take a couple of sleeping-tablets. I bet you've got those too."

"You don't seem," said Alan, "to be too bad of a bloke, really. Have you got children?"

"None. Nor a wife."

"A lone wolf," said Alan. "The cat that walks alone. I only wish you'd be straight with me. I'd like to strip the disguise off and find out what you really are."

Miss Devi again. "Tomorrow," said Hillier. "Everything will seem different tomorrow. Which is your cabin?"

"That one there. Come in and have a nightcap."

"Many thanks," said Hillier. "But I have some rather urgent business to attend to." He writhed as with bowel pain.

"That's all the eating," said Alan. "I saw that and I heard about the rest of it. Don't trust that man," he whispered. "He's a foreigner. He can't kid me with his posh accent." And then, in an officer-tone: "All right. Off you go." And he returned to his cabin. Wriste had also gone. Hillier padded to Cabin No. 58. As he had expected, the door was not locked. He knocked and at once entered. Again as he had expected, Miss Devi said: "You're late."

"Delayed," gulped Hillier. Miss Devi was lying on her bunk, naked except for her silver nose-ring. "Unavoidably." She had loosened her hair and her body was framed in it as far as the knees. Her body was superb, brown as though cooked, with the faintest shimmer of a glaze upon it; the jet-black bush answered the magnificent hair like a cheeky parody; the breasts, though full, did not loll but sat firmly as though moulded out of some celestial rubber; the nipples had already started upright. She reached out her arms, golden swords, towards him. He kicked off his slippers and let his bathrobe fall to the floor. "The light," he gasped. "I must put out the—"

"Leave it on. I want to see."

Hillier engaged. *"Araikkul va,"* she whispered. Tamil? A southern woman then, Dravidian not Aryan. She had been trained out of some manual, but it was not that coarse *Kama Sutra*. Was it the rare book called *Pokam,* whose title Hillier had always remembered for its facetious English connotation? What now began was agonisingly exquisite, something he had forgotten existed. She gently inflamed him with the *mayil* or peacock embrace, moved on to the *matakatham,* the *poththi,* the *putanai.* Hillier started to pass out of time, nodding to himself as he saw himself begin to take flight. Goodbye, Hillier. A voice beyond, striking like light, humorously catechised him, and he knew all the answers. Holy Cross Day? The festival of the exaltation of the Cross, September 14th. The year of the publication of *Hypatia?* 1853. The Mulready Envelope, the Morall Philosophie of Doni, the Kennington

Oval laid out in 1845, The White Doe of Rylstone, Markheim, Thrawn Janet, Wade's magic boat called Wingelock, Pontius Pilate's porter was named Cartaphilus the wandering Jew. When did Queen Elizabeth come to the throne? November, 1558. Something there tried to tug him back, some purpose on earth, connected with now, his job, but he was drawn on and on, beyond, to the very source of the voice. He saw the lips moving, opening as to devour him. The first is the fifth and the fifth is the eighth, he was told by a niggling earth-voice, but he shouted it down. He let himself be lipped in by the chewing mouth, then was masticated strongly till he was resolved into a juice, willing this, wanting it. *Mani, mani* was the word he remembered. The *mani* was tipped, gallons of it, into a vessel that throbbed as if it were organic and alive, and then the vessel was sealed with hot wax. He received his instructions in the name of man, addressed as Johnrobert-jameswilliam (the brothers Maryburgh playing a fife over Pompeii, Spalato, Kenwood, Osterley) Bedebellblair: *Cast forth doughtily!* So to cast forth in that one narrow sweet cave would be to wreck all the ships of the world—Alabama, Ark, Beagle, Bellerophon, Bounty, Cutty Sark, Dreadnought, Endeavour, Erebus, Fram, Golden Hind, Great Eastern, Great Harry, Marie Celeste, Mayflower, Revenge, Skidbladnir, Victory. But it was the one way to refertilise all the earth, for the cave opened into myriad channels below ground, mapped before him like the tree of man in an *Anatomy*. The gallons of *mani* had swollen to a scalding ocean on which navies cheered, their masts cracking. The eighty-foot tower that crowed from his loins glowed whitehot and then disintegrated into a million flying bricks. He pumped the massive burden out. Uriel, Raphael, Raguel, Michael, Sariel, Gabriel and Jerahmeel cried with sevenfold main voice, a common chord that was yet seven distinct and different notes. But, miracle, at once, from unknown reservoirs, the vessel began to fill again.

"Madu, madu!" she seemed to call. It was then now to be the gross way of the south. She bloated herself by magic to massive earth-mother, the breasts ever growing too big for his grasp, so that his fingers must grow and he grow new fingers. The nipples were rivets boring through the middle metacarpal bones. His soreness was first cooled then anointed by the heat of a beneficent hell that (Dante was

right) found its location at earth's centre. He was caught in a clef between great hills. He worked slowly, then faster, then let the cries of birds possess his ears—gannet, cormorant, bittern, ibis, spoonbill, flamingo, curassow, quail, rail, coot, trumpeter, bustard, plover, avocet, oystercatcher, curlew, oriole, crossbill, finch, shrike, godwit, wheatear, bluethroat. The cries condensed to a great roar of blood. The cabin soared, its ceiling blew off in the stratosphere and released them both. He clung, riding her, fearful of being dislodged, then, as the honeyed cantilena broke and flowed, he was ready to sink with her, she deflating herself to what she had been, her blown river of hair settling after the storm and flood.

But even now it was not all over. The last fit was in full awareness of time and place, the mole on the left shoulder noted, the close weave of the skin, the sweat that gummed body to body. The aim was to slice off the externals of the *jaghana* of each, so that viscera engaged, coiling and knotting into one complex of snakes. Here nature must allow of total penetration, both bodies lingam and yoni. "Now pain," she said. Her talons attacked his back; it was as if she were nailing him to herself. When she perceived his sinking, she broke away—viscera of each retreating and coiling in again, each polished belly slamming to, a door with secret hinges. She gave his neck and chest the sounding touch, so that the hairs stood erect, passed on to the half-moon on the buttocks, then the tiger's claw, the peacock's foot, the hare's jump, the blue lotus-leaf. She was essaying the man's part, and now she took it wholly, but not before Hillier had nearly swooned with the delectable agony of a piercing in his perineum so intense that it was as if he were to be spitted. She was on him then, and though he entered her it seemed she was entering him. He seemed raised from the surface of the bed by his tweaked and moulded nipples. He in his turn dug deep with plucking fingers into the fires that raged in the interlunar cavern, and soon what must be the ultimate accession gathered to its head. With athletic swiftness he turned her to the primal position and then, whinnying like a whole herd of wild horses, shivering as if transformed to protoplasm save for that plunging sword, he released lava like a mountain in a single thrust of destruction, so that she screamed like a burning city. Hillier lay on her still, sucked dry by vampires, moaning. The galaxies

wheeled, history shrieked then settled, familiar sensations crept back into the body, common hungers began to bite. He fell from her dripping as from a sea-bathe and, as also from that, tasting salt. He sought his bathrobe, but she grabbed it first, covering herself with it. She smiled—not kindly but with malice, so that he frowned in puzzlement—and then she called:

"Come in!"

And so he entered, still in evening clothes, huge, bald, smiling. Mr. Theodorescu. "Ah, yes," he organ-stopped. "Accept only this brand. The genuine article." The S burned on wet nakedness; it was too late now to attempt to hide it. "Mr. Hillier," beamed Theodorescu. "I thought it must be Mr. Hillier. Now I definitely know."

6

"Yes," said Theodorescu, "now I definitely know." He was carrying, Hillier now noticed, the kind of stick known as a Penang lawyer. "You, of course, Miss Devi, have known a little longer. That branded S tells all. Soskice's work, a cruel operator. The face of Hillier still unknown, but that signature snaking all over Europe, revealed only to the debagger—and your enemies, Mr. Hillier, do not go in for debagging, not having been educated in British public schools—to them, I say, or to a lady with the manifold talents of Miss Devi here."

"I was a bloody fool," said Hillier. "There's no point in my denying my identity. Look, I feel as though I'm having a medical. Can I put something on?"

"I think not," said Theodorescu. Miss Devi still had Hillier's robe about her; she was also sitting on her bunk, so that Hillier could not tug a sheet or blanket off. Hillier sat down on the cabin's solitary chair, set under the porthole. To his left was a dressing-table. In those drawers would be garments. Even now, the prospect of wearing one of Miss Devi's saris or wisp of her underwear met a physical response he had to hide with both hands. Again, in one of those drawers might be a gun. He risked putting out a hand to a drawer-handle, tugged, but the drawer was locked. "It is better, Mr. Hillier, that you sit there *in puris*

naturalibus, delightful coy phrase. Let us see you as you are. Dear dear dear, how scarred your body has been in war's or love's lists. But I would like to see the face. Pads of wax in the cheeks, I should imagine; the mouth-corner drawn down in a sneer—by simple stitching? Is that moustache real? Why do your eyes glitter so? Never mind, never mind. The time for talk is short. Let us talk then."

"First," said naked Hillier, "tell me who you are."

"I operate under my own name," said Theodorescu, leaning against the wardrobe. "I am utterly neutral, in the pay of no power, major or minor. I collect information and sell it to the highest—or shall I say higher?—bidder. I see only two men, usually in Lausanne. They bid according to the funds their respective organisations render available. It is a tolerably profitable trade, relatively harmless. Occasionally I make a direct sale, no auctioning. Well, now. Would you, Miss Devi, be good enough to dress? We will both look the other way, being gentlemen. And then I'd be glad if you'd proceed at once to the radio-room. You know what message to send."

"What is all this?" asked Hillier. "Something about me?"

Miss Devi rose from her bed, bundling up sheets and blankets as she did so. These she threw, a billow of white and brown, on to the space between Theodorescu and the cabin-door, so that Hillier could not get at them. Theodorescu then stepped gracefully aside, that she might take garments from the wardrobe. She chose black slacks and a white jumper. Hillier, naked, no gentleman, watched. She drew on the slacks without removing the bathrobe. Then she removed and threw it among the sheets and blankets, making Hillier gulp with the nostalgia of shared passion. She pulled the sweater on. Her hair, still flowing, was trapped in it. She released it with a long electric crackle. Hillier gulped and gulped. Theodorescu had kept his eyes averted, looking through the porthole at the deep Adriatic night. Miss Devi smiled at nothing, thrust her feet into sandals, then silently left. Theodorescu came to sit heavily upon the bunk. He said:

"You will have guessed what the message is. You are, if my informants in Trieste have not lied, now on your final assignment. I do not know what the assignment is, nor do I much care. The fact is that you will not be landing in Yarylyuk. Miss Devi is informing

the authorities—in a suitably cryptic form they will know how to interpret—that you are on your way. They will be awaiting you on the quayside. I am not doing this for money, Mr. Hillier, for, of course, you will not be landing. There will be men waiting for Mr. Jagger or whatever new persona you might consider assuming, and they will find nobody answering your description. They may, of course, find it necessary to strip one or two of the male passengers, looking for a tell-tale S. Those who *are* stripped—and they will not be many, most of our *compagnons de voyage* being old and fat—those who *are* will not object: it will be a story about adventures in a brutal police-state to retail over brandy and cigars back home. You would, if you were to stay on board instead of landing, also be in some slight danger. For these dear people are efficient at winkling out their quarry, as you well know. Visitors are allowed aboard, in the interests of the promotion of international friendship. This port of call is the sweet-sour sauce of the whole meaty trip. A British meal, British whisky, a few little purchases in the ship's gift-shop—there are encouragements to keep the Black Sea open to British cruises. There will be people wandering the ship looking for you, Mr. Hillier. There may even be police-warrants, trumped-up charges. The Captain will not want too much trouble."

"You do talk a lot," said Hillier.

"Do I? Do I?" Theodorescu seemed pleased. "Well, I'd better come to the point or points, had I not? Tomorrow a helicopter will be picking up Miss Devi and myself. We shall be sailing quite near the island of Zakynthos. You are cordially invited to come with us, Mr. Hillier."

"Where to?"

"Oh, I have no one headquarters. We could spend a pleasant enough time, the three of us, in my little villa near Amalias."

"And then, of course, I would be sold."

"Sold? *Sold?* Could I not sell you now if I wished? No, Mr. Hillier, I trade only in information. You must be a repository of a great deal of that. We could take our time over it. And then you could go, free as the air, well-rewarded. What do you say?"

"No."

Theodorescu sighed. "I expected that. Well, well. The delights that Miss Devi is qualified to purvey are, as you already know, very consid-

erable. Or rather you do not yet know. You've had time to touch only their fringes. Women I do not much care for myself—I prefer little Greek shepherd-boys—but Miss Devi—this I have been assured of by some whose judgment I respect on other matters of a hedonistic kind—Miss Devi is altogether exceptional. Think, Mr. Hillier. You're retiring from the hazardous work of espionage. What have you to look forward to? A tiny pension, no golden handshake—"

"I'm promised a sizeable bonus if I do this last job."

"If, Mr. Hillier, if. You know you won't do it now. Soon you will not say even 'if.' I offer you money and Miss Devi offers herself. What do you say to that? I am not likely to be less generous in my own bestowals than Miss Devi is in hers."

"I could think better," said Hillier, "if I had some clothes on."

"That's good," said Theodorescu. "That's a beginning. You talk of thinking, you see."

"As for that, I've thought about it. I'm not coming with you."

"Like yourself," said Theodorescu, "I believe in free will. I hate coercion. Bribery, of course, is altogether different. Well, there are certain things I wish to know now. I shall pay well. As an earnest of my generosity I start by rescinding the debt you owe me. The Trencherman Stakes." He laughed. "You need not pay me the thousand pounds."

"Thank you," said Hillier.

As if Hillier had really done him a favour, Theodorescu pulled a big cigar-case from his inner pocket. At the same time he allowed to peep out coyly bundles of American currency. "Hundred-dollar bills, Mr. Hillier. 'C's,' I think they call them. Do have a cigar." He disclosed fat Romeo and Juliets. Hillier took one; he'd been dying for a smoke. Theodorescu donated fire from a gold Ronson. They both puffed. The feminine odours of Miss Devi's cabin were overlaid with blue wraiths of Edwardian clubmen. "Do you remember," said Theodorescu dreamily, "a certain passage in the transports you seemed to be sharing with Miss Devi—an excruciatingly pleasurable one, in which it seemed that a claw sharpened to a needle-point pierced a most intimate part of your person?"

"How do you know about that?"

"It was arranged. It was a special injection, slow-working but efficacious. A substance developed by Dr. Pobedonostev of Yuzovo called, I believe, B-type vellocet. That has entered your body. In about fifteen minutes you will answer any question I put to you with perfect truth. Please, please, Mr. Hillier, give me the credit for a little sense, more— a little honesty, before you say that this is sheer bluff. You see, you will not fall into a trance, answering from a dream, as with so many of the so-called truth-drugs. You will be thoroughly conscious but possessed of a euphoria which will make concealment of the truth seem a crime against the deep and lasting friendship you will be convinced subsists between us. All I have to do is to wait."

Hillier said, "Bastard," and tried to get up from the chair. Theodorescu immediately cracked him on the *glans penis* with his Penang lawyer. Hillier tried to punch Theodorescu, but Theodorescu parried the blow easily with his stick, puffing at his cigar with enjoyment. Hillier then had time to attend to his privy agony, sitting again, rocking and moaning.

"It is because I believe in free will as you do," said Theodorescu, "that I want you to answer certain questions totally of your volition. The first question is for five thousand dollars. It is rather like one of these stupid television quiz-games, isn't it? Note, Mr. Hillier, that I needn't pay you anything at all. But I've robbed you of your chance of a bonus and I must make amends."

"I won't answer, you bastard."

"But you will, you will, nothing is more certain. Is it not better to answer with the exalted and, yes, totally *human* awareness that you yourself are choosing, not having information extracted from you with the aid of a silly little drug?"

"What's the first question?" asked Hillier, thinking: I needn't answer, I needn't answer, I have a choice.

"First of all, and for five thousand dollars, remember, I want to know the exact location of the East German escape route known, I believe, as Karl Otto."

"I don't know. I honestly don't know."

"Oh, surely. Well, think about it, but think quickly. Time is short for you, if not for me. Second, for six thousand dollars, I wish to be told

the identities of the members of the terrorist organisation called Vol-russ in Kharkov."

"Oh, God, you can't—"

"Wait, Mr. Hillier. I haven't said anything about selling this in-formation to the Soviet authorities. It's a matter of auctioning. So it's essential that, on top of this particular disclosure, you also reveal the code that I need to contact them. I understand it's a matter of putting a personal message in your British *Daily Worker*. The only British news-paper allowed in the Soviet Union, as you know, hence invaluable for conveying messages to those disaffected and vigorous bodies which are so annoying—though perhaps only annoying as a mosquito-sting is annoying—annoying, I say, to the MGB. I doubt if their representa-tive will outbid the émigré sponsors of Volruss."

Hillier, who now felt no pain, who no longer saw any embarrass-ment in his nakedness, who felt warm and rested and confident, smiled at Theodorescu. An intelligent and able man, he thought. A good eater and drinker. A man you could have a bloody good night out with. No enemy; a mere neutral who was wisely making money out of the whole stupid business that he, Hillier, was opting out of because the stupidity had recently become rather nasty. And then he saw that this must be the drug beginning to take effect. It was necessary to hate Theodor-escu again, and quickly. He got up from his chair, though smiling ami-ably, and said: "I'm going to get my bathrobe, and you're not bloody well going to stop me." Theodorescu at once, and without malice, cracked both shins hard with the Penang lawyer. Pain flowed like scalding water. "You fucking swine, Theodorescu," he gritted. And then he was grateful to Theodorescu for turning himself into the enemy again. He was a good man to be willing to do that. He saw what was happening; he saw that he would have to be quick. "Give me the money," he said. "Eleven thousand dollars." Theodorescu whipped out all his notes. "Karl Otto," he said, "starts in the cellar of Nummer Dreiundvierzig, Schlegelstrasse, Salzwedel."

"Good, good."

"I can only name five members of Volruss in Kharkov. They are N. A. Brussilov, I. R. Stolypin, F. Guchkov—I can't remember his patronymic—"

"Good, good, good."

"Aren't you going to take this down?"

"It's going down. This top button in my flies is a microphone. I have a tape-recorder in my left inside pocket. I was not scratching my armpit just then. I was switching it on."

"The others are F. T. Krylenko and H. K. Skovaioda."

"Ah, a Ukrainian that last one. Excellent. And the code?"

"Elkin."

"Elkin? Hm. And now, for twelve thousand dollars, the exact location—*exact*, mind—of Department 9A in London."

"I can't tell you that."

"But you must, Mr. Hillier. More, you will. Any moment now."

"I can't. That would be treason."

"Nonsense. There is no war. There is not going to be any war. This is all a great childish game on the floor of the world. It's absurd to talk about treason, isn't it?" He smiled kindly with the huge polished lamps of his eyes. Hillier started to smile back. Then he stood up again and lunged at Theodorescu. Theodorescu himself stood and towered high. He took both of Hillier's punching hands gently in his, still savouring his cigar. "Don't, Mr. Hillier. What's your first name? Ah, yes, I remember. Denis. We're friends, Denis, friends. If you don't tell me at once for twelve thousand dollars, you will tell me in a very few minutes for nothing."

"For God's sake hit me. Hit me hard."

"Oh no. Oh dear me no." Theodorescu spoke prissily. "Now come along, my dear Denis. Department 9A of Intercep. The exact location."

"If you hit me," said Hillier, "I shall hate you, and then when I tell you I shall be telling you of my own volition. That's what you want, isn't it? Free will."

"You're approaching the crepuscular zone, but you've not yet entered it. You'll be telling me because you want to tell me. See, here is the money. Twelve thousand dollars." He fanned the notes before Hillier's swimming eyes. "But be quick."

"It's off Devonshire Road in Chiswick, W.4. Globe Street. From Number 24 to the dairy at the end. Oh, God. Oh, God forgive me."

"He'll do that," nodded Theodorescu. "Sit down, my dear Denis. A pleasant name, Denis. It comes from Dionysus, you know. Sit down and rest. You seem to have nowhere to put this money. Perhaps I'd better keep it for you and give it you when you have clothes on."

"Give it me now. It's mine. I earned it."

"And you shall earn more." Hillier grabbed the money and held it, like figleaves, over his blushing genitals. "It's a pity you won't come with Miss Devi and me tomorrow. But we'll find you, never fear. There aren't very many places you can retire to. We shall be looking for you. Though," he said thoughtfully, "it's quite conceivable that you will come looking for Miss Devi."

Abject shame and rising euphoria warred in Hillier. He kept his eyes tight shut, biting his mouth so as not to smile.

"You're not a good subject for B-type vellocet," said Theodorescu. "There are certain powerful reserves in your bloodstream. You should now be slobbering all over me with love."

"I hate you," smiled Hillier warmly. "I loathe your bloody fat guts."

Theodorescu shook his head. "You'll hate me tomorrow. But tomorrow will be too late. You'll sleep very soundly tonight, I think. You won't wake early. But if you do, and if Miss Devi and I are not yet helicoptering off to the isles of Greece at the time of your awakening, it will be futile to attempt to do me harm. I shall be with the Captain on the bridge most of the morning. Moreover you have nothing with which to do me harm. I took the precaution of entering your cabin and stealing your Aiken and silencer. A very nice little weapon. I have it here." He took it from his left side-pocket. Hillier winced but then smiled. He nearly said that Theodorescu could keep it as a present. As if he had actually said that, Theodorescu put it back, patting the pocket. "As for the ampoules you had in the same stupid hiding-place—it was stupid, wasn't it? So obvious—as for those, you can keep them, whatever they are. Perhaps lethal—I don't know. I found your hypodermic in one of your suitcases. I took the precaution of smashing it. It's best to be on the safe side, don't you agree?"

"Oh, yes, yes," smiled Hillier. "How did you get into my cabin?"

Theodorescu sighed. "My dear fellow. There are duplicates in the

purser's office. I said I'd lost my key and I was made free of the board
on which the duplicates hang."

"You're a bloody good bloke," said Hillier sincerely.

Theodorescu, looking down on Hillier by the porthole, heard the
door behind him open. "Miss Devi," he said without turning. "You've
been rather a long time."

"I have, have I?" said Wriste in a girlish voice. He pouted, toothless,
towards turning Theodorescu. "What you doing with him there? He'll
catch his death sat like that."

"He likes to sit like that, don't you, Denis?"

"Oh yes, yes, Theo, I do."

"Just because a bloke's had a bit of a dip in the jampot," said Wriste,
"there's no call to get vindictive and sarky. She said she was your secretary. Now we know better, don't we?"

"This," said Theodorescu, "is a lady's cabin. You've no right to enter
without knocking. Now please leave."

"I'll leave all right," said Wriste. "But he's coming with me. I can see
what you've been doing, beating him to a pulp with that bloody stick.
Just because your bit can stand his weight better than yours."

"I shall report you to the purser."

"Report away." Wriste saw that Hillier had money grasped tight at
his groin. "Oh," he said, "that's possible. I hadn't thought of that. Has
he," he asked Hillier, "been giving you cabbage to let him bash you
about a bit?"

"Not at all," said Hillier, smiling truthfully. "Nothing like that at all.
He gave me this money for giving him—"

"He had it under the pillow," organed Theodorescu. "That's where
he had it. All right, take him away." He picked up the bathrobe from
the floor and threw it at Hillier.

"Thank you so very much, Theo. That's awfully kind."

"I'll take him away all right," said Wriste, "but not on your bleeding
orders. Come on, old boy," he said to Hillier as to a dog. "Why did he
have it under the pillow?" he beetled at Theodorescu. "There's something about all this that I don't get."

"He doesn't trust anybody," cried Theodorescu. "He won't go anywhere without his money."

"He can trust me," said Wriste, taking Hillier's hand. "You trust me, don't you?"

"Oh, yes. I trust you."

"That's all right, then. Now let Daddy put you to bed." He led his charge out. Hillier smiled, just starting to drop off.

FROM *UNDER WESTERN EYES* (1911)

Joseph Conrad (1857–1924)

Born in Lodz as Józef Korzeniowski, at a time when Poland existed only as part of the Russian empire, Conrad went to sea at the age of sixteen, served in the French navy, then the English merchant fleet, rose to the rank of captain, and commanded ships in the Orient and on the Congo River. He left the sea when he was thirty-two and became a writer. His novels are framed as adventure stories—of storms and wars, exotic locations, scoundrels and heroes. But Conrad sought throughout his fiction to operate at a great moral depth, so that the actions of humans are seen to be significant, and defining, and his work might be characterized as determinedly anti-existentialist. Under Western Eyes, *with* The Secret Agent *and* Nostromo, *forms a trilogy about political conflict and clandestine conspiracy.*

————

I

The origin of Mr. Razumov's record is connected with an event characteristic of modern Russia in the actual fact: the assassination of a

prominent statesman—and still more characteristic of the moral corruption of an oppressed society where the noblest aspirations of humanity, the desire of freedom, an ardent patriotism, the love of justice, the sense of pity, and even the fidelity of simple minds are prostituted to the lusts of hate and fear, the inseparable companions of an uneasy despotism.

The fact alluded to above is the successful attempt on the life of Mr. de P——, the President of the notorious Repressive Commission of some years ago, the Minister of State invested with extraordinary powers. The newspapers made noise enough about that fanatical, narrow-chested figure in gold-laced uniform, with a face of crumpled parchment, insipid, bespectacled eyes, and the cross of the Order of St. Procopius hung under the skinny throat. For a time, it may be remembered, not a month passed without his portrait appearing in some one of the illustrated papers of Europe. He served the monarchy by imprisoning, exiling, or sending to the gallows men and women, young and old, with an equable, unwearied industry. In his mystic acceptance of the principle of autocracy he was bent on extirpating from the land every vestige of anything that resembled freedom in public institutions; and in his ruthless persecution of the rising generation he seemed to aim at the destruction of the very hope of liberty itself.

It is said that this execrated personality had not enough imagination to be aware of the hate he inspired. It is hardly credible; but it is a fact that he took very few precautions for his safety. In the preamble of a certain famous State paper he had declared once that "the thought of liberty has never existed in the Act of the Creator. From the multitude of men's counsel nothing could come but revolt and disorder; and revolt and disorder in a world created for obedience and stability is sin. It was not Reason but Authority which expressed the Divine Intention. God was the Autocrat of the Universe...." It may be that the man who made this declaration believed that heaven itself was bound to protect him in his remorseless defence of Autocracy on this earth.

No doubt the vigilance of the police saved him many times; but, as a matter of fact, when his appointed fate overtook him, the competent authorities could not have given him any warning. They had no

knowledge of any conspiracy against the Minister's life, had no hint of any plot through their usual channels of information, had seen no signs, were aware of no suspicious movements or dangerous persons.

Mr. de P—— was being driven towards the railway station in a two-horse uncovered sleigh with footman and coachman on the box. Snow had been falling all night, making the roadway, uncleared as yet at this early hour, very heavy for the horses. It was still falling thickly. But the sleigh must have been observed and marked down. As it drew over to the left before taking a turn, the footman noticed a peasant walking slowly on the edge of the pavement with his hands in the pockets of his sheepskin coat and his shoulders hunched up to his ears under the falling snow. On being overtaken this peasant suddenly faced about and swung his arm. In an instant there was a terrible shock, a detonation muffled in the multitude of snowflakes; both horses lay dead and mangled on the ground and the coachman, with a shrill cry, had fallen off the box mortally wounded. The footman (who survived) had no time to see the face of the man in the sheepskin coat. After throwing the bomb this last got away, but it is supposed that, seeing a lot of people surging up on all sides of him in the falling snow, and all running towards the scene of the explosion, he thought it safer to turn back with them.

In an incredibly short time an excited crowd assembled round the sledge. The Minister-President, getting out unhurt into the deep snow, stood near the groaning coachman and addressed the people repeatedly in his weak, colourless voice: "I beg of you to keep off. For the love of God, I beg of you good people to keep off."

It was then that a tall young man who had remained standing perfectly still within a carriage gateway, two houses lower down, stepped out into the street and walking up rapidly flung another bomb over the heads of the crowd. It actually struck the Minister-President on the shoulder as he stooped over his dying servant, then falling between his feet exploded with a terrific concentrated violence, striking him dead to the ground, finishing the wounded man and practically annihilating the empty sledge in the twinkling of an eye. With a yell of horror the crowd broke up and fled in all directions, except for those who fell dead or dying where they stood nearest to the Minister-

President, and one or two others who did not fall till they had run a little way.

The first explosion had brought together a crowd as if by enchantment, the second made as swiftly a solitude in the street for hundreds of yards in each direction. Through the falling snow people looked from afar at the small heap of dead bodies lying upon each other near the carcasses of the two horses. Nobody dared to approach till some Cossacks of a street-patrol galloped up and, dismounting, began to turn over the dead. Amongst the innocent victims of the second explosion laid out on the pavement there was a body dressed in a peasant's sheepskin coat; but the face was unrecognizable, there was absolutely nothing found in the pockets of its poor clothing, and it was the only one whose identity was never established.

That day Mr. Razumov got up at his usual hour and spent the morning within the University buildings listening to the lectures and working for some time in the library. He heard the first vague rumour of something in the way of bomb-throwing at the table of the students' ordinary, where he was accustomed to eat his two o'clock dinner. But this rumour was made up of mere whispers, and this was Russia, where it was not always safe, for a student especially, to appear too much interested in certain kinds of whispers. Razumov was one of those men who, living in a period of mental and political unrest, keep an instinctive hold on normal, practical, everyday life. He was aware of the emotional tension of his time; he even responded to it in an indefinite way. But his main concern was with his work, his studies, and with his own future.

Officially and in fact without a family (for the daughter of the Archpriest had long been dead), no home influences had shaped his opinions or his feelings. He was as lonely in the world as a man swimming in the deep sea. The word Razumov was the mere label of a solitary individuality. There were no Razumovs belonging to him anywhere. His closest parentage was defined in the statement that he was a Russian. Whatever good he expected from life would be given to or withheld from his hopes by that connexion alone. This immense parentage suffered from the throes of internal dissensions, and he

shrank mentally from the fray as a good-natured man may shrink from taking definite sides in a violent family quarrel.

Razumov, going home, reflected that having prepared all the matters of the forthcoming examination, he could now devote his time to the subject of the prize essay. He hankered after the silver medal. The prize was offered by the Ministry of Education; the names of the competitors would be submitted to the Minister himself. The mere fact of trying would be considered meritorious in the higher quarters; and the possessor of the prize would have a claim to an administrative appointment of the better sort after he had taken his degree. The student Razumov in an access of elation forgot the dangers menacing the stability of the institutions which give rewards and appointments. But remembering the medallist of the year before, Razumov, the young man of no parentage, was sobered. He and some others happened to be assembled in their comrade's rooms at the very time when that last received the official advice of his success. He was a quiet, unassuming young man: "Forgive me," he had said with a faint apologetic smile and taking up his cap, "I am going out to order up some wine. But I must first send a telegram to my folk at home. I say! Won't the old people make it a festive time for the neighbours for twenty miles around our place."

Razumov thought there was nothing of that sort for him in the world. His success would matter to no one. But he felt no bitterness against the nobleman his protector, who was not a provincial magnate as was generally supposed. He was in fact nobody less than Prince K——, once a great and splendid figure in the world and now, his day being over, a Senator and a gouty invalid, living in a still spendid but more domestic manner. He had some young children and a wife as aristocratic and proud as himself.

In all his life Razumov was allowed only once to come into personal contact with the Prince.

It had the air of a chance meeting in the little attorney's office. One day Razumov, coming in by appointment, found a stranger standing there—a tall, aristocratic-looking personage with silky, grey sidewhiskers. The bald-headed, sly little lawyer-fellow called out, "Come in—come in, Mr. Razumov," with a sort of ironic heartiness. Then

turning deferentially to the stranger with the grand air, "A ward of mine, your Excellency. One of the most promising students of his faculty in the St. Petersburg University."

To his intense surprise Razumov saw a white shapely hand extended to him. He took it in great confusion (it was soft and passive) and heard at the same time a condescending murmur in which he caught only the words "Satisfactory" and "Persevere." But the most amazing thing of all was to feel suddenly a distinct pressure of the white shapely hand just before it was withdrawn: a light pressure like a secret sign. The emotion of it was terrible. Razumov's heart seemed to leap into his throat. When he raised his eyes the aristocratic personage, motioning the little lawyer aside, had opened the door and was going out.

The attorney rummaged amongst the papers on his desk for a time. "Do you know who that was?" he asked suddenly.

Razumov, whose heart was thumping hard yet, shook his head in silence.

"That was Prince K———. You wonder what he could be doing in the hole of a poor legal rat like myself—eh? These awfully great people have their sentimental curiosities like common sinners. But if I were you, Kirylo Sidorovitch," he continued, leering and laying a peculiar emphasis on the patronymic, "I wouldn't boast at large of the introduction. It would not be prudent, Kirylo Sidorovitch. Oh dear no! It would be in fact dangerous for your future."

The young man's ears burned like fire; his sight was dim. "That man!" Razumov was saying to himself. "He!"

Henceforth it was by this monosyllable that Mr. Razumov got into the habit of referring mentally to the stranger with grey silky side-whiskers. From that time too, when walking in the more fashionable quarters, he noted with interest the magnificent horses and carriages with Prince K———'s liveries on the box. Once he saw the Princess get out—she was shopping—followed by two girls, of which one was nearly a head taller than the other. Their fair hair hung loose down their backs in the English style; they had merry eyes, their coats, muffs, and little fur caps were exactly alike, and their cheeks and noses were tinged a cheerful pink by the frost. They crossed the pavement in front

of him, and Razumov went on his way smiling shyly to himself. "His" daughters. They resembled "Him." The young man felt a glow of warm friendliness towards these girls who would never know of his existence. Presently they would marry Generals or Kammerherrs and have girls and boys of their own, who perhaps would be aware of him as a celebrated old professor, decorated, possibly a Privy Councillor, one of the glories of Russia—nothing more!

But a celebrated professor was a somebody. Distinction would convert the label Razumov into an honoured name. There was nothing strange in the student Razumov's wish for distinction. A man's real life is that accorded to him in the thoughts of other men by reason of respect or natural love. Returning home on the day of the attempt on Mr. de P——'s life, Razumov resolved to have a good try for the silver medal.

Climbing slowly the four flights of the dark, dirty staircase in the house where he had his lodgings, he felt confident of success. The winner's name would be published in the papers on New Year's Day. And at the thought that "He" would most probably read it there, Razumov stopped short on the stairs for an instant, then went on smiling faintly at his own emotion. "This is but a shadow," he said to himself, "but the medal is a solid beginning."

With those ideas of industry in his head the warmth of his room was agreeable and encouraging. "I shall put in four hours of good work," he thought. But no sooner had he closed the door than he was horribly startled. All black against the usual tall stove of white tiles gleaming in the dusk, stood a strange figure, wearing a skirted, close-fitting, brown cloth coat strapped round the waist, in long boots, and with a little Astrakhan cap on its head. It loomed lithe and martial. Razumov was utterly confounded. It was only when the figure advancing two paces asked in an untroubled, grave voice if the outer door was closed that he regained his power of speech.

"Haldin! . . . Victor Victorovitch! . . . Is that you? . . . Yes. The outer door is shut all right. But this is indeed unexpected."

Victor Haldin, a student older than most of his contemporaries at the University, was not one of the industrious set. He was hardly ever seen at lectures; the authorities had marked him as "restless" and

"unsound"—very bad notes. But he had a great personal prestige with his comrades and influenced their thoughts. Razumov had never been intimate with him. They had met from time to time at gatherings in other students' houses. They had even had a discussion together—one of those discussions on first principles dear to the sanguine minds of youth.

Razumov wished the man had chosen some other time to come for a chat. He felt in good trim to tackle the prize essay. But as Haldin could not be slightingly dismissed Razumov adopted the tone of hospitality, asking him to sit down and smoke.

"Kirylo Sidorovitch," said the other, flinging off his cap, "we are not perhaps in exactly the same camp. Your judgment is more philosophical. You are a man of few words, but I haven't met anybody who dared to doubt the generosity of your sentiments. There is a solidity about your character which cannot exist without courage."

Razumov felt flattered and began to murmur shyly something about being very glad of his good opinion, when Haldin raised his hand.

"That is what I was saying to myself," he continued, "as I dodged in the woodyard down by the river-side. 'He has a strong character this young man,' I said to myself. 'He does not throw his soul to the winds.' Your reserve has always fascinated me, Kirylo Sidorovitch. So I tried to remember your address. But look here—it was a piece of luck. Your dvornik was away from the gate talking to a sleigh-driver on the other side of the street. I met no one on the stairs, not a soul. As I came up to your floor I caught sight of your landlady coming out of your rooms. But she did not see me. She crossed the landing to her own side, and then I slipped in. I have been here two hours expecting you to come in every moment."

Razumov had listened in astonishment; but before he could open his mouth Haldin added, speaking deliberately, "It was I who removed de P—— this morning."

Razumov kept down a cry of dismay. The sentiment of his life being utterly ruined by this contact with such a crime expressed itself quaintly by a sort of half-derisive mental exclamation, "There goes my silver medal!"

Haldin continued after waiting a while—

"You say nothing, Kirylo Sidorovitch! I understand your silence. To be sure, I cannot expect you with your frigid English manner to embrace me. But never mind your manners. You have enough heart to have heard the sound of weeping and gnashing of teeth this man raised in the land. That would be enough to get over any philosophical hopes. He was uprooting the tender plant. He had to be stopped. He was a dangerous man—a convinced man. Three more years of his work would have put us back fifty years into bondage—and look at all the lives wasted, at all the souls lost in that time."

His curt, self-confident voice suddenly lost its ring and it was in a dull tone that he added, "Yes, brother, I have killed him. It's weary work."

Razumov had sunk into a chair. Every moment he expected a crowd of policemen to rush in. There must have been thousands of them out looking for that man walking up and down in his room. Haldin was talking again in a restrained, steady voice. Now and then he flourished an arm, slowly, without excitement.

He told Razumov how he had brooded for a year; how he had not slept properly for weeks. He and "Another" had a warning of the Minister's movements from "a certain person" late the evening before. He and that "Another" prepared their "engines" and resolved to have no sleep till "the deed" was done. They walked the streets under the falling snow with the "engines" on them, exchanging not a word the livelong night. When they happened to meet a police patrol they took each other by the arm and pretended to be a couple of peasants on the spree. They reeled and talked in drunken hoarse voices. Except for these strange outbreaks they kept silence, moving on ceaselessly. Their plans had been previously arranged. At daybreak they made their way to the spot which they knew the sledge must pass. When it appeared in sight they exchanged a muttered good-bye and separated. The "other" remained at the corner, Haldin took up a position a little farther up the street. . . .

After throwing his "engine" he ran off and in a moment was overtaken by the panic-struck people flying away from the spot after the second explosion. They were wild with terror. He was jostled once or

twice. He slowed down for the rush to pass him and then turned to the left into a narrow street. There he was alone.

He marvelled at this immediate escape. The work was done. He could hardly believe it. He fought with an almost irresistible longing to lie down on the pavement and sleep. But this sort of faintness—a drowsy faintness—passed off quickly. He walked faster, making his way to one of the poorer parts of the town in order to look up Ziemianitch.

This Ziemianitch, Razumov understood, was a sort of town-peasant who had got on; owner of a small number of sledges and horses for hire. Haldin paused in his narrative to exclaim—

"A bright spirit! A hardy soul! The best driver in St. Petersburg. He has a team of three horses there. . . . Ah! He's a fellow!"

This man had declared himself willing to take out safely, at any time, one or two persons to the second or third railway station on one of the southern lines. But there had been no time to warn him the night before. His usual haunt seemed to be a low-class eating-house on the outskirts of the town. When Haldin got there the man was not to be found. He was not expected to turn up again till the evening. Haldin wandered away restlessly.

He saw the gate of a woodyard open and went in to get out of the wind which swept the bleak broad thoroughfare. The great rectangular piles of cut wood loaded with snow resembled the huts of a village. At first the watchman who discovered him crouching amongst them talked in a friendly manner. He was a dried-up old man wearing two ragged army coats one over the other; his wizened little face, tied up under the jaw and over the ears in a dirty red handkerchief, looked comical. Presently he grew sulky, and then all at once without rhyme or reason began to shout furiously.

"Aren't you ever going to clear out of this, you loafer? We know all about factory hands of your sort. A big, strong, young chap! You aren't even drunk. What do you want here? You don't frighten us. Take yourself and your ugly eyes away."

Haldin stopped before the sitting Razumov. His supple figure, with the white forehead above which the fair hair stood straight up, had an aspect of lofty daring.

"He did not like my eyes," he said. "And so . . . here I am."

Razumov made an effort to speak calmly.

"But pardon me, Victor Victorovitch. We know each other so little. . . . I don't see why you . . ."

"Confidence," said Haldin.

This word sealed Razumov's lips as if a hand had been clapped on his mouth. His brain seethed with arguments.

"And so—here you are," he muttered through his teeth.

The other did not detect the tone of anger. Never suspected it.

"Yes. And nobody knows I am here. You are the last person that could be suspected—should I get caught. That's an advantage, you see. And then—speaking to a superior mind like yours I can well say all the truth. It occurred to me that you—you have no one belonging to you—no ties, no one to suffer for it if this came out by some means. There have been enough ruined Russian homes as it is. But I don't see how my passage through your rooms can be ever known. If I should be got hold of, I'll know how to keep silent—no matter what they may be pleased to do to me," he added grimly.

He began to walk again while Razumov sat still, appalled.

"You thought that——" he faltered out almost sick with indignation.

"Yes, Razumov. Yes, brother. Some day you shall help to build. You suppose that I am a terrorist, now—a destructor of what is. But consider that the true destroyers are they who destroy the spirit of progress and truth, not the avengers who merely kill the bodies of the persecutors of human dignity. Men like me are necessary to make room for self-contained, thinking men like you. Well, we have made the sacrifice of our lives, but all the same I want to escape if it can be done. It is not my life I want to save, but my power to do. I won't live idle. Oh no! Don't make any mistake, Razumov. Men like me are rare. And, besides, an example like this is more awful to oppressors when the perpetrator vanishes without a trace. They sit in their offices and palaces and quake. All I want you to do is to help me to vanish. No great matter that. Only to go by and by and see Ziemianitch for me at that place where I went this morning. Just tell him, 'He whom you know wants a well-horsed sledge to pull up half an hour after mid-

night at the seventh lamp-post on the left counting from the upper end of Karabelnaya. If nobody gets in, the sledge is to run round a block or two, so as to come back past the same spot in ten minutes' time.' "

Razumov wondered why he had not cut short that talk and told this man to go away long before. Was it weakness or what?

He concluded that it was a sound instinct. Haldin must have been seen. It was impossible that some people should not have noticed the face and appearance of the man who threw the second bomb. Haldin was a noticeable person. The police in their thousands must have had his description within the hour. With every moment the danger grew. Sent out to wander in the streets he could not escape being caught in the end.

The police would very soon find out all about him. They would set about discovering a conspiracy. Everybody Haldin had ever known would be in the greatest danger. Unguarded expressions, little facts in themselves innocent would be counted for crimes. Razumov remembered certain words he said, the speeches he had listened to, the harmless gatherings he had attended—it was almost impossible for a student to keep out of that sort of thing, without becoming suspect to his comrades.

Razumov saw himself shut up in a fortress, worried, badgered, perhaps ill-used. He saw himself deported by an administrative order, his life broken, ruined, and robbed of all hope. He saw himself—at best—leading a miserable existence under police supervision, in some small, far-away provincial town, without friends to assist his necessities or even take any steps to alleviate his lot—as others had. Others had fathers, mothers, brothers, relations, connexions, to move heaven and earth on their behalf—he had no one. The very officials that sentenced him some morning would forget his existence before sunset.

He saw his youth pass away from him in misery and half starvation—his strength give way, his mind become an abject thing. He saw himself creeping, broken down and shabby, about the streets—dying unattended in some filthy hole of a room, or on the sordid bed of a Government hospital.

He shuddered. Then the peace of bitter calmness came over him. It was best to keep this man out of the streets till he could be got rid of

with some chance of escaping. That was the best that could be done. Razumov, of course, felt the safety of his lonely existence to be permanently endangered. This evening's doings could turn up against him at any time as long as this man lived and the present institutions endured. They appeared to him rational and indestructible at that moment. They had a force of harmony—in contrast with the horrible discord of this man's presence. He hated the man. He said quietly—

"Yes, of course, I will go. You must give me precise directions, and for the rest—depend on me."

"Ah! You are a fellow! Collected—cool as a cucumber. A regular Englishman. Where did you get your soul from? There aren't many like you. Look here, brother! Men like me leave no posterity, but their souls are not lost. No man's soul is ever lost. It works for itself—or else where would be the sense of self-sacrifice, of martyrdom, of conviction, of faith—the labours of the soul? What will become of my soul when I die in the way I must die—soon—very soon perhaps? It shall not perish. Don't make a mistake, Razumov. This is not murder—it is war, war. My spirit shall go on warring in some Russian body till all falsehood is swept out of the world. The modern civilization is false, but a new revelation shall come out of Russia. Ha! you say nothing. You are a sceptic. I respect your philosophical scepticism, Razumov, but don't touch the soul. The Russian soul that lives in all of us. It has a future. It has a mission, I tell you, or else why should I have been moved to do this—reckless—like a butcher—in the middle of all these innocent people—scattering death—I! I! . . . I wouldn't hurt a fly!"

"Not so loud," warned Razumov harshly.

Haldin sat down abruptly, and leaning his head on his folded arms burst into tears. He wept for a long time. The dusk had deepened in the room. Razumov, motionless in sombre wonder, listened to the sobs.

The other raised his head, got up and with an effort mastered his voice.

"Yes. Men like me leave no posterity," he repeated in a subdued tone. "I have a sister though. She's with my old mother—I persuaded them to go abroad this year—thank God. Not a bad little girl my sister. She has the most trustful eyes of any human being that ever walked this earth. She will marry well, I hope. She may

have children—sons perhaps. Look at me. My father was a Government official in the provinces. He had a little land too. A simple servant of God—a true Russian in his way. His was the soul of obedience. But I am not like him. They say I resemble my mother's eldest brother, an officer. They shot him in '28. Under Nicholas, you know. Haven't I told you that this is war, war. . . . But God of Justice! This is weary work."

Razumov, in his chair, leaning his head on his hand, spoke as if from the bottom of an abyss.

"You believe in God, Haldin?"

"There you go catching at words that are wrung from one. What does it matter? What was it the Englishman said: 'There is a divine soul in things . . .' Devil take him—I don't remember now. But he spoke the truth. When the day of you thinkers comes don't you forget what's divine in the Russian soul—and that's resignation. Respect that in your intellectual restlessness and don't let your arrogant wisdom spoil its message to the world. I am speaking to you now like a man with a rope round his neck. What do you imagine I am? A being in revolt? No. It's you thinkers who are in everlasting revolt. I am one of the resigned. When the necessity of this heavy work came to me and I understood that it had to be done—what did I do? Did I exult? Did I take pride in my purpose? Did I try to weigh its worth and consequences? No! I was resigned. I thought 'God's will be done.' "

He threw himself full length on Razumov's bed and putting the backs of his hands over his eyes remained perfectly motionless and silent. Not even the sound of his breathing could be heard. The dead stillness of the room remained undisturbed till in the darkness Razumov said gloomily—

"Haldin."

"Yes," answered the other readily, quite invisible now on the bed and without the slightest stir.

"Isn't it time for me to start?"

"Yes, brother." The other was heard, lying still in the darkness as though he were talking in his sleep. "The time has come to put fate to the test."

He paused, then gave a few lucid directions in the quiet impersonal

voice of a man in a trance. Razumov made ready without a word of answer. As he was leaving the room the voice in the bed said after him—
"Go with God, thou silent soul."

On the landing, moving softly, Razumov locked the door and put the key in his pocket. . . .

III

. . . Razumov woke up for the tenth time perhaps with a heavy shiver. Seeing the light of day in his window, he resisted the inclination to lay himself down again. He did not remember anything, but he did not think it strange to find himself on the sofa in his cloak and chilled to the bone. The light coming through the window seemed strangely cheerless, containing no promise as the light of each new day should for a young man. It was the awakening of a man mortally ill, or of a man ninety years old. He looked at the lamp, which had burnt itself out. It stood there, the extinguished beacon of his labours, a cold object of brass and porcelain, amongst the scattered pages of his notes and small piles of books—a mere litter of blackened paper—dead matter—without significance or interest.

He got on his feet, and divesting himself of his cloak hung it on the peg, going through all the motions mechanically. An incredible dullness, a ditch-water stagnation was sensible to his perceptions, as though life had withdrawn itself from all things and even from his own thoughts. There was not a sound in the house.

Turning away from the peg, he thought in that same lifeless manner that it must be very early yet; but when he looked at the watch on his table he saw both hands arrested at twelve o'clock.

"Ah, yes," he mumbled to himself, and as if beginning to get roused a little he took a survey of his room. The paper stabbed to the wall arrested his attention. He eyed it from the distance without approval or perplexity; but when he heard the servant-girl beginning to bustle about in the outer room with the samovar for his morning tea, he walked up to it and took it down with an air of profound indifference.

While doing this he glanced down at the bed on which he had not

slept that night. The hollow in the pillow made by the weight of Haldin's head was very noticeable.

Even his anger at this sign of the man's passage was dull. He did not try to nurse it into life. He did nothing all that day; he neglected even to brush his hair. The idea of going out never occurred to him—and if he did not start a connected train of thought it was not because he was unable to think. It was because he was not interested enough.

He yawned frequently. He drank large quantities of tea, he walked about aimlessly, and when he sat down he did not budge for a long time. He spent some time drumming on the window with his finger-tips quietly. In his listless wanderings round about the table he caught sight of his own face in the looking-glass and that arrested him. The eyes which returned his stare were the most unhappy eyes he had ever seen. And this was the first thing which disturbed the mental stagnation of that day.

He was not affected personally. He merely thought that life without happiness is impossible. What was happiness? He yawned and went on shuffling about and about between the walls of his room. Looking forward was happiness—that's all—nothing more. To look forward to the gratification of some desire, to the gratification of some passion, love, ambition, hate—hate, too, indubitably. Love and hate. And to escape the dangers of existence, to live without fear, was also happiness. There was nothing else. Absence of fear—looking forward. "Oh! the miserable lot of humanity!" he exclaimed mentally; and added at once in his thought, "I ought to be happy enough as far as that goes." But he was not excited by that assurance. On the contrary, he yawned again as he had been yawning all day. He was mildly surprised to discover himself being overtaken by night. The room grew dark swiftly though time had seemed to stand still. How was it that he had not noticed the passing of that day? Of course, it was the watch being stopped. . . .

He did not light his lamp, but went over to the bed and threw himself on it without any hesitation. Lying on his back, he put his hands under his head and stared upward. After a moment he thought, "I am lying here like that man. I wonder if he slept while I was struggling with the blizzard in the streets. No, he did not sleep. But why should I

not sleep?" and he felt the silence of the night press upon all his limbs like a weight.

In the calm of the hard frost outside, the clear-cut strokes of the town clock counting off midnight penetrated the quietness of his suspended animation.

Again he began to think. It was twenty-four hours since that man left his room. Razumov had a distinct feeling that Haldin in the fortress was sleeping that night. It was a certitude which made him angry because he did not want to think of Haldin, but he justified it to himself by physiological and psychological reasons. The fellow had hardly slept for weeks on his own confession, and now every incertitude was at an end for him. No doubt he was looking forward to the consummation of his martyrdom. A man who resigns himself to kill need not go very far for resignation to die. Haldin slept perhaps more soundly than General T——, whose task—weary work too— was not done, and over whose head hung the sword of revolutionary vengeance.

Razumov, remembering the thick-set man with his heavy jowl resting on the collar of his uniform, the champion of autocracy, who had let no sign of surprise, incredulity, or joy escape him, but whose goggle eyes could express a mortal hatred of all rebellion—Razumov moved uneasily on the bed.

"He suspected me," he thought. "I suppose he must suspect everybody. He would be capable of suspecting his own wife, if Haldin had gone to her boudoir with his confession."

Razumov sat up in anguish. Was he to remain a political suspect all his days? Was he to go through life as a man not wholly to be trusted— with a bad secret police note tacked on to his record? What sort of future could he look forward to?

"I am now a suspect," he thought again; but the habit of reflection and that desire of safety, of an ordered life, which was so strong in him came to his assistance as the night wore on. His quiet, steady, and laborious existence would vouch at length for his loyalty. There were many permitted ways to serve one's country. There was an activity that made for progress without being revolutionary. The field of influence was great and infinitely varied—once one had conquered a name.

His thought, like a circling bird, reverted after four-and-twenty hours to the silver medal, and as it were poised itself there.

When the day broke he had not slept, not for a moment, but he got up not very tired and quite sufficiently self-possessed for all practical purposes.

He went out and attended three lectures in the morning. But the work in the library was a mere dumb show of research. He sat with many volumes open before him trying to make notes and extracts. His new tranquillity was like a flimsy garment, and seemed to float at the mercy of a casual word. Betrayal! Why! the fellow had done all that was necessary to betray himself. Precious little had been needed to deceive him.

"I have said no word to him that was not strictly true. Not one word," Razumov argued with himself.

Once engaged on this line of thought there could be no question of doing useful work. The same ideas went on passing through his mind, and he pronounced mentally the same words over and over again. He shut up all the books and rammed all his papers into his pocket with convulsive movements, raging inwardly against Haldin.

As he was leaving the library, a long bony student in a threadbare overcoat joined him, stepping moodily by his side. Razumov answered his mumbled greeting without looking at him at all.

"What does he want with me?" he thought, with a strange dread of the unexpected which he tried to shake off lest it should fasten itself upon his life for good and all. And the other, muttering cautiously with downcast eyes, supposed that his comrade had seen the news of de P——'s executioner—that was the expression he used—having been arrested the night before last. . . .

"I've been ill—shut up in my rooms," Razumov mumbled through his teeth.

The tall student, raising his shoulders, shoved his hands deep into his pockets. He had a hairless, square, tallowy chin which trembled slightly as he spoke, and his nose nipped bright red by the sharp air looked like a false nose of painted cardboard between the sallow cheeks. His whole appearance was stamped with the mark of cold and

hunger. He stalked deliberately at Razumov's elbow with his eyes on the ground.

"It's an official statement," he continued in the same cautious mutter. "It may be a lie. But there was somebody arrested between midnight and one in the morning on Tuesday. This is certain."

And talking rapidly under the cover of his downcast air, he told Razumov that this was known through an inferior Government clerk employed at the Central Secretariat. That man belonged to one of the revolutionary circles. "The same, in fact, I am affiliated to," remarked the student.

They were crossing a wide quadrangle. An infinite distress possessed Razumov, annihilated his energy, and before his eyes everything appeared confused and as if evanescent. He dared not leave the fellow there. "He may be affiliated to the police," was the thought that passed through his mind. "Who could tell?" But eyeing the miserable frost-nipped, famine-struck figure of his companion he perceived the absurdity of his suspicion.

"But I—you know—I don't belong to any circle. I . . ."

He dared not say any more. Neither dared he mend his pace. The other, raising and setting down his lamentably shod feet with exact deliberation, protested in a low tone that it was not necessary for everybody to belong to an organisation. The most valuable personalities remained outside. Some of the best work was done outside the organisation. Then very fast, with whispering, feverish lips:

"The man arrested in the street was Haldin."

And accepting Razumov's dismayed silence as natural enough, he assured him that there was no mistake. That Government clerk was on night duty at the Secretariat. Hearing a great noise of footsteps in the hall and aware that political prisoners were brought over sometimes at night from the fortress, he opened the door of the room in which he was working, suddenly. Before the gendarme on duty could push him back and slam the door in his face, he had seen a prisoner being partly carried, partly dragged along the hall by a lot of policemen. He was being used very brutally. And the clerk had recognised Haldin perfectly. Less than half an hour afterwards General T—— arrived at the Secretariat to examine that prisoner personally.

"Aren't you astonished?" concluded the gaunt student.

"No," said Razumov roughly—and at once regretted his answer.

"Everybody supposed Haldin was in the provinces—with his people. Didn't you?"

The student turned his big hollow eyes upon Razumov, who said unguardedly:

"His people are abroad."

He could have bitten his tongue out with vexation. The student pronounced in a tone of profound meaning:

"So! You alone were aware . . ." and stopped.

"They have sworn my ruin," thought Razumov. "Have you spoken of this to any one else?" he asked with bitter curiosity.

The other shook his head.

"No, only to you. Our circle thought that as Haldin had been often heard expressing a warm appreciation of your character . . ."

Razumov could not restrain a gesture of angry despair which the other must have misunderstood in some way, because he ceased speaking and turned away his black, lack-lustre eyes.

They moved side by side in silence. Then the gaunt student began to whisper again, with averted gaze:

"As we have at present no one affiliated inside the fortress so as to make it possible to furnish him with a packet of poison, we have considered already some sort of retaliatory action—to follow very soon . . ."

Razumov trudging on interrupted:

"Were you acquainted with Haldin? Did he know where you live?"

"I had the happiness to hear him speak twice," his companion answered in the feverish whisper contrasting with the gloomy apathy of his face and bearing. "He did not know where I live. . . . I am lodging poorly . . . with an artisan family. . . . I have just a corner in a room. It is not very practicable to see me there, but if you should need me for anything I am ready. . . ."

Razumov trembled with rage and fear. He was beside himself, but kept his voice low.

"You are not to come near me. You are not to speak to me. Never address a single word to me. I forbid you."

"Very well," said the other submissively, showing no surprise whatever at this abrupt prohibition. "You don't wish for secret reasons . . . perfectly . . . I understand."

He edged away at once, not looking up even; and Razumov saw his gaunt, shabby, famine-stricken figure cross the street obliquely with lowered head and that peculiar exact motion of the feet.

He watched him as one would watch a vision out of a nightmare, then he continued on his way, trying not to think. On his landing the landlady seemed to be waiting for him. She was a short, thick, shapeless woman with a large yellow face wrapped up everlastingly in a black woollen shawl. When she saw him come up the last flight of stairs she flung both her arms up excitedly, then clasped her hands before her face.

"Kirylo Sidorovitch—little father—what have you been doing? And such a quiet young man, too! The police have just gone this moment after searching your rooms."

Razumov gazed down at her with silent, scrutinising attention. Her puffy yellow countenance was working with emotion. She screwed up her eyes at him entreatingly.

"Such a sensible young man! Anybody can see you are sensible. And now—like this—all at once. . . . What is the good of mixing yourself up with these Nihilists? Do give over, little father. They are unlucky people."

Razumov moved his shoulders slightly.

"Or is it that some secret enemy has been calumniating you, Kirylo Sidorovitch? The world is full of black hearts and false denunciations nowadays. There is much fear about."

"Have you heard that I have been denounced by some one?" asked Razumov, without taking his eyes off her quivering face.

But she had not heard anything. She had tried to find out by asking the police captain while his men were turning the room upside down. The police captain of the district had known her for the last eleven years and was a humane person. But he said to her on the landing, looking very black and vexed:

"My good woman, do not ask questions. I don't know anything myself. The order comes from higher quarters."

And indeed there had appeared, shortly after the arrival of the policeman of the district, a very superior gentleman in a fur coat and a shiny hat, who sat down in the room and looked through all the papers himself. He came alone and went away by himself, taking nothing with him. She had been trying to put things straight a little since they left.

Razumov turned away brusquely and entered his rooms.

All his books had been shaken and thrown on the floor. His landlady followed him, and stooping painfully began to pick them up into her apron. His papers and notes, which were kept always neatly sorted (they all related to his studies), had been shuffled up and heaped together into a ragged pile in the middle of the table.

This disorder affected him profoundly, unreasonably. He sat down and stared. He had a distinct sensation of his very existence being undermined in some mysterious manner, of his moral supports falling away from him one by one. He even experienced a slight physical giddiness and made a movement as if to reach for something to steady himself with.

The old woman, rising to her feet with a low groan, shot all the books she had collected in her apron on to the sofa and left the room muttering and sighing.

It was only then that he noticed that the sheet of paper which for one night had remained stabbed to the wall above his empty bed was lying on top of the pile.

When he had taken it down the day before, he had folded it in four, absent-mindedly, before dropping it on the table. And now he saw it lying uppermost, spread out, smoothed out even and covering all the confused pile of pages, the record of his intellectual life for the last three years. It had not been flung there. It had been placed there—smoothed out, too! He guessed in that an intention of profound meaning—or perhaps some inexplicable mockery.

He sat staring at the piece of paper till his eyes began to smart. He did not attempt to put his papers in order, either that evening or the next day—which he spent at home in a state of peculiar irresolution. This irresolution bore upon the question whether he should continue to live—neither more nor less. But its nature was very far removed from the hesitation of a man contemplating suicide. The idea of lay-

ing violent hands upon his body did not occur to Razumov. The unrelated organism bearing that label, walking, breathing, wearing these clothes, was of no importance to any one, unless maybe to the landlady. The true Razumov had his being in the willed, in the determined future—in that future menaced by the lawlessness of autocracy—for autocracy knows no law—and the lawlessness of revolution. The feeling that his moral personality was at the mercy of these lawless forces was so strong that he asked himself seriously if it were worth while to go on accomplishing the mental functions of that existence which seemed no longer his own.

"What is the good of exerting my intelligence, of pursuing the systematic development of my faculties and all my plans of work?" he asked himself. "I want to guide my conduct by reasonable convictions, but what security have I against something—some destructive horror—walking in upon me as I sit here? . . ."

Razumov looked apprehensively towards the door of the outer room as if expecting some shape of evil to turn the handle and appear before him silently.

"A common thief," he said to himself, "finds more guarantees in the law he is breaking, and even a brute like Ziemianitch has his consolation." Razumov envied the materialism of the thief and the passion of the incorrigible lover. The consequences of their actions were always clear and their lives remained their own.

But he slept as soundly that night as though he had been consoling himself in the manner of Ziemianitch. He dropped off suddenly, lay like a log, remembered no dream on waking. But it was as if his soul had gone out in the night to gather the flowers of wrathful wisdom. He got up in a mood of grim determination and as if with a new knowledge of his own nature. He looked mockingly on the heap of papers on his table; and left his room to attend the lectures, muttering to himself, "We shall see."

He was in no humour to talk to anybody or hear himself questioned as to his absence from lectures the day before. But it was difficult to repulse rudely a very good comrade with a smooth pink face and fair hair, bearing the nickname amongst his fellow-students of "Madcap Kostia." He was the idolised only son of a very wealthy and illiterate Govern-

ment contractor, and attended the lectures only during the periodical fits of contrition following upon tearful paternal remonstrances. Noisily blundering like a retriever puppy, his elated voice and great gestures filled the bare academy corridors with the joy of thoughtless animal life, provoking indulgent smiles at a great distance. His usual discourses treated of trotting horses, wine-parties in expensive restaurants, and the merits of persons of easy virtue, with a disarming artlessness of outlook. He pounced upon Razumov about midday, somewhat less uproariously than his habit was, and led him aside.

"Just a moment, Kirylo Sidorovitch. A few words here in this quiet corner."

He felt Razumov's reluctance, and insinuated his hand under his arm caressingly.

"No—pray do. I don't want to talk to you about any of my silly scrapes. What are my scrapes? Absolutely nothing. Mere childishness. The other night I flung a fellow out of a certain place where I was having a fairly good time. A tyrannical little beast of a quill-driver from the Treasury department. . . . He was bullying the people of the house. I rebuked him. 'You are not behaving humanely to God's creatures that are a jolly sight more estimable than yourself,' I said. I can't bear to see any tyranny, Kirylo Sidorovitch. Upon my word I can't. He didn't take it in good part at all. 'Who's that impudent puppy?' he begins to shout. I was in excellent form as it happened, and he went through the closed window very suddenly. He flew quite a long way into the yard. I raged like—like a—minotaur. The women clung to me and screamed, the fiddlers got under the table. . . . Such fun! My dad had to put his hand pretty deep into his pocket, I can tell you."

He chuckled.

"My dad is a very useful man. Jolly good thing it is for me, too. I do get into unholy scrapes."

His elation fell. That was just it. What was his life? Insignificant; no good to any one; a mere festivity. It would end some fine day in his getting his skull split with a champagne bottle in a drunken brawl. At such times, too, when men were sacrificing themselves to ideas. But he could never get any ideas into his head. His head wasn't worth anything better than to be split by a champagne bottle.

Razumov, protesting that he had no time, made an attempt to get away. The other's tone changed to confidential earnestness.

"For God's sake, Kirylo, my dear soul, let me make some sort of sacrifice. It would not be a sacrifice really. I have my rich dad behind me. There's positively no getting to the bottom of his pocket."

And rejecting indignantly Razumov's suggestion that this was drunken raving, he offered to lend him some money to escape abroad with. He could always get money from his dad. He had only to say that he had lost it at cards or something of that sort, and at the same time promise solemnly not to miss a single lecture for three months on end. That would fetch the old man; and he, Kostia, was quite equal to the sacrifice. Though he really did not see what was the good for him to attend the lectures. It was perfectly hopeless.

"Won't you let me be of some use?" he pleaded to the silent Razumov, who, with his eyes on the ground and utterly unable to penetrate the real drift of the other's intention, felt a strange reluctance to clear up the point.

"What makes you think I want to go abroad?" he asked at last very quietly.

Kostia lowered his voice.

"You had the police in your rooms yesterday. There are three or four of us who have heard of that. Never mind how we know. It is sufficient that we do. So we have been consulting together."

"Ah! You got to know that so soon," muttered Razumov negligently.

"Yes. We did. And it struck us that a man like you . . ."

"What sort of a man do you take me to be?" Razumov interrupted him.

"A man of ideas—and a man of action too. But you are very deep, Kirylo. There's no getting to the bottom of your mind. Not for fellows like me. But we all agreed that you must be preserved for our country. Of that we have no doubt whatever—I mean all of us who have heard Haldin speak of you on certain occasions. A man doesn't get the police ransacking his rooms without there being some devilry hanging over his head. . . . And so if you think that it would be better for you to bolt at once . . ."

Razumov tore himself away and walked down the corridor, leaving

the other motionless with his mouth open. But almost at once he returned and stood before the amazed Kostia, who shut his mouth slowly. Razumov looked him straight in the eyes, before saying with marked deliberation and separating his words:

"I thank—you—very—much."

He went away again rapidly. Kostia, recovering from his surprise at these manœuvres, ran up behind him pressingly.

"No! Wait! Listen. I really mean it. It would be like giving your compassion to a starving fellow. Do you hear, Kirylo? And any disguise you may think of, that too I could procure from a costumier, a Jew I know. Let a fool be made serviceable according to his folly. Perhaps also a false beard or something of that kind may be needed."

Razumov turned at bay.

"There are no false beards needed in this business, Kostia—you good-hearted lunatic, you. What do you know of my ideas? My ideas may be poison to you."

The other began to shake his head in energetic protest.

"What have you got to do with ideas? Some of them would make an end of your dad's money-bags. Leave off meddling with what you don't understand. Go back to your trotting horses and your girls, and then you'll be sure at least of doing no harm to anybody, and hardly any to yourself."

The enthusiastic youth was overcome by this disdain.

"You're sending me back to my pig's trough, Kirylo. That settles it. I am an unlucky beast—and I shall die like a beast too. But mind—it's your contempt that has done for me."

Razumov went off with long strides. That this simple and grossly festive soul should have fallen too under the revolutionary curse affected him as an ominous symptom of the time. He reproached himself for feeling troubled. Personally he ought to have felt reassured. There was an obvious advantage in this conspiracy of mistaken judgment taking him for what he was not. But was it not strange?

Again he experienced that sensation of his conduct being taken out of his hands by Haldin's revolutionary tyranny. His solitary and laborious existence had been destroyed—the only thing he could call his

own on this earth. By what right? he asked himself furiously. In what name?

What infuriated him most was to feel that the "thinkers" of the university were evidently connecting him with Haldin—as a sort of confidant in the background apparently. A mysterious connection! Ha, ha! . . . He had been made a personage without knowing anything about it. How that wretch Haldin must have talked about him! Yet it was likely that Haldin had said very little. The fellow's casual utterances were caught up and treasured and pondered over by all these imbeciles. And was not all secret revolutionary action based upon folly, self-deception, and lies?

"Impossible to think of anything else," muttered Razumov to himself. "I'll become an idiot if this goes on. The scoundrels and the fools are murdering my intelligence."

He lost all hope of saving his future, which depended on the free use of his intelligence.

He reached the doorway of his house in a state of mental discouragement which enabled him to receive with apparent indifference an official-looking envelope from the dirty hand of the dvornik.

"A gendarme brought it," said the man. "He asked if you were at home. I told him, 'No, he's not at home.' So he left it. 'Give it into his own hand,' says he. Now you've got it—eh?"

He went back to his sweeping, and Razumov climbed his stairs, envelope in hand. Once in his room he did not hasten to open it. Of course this official missive was from the superior direction of the police. A suspect! A suspect!

He stared in dreary astonishment at the absurdity of his position. He thought with a sort of dry, unemotional melancholy; three years of good work gone, the course of forty more perhaps jeopardised—turned from hope to terror, because events started by human folly link themselves into a sequence which no sagacity can foresee and no courage can break through. Fatality enters your rooms while your landlady's back is turned; you come home and find it in possession bearing a man's name, clothed in flesh—wearing a brown cloth coat and long boots—lounging against the stove. It asks you, "Is the outer door closed?"—and you don't know enough to take it by the throat and

fling it downstairs. You don't know. You welcome the crazy fate. "Sit down," you say. And it is all over. You cannot shake it off any more. It will cling to you for ever. Neither halter nor bullet can give you back the freedom of your life and the sanity of your thought. . . . It was enough to dash one's head against a wall.

Razumov looked slowly all round the walls as if to select a spot to dash his head against. Then he opened the letter. It directed the student Kirylo Sidorovitch Razumov to present himself without delay at the General Secretariat.

Razumov had a vision of General T——'s goggle eyes waiting for him—the embodied power of autocracy, grotesque and terrible. He embodied the whole power of autocracy because he was its guardian. He was the incarnate suspicion, the incarnate anger, the incarnate ruthlessness of a political and social régime on its defence. He loathed rebellion by instinct. And Razumov reflected that the man was simply unable to understand a reasonable adherence to the doctrine of absolutism.

"What can he want with me precisely—I wonder?" he asked himself.

As if that mental question had evoked the familiar phantom, Haldin stood suddenly before him in the room with an extraordinary completeness of detail. Though the short winter day had passed already into the sinister twilight of a land buried in snow, Razumov saw plainly the narrow leather strap round the Tcherkess coat. The illusion of that hateful presence was so perfect that he half expected it to ask, "Is the outer door closed?" He looked at it with hatred and contempt. Souls do not take a shape of clothing. Moreover, Haldin could not be dead yet. Razumov stepped forward menacingly; the vision vanished—and turning short on his heel he walked out of his room with infinite disdain.

But after going down the first flight of stairs it occurred to him that perhaps the superior authorities of police meant to confront him with Haldin in the flesh. This thought struck him like a bullet, and had he not clung with both hands to the banister he would have rolled down to the next landing most likely. His legs were of no use for a considerable time. . . . But why? For what conceivable reason? To what end?

There could be no rational answer to these questions; but Razumov remembered the promise made by the general to Prince K——. His action was to remain unknown.

He got down to the bottom of the stairs, lowering himself as it were from step to step, by the banister. Under the gate he regained much of his firmness of thought and limb. He went out into the street without staggering visibly. Every moment he felt steadier mentally. And yet he was saying to himself that General T—— was perfectly capable of shutting him up in the fortress for an indefinite time. His temperament fitted his remorseless task, and his omnipotence made him inaccessible to reasonable argument.

But when Razumov arrived at the Secretariat he discovered that he would have nothing to do with General T——. It is evident from Mr. Razumov's diary that this dreaded personality was to remain in the background. A civilian of superior rank received him in a private room after a period of waiting in outer offices where a lot of scribbling went on at many tables in a heated and stuffy atmosphere.

The clerk in uniform who conducted him said in the corridor:

"You are going before Gregory Matvieitch Mikulin."

There was nothing formidable about the man bearing that name. His mild, expectant glance was turned on the door already when Razumov entered. At once, with the penholder he was holding in his hand, he pointed to a deep sofa between two windows. He followed Razumov with his eyes while that last crossed the room and sat down. The mild gaze rested on him, not curious, not inquisitive—certainly not suspicious—almost without expression. In its passionless persistence there was something resembling sympathy.

Razumov, who had prepared his will and his intelligence to encounter General T—— himself, was profoundly troubled. All the moral bracing up against the possible excesses of power and passion went for nothing before this sallow man, who wore a full unclipped beard. It was fair, thin, and very fine. The light fell in coppery gleams on the protuberances of a high, rugged forehead. And the aspect of the broad, soft physiognomy was so homely and rustic that the careful middle parting of the hair seemed a pretentious affectation.

The diary of Mr. Razumov testifies to some irritation on his part. I

may remark here that the diary proper, consisting of the more or less daily entries, seems to have been begun on that very evening after Mr. Razumov had returned home.

Mr. Razumov, then, was irritated. His strung-up individuality had gone to pieces within him very suddenly.

"I must be very prudent with him," he warned himself in the silence during which they sat gazing at each other. It lasted some little time, and was characterised (for silences have their character) by a sort of sadness imparted to it perhaps by the mild and thoughtful manner of the bearded official. Razumov learned later that he was the chief of a department in the General Secretariat, with a rank in the Civil Service equivalent to that of a colonel in the Army.

Razumov's mistrust became acute. The main point was, not to be drawn into saying too much. He had been called there for some reason. What reason? To be given to understand that he was a suspect—and also no doubt to be pumped. As to what precisely? There was nothing. Or perhaps Haldin had been telling lies. . . . Every alarming uncertainty beset Razumov. He could bear the silence no longer, and cursing himself for his weakness spoke first, though he had promised himself not to do so on any account.

"I haven't lost a moment's time," he began in a hoarse, provoking tone; and then the faculty of speech seemed to leave him and enter the body of Councillor Mikulin, who chimed in approvingly:

"Very proper. Very proper. Though as a matter of fact . . ."

But the spell was broken, and Razumov interrupted him boldly, under a sudden conviction that this was the safest attitude to take. With a great flow of words he complained of being totally misunderstood. Even as he talked with a perception of his own audacity he thought that the word "misunderstood" was better than the word "mistrusted," and he repeated it again with insistence. Suddenly he ceased, being seized with fright before the attentive immobility of the official. "What am I talking about?" he thought, eyeing him with a vague gaze. Mistrusted—not misunderstood—was the right symbol for these people. Misunderstood was the other kind of curse. Both had been brought on his head by that fellow Haldin. And his head ached terribly. He passed his hand over his brow—an involuntary

gesture of suffering, which he was too careless to restrain. At that moment Razumov beheld his own brain suffering on the rack—a long, pale figure drawn asunder horizontally with terrific force in the darkness of a vault, whose face he failed to see. It was as though he had dreamed for an infinitesimal fraction of time of some dark print of the Inquisition. . . .

It is not to be seriously supposed that Razumov had actually dozed off and had dreamed in the presence of Councillor Mikulin, of an old print of the Inquisition. He was indeed extremely exhausted, and he records a remarkably dreamlike experience of anguish at the circumstance that there was no one whatever near the pale and extended figure. The solitude of the racked victim was particularly horrible to behold. The mysterious impossibility to see the face, he also notes, inspired a sort of terror. All these characteristics of an ugly dream were present. Yet he is certain that he never lost the consciousness of himself on the sofa, leaning forward with his hands between his knees and turning his cap round and round in his fingers. But everything vanished at the voice of Councillor Mikulin. Razumov felt profoundly grateful for the even simplicity of its tone.

"Yes. I have listened with interest. I comprehend in a measure your . . . But, indeed, you are mistaken in what you . . ." Councillor Mikulin uttered a series of broken sentences. Instead of finishing them he glanced down his beard. It was a deliberate curtailment which somehow made the phrases more impressive. But he could talk fluently enough, as became apparent when changing his tone to persuasiveness he went on: "By listening to you as I did, I think I have proved that I do not regard our intercourse as strictly official. In fact, I don't want it to have that character at all. . . . Oh yes! I admit that the request for your presence here had an official form. But I put it to you whether it was a form which would have been used to secure the attendance of a . . ."

"Suspect," exclaimed Razumov, looking straight into the official's eyes. They were big with heavy eyelids, and met his boldness with a dim, steadfast gaze. "A suspect." The open repetition of that word which had been haunting all his waking hours gave Razumov a strange sort of satisfaction. Councillor Mikulin shook his head

slightly. "Surely you do know that I've had my rooms searched by the police?"

"I was about to say a 'misunderstood person,' when you interrupted me," insinuated quietly Councillor Mikulin.

Razumov smiled without bitterness. The renewed sense of his intellectual superiority sustained him in the hour of danger. He said a little disdainfully:

"I know I am but a reed. But I beg you to allow me the superiority of the thinking reed over the unthinking forces that are about to crush him out of existence. Practical thinking in the last instance is but criticism. I may perhaps be allowed to express my wonder at this action of the police being delayed for two full days during which, of course, I could have annihilated everything compromising by burning it—let us say—and getting rid of the very ashes, for that matter."

"You are angry," remarked the official, with an unutterable simplicity of tone and manner. "Is that reasonable?"

Razumov felt himself colouring with annoyance.

"I am reasonable. I am even—permit me to say—a thinker, though, to be sure, this name nowadays seems to be the monopoly of hawkers of revolutionary wares, the slaves of some French or German thought—devil knows what foreign notions. But I am not an intellectual mongrel. I think like a Russian. I think faithfully—and I take the liberty to call myself a thinker. It is not a forbidden word, as far as I know."

"No. Why should it be a forbidden word?" Councillor Mikulin turned in his seat with crossed legs, and resting his elbow on the table propped his head on the knuckles of a half-closed hand. Razumov noticed a thick forefinger clasped by a massive gold band set with a blood-red stone—a signet ring that, looking as if it could weigh half a pound, was an appropriate ornament for that ponderous man with the accurate middle-parting of glossy hair above a rugged Socratic forehead.

"Could it be a wig?" Razumov detected himself wondering with an unexpected detachment. His self-confidence was much shaken. He resolved to chatter no more. Reserve! Reserve! All he had to do was to keep the Ziemianitch episode secret with absolute determination,

when the question came. Keep Ziemianitch strictly out of all the answers.

Councillor Mikulin looked at him dimly. Razumov's self-confidence abandoned him completely. It seemed impossible to keep Ziemianitch out. Every question would lead to that, because, of course, there was nothing else. He made an effort to brace himself up. It was a failure. But Councillor Mikulin was surprisingly detached too.

"Why should it be forbidden?" he repeated. "I too consider myself a thinking man, I assure you. The principal condition is to think correctly. I admit it is difficult sometimes at first for a young man abandoned to himself—with his generous impulses undisciplined, so to speak—at the mercy of every wild wind that blows. Religious belief, of course, is a great..."

Councillor Mikulin glanced down his beard, and Razumov, whose tension was relaxed by that unexpected and discursive turn, murmured with gloomy discontent:

"That man, Haldin, believed in God."

"Ah! You are aware," breathed out Councillor Mikulin, making the point softly, as if with discretion, but making it nevertheless plainly enough, as if he too were put off his guard by Razumov's remark. The young man preserved an impassive, moody countenance, though he reproached himself bitterly for a pernicious fool, to have given thus an utterly false impression of intimacy. He kept his eyes on the floor. "I must positively hold my tongue unless I am obliged to speak," he admonished himself. And at once against his will the question, "Hadn't I better tell him everything?" presented itself with such force that he had to bite his lower lip. Councillor Mikulin could not, however, have nourished any hope of confession. He went on:

"You tell me more than his judges were able to get out of him. He was judged by a commission of three. He would tell them absolutely nothing. I have the report of the interrogatories here, by me. After every question there stands 'Refuses to answer—refuses to answer.' It's like that, page after page. You see, I have been entrusted with some further investigations around and about this affair. He has left me nothing to begin my investigations on. A hardened miscreant. And so, you say, he believed in..."

Again Councillor Mikulin glanced down his beard with a faint grimace; but he did not pause for long. Remarking with a shade of scorn that blasphemers also had that sort of belief, he concluded by supposing that Mr. Razumov had conversed frequently with Haldin on the subject.

"No," said Razumov loudly, without looking up. "He talked and I listened. That is not a conversation."

"Listening is a great art," observed Mikulin parenthetically.

"And getting people to talk is another," mumbled Razumov.

"Well, no—that is not very difficult," Mikulin said innocently, "except, of course, in special cases. For instance, this Haldin. Nothing could induce him to talk. He was brought four times before the delegated judges. Four secret interrogatories—and even during the last, when your personality was put forward . . ."

"My personality put forward?" repeated Razumov, raising his head brusquely. "I don't understand."

Councillor Mikulin turned squarely to the table, and taking up some sheets of grey foolscap dropped them one after another, retaining only the last in his hand. He held it before his eyes while speaking.

"It was—you see—judged necessary. In a case of that gravity no means of action upon the culprit should be neglected. You understand that yourself, I am certain."

Razumov stared with enormous wide eyes at the side view of Councillor Mikulin, who now was not looking at him at all.

"So it was decided (I was consulted by General T——) that a certain question should be put to the accused. But in deference to the earnest wishes of Prince K—— your name has been kept out of the documents and even from the very knowledge of the judges themselves. Prince K—— recognised the propriety, the necessity of what we proposed to do, but he was concerned for your safety. Things do leak out—that we can't deny. One cannot always answer for the discretion of inferior officials. There was, of course, the secretary of the special tribunal—one or two gendarmes in the room. Moreover, as I have said, in deference to Prince K—— even the judges themselves were to be left in ignorance. The question ready framed was sent to them by General T—— (I wrote it out with my

own hand) with instructions to put it to the prisoner the very last of all. Here it is."

Councillor Mikulin threw back his head into proper focus and went on reading monotonously: "Question—Was the man well known to you, in whose rooms you remained for several hours on Monday and on whose information you have been arrested—has he had any previous knowledge of your intention to commit a political murder? . . . Prisoner refuses to reply.

"Question repeated. Prisoner preserves the same stubborn silence.

"The venerable Chaplain of the Fortress being then admitted and exhorting the prisoner to repentance, entreating him also to atone for his crime by an unreserved and full confession which should help to liberate from the sin of rebellion against the Divine laws and the sacred Majesty of the Ruler of our Christ-loving land—the prisoner opens his lips for the first time during this morning's audience and in a loud, clear voice rejects the venerable Chaplain's ministrations.

"At eleven o'clock the Court pronounces in summary form the death sentence.

"The execution is fixed for four o'clock in the afternoon, subject to further instructions from superior authorities."

Councillor Mikulin dropped the page of foolscap, glanced down his beard, and turning to Razumov, added in an easy, explanatory tone:

"We saw no object in delaying the execution. The order to carry out the sentence was sent by telegraph at noon. I wrote out the telegram myself. He was hanged at four o'clock this afternoon."

The definite information of Haldin's death gave Razumov the feeling of general lassitude which follows a great exertion or a great excitement. He kept very still on the sofa, but a murmur escaped him:

"He had a belief in a future existence."

Councillor Mikulin shrugged his shoulders slightly, and Razumov got up with an effort. There was nothing now to stay for in that room. Haldin had been hanged at four o'clock. There could be no doubt of that. He had, it seemed, entered upon his future existence, long boots, Astrakhan fur cap and all, down to the very leather strap round his waist. A flickering, vanishing sort of existence. It was not his soul, it was his mere phantom he had left behind on this earth—thought Razumov,

smiling caustically to himself while he crossed the room, utterly forgetful of where he was and of Councillor Mikulin's existence. The official could have set a lot of bells ringing all over the building without leaving his chair. He let Razumov go quite up to the door before he spoke:

"Come, Kirylo Sidorovitch—what are you doing?"

Razumov turned his head and looked at him in silence. He was not in the least disconcerted. Councillor Mikulin's arms were stretched out on the table before him and his body leaned forward a little with an effort of his dim gaze.

"Was I actually going to clear out like this?" Razumov wondered at himself with an impassive countenance. And he was aware of this impassiveness concealing a lucid astonishment.

"Evidently I was going out if he had not spoken," he thought. "What would he have done then? I must end this affair one way or another. I must make him show his hand."

For a moment longer he reflected behind the mask as it were, then let go the door-handle and came back to the middle of the room.

"I'll tell you what you think," he said explosively, but not raising his voice. "You think that you are dealing with a secret accomplice of that unhappy man. No, I do not know that he was unhappy. He did not tell me. He was a wretch from my point of view, because to keep alive a false idea is a greater crime than to kill a man. I suppose you will not deny that? I hated him! Visionaries work everlasting evil on earth. Their Utopias inspire in the mass of mediocre minds a disgust of reality and a contempt for the secular logic of human development."

Razumov shrugged his shoulders and stared. "What a tirade!" he thought. The silence and immobility of Councillor Mikulin impressed him. The bearded bureaucrat sat at his post, mysteriously self-possessed like an idol with dim, unreadable eyes. Razumov's voice changed involuntarily.

"If you were to ask me where is the necessity of my hate for such as Haldin, I would answer you—there is nothing sentimental in it. I did not hate him because he had committed the crime of murder. Abhorrence is not hate. I hated him simply because I am sane. It is in that character that he outraged me. His death . . ."

Razumov felt his voice growing thick in his throat. The dimness of Councillor Mikulin's eyes seemed to spread all over his face and made it indistinct to Razumov's sight. He tried to disregard these phenomena.

"Indeed," he pursued, pronouncing each word carefully, "what is his death to me? If he were lying here on the floor I could walk over his breast. . . . The fellow is a mere phantom. . . ."

Razumov's voice died out very much against his will. Mikulin behind the table did not allow himself the slightest movement. The silence lasted for some little time before Razumov could go on again.

"He went about talking of me. . . . Those intellectual fellows sit in each other's rooms and get drunk on foreign ideas in the same way young Guards' officers treat each other with foreign wines. Merest debauchery. . . . Upon my word,"—Razumov, enraged by a sudden recollection of Ziemianitch, lowered his voice forcibly,—"upon my word, we Russians are a drunken lot. Intoxication of some sort we must have: to get ourselves wild with sorrow or maudlin with resignation; to lie inert like a log or set fire to the house. What is a sober man to do, I should like to know? To cut oneself entirely from one's kind is impossible. To live in a desert one must be a saint. But if a drunken man runs out of the grog-shop, falls on your neck and kisses you on both cheeks because something about your appearance has taken his fancy, what then—kindly tell me? You may break, perhaps, a cudgel on his back and yet not succeed in beating him off. . . ."

Councillor Mikulin raised his hand and passed it down his face deliberately.

"That's . . . of course," he said in an undertone.

The quiet gravity of that gesture made Razumov pause. It was so unexpected too. What did it mean? It had an alarming aloofness. Razumov remembered his intention of making him show his hand.

"I have said all this to Prince K——," he began, with assumed indifference, but lost it on seeing Councillor Mikulin's slow nod of assent. "You know it? You've heard . . . Then why should I be called here to be told of Haldin's execution? Did you want to confront me with his silence now that the man is dead? What is his silence to me? This is incomprehensible. You want in some way to shake my moral balance."

"No. Not that," murmured Councillor Mikulin, just audibly. "The service you have rendered is appreciated . . ."

"Is it?" interrupted Razumov ironically.

". . . and your position too." Councillor Mikulin did not raise his voice. "But only think! You fall into Prince K——'s study as if from the sky with your startling information. . . . You are studying yet, Mr. Razumov, but we are serving already—don't forget that. . . . And naturally some curiosity was bound to . . ."

Councillor Mikulin looked down his beard. Razumov's lips trembled.

"An occurrence of that sort marks a man," the homely murmur went on. "I admit I was curious to see you. General T—— thought it would be useful too. . . . Don't think I am incapable of understanding your sentiments. When I was young like you I studied . . ."

"Yes—you wished to see me," said Razumov in a tone of profound distaste. "Naturally you have the right—I mean the power. It all amounts to the same thing. But it is perfectly useless, if you were to look at me and listen to me for a year. I begin to think there is something about me which people don't seem able to make out. It's unfortunate. I imagine, however, that Prince K—— understands. He seems to."

Councillor Mikulin moved slightly and spoke.

"Prince K—— is aware of everything that is being done, and I don't mind informing you that he approved my intention of becoming personally acquainted with you."

Razumov concealed an immense disappointment under the accents of railing surprise.

"So he is curious too! . . . Well—after all, Prince K—— knows me very little. It is really very unfortunate for me, but—it is not exactly my fault."

Councillor Mikulin raised a hasty deprecatory hand and inclined his head slightly over his shoulder.

"Now, Mr. Razumov—is it necessary to take it in that way? Everybody I am sure can . . ."

He glanced rapidly down his beard, and when he looked up again there was for a moment an interested expression in his misty gaze. Razumov discouraged it with a cold, repellent smile.

"No. That's of no importance, to be sure—except that in respect of all this curiosity being aroused by a very simple matter.... What is to be done with it? It is unappeasable. I mean to say there is nothing to appease it with. I happen to have been born a Russian with patriotic instincts—whether inherited or not I am not in a position to say."

Razumov spoke consciously with elaborate steadiness.

"Yes, patriotic instincts developed by a faculty of independent thinking—of detached thinking. In that respect I am more free than any social democratic revolution could make me. It is more than probable that I don't think exactly as you are thinking. Indeed, how could it be? You would think most likely at this moment that I am elaborately lying to cover up the track of my repentance."

Razumov stopped. His heart had grown too big for his breast. Councillor Mikulin did not flinch.

"Why so?" he said simply. "I assisted personally at the search of your rooms. I looked through all the papers myself. I have been greatly impressed by a sort of political confession of faith. A very remarkable document. Now may I ask for what purpose ..."

"To deceive the police naturally," said Razumov savagely.... "What is all this mockery? Of course, you can send me straight from this room to Siberia. That would be intelligible. To what is intelligible I can submit. But I protest against this comedy of persecution. The whole affair is becoming too comical altogether for my taste. A comedy of errors, phantoms, and suspicions. It's positively indecent ..."

Councillor Mikulin turned an attentive ear.

"Did you say phantoms?" he murmured.

"I could walk over dozens of them." Razumov, with an impatient wave of his hand, went on headlong. "But, really, I must claim the right to be done once for all with that man. And in order to accomplish this I shall take the liberty ..."

Razumov on his side of the table bowed slightly to the seated bureaucrat.

"... To retire—simply to retire," he finished with great resolution.

He walked to the door, thinking, "Now he must show his hand. He must ring and have me arrested before I am out of the building, or he must let me go. And either way ..."

An unhurried voice said:

"Kirylo Sidorovitch."

Razumov at the door turned his head.

"To retire," he repeated.

"Where to?" asked Councillor Mikulin softly.

FROM *THE SPY* (1908)

Maxim Gorky (1868–1936)

Gorky is considered the founder of Soviet—as opposed to Russian—literature, a genre called socialist realism. *A serious revolutionary, Gorky eventually fell into opposition to Lenin and the Bolsheviks, and especially Stalin. Gorky was, at heart, a compassionate humanist, and may well have paid for it—his death, in 1936, was rumored to have been arranged by the Soviet secret service at the direction of Stalin himself.*

The events of The Spy *take place at the time of the first, failed, attempt to overthrow the czarist government, in 1905. The novel begins with the humble, sorrowful childhood of the* agent provocateur *Yevsey Klimkov, and follows his vocational ascent, and spiritual descent, to the point where our selection begins.*

———

CHAPTER XV

A few weeks later Klimkov began to feel freer and more at ease. Every morning, warmly and comfortably dressed, with a box of small wares on his breast, he went to receive orders either at one of the cafés where

the spies gathered or at a police office, or at the lodging of one of the spies. The directions given him were simple and distinct.

"Go to such and such a house; get acquainted with the servants; find out how the masters live."

If he succeeded in penetrating to the kitchen of the given house, he would first try to bribe the servants by the cheap price of the goods and by little presents. Then he would carefully question them about what he had been ordered to learn. When he felt that the information gathered was insufficient, he filled up the deficiency from his own head, thinking it out according to the plan draughted for him by the old, fat, and sensual Solovyov.

"These men in whom we are interested," Solovyov once said in a smug, honey-sweet voice, "all have the same habits. They do not believe in God, they do not go to church, they dress poorly, but they are civil in their manners. They read many books, sit up late at night, often have gatherings of guests in their lodgings, but drink very little wine, and do not play cards. They speak about foreign countries, about systems of government, working men's Socialism, and full liberty for the people; also about the poor masses, declaring it is necessary to stir them up to revolt against our Czar, to kill off the entire administration, take possession of the highest offices, and by means of Socialism again introduce serfdom, in which they will have complete liberty." The warm voice of the spy broke off. He coughed, and heaved a sentimental sigh. "Liberty—everybody likes and wants to have liberty. But if you give me liberty, maybe I'll become the first villain in the world. That's it. It is impossible to give even a child full liberty. The Church Fathers, God's saints, even they were subject to the temptations of the flesh, and they sinned in the very highest. People's lives are held together, not by liberty, but by fear. Submission to law is essential to man. But the revolutionists reject law. They form two parties. One wants to make quick work with the Ministers and the faithful subjects of the Czar by means of bombs, etc. The other party is willing to wait a little; first they'll have a general uprising, then they'll kill off everybody at once." Solovyov raised his eyes pensively, and paused an instant. "It is difficult for us to comprehend their politics. Maybe they really understand something. But for us, everything they propose is an obnoxious

delusion. We fulfill the will of the Czar, the anointed sovereign of God. And he is responsible for us before God, so we ought to do what he bids us. In order to gain the confidence of the revolutionists, you must complain: 'Life is very hard for the poor; the police insult them, and there's no sort of law.' Although they are people of villainous intent, yet they are credulous, and you can always catch them with that bait. Behave cannily towards their servants; for their servants aren't stupid, either. Whenever necessary, reduce the price of your goods, so that they will get used to you and value you. But guard against exciting suspicion. They will begin to think, 'What is it? He sells very cheap, and asks prying questions.' The best thing for you to do is to strike up friendships. Take a little dainty, hot, full-breasted thing, and you get all sorts of good information from her. She will sew shirts for you, and invite you to spend the night with her, and she will find out whatever you order her to. You know—a tiny, soft little mouse. You can stretch your arm a long distance, through a woman."

This round man, hairy-handed, thick-lipped, and pock-marked, spoke about women more frequently than the others. He would lower his soft voice to a whisper, his neck would perspire, his feet would shuffle uneasily, and his eyes, minus eyebrows and eyelashes, would fill with warm, oily moisture. Yevsey, with his sharp scent, observed that Solovyov always smelt of hot, greasy, decayed meat.

In the chancery the spies had been spoken of as people who know everything, hold everything in their hands, and have friends and helpers everywhere. Though they could seize all the dangerous people at once, they were not doing so simply because they did not wish to deprive themselves of a position. On entering the Department of Safety, everyone swore an oath to pity nobody—neither father, mother, nor brother—nor to speak a word to one another about the sacred and awful business which they vowed they would serve all their lives.

Consequently Yevsey had expected to find sullen personalities. He had pictured them as speaking little, in words unintelligible to simple people, as possessing the miraculous perspicacity of a sorcerer, able to read man's thoughts and divine all the secrets of his life.

Now, from his sharp observation of them, he clearly saw they were

not unusual, nor for him either worse or more dangerous than others. In fact, they seemed to live in a more comradely fashion than was common. They frankly spoke of their mistakes and failures, even laughed over them. All, without exception, were equally fervent in swearing at their superiors, though with varying degrees of malice.

Conscious of a close bond uniting them, they were solicitous for one another. When it happened that someone was late for a meeting, or failed to appear at all, there was a general sense of uneasiness about the absentee, and Yevsey, Zarubin, or someone of the numerous group of "novices," or "assistants," was sent to look for the lost man at another gathering-place.

A stranger, observing them, would have been instantly struck by the lack of greed for money among the majority, and the readiness to share money with comrades who had gambled it away or squandered it in some other fashion. They all loved games of hazard, took a childish interest in card tricks, and envied the cleverness of the card-sharper.

They spoke to one another with ecstasy and acute envy of the revelries of the officials, described in detail the lewd women known to them, and hotly discussed their various relations with them. Most of them were unmarried, almost all were young, and for every one of them a woman was something in the nature of whisky—to give him ease and lull him to sleep. Woman brought them relief from the anxiety of their dog's work. Their discussions roused in Yevsey a sharp, intoxicating curiosity, sometimes incredulity and nausea. They all drank a lot, mixing wine with beer, and beer with cognac, in an effort to get drunk as quickly as possible.

Only a few of them put hot enthusiasm, the passion of the hunter, into their work. These boasted of their skill, swelling with pride as they described themselves as heroes. The majority, however, did their work wearily, with an air of being bored.

Their talks about the people whom they hunted down like beasts were seldom marked by the fierce hatred that boiled in Sasha's conversation like a seething hot-spring. One who was different from the rest was Melnikov, a heavy, hairy man with a thick, bellowing voice, who walked with oddly bent neck and spoke little. His dark eyes were always straining, as if in constant search. The man seemed to Yevsey

ever to be thinking of something terrible. Krasavin and Solovyov also contrasted with the others, the one by his cold malice, the other by the complacent satisfaction with which he spoke about fights, bloodshed, and women.

Among the youth, the most noticeable was Yakov Zarubin, who was constantly fidgeting about, and constantly running up to the others with questions. When he listened to the conversations about the revolutionists, he knitted his brows in anger, and jotted down notes in his little notebook. He tried to be of service to all the important spies, though it was evident that no one liked him, and that his book was regarded with suspicion.

The larger number spoke indifferently about the revolutionists, sometimes denouncing them as incomprehensible men of whom they were sick, sometimes referring to them in fun as to amusing cranks. Occasionally, too, they spoke in anger as one speaks of a child who deserves punishment for impudence. Yevsey began to imagine that all the revolutionists were empty people, who were not serious, and did not themselves know what they wanted, but merely brought disturbance and disorder into life.

Once Yevsey asked Piotr:

"There, you said the revolutionists are being bribed by the Germans, and now they say differently."

"What do you mean by 'differently'?" Piotr demanded angrily.

"That they are poor and stupid, and nobody says anything about the Germans."

"Go to the devil! Isn't it all the same to you? Do what you are told. Your colour is the diamond, and you go with diamonds."

Matters of business were discussed in a lazy, unwilling way, and, "You don't understand anything, brother," was a common rejoinder of one spy to another.

"And you?" would be the counter-retort.

"I keep quiet."

Klimkov tried to keep as far away as possible from Sasha. The ominous face of the sick man frightened him, and the smell of iodoform and the snuffling, cantankerous voice disgusted him.

"Villains!" cried Sasha, swearing at the officials. "They are given mil-

lions, and toss us pennies. They squander hundreds of thousands on women and on various genteel folk, who, they want us to believe, work for the good of society. But it's not the gentry that make revolutions—you must know that, idiots—the revolution grows underneath, in the ground, among the people. Give me five millions, and in one month I'll lift the revolution up above-ground into the street. I'll carry it out of the dark corners into the light of day, then—choke it!"

Sasha always contrived horrible schemes for the extermination of the noxious people. While devising them he stamped his feet, extended his trembling arms, and tore the air with his yellow fingers, while his face turned leaden, his red eyes grew strangely dim, and the spittle spurted from his mouth.

All, it was evident, looked upon him with aversion and feared him, though they were anxious to conceal the repulsion produced by his disease. Maklakov alone calmly avoided close intercourse with the sick man. He did not even give him his hand in greeting. Sasha, in his turn, who ridiculed everybody, who swore at all his comrades, setting them down as fools, plainly put Maklakov in a category by himself. He was always serious in his intercourse with this spy, and apparently spoke to him with greater will than to the rest. He did not abuse him even behind his back.

Once, when Maklakov had walked out without, as usual, taking leave of him, he cried:

"The nobleman is squeamish. He doesn't want to come near me. He has the right to be, the devil take him! His ancestors lived in lofty rooms; they breathed rarefied air, ate wholesome food, wore clean undergarments—he, too, for that matter. But I am a muzhik. I was born and brought up like an animal, in filth, among lice, on coarse black bread made of unbolted meal. His blood is better than mine—yes, indeed, both the blood and the brain, and the brain is the soul." After a pause he added in a lower voice, gloomily, without ridicule: "Idiots and impostors speak of the equality of man. The aristocrat preaches equality because he is an impudent scoundrel, and can't do anything himself. So, of course, he says: 'You are just as good a man as I am. Act so that I shall be able to live better.' This is the theory of equality."

Sasha's talks did not evoke a response from the other spies. They

failed to be moved by his excitement, and listened to his growling in indifferent silence. He received sulky support, however, from one—the large Melnikov, who acted as a detective among working men.

"Yes," Melnikov would say, "they are all deceivers," and nod his dark, unkempt head in confirmation while vigorously clenching his hairy fist.

"They ought to be killed, as the muzhiks kill horse-thieves," screamed Sasha.

"To kill may be a little too much, but sometimes it would be delicious to give a gentleman a box on the ear," said Chashin, a celebrated billiard-player, curly-haired, thin, and sharp-nosed. "Let's take this example. About a week ago I was playing in Kononov's hotel with a gentleman. I saw his face was familiar to me, but all chickens have feathers. He stared at me in his turn. 'Well,' thinks I, 'look. I don't change colour.' I fixed him for three rubles and half a dozen beers, and while we were drinking he suddenly rose, and said: 'I recognize you. You are a spy. When I was in the University,' said he, 'thanks to you,' he said, 'I had to stick in prison four months. You are,' he said, 'a scoundrel.' At first I was frightened, but soon the insult gnawed at my heart. 'You sat in prison not at all thanks to me, but to your politics. And your politics do not concern me personally. But let me tell you that on your account I had to run about day and night hunting you in all sorts of weather. I had to stick in the hospital thirteen days.' That's the truth. The idea, of him jumping on me! The pig, he had eaten himself fat as a priest, wore a gold watch, and had a diamond pin stuck in his tie!"

Akim Grokhotov, a handsome fellow, with a face mobile as an actor's, observed:

"I know men like that, too. When they are young, they walk on their heads; when the serious years come, they stay at home peacefully with their wives, and for the sake of a livelihood are even ready to enter our Department of Safety. The law of Nature."

"Among them are some who can't do anything besides revolutionary work. Those are the most dangerous," said Melnikov.

"Yes, yes," shot from Krasavin, who greedily rolled his oblique eyes.

Once Piotr lost a great deal in cards. He asked in a wearied, exasperated tone:

"When will this dog's life of ours end?"

Solovyov looked at him, and chewed his thick lips.

"We are not called upon to judge of such matters. Our business is simple. All we have to do is to take note of a certain face pointed out by the officials, or to find it ourselves, gather information, make observations, give a report to the authorities, and let them do as they please. For all we care, they may flay people alive. Politics do not concern us. Once there was an agent in our department, Grisha Sokovnin, who also thought about such things, and ended his life in a prison hospital, where he died of consumption."

Oftenest the conversation took some such course as the following:

Viekov, a wig-maker, always gaily and fashionably dressed, a modest, quiet person, announced:

"Three fellows were arrested yesterday."

"Great news!" someone responded indifferently.

But Viekov, whether or no, would tell his comrades all he knew. A spark of quiet stubbornness flared up in his small eyes, and his voice sounded inquisitive.

"The gentlemen revolutionists, it seems, are again hatching plots on Nikitskaya Street—great goings-on."

"Fools! All the dvorniks there are old hands in the service."

"Much help they are, the dvorniks!"

"H'm, yes, indeed."

"However," said Viekov cautiously, "a dvornik can be bribed."

"And you, too. Every man can be bribed—a mere matter of price."

"Did you hear, boys, Siekachev won seven hundred rubles in cards yesterday?"

"How he packs the cards!"

"Yes, yes. He's no sharper, but a young wizard."

Viekov looked around, smiled in embarrassment, then silently and carefully smoothed his clothes.

"A new proclamation has appeared," he announced another time.

"There are lots of proclamations. The devil knows which of them is new."

"There's a great deal of evil in them."

"Did you read it?"

"No. Philip Philippovich says there's a new one, and he's mad."

"The authorities are always mad. Such is the law of Nature," remarked Grokhotov with a smile.

"Who reads those proclamations?"

"They're read all right—very much so."

"Well, what of it? I have read them, too, yet I didn't turn black. I remained what I was, a red-haired fellow. It's not a matter of proclamations, it's a matter of bombs."

"Of course."

"A proclamation doesn't explode."

Evidently, however, the spies did not like to speak of bombs, for each time they were mentioned all made a strenuous effort to change the subject.

"Forty thousand dollars' worth of gold articles were stolen in Kazan."

"There's something for you!"

"Forty thousand! Whew!"

"Did they catch the thieves?" someone asked in great excitement.

"They'll get caught," prophesied another sorrowfully.

"Well, before that happens they'll have a good time."

A mist of envy enveloped the spies, who sank into dreams of revelries, of big stakes, and costly women.

Melnikov was more interested than the others in the course of the war. Often he asked Maklakov, who read the newspapers carefully:

"Are they still licking us?"

"They are."

"But what's the cause?" Melnikov exclaimed in perplexity, rolling his eyes. "Aren't there people enough, or what?"

"Not enough sense," Maklakov retorted dryly.

"The working men are dissatisfied. They do not understand. They say the generals have been bribed."

"That's certainly true," Krasavin broke in. "None of them are Russians." He muttered an ugly oath. "What's our blood to them?"

"Blood is cheap," said Solovyov, and smiled strangely.

As a rule the spies spoke of the war unwillingly, as if constrained in

one another's presence, and afraid of uttering some dangerous word. On the day of a defeat they all drank more whisky than usual, and having got drunk, quarrelled over trifles.

On such days Yevsey, trying to avoid possible brawls, made his escape unnoticed to his empty room, and there thought about the life of the spies. All of them—and there were many, their numbers constantly increasing—all of them seemed unhappy to Klimkov. They were all solitary, and he pitied them with his colourless pity. Nevertheless he liked to be among them and listen to their talk.

At the meetings Sasha boiled over and swore.

"Monstrosities! You understand nothing. You can't understand the significance of the business. Monstrosities!"

In answer some smiled deprecatingly, others maintained sullen silence.

"For forty rubles a month you can't be expected to understand very much," one would sometimes mutter.

"You ought to be wiped off the face of the earth," shrieked Sasha.

Klimkov began to dislike Sasha more and more, strengthened in his ill-will by the fact that nobody else cared for the diseased man.

Many of the spies were actually sick from the constant dread of attacks and death. Fear drove some, as it had Yelizar Titov, into an insane asylum.

"I was playing in the club yesterday," said Piotr in a disconcerted tone, "when I felt something pressing on the nape of my neck, and a cold shiver running up and down my backbone. I looked around. There in the corner stood a tall man looking at me as if he were measuring me inch by inch. I could not play. I rose from the table, and I saw him move. I backed out, and ran down the stairs into the yard and out into the street. I took a cab, sat in it sidewise, and looked back. Suddenly the man appeared from somewhere in front of me, and crossed the street under the horse's very nose. Maybe it wasn't he. But in such a case you can't think. How I yelled! He stopped, and I jumped out of the cab, and off I went at a gallop, the cabmen after me. Well, how I did run, the devil take it!"

"Such things happen," said Grokhotov, smiling. "I once hid myself for a similar reason in the yard. But it was still more horrible there, so

I climbed up to a roof, and sat there behind the chimney until day-break. A man must guard himself against another man. Such is the law of Nature."

Krasavin once entered pale and sweating, with staring eyes.

"They were following me," he announced gloomily, pressing his temples.

"Who?"

"They."

Solovyov endeavoured to calm him.

"Lots of people walk the streets, Gavrilo. What's that to you?"

"I could tell by the way they walked they were after me."

For more than two weeks Yevsey did not see Krasavin.

The spies treated Klimkov good-naturedly, and their occasional laughter at his expense did not offend him, for when he was grieved over his mistakes they comforted him.

"You'll get used to the work."

He was puzzled as to when the spies did their work, and tried to un-riddle the problem. They seemed to pass the greater part of their time in the cafés, sending novices and such insignificant fellows as himself out for observations.

He knew that, beside all the spies with whom he was acquainted, there were still others, desperate, fearless men, who mingled with the revolutionists, and were known by the name of provocators. There were only a few such men, but these few did most of the work, and di-rected it entirely. The authorities prized them very highly, while the street spies, envious of them, were unanimous in their dislike of the provocators because of their haughtiness.

Once in the street Grokhotov pointed out a provocator to Yev-sey.

"Look, Klimkov, quick!"

A tall, sturdy man was walking along the pavement. His fair hair, combed back, fell down beautifully from under his hat to his shoul-ders. His face was large and handsome, his moustache luxuriant. His soberly-clad person produced the impression of that of an important, well-fed gentleman of the nobility.

"You see what a fellow?" said Grokhotov with pride. "Fine, isn't he?

Our guard. He handed over twenty makers of bombs. He made the bombs with them himself. They wanted to blow up a Minister. He taught them, then delivered them up. Clever piece of business, wasn't it?"

"Yes," said Yevsey, amazed at the man's stately appearance, so unlike that of the busy bustling street spies.

"That's the kind they are, the real ones," said Grokhotov. "Why, he would do for a Minister; he has the face and figure for it. And we—what are we? Poverty-stricken dependents upon a hungry nobleman."

Yevsey sighed. The magnificent spy aroused his envy.

Ready to serve anybody and everybody for a good look or a kind word, he ran about the city obediently, searched, questioned, and informed. If he succeeded in pleasing, he rejoiced sincerely, and grew in his own estimation. He worked much, made himself very tired, and had no time to think.

Maklakov, reserved and serious, seemed better and purer to Yevsey than any person he had met up to that time. He always wanted to ask him about something, and tell him about himself—such an attractive and engaging face did this young spy have.

Once Yevsey actually put a question to him:

"Timofey Vasilyevich, how much do the revolutionists receive a month?"

A light shadow passed over Maklakov's bright eyes.

"You are talking nonsense," he answered, not in a loud voice, but angrily.

The days passed quickly, in a constant stir, one just like the other. At times Yevsey felt they would file on in the same way far into the future—vari-coloured, boisterous, filled with the talk now become familiar to him, and with the running about to which he had already grown accustomed. This thought enwrapped his heart with cold tedium, his body in enfeebling languor. Everything within and without became empty. Klimkov seemed to be sliding down into a bottomless pit.

CHAPTER XVI

In the middle of the winter everything suddenly trembled and shook. People anxiously opened their eyes, gesticulated, disputed furiously, and swore. As though severely wounded and blinded by a blow, they all stampeded to one place.

It began in this way. One evening, on reaching the Department of Safety to hand in a hurried report of his investigations, Klimkov found something unusual and incomprehensible in the place. The officials, agents, and clerks appeared to have put on new faces. All seemed strangely unlike themselves. They wore an air of astonishment and rejoicing. They spoke now in very low tones and mysteriously, now aloud and angrily. There was a senseless running from room to room, a listening to one another's words, a suspicious screwing-up of anxious eyes, a shaking of heads and sighing, a sudden cessation of talk, and an equally sudden burst of disputing. A whirlwind of fear and perplexity swept the room in broad circles. Playing with these people's impotence, it drove them about like dust, first blowing them into a pile, then scattering them on all sides. Klimkov, stationed in a corner, looked with vacant eyes upon this state of consternation, and listened to the conversation with strained attention.

He saw Melnikov, with his powerful neck bent and his head stuck forward, place his hairy hands on different persons' shoulders, and demand in his low, hollow voice:

"Why did the people do it?"

"What of it? The people must live. Hundreds were killed, eh? Wounded!" shouted Solovyov.

From somewhere came the repulsive voice of Sasha, cutting the ear.

"The priest ought to have been caught. That before everything else. The idiots!"

Krasavin walked about with his hands folded behind his back, biting his lips and rolling his eyes in every direction.

Quiet Viekov took up his stand beside Yevsey, and picked at the buttons of his vest.

"So this is the point we've reached," he said. "My God! Bloodshed! What do you think, eh?"

"What happened?" Yevsey asked.

Viekov looked around warily, took Klimkov by the hand, and whispered:

"This morning the people in St. Petersburg, with a priest and sacred banners, marched to the Czar Emperor. You understand? But they were not admitted. The soldiers were stationed about, and blood was spilled."

A handsome, staid gentleman, Leontyev, ran past them, glanced back at Viekov through his pince-nez, and asked:

"Where is Philip Philippovich?" But he disappeared without waiting for the information he wanted, and Viekov ran after him.

Yevsey closed his eyes for a minute, in order to try in the darkness to get at the meaning of what had been told him. He could easily represent to himself a mass of people walking through the streets in a sacred procession, but since he could not understand why the soldiers had shot at them, he was sceptical about the affair. However, the general agitation seized him, too, and he felt disturbed and ill at ease. He wanted to bustle about with the spies, but, unable to make up his mind to approach those he knew, he merely retreated still farther into his corner.

Many persons passed by him, all of whom, he fancied, were quickly searching for a little cosy corner where they might stand to collect their thoughts.

Maklakov appeared. He remained near the door, with his hands thrust into his pockets, and looked sideways at everybody. Melnikov approached him.

"Did they do it on account of the war?"

"I don't know."

"For what else? If it was really the people. But maybe it was simply some mistake. Eh? What did they ask for, do you know?"

"A constitution," replied Maklakov.

The sullen spy shook his head.

"I don't believe it."

"As you please."

Then Melnikov turned heavily, like a bear, and walked away grumbling:

"No one understands anything. They stir about, make a big noise——"

Yevsey went up to Maklakov, who looked at him.

"What is it?"

"I have a report."

Maklakov waived him aside.

"Who wants to bother about reports to-day?"

Yevsey drew still nearer, and asked:

"Timofey Vasilyevich, what does 'constitution' mean?"

"A different order of life," answered the spy in a low voice.

Solovyov, perspiring and red, came running up.

"Have you heard whether they are going to send us to St. Petersburg?"

"No, I haven't."

"I think they probably will. Such an event! Why, it's a revolt, a real revolt."

"To-morrow we will know."

"How much blood has been shed! What is it?"

Maklakov's eyes ran about uneasily. To-day his shoulders seemed more stooping than ever, and the ends of his moustache dropped downward.

Something seemed to be revolving in Yevsey's brain, and Maklakov's grim words kept repeating themselves.

"A different order of life—different."

They gripped at his heart, arousing a sharp desire to extract their meaning. But everything around him turned and darted hither and thither. Melnikov's angry, resonant voice sounded sickeningly:

"The thing is, to know what people did it. The working people are one thing, simply residents another. This differentiation must be made."

And Krasavin spoke distinctly:

"If even the people begin to revolt against the Czar, then there are no people any more, only rebels."

"Wait, and suppose there's deception here."

"Hey, you old devil," whispered Zarubin, hastening up to Yevsey. "I've struck a vein of business. Come on, I'll tell you."

Klimkov followed him in silence for a space, then stopped.

"Where shall I go?"

"To a beer saloon. You understand? There's a girl there—Margarita. She has an acquaintance, a milliner. At the milliner's lodging they read books on Saturdays—students and various other people like that. So I'm going to cut them up. Ugh!"

"I won't go," said Yevsey.

"Oh, you! Ugh!"

The long ribbon of strange impressions quickly enmeshed Yevsey's heart, hindering him from an understanding of what was happening. He walked off home unobserved, carrying away with him the premonition of impending misfortune—a misfortune that already lay in hiding, and was stretching out irresistible arms to clutch him. It filled his heart with new fear and grief. In expectation of this misfortune he endeavoured to walk in the obscurity close against the houses. He recalled the agitated faces and excited voices, the disconnected talk about death, about blood, about the huge graves into which dozens of bodies had been flung like rubbish.

At home he stood at the window a long time looking at the yellow light of the street-lamp. The pedestrians quickly walked into the circle of its light, then plunged into the darkness again. So in Yevsey's head a faint timid light was casting a pale illumination upon a narrow circle, into which ignorant, cautious grey thoughts, helplessly holding on to one another like blind people, were slowly creeping. Small and lame, they gathered into a shy group driven into one place like a swarm of mosquitoes. But suddenly, loosing hold of the bond uniting them, they disappeared without leaving a trace, and his soul, devoid of them, remained like a desert illuminated by a solitary ray from a sorrowful moon.

The days passed as in a delirium, filled with terrible tales of the fierce destruction of people. For Yevsey these days crawled slowly over the earth like black eyeless monsters, swollen with the blood they had devoured. They crawled with their huge jaws wide open, poisoning the air with their stifling, salty odour. People ran and fell, shouted and wept, mingling their tears with their blood. And the blind monster destroyed them, crushed old and young, women and children. They

were pushed forward to their destruction by the ruler of their life, fear—fear leaden-grey as a storm-cloud, powerful as the current of a broad stream.

Though the thing had happened far away, in a strange city, Yevsey knew that fear was alive everywhere. He felt it all over round about him.

No one understood the event, no one was able to explain it. It stood before the people like a huge riddle and frightened them. The spies stuck in their meeting-places from morning until night, and did much reading of newspapers and drinking of whisky. They also crowded into the Department of Safety, where they disputed, and pressed close against one another. They were impatiently awaiting something.

"Can anybody explain the truth?" Melnikov kept asking.

One evening a few weeks after the event they assembled in the Department of Safety. Sasha said sharply:

"Stop this nonsensical talk! It's a scheme of the Japs. The Japs gave eighteen million rubles to Father Gapon to stir the people up to revolt. You understand? The people were made drunk on the road to the palace; the revolutionists had ordered a few wine-shops to be broken into. You understand?" He let his red eyes rove about the company as if seeking those of his listeners who disagreed with him. "They thought the Czar, loving the people, would come out to them. And at that time it was decided to kill him. Is it clear to you?"

"Yes, it's clear," shouted Yakov Zarubin, and began to jot something down in his notebook.

"Jackass!" shouted Sasha in a surly voice. "I'm not asking you. Melnikov, do you understand?"

Melnikov was sitting in a corner, clutching his head with both hands, and swaying to and fro as if he had the toothache. Without changing his position he answered:

"A deception!" His voice struck the floor dully, as if something soft, yet heavy, had fallen.

"Yes, a deception," repeated Sasha, and began again to speak quickly and fluently. Sometimes he carefully touched his forehead, then looked at his fingers, and wiped them on his knee. Yevsey had the sensation that even his words reeked with a putrid odour. He listened,

wrinkling his forehead painfully. He understood everything the spy said, but he felt that his speech did not efface—in fact, could not efface—from his mind the black picture of the bloody holiday.

All were silent, now and then shaking their heads, and refraining from looking at one another. It was quiet and gloomy. Sasha's words floated a long time over his auditors' heads, touching nobody.

"If it was known that the people had been deceived, then why were they killed?" the unexpected question suddenly burst from Melnikov.

"Fool!" screamed Sasha. "Suppose you had been told that I was your wife's paramour, and you got drunk and came at me with a knife, what should I do? Should I tell you 'Strike!' even though you had been duped, and I was not guilty?"

Melnikov started to his feet, stretched himself, and bawled:

"Don't bark, you dog!"

A tremor ran through Yevsey at his words, and Viekov, thin and nerveless, who sat beside him, whispered in fright:

"O God! Hold him!"

Sasha clenched his teeth, thrust one hand into his pocket, and drew back. All the spies—there were many in the room—sat silent and motionless, and waited, watching Sasha's hand. Melnikov waved his hat, and walked slowly to the door.

"I'm not afraid of your pistol."

He slammed the door after him noisily. Viekov went to lock it, and said as he returned to his place:

"What a dangerous man!"

"So," continued Sasha, pulling a revolver from his pocket and examining it, "to-morrow morning you are each of you to get down to business, do you hear? And bear in mind that now you will all have more to do than before. Part of us will have to go to St. Petersburg. That's number one. Secondly, this is the very time that you'll have to keep your eyes and ears particularly wide open, because people will begin to babble all sorts of nonsense in regard to this affair. The revolutionists will not be so careful now, you understand?"

Handsome Grokhotov drew a loud breath, and said:

"We understand, never mind! If it's true that the Japs gave such large sums of money, that explains it, of course."

"Without any explanation, it's very hard," said someone.

"Ye-e-e-s."

"People cry, 'What does it mean?' And they give you poisonous talk, and you don't know how to answer back."

"The people are very much interested in this revolt."

All these remarks were made in an indolent, bloodless fashion, and with an air of constraint.

"Well, now you know what you are about, and how you should reply to the fools," said Sasha angrily. "And if some donkey should begin to bray, take him by the neck, whistle for a policeman, and off with him to the police-station. There they have instructions as to what's to be done with such people. Ho, Viekov, or somebody, ring the bell, and order some seltzer."

Yakov Zarubin rushed to the bell.

Sasha looked at him, and said, showing his teeth:

"I say, pup, don't be mad with me for having cut you off."

"I'm not mad, Aleksandr Nikitich."

"Ye-e-s," Grokhotov drawled pensively. "Still they are a power, after all! Consider what they accomplished—raised a hundred thousand people."

"Stupidity is light; it's easy to raise," Sasha interrupted him. "They had the means to raise a hundred thousand people—they had the money. Just you give me such a sum of money, and I'll show you how to make history." Sasha uttered an ugly oath, lifted himself slightly from the sofa, stretched out the thin yellow hand which held the revolver, screwed up his eyes, and aiming at the ceiling, cried through his teeth in a yearning whine: "I would show you!"

All these things—Sasha's words and gestures, his eyes and his smiles—were familiar to Yevsey, but now they seemed impotent, useless, as infrequent drops of rain in extinguishing a conflagration. They did not extinguish fear, and were powerless to stop the quiet growth of a premonition of misfortune.

At this time a new view of the life of the people unconsciously developed in Yevsey's mind. He learned that on the one hand some people might gather in the streets by the tens of thousands in order to go to the rich and powerful Czar and ask him for help, while others might

kill these tens of thousands for doing so. He recalled everything the Smokestack had said about the poverty of the people and the wealth of the Czar, and was convinced that both sides acted in the manner they did from fear.

Nevertheless the people astonished him by their desperate bravery, and aroused in him a feeling with which he had hitherto been unfamiliar.

Now as before, when walking the streets with the box of goods on his breast, he carefully stepped aside for the passers-by, either taking to the middle of the street or pressing against the walls of the houses. However, he began to look into the people's faces more attentively, with a feeling akin to respect, and his fear of them seemed to have diminished slightly. Men's faces had suddenly changed, acquiring more variety and significance of expression. All began to talk with one another more willingly and simply, and to walk the streets more briskly, with a firmer tread.

CHAPTER XVII

Yevsey often entered a house occupied by a physician and a journalist upon whom he was assigned to spy. The physician employed a wet-nurse named Masha, a full, round little woman with merry, sky-blue eyes, who was always neat and clean, and wore a white or blue sarafan with a string of beads around her bare neck. Her full-breasted figure gave the impression of a luscious, healthy creature, and won the fancy of Yevsey, who imagined that a strong savoury odour, as of hot rye-bread, emanated from her. She was an affectionate little person. He loved to question her about the village, and hear her replies in a rapid singsong. He soon came to know all her relatives— where each one lived, what was the occupation of each, and what the wages.

He paid her one of his visits five days after Sasha had explained the cause of the uprising. He found her sitting on the bed in the cook's room adjoining the kitchen. Her face was swollen, her eyes were red, and her lower lip stuck out comically.

"Good morning," she said sullenly. "We don't want anything. Go. We don't want anything."

"Did the master insult you?" Yevsey asked. Though he knew the master had not insulted her, he regarded it as his professional duty to ask just such questions. His next duty was to sigh and add: "That's the way they always are. You've got to work for them your whole life long."

Anfisa Petrovna, the cook, a thin, ill-tempered body, suddenly cried out:

"Her brother-in-law was killed, and her sister was knouted. She had to be taken to the hospital."

"In St. Petersburg?" Yevsey inquired quietly.

"Yes."

Masha drew a deep breath, and groaned, holding her head in her hands.

"What for?" asked Yevsey.

"Who knows them? A curse upon them!" shrieked the cook, rattling the dishes in her exasperation. "Why did they kill all those people? That's what I would like to know."

"It wasn't his fault," Masha sobbed. "I know him. O God! he was a book-binder, a peaceful fellow. He didn't drink. He made forty rubles a month. O God! they beat Tania, and she's soon to have a child. It will be her second child. 'If it's a boy,' she said, 'I'll christen him Foma, in honour of my husband's friend.' And she wanted the friend to be the child's godfather, too. But they put a bullet through his leg, and broke his head open, the cursed monsters! May they have neither sleep nor rest! May they be torn with anguish and with shame! May they choke in blood, the infernal devils!"

Her words and tears flowed in tempestuous streams. Dishevelled and pitiful, she screamed in desperate rage, and scratched her shoulders and her breast with her nails. Then she flung herself on the bed, and buried her head in the pillow, moaning and trembling convulsively.

"Her uncle sent her a letter from there," said the cook, running about in the kitchen from the table to the stove and back again. "You ought to see what he writes! The whole street is reading the letter. Nobody can understand it. The people marched with ikons, with their

holy man; they had priests. Everything was done in a Christian fashion. They went to the Czar to tell him: 'Father, our Emperor, reduce the number of officials a little. We cannot live with so many officers and such burdensome taxes on our shoulders. We haven't enough to pay their salaries, and they take such liberties with us—the extremest of liberties. They squeeze everything out of us they want.' Everything was honest and open. They had been preparing for this a long time—a whole month. The police knew of it, yet no one interfered. They went out, and marched along the streets, when suddenly off go the soldiers, shooting at them! The soldiers surrounded them on all sides, and fired at them; hacked them and trampled them down with their horses—everybody, even the little children! They kept up the massacre for two days. Think of it! What does it mean? That the people are not wanted any more? That they have decided to exterminate them?"

Anfisa's cutting, unpleasant voice sank into a whisper, above which could now be heard the sputtering of the butter on the stove, the angry gurgle of the boiling water in the kettle, the dull roaring of the fire, and Masha's groans. Yevsey felt obliged to answer the sharp questions of the cook, and he wanted to soothe Masha. He coughed carefully, and said, without looking at anybody:

"They say the Japs arranged the affair."

"S-s-s-o?" the cook cried ironically. "The Japs, the Japs, of course! We know the Japs. They keep to themselves; they stick in their own home. Our master explained to us who they are. You just tell my brother about the Japs. He knows all about them, too. It was scoundrels, not Japs!"

From what Melnikov had said, Yevsey knew that the cook's brother, Matvey Zimin, worked in a furniture factory, and read prohibited books. Now, all of a sudden, he was seized with the desire to tell her that the police knew about Zimin's infidelity to the Czar. But at that minute Masha jumped down from the bed, and cried out, while arranging her hair:

"Of course, they have no way of justifying themselves, so they hit upon the Japs as an excuse."

"The blackguards!" drawled the cook. "Yesterday, in the market, somebody also made a speech about the Japs. Evidently he had been

bribed to justify the officials. One old man was listening, and then you should have heard what he said about the generals, about the Ministers, and even about the Czar himself. How he could do it without putting the least check upon himself—— No, you can't fool the people. They'll catch the truth, no matter into what corner you drive it."

Klimkov looked at the floor, and was silent. The desire to tell the cook that watch was being kept upon her brother now left him. He involuntarily thought that every person killed had relatives who were now just as puzzled as Masha and Anfisa, and asked one another "Why?" He realized that they were crying and grieving in dark perplexity, with hatred secretly springing up in their hearts—hatred of the murderers and of those who endeavoured to justify the crime. He sighed and said:

"A horrible deed has been done." At the same time he thought: "But I, too, am compelled to protect the officials."

Masha giving the door to the kitchen a push with her foot, Yevsey remained alone with the cook, who looked at the door sidewise, and grumbled:

"The woman is killing herself. Even her milk is spoiled. This is the third day she hasn't given nourishment. Look here, Thursday next week is her birthday, and I'll celebrate my birthday then, too. Suppose you come here as a guest, and make her a present, say, of a good string of beads. You must comfort a person some way or other."

"Very well; I'll come."

"All right."

Klimkov walked off slowly, revolving in his mind what the woman had said to him. The cook's talk was too noisy, too forward, instantly creating the impression that she did not speak her own sentiments, but echoed those of another. As for Masha, her grief did not touch him. He had no relatives; moreover, he rarely experienced pity for people. Nevertheless, he felt that the general revolt everywhere noticeable was reflected in the outcries of these women, and—the main thing—that such talk was unusual, inhumanly brave. Yevsey had his own explanation of the event: fear pushed people one against the other. Then those who were armed and had lost their senses exterminated those

who were unarmed and foolish. But this explanation did not stand firm in Yevsey's mind, and failed to calm his soul. He clearly realized from what he had seen and heard that the people were beginning to free themselves from the thraldom of fear, and were insistently and fearlessly seeking the guilty, whom they found and judged. Everywhere large quantities of leaflets appeared, in which the revolutionists described the bloody days in St. Petersburg, and cursed the Czar, and urged the people not to believe in the administration. Yevsey read a few such leaflets. Though their language was unintelligible to him, he scented something dangerous in them—something that irresistibly made its way into his heart and filled him with fresh alarm. He resolved not to read any leaflets again.

Strict orders were given to find the printing-office in which the leaflets were printed, and to catch the persons who distributed them. Sasha swore, and even gave Viekov a slap in the face for something he had done. Philip Philippovich invited the agents to come to him in the evenings, in order to deliver speeches to them. He usually sat in the middle of the room behind his desk, resting the lower half of his arms upon it, and keeping his long fingers engaged in quietly toying with the pencils, pens, and papers. The various gems on his hands sparkled in different colours. From under his black beard gleamed a large yellow medal. He moved his short neck slowly, and his blue spectacles rested in turn upon the faces of all present, who meekly and silently sat against the wall. He scarcely ever rose from his arm-chair. Nothing but his fingers and his neck moved. His heavy face, bloated and white, looked like a face in a portrait; the hairs of his beard seemed glued together. When silent, he was calm and staid, but the instant he spoke in his thin voice, which screeched like an iron saw while being filed, everything about him—the black frock-coat, and the order, the gems, and the beard—seemed to be stuck upon somebody else. Sometimes Yevsey fancied that an artificial puppet sat in front of him, inside of which was hidden a little shrivelled-up fellow, resembling a little red devil. If someone were to shout at the puppet, he imagined, the little devil would be frightened, and would jump out with a squeak and leap through the window.

Nevertheless, Yevsey was afraid of Philip Philippovich. In order not

to attract to himself the gobbling look of his blue glasses, he sat as far as possible from him, trying the entire time not to move.

"Gentlemen"—the thin voice trembled in the air; it drove against Yevsey's breast unpleasantly and coldly, like a gleaming steel rod—"gentlemen, you must listen to me carefully. You must remember my words. In these days every one of you should put your entire mind, your entire soul, into the war with the secret and cunning enemy. You should listen to your orders and fulfil them strictly, though you may act on your own initiative, too. In the secret war for the life of your mother Russia, you must know, all means are permissible. The revolutionists are not squeamish as to the means they employ; they do not stop at murder. Remember how many of your comrades have perished at their hands. I do not tell you to kill—no, of course not. I cannot advise such measures. To kill a man requires no cleverness. Any fool can kill. Yet the law is with you. You go against the lawless. It would be criminal to be merciful toward them. They must be rooted out like noxious weeds. I say, you must for yourselves find out what is the best way to stifle the rising revolution. It isn't I who demand this of you; it is the Czar and the country." After a pause, during which he examined his rings, he went on: "You, gentlemen, have too little energy, too little love for your honest calling. For instance, you have let the old revolutionist Saydakov slip. I now know that he lived in our city for three and a half months. Secondly, up to this time you have failed to find the printing-office."

"Without provocation it is hard," someone ventured in an offended tone.

"Don't interrupt, if you please. I myself know what is hard, and what is easy. Up to this time you have not been able to gather serious evidence against a whole lot of people known for their seditious tendencies, and you cannot give me any grounds for their arrest."

"Arrest them without grounds," said Piotr with a laugh.

"What is the object of your facetiousness? I am speaking seriously. If you were to arrest them without grounds, we should simply have to let them go again. That's all. And to you personally, Piotr Petrovich, I want to remark that you promised something a long time ago. Do you remember? You likewise, Krasavin. You said you had succeeded in be-

coming acquainted with a man who might lead you to the Terrorists. Well, and what has come of it?"

"He turned out to be a cheat. You just wait. I'll do my business," Krasavin answered calmly.

"I have no doubt of it whatsoever, but I beg all of you to understand that we must work more energetically; we must hurry matters up."

Philip Philippovich discoursed a long time—sometimes a whole hour—without taking breath, calmly, in the same level tone. The only words that varied the monotonous flow were "You must." The "you" came out resonantly like a long-drawn hammer-blow, the "must" in a drawled hiss. He embraced everybody with his glassy blue stare. His words fairly choked Yevsey.

Once at the end of a meeting, when Sasha and Yevsey were the only ones who remained with Philip Philippovich, Yevsey heard the following colloquy:

PHILIP PHILIPPOVICH (glumly, dejectedly). "What idiots they are, though!"

SASHA (snuffling). "Aha!"

PHILIP PHILIPPOVICH. "Yes, yes, what *can* they do?"

SASHA. "It seems that now you are going to learn the value of decent people."

PHILIP PHILIPPOVICH. "Well, give them to me—give them to me."

SHASHA. "Ah, they cost dear!"

Klimkov was neither surprised nor offended. This was not the first time he had heard the authorities swear at their subordinates. He counted it in the regular order of life.

The spies after the meetings spoke to one another thus:

"Um, yes, a converted Jew, and just look at him!"

"They say he got a rise of six hundred rubles on the first of January."

"The value of our labour is growing."

Sometimes a handsome, richly-dressed gentleman by the name of Leontyev addressed the spies in place of Philip Philippovich. He did not remain seated, but walked up and down the room holding his hands in his pockets, politely stepping out of everybody's way. His smooth face, always drawn in a frown, was cold and repellent; his thin lips moved reluctantly, and his eyes were veiled.

Another man named Yasnogursky came from St. Petersburg for the same purpose. He was a low, broad-shouldered, bald man with an order on his breast. He had a large mouth, a wizened face, heavy eyes, like two little stones, and long hands. He spoke in a loud voice, smacking his lips, and pouring out streams of strong oaths. One sentence of his particularly impressed itself on Yevsey's memory:

"They say to the people, 'You can arrange another, an easy life for yourselves.' They lie, my children. The Emperor, our Czar, and our Holy Church arrange life, while the people can change nothing—nothing."

All the speakers said the same thing. The political agents must serve more zealously, must work more, must be cleverer, because the revolutionists were growing more and more powerful. Sometimes they told about the Czars—how good and wise they were, how the foreigners feared them and envied them because they had liberated various nations from the foreign yoke. They had freed the Bulgarians and the Servians from the oppression of the Turkish Sultan, the Khivans, the Bokharans, and the Turkomans from the Persian Shah, and the Manchurians from the Chinese Emperor. As a result, the Germans and the English, along with the Japanese, who were bribed by them, were dissatisfied. They would like to get the nations Russia had liberated into their own power. But they knew the Czar would not permit this, and that was why they hated him, why they wished him all evil, and endeavoured to bring about the revolution in Russia.

Yevsey listened to these speeches with interest, waiting for the moment when the speakers would begin to tell about the Russian people, and explain why all of them were unpleasant and cruel; why they loved to torture one another, and lived such a restless, uncomfortable life. He wanted to hear what the cause was of such poverty, of the universal fear, and the angry groans heard on all sides. But of such things no one spoke.

After one of the meetings Viekov said to Yevsey as the two were walking in the street:

"So it means that they are getting into power. Did you hear? It's impossible to understand what it signifies. Just see: here you have secret people who live hidden, and suddenly they cause general alarm, and

shake everything up. It's very hard to comprehend. From where, I'd like to know, do they get their power?"

Melnikov, now even more morose and taciturn, grown thin and all dishevelled, once hit his fist on his knee, and shouted:

"I want to know where the truth is!"

"What's the matter?" asked Maklakov angrily.

"What's the matter? This is the matter. I understand it this way. One class of officials has grown weak—our class. Now another class gets the power over the people—that's all."

"And the result is—fiddlesticks!" said Maklakov, laughing.

Melnikov looked at him, and sighed:

"Don't lie, Timofey Vasilyevich. You lie out and out. You are a wise man, and you lie. I understand."

Thoughts instinctively arose in the dark depths of Yevsey's soul. He did not realize how they formed themselves, did not feel their secret growth. They appeared suddenly, in perfect array, and frightened him by their unexpected apparition. He endeavoured to hide them, to extinguish them for a time, but unsuccessfully. They quietly flashed up again, and shone more clearly, though their light only cast life into still greater obscurity. The frequent conversations about the revolutionists became interwoven in his brain, creating an insensible sediment in his mind, a thin strata of fresh soil for the growth of puny thoughts. These thoughts disquieted him, and drew him gently to something unknown.

FROM *THE QUIET AMERICAN* (1955)

Graham Greene (1904–1991)

Graham Greene wrote The Quiet American *before the United States made a serious commitment to defend South Vietnam; the book is essentially an attack on American innocence, and the almost incidental brutality of American power—both personified by the American intelligence officer Alden Pyle—during the last days of French colonial administration in that country. Greene claimed to write "entertainments" along with serious novels.* The Quiet American *is, in fact, a highly seductive mixture of both. Greene wrote the screenplay for the film* The Third Man— *one of the greatest films of intrigue ever made, and never, alas, a novel.*

CHAPTER II

1

At least once a year the Caodaists hold a festival at the Holy See in Tanyin, which lies eighty kilometres to the north-west of Saigon, to celebrate such and such a year of liberation, or of conquest, or even a Buddhist, Confucian, or Christian festival. Caodaism was always the favourite chapter of my briefing to visitors. Caodaism, the invention

of a Cochin civil servant, was a synthesis of the three religions. The Holy See was at Tanyin. A pope and female cardinals. Prophecy by planchette. Saint Victor Hugo. Christ and Buddha looking down from the roof of the cathedral on a Walt Disney fantasia of the East, dragons and snakes in Technicolor. Newcomers were always delighted with the description. How could one explain the dreariness of the whole business: the private army of twenty-five thousand men, armed with mortars made out of the exhaust pipes of old cars, allies of the French who turned neutral at the moment of danger? To these celebrations, which helped to keep the peasants quiet, the Pope invited members of the government (who would turn up if the Caodaists at the moment held office), the diplomatic corps (who would send a few second secretaries with their wives or girls), and the French commander-in-chief, who would detail a two-star general from an office job to represent him.

Along the route to Tanyin flowed a fast stream of staff and C.D. cars, and on the more exposed sections of the road Foreign Legionaries threw out cover across the rice fields. It was always a day of some anxiety for the French high command, and perhaps of a certain hope for the Caodaists, for what could more painlessly emphasize their own loyalty than to have a few important guests shot outside their territory?

Every kilometre a small mud watch-tower stood up above the flat fields like an exclamation mark, and every ten kilometres there was a larger fort manned by a platoon of Legionaries, Moroccans or Senegalese. Like the traffic into New York, the cars kept one pace—and as with the traffic into New York you had a sense of controlled impatience, watching the next car ahead and, in the mirror, the car behind. Everybody wanted to reach Tanyin, see the show, and get back as quickly as possible: curfew was at seven.

One passed out of the French-controlled rice fields into the rice fields of the Hoa Haos and thence into the rice fields of the Caodaists, who were usually at war with the Hoa Haos; only the flags changed on the watch-towers. Small naked boys sat on the buffaloes which waded genital deep among the irrigated fields; where the gold harvest was ready, the peasants in their hats like limpets winnowed the rice against

little curved shelters of plaited bamboo. The cars drove rapidly by, belonging to another world.

Now the churches of the Caodaists would catch the attention of strangers in every village: pale blue and pink plasterwork and a big Eye of God over the door. Flags increased; troops of peasants made their way along the road; we were approaching the Holy See. In the distance the sacred mountain stood like a green bowler hat above Tanyin—that was where General Thé held out, the dissident chief of staff who had recently declared his intention of fighting both the French and the Vietminh. The Caodaists made no attempt to capture him, although he had kidnapped a cardinal—it was rumoured that he had done it with the Pope's connivance.

It always seemed hotter in Tanyin than anywhere else in the Southern Delta; perhaps it was the absence of water, perhaps it was the sense of interminable ceremonies which made one sweat vicariously, sweat for the troops standing to attention through the long speeches in a language they didn't understand, sweat for the Pope in his heavy Chu Chin Chow chinoiserie robes. Only the female cardinals in their white silk trousers, chatting to the priests in sun helmets, gave an impression of coolness under the sun glare; you couldn't believe it would ever be seven o'clock and cocktail time on the roof of the Majestic, with a wind from Saigon River.

After the parade I interviewed the Pope's deputy. I didn't expect to get anything out of him and I was right; it was a convention on both sides. I asked him about General Thé.

"A rash man," he said and dismissed the subject. He began his set speech, forgetting that I had heard it two years before; it reminded me of my own gramophone records for newcomers: Caodaism was a religious synthesis . . . the best of all religions . . . missionaries had been dispatched to Los Angeles . . . the secrets of the Great Pyramid. He wore a long white soutane and he chain-smoked. There was something cunning and corrupt about him; the word "love" occurred often. I was certain he knew that all of us were there to laugh at his movement; our air of respect was as corrupt as his phony hierarchy, but we were less cunning. Our hypocrisy gained us nothing—not even a reliable ally— while theirs had procured arms, supplies, even cash down.

"Thank you, Your Eminence." I got up to go. He came with me to the door, scattering cigarette ash.

"God's blessing on your work," he said unctuously. "Remember, God loves the truth."

"Which truth?" I asked.

"In the Caodaist faith all truths are reconciled, and truth is love."

He had a large ring on his finger, and when he held out his hand I really think he expected me to kiss it, but I am not a diplomat.

Under the bleak vertical sunlight I saw Pyle; he was trying in vain to make his Buick start. Somehow, during the last two weeks, at the bar of the Continental, in the only good bookshop, in the rue Catinat, I had continually run into Pyle. The friendship, which he had imposed from the beginning, he now emphasized more than ever. His sad eyes would inquire mutely after Phuong, while his lips expressed with even more fervour the strength of his affection and of his admiration—God save the mark!—for me.

A Caodaist commandant stood beside the car, talking rapidly. He stopped when I came up. I recognized him—he had been one of Thé's assistants before Thé took to the hills.

"Hullo, commandant," I said, "how's the general?"

"Which general?" he asked with a shy grin.

"Surely in the Caodaist faith," I said, "all generals are reconciled."

"I can't make this car move, Thomas," Pyle said.

"I will get a mechanic," the commandant said and left us.

"I interrupted you."

"Oh, it was nothing," Pyle said. "He wanted to know how much a Buick cost. These people are so friendly when you treat them right. The French don't seem to know how to handle them."

"The French don't trust them."

Pyle said solemnly, "A man becomes trustworthy when you trust him." It sounded like a Caodaist maxim. I began to feel the air of Tanyin was too ethical for me to breathe.

"Have a drink," Pyle said.

"There's nothing I'd like better."

"I brought a Thermos of lime juice with me." He leaned over and busied himself with a basket in the back.

"Any gin?"

"No. I'm awfully sorry. You know," he said encouragingly, "lime juice is very good for you in this climate. It contains—I'm not sure which vitamins." He held out a cup to me and I drank.

"Anyway, it's wet," I said.

"Like a sandwich? They're really awfully good. A new sandwich mixture called Vit-Health. My mother sent it from the States."

"No thanks, I'm not hungry."

"It tastes rather like Russian dressing—only sort of drier."

"I don't think I will."

"You don't mind if I do?"

"No, no, of course not."

He took a large mouthful and it crunched and crackled. In the distance Buddha in white and pink stone rode away from his ancestral home, and his valet—another statue—pursued him running. The female cardinals were drifting back to their house and the Eye of God watched us from above the cathedral door.

"You know they are serving lunch here?" I said.

"I thought I wouldn't risk it. The meat—you have to be careful in this heat."

"You are quite safe. They are vegetarian."

"I suppose it's all right—but I like to know what I'm eating." He took another munch at his Vit-Health. "Do you think they have any reliable mechanics?"

"They know enough to turn your exhaust pipe into a mortar. I believe Buicks make the best mortars."

The commandant returned and, saluting us smartly, said he had sent to the barracks for a mechanic. Pyle offered him a Vit-Health sandwich, which he refused politely. He said with a man-of-the-world air, "We have so many rules here about food." (He spoke excellent English.) "So foolish. But you know what it is in a religious capital. I expect it is the same thing in Rome—or Canterbury," he added with a neat natty little bow to me. Then he was silent. They were both silent. I had a strong impression that my company was not wanted. I couldn't resist the temptation to tease Pyle—it is after all the weapon of weakness, and I was weak. I hadn't youth, seri-

ousness, integrity, a future. I said, "Perhaps after all I'll have a sandwich."

"Oh, of course," Pyle said, "of course." He paused before turning to the basket in the back.

"No, no," I said. "I was only joking. You two want to be alone."

"Nothing of the kind," Pyle said. He was one of the most inefficient liars I have ever known—it was an art he had obviously never practised. He explained to the commandant, "Thomas here's the best friend I have."

"I know Mr. Fowler," the commandant said.

"I'll see you before I go, Pyle." And I walked away to the cathedral. I could get some coolness there.

Saint Victor Hugo in the uniform of the French Academy with a halo round his tricorn hat pointed at some noble sentiment Sun Yat Sen was inscribing on a tablet, and then I was in the nave. There was nowhere to sit except in the papal chair, round which a plaster cobra coiled; the marble floor glittered like water; and there was no glass in the windows— We make a cage for air with holes, I thought, and man makes a cage for his religion in much the same way, with doubts left open to the weather and creeds opening on innumerable interpretations. My wife had found her cage with holes, and sometimes I envied her. There is a conflict between sun and air; I lived too much in the sun.

I walked the long empty nave—this was not the Indochina I loved. The dragons with lionlike heads climbed the pulpit; on the roof Christ exposed his bleeding heart. Buddha sat, as Buddha always sits, with his lap empty; Confucius's beard hung meagrely down, like a waterfall in the dry season. This was play-acting: the great globe above the altar was ambition; the basket with the movable lid in which the Pope worked his prophecies was trickery. If this cathedral had existed for five centuries instead of two decades, would it have gathered a kind of convincingness with the scratches of feet and the erosion of weather? Would somebody who was convincible like my wife find here a faith she couldn't find in human beings? And if I had really wanted faith would I have found it in her Norman church? But I had never desired faith. The job of a reporter is to expose and record. I had never in my

career discovered the inexplicable. The Pope worked his prophecies with a pencil in a movable lid and the people believed. In any vision somewhere you could find the planchette. I had no visions or miracles in my repertoire of memory.

I turned my memories over at random like pictures in an album: a fox I had seen by the light of an enemy flare over Orpington, stealing along beside a fowl run, out of his russet place in the marginal country; the body of a bayoneted Malay which a Gurkha patrol had brought at the back of a lorry into a mining camp in Pahang, and the Chinese coolies stood by and giggled with nerves, while a brother Malay put a cushion under the dead head; a pigeon on a mantel-piece, poised for flight in a hotel bedroom; my wife's face at a window when I came home to say good-bye for the last time. My thoughts had begun and ended with her. She must have received my letter more than a week ago, and the cable I did not expect had not come. But they say if a jury remains out for long enough there is hope for the prisoner. In another week if no letter arrived could I begin to hope? All round me I could hear the cars of the soldiers and the diplomats revving up; the party was over for another year. The stampede back to Saigon was beginning, and curfew called. I went out to look for Pyle.

He was standing in a patch of shade with the commandant, and no one was doing anything to his car. The conversation seemed to be over, whatever it had been about, and they stood silently there, constrained by mutual politeness. I joined them.

"Well," I said, "I think I'll be off. You'd better be leaving too if you want to be in before curfew."

"The mechanic hasn't turned up."

"He will come soon," the commandant said. "He was in the parade."

"You could spend the night," I said. "There's a special Mass—you'll find it quite an experience. It lasts three hours."

"I ought to get back."

"You won't get back unless you start now." I added unwillingly, "I'll give you a lift if you like, and the commandant can have your car sent in to Saigon tomorrow."

"You need not bother about curfew in Caodaist territory," the com-

mandant said smugly. "But beyond— Certainly I will have your car sent tomorrow."

"Exhaust intact," I said, and he smiled, brightly, neatly, efficiently, a military abbreviation of a smile.

2

The procession of cars was well ahead of us by the time we started. I put on speed to try to overtake it, but we had passed out of the Caodaist zone into the zone of the Hoa Haos with not even a dust cloud ahead of us. The world was flat and empty in the evening.

It was not the kind of country one associates with ambush, but men could conceal themselves neck deep in the drowned fields within a few yards of the road.

Pyle cleared his throat and it was the signal for an approaching intimacy. "I hope Phuong's well," he said.

"I've never known her ill." One watch-tower sank behind, another appeared, like weights on a balance.

"I saw her sister out shopping yesterday."

"And I suppose she asked you to look in," I said.

"As a matter of fact, she did."

"She doesn't give up hope easily."

"Hope?"

"Of marrying you to Phuong."

"She told me you are going away."

"These rumours get about."

Pyle said, "You'd play straight with me, Thomas, wouldn't you?"

"Straight?"

"I've applied for a transfer," he said. "I wouldn't want her to be left without either of us."

"I thought you were going to see your time out."

He said without self-pity, "I found I couldn't stand it."

"When are you leaving?"

"I don't know. They thought something could be arranged in six months."

"You can stand six months?"

"I've got to."

"What reason did you give?"

"I told the Economic Attaché—you met him—Joe—more or less the facts."

"I suppose he thinks I'm a bastard not to let you walk off with my girl."

"Oh, no, he rather sided with you."

The car was spluttering and heaving—it had been spluttering for a minute, I think, before I noticed it, for I had been examining Pyle's innocent question: Are you playing straight? It belonged to a psychological world of great simplicity, where you talked of Democracy and Honor without the "u," as it's spelled on old tombstones, and you meant what your father meant by the same words.

I said, "We've run out."

"Gas?"

"There was plenty. I crammed it full before I started. Those bastards in Tanyin have syphoned it out. I ought to have noticed. It's like them to leave us enough to get out of their zone."

"What shall we do?"

"We can just make the next watch-tower. Let's hope they have a little."

But we were out of luck. The car reached within thirty yards of the tower and gave up. We walked to the foot of the tower, and I called up in French to the guards that we were friends, that we were coming up. I had no wish to be shot by a Vietnamese sentry. There was no reply; nobody looked out. I said to Pyle, "Have you a gun?"

"I never carry one."

"Nor do I."

The last colours of sunset, green and gold like the rice, were dripping over the edge of the flat world; against the grey neutral sky the watch-tower looked as black as print. It must be nearly the hour of curfew. I shouted again, and nobody answered.

"Do you know how many towers we passed since the last fort?"

"I wasn't noticing."

"Nor was I." It was probably at least six kilometres to the next fort—an hour's walk. I called a third time, and silence repeated itself like an answer.

I said, "It seems to be empty; I'd better climb up and see." The yellow flag with red stripes faded to orange showed that we were out of the territory of the Hoa Haos and in the territory of the Vietnamese army.

Pyle said, "Don't you think if we waited here a car might come?"

"It might, but *they* might come first."

"Shall I go back and turn on the lights? For a signal."

"Good God, no. Let it be." It was dark enough now to stumble, looking for the ladder. Something cracked under foot; I could imagine the sound travelling across the fields of paddy, listened to by whom? Pyle had lost his outline and was a blur at the side of the road. Darkness, when once it fell, fell like a stone.

I said, "Stay there until I call." I wondered whether the guard would have drawn up his ladder, but there it stood—though an enemy might climb it, it was their only way of escape. I began to mount.

I have read so often of people's thoughts in the moment of fear: of God, or family, or a woman. I admire their control. I thought of nothing, not even of the trapdoor above me; I ceased, for those seconds, to exist; I was fear taken neat. At the top of the ladder I banged my head because fear couldn't count steps, hear, or see. Then my head came over the earth floor and nobody shot at me and fear seeped away.

3

A small oil lamp burned on the floor, and two men crouched against the wall, watching me. One had a sten gun and one a rifle, but they were as scared as I'd been. They looked like schoolboys, but with the Vietnamese, age drops suddenly like the sun—they are boys and then they are old men. I was glad that the colour of my skin and the shape of my eyes were a passport—they wouldn't shoot now even from fear.

I came up out of the floor, talking to reassure them, telling them that my car was outside, that I had run out of petrol. Perhaps they had a little I could buy—somewhere; it didn't seem likely as I stared around. There was nothing in the little round room except a box of ammunition for the sten gun, a small wooden bed, and two packs hanging on a nail. A couple of pans with the remains of rice and some

wooden chopsticks showed they had been eating without much appetite.

"Just enough to get us to the next fort?" I said.

One of the men sitting against the wall—the one with the rifle—shook his head.

"If you can't we'll have to stay the night here."

"C'est défendu."

"Who by?"

"You are a civilian."

"Nobody's going to make me sit out there on the road and have my throat cut."

"Are you French?"

Only one man had spoken. The other sat with his head turned sideways, watching the slit in the wall. He could have seen nothing but a postcard of sky; he seemed to be listening, and I began to listen too. The silence became full of sound: noises you couldn't put a name to—a crack, a creak, a rustle, something like a cough, and a whisper. Then I heard Pyle; he must have come to the foot of the ladder. "You all right, Thomas?"

"Come up," I called back. He began to climb the ladder, and the silent soldier shifted his sten gun—I don't believe he'd heard a word of what we'd said. It was an awkward, jumpy movement. I realized that fear had paralysed him. I rapped out at him like a sergeant major, "Put that gun down!" and I used the kind of French obscenity I thought he would recognize. He obeyed me automatically. Pyle came up into the room. I said, "We've been offered the safety of the tower till morning."

"Fine," Pyle said. His voice was a little puzzled. He said, "Shouldn't one of those mugs be on sentry?"

"They prefer not to be shot at. I wish you'd brought something stronger than lime juice."

"I guess I will next time," Pyle said.

"We've got a long night ahead." Now that Pyle was with me, I didn't hear the noises. Even the two soldiers seemed to have relaxed a little.

"What happens if the Viets attack them?" Pyle asked.

"They'll fire a shot and run. You read it every morning in the

Extrême-Orient. 'A post south-west of Saigon was temporarily occupied last night by the Vietminh.' "

"It's a bad prospect."

"There are forty towers like this between us and Saigon. The chances always are that it's the other chap who's hurt."

"We could have done with those sandwiches," Pyle said. "I do think one of them should keep a look-out."

"He's afraid a bullet might look in." Now that we too had settled on the floor, the Vietnamese relaxed a little. I felt some sympathy for them; it wasn't an easy job for a couple of ill-trained men to sit up here night after night, never sure of when the Viets might creep up on the road through the fields of paddy. I said to Pyle, "Do you think they know they are fighting for democracy? We ought to have York Harding here to explain it to them."

"You always laugh at York," Pyle said.

"I laugh at anyone who spends so much time writing about what doesn't exist—mental concepts."

"They exist for him. Haven't you got any mental concepts? God, for instance."

"I've no reason to believe in a God. Do you?"

"Yes. I'm a Unitarian."

"How many hundred million Gods do people believe in? Why, even a Roman Catholic believes in quite a different God when he's scared or happy or hungry."

"Maybe if there is a God, he'd be so vast he'd look different to everyone."

"Like the great Buddha in Bangkok," I said. "You can't see all of him at once. Anyway, *he* keeps still."

"I guess you're just trying to be tough," Pyle said. "There must be something you believe in. Nobody can go on living without some belief."

"Oh, I'm not a Berkeleian. I believe my back's against this wall. I believe there's a sten gun over there."

"I didn't mean that."

"I even believe what I report, which is more than most of your correspondents do."

"Cigarette?"

"I don't smoke—except opium. Give one to the guards. We'd better stay friends with them." Pyle got up and lit their cigarettes and came back. I said, "I wish cigarettes had a symbolic significance, like salt."

"Don't you trust them?"

"No French officer," I said, "would care to spend the night alone with two scared guards in one of these towers. Why, even a platoon have been known to hand over their officers. Sometimes the Viets have a better success with a megaphone than a bazooka. I don't blame them. They don't believe in anything either. You and your like are trying to make a war with the help of people who just aren't interested."

"They don't want communism."

"They want enough rice," I said. "They don't want to be shot at. They want one day to be much the same as another. They don't want our white skins around telling them what they want."

"If Indochina goes—"

"I know that record. Siam goes. Malaya goes. Indonesia goes. What does 'go' mean? If I believed in your God and another life, I'd bet my future harp against your golden crown that in five hundred years there may be no New York or London, but they'll be growing paddy in these fields, they'll be carrying their produce to market on long poles, wearing their pointed hats. The small boys will be sitting on the buffaloes. I like the buffaloes, they don't like our smell, the smell of Europeans. And remember—from a buffalo's point of view you are a European too."

"They'll be forced to believe what they are told; they won't be allowed to think for themselves."

"Thought's a luxury. Do you think the peasant sits and thinks of God and democracy when he gets inside his mud hut at night?"

"You talk as if the whole country were peasant. What about the educated? Are they going to be happy?"

"Oh, no," I said, "we've brought them up in *our* ideas. We've taught them dangerous games, and that's why we are waiting here, hoping we don't get our throats cut. We deserve to have them cut. I wish your friend York was here too. I wonder how he'd relish it."

"York Harding's a very courageous man. Why, in Korea—"

"He wasn't an enlisted man, was he? He had a return ticket. With a return ticket, courage becomes an intellectual exercise, like a monk's flagellation. How much can I stick? Those poor devils can't catch a plane home. Hi," I called to them, "what are your names?" I thought that knowledge somehow would bring them into the circle of our conversation. They didn't answer, just glowered back at us behind the stumps of their cigarettes. "They think we are French," I said.

"That's just it," Pyle said. "You shouldn't be against York, you should be against the French. Their colonialism."

"Isms and ocracies. Give me facts. A rubber planter beats his labourer—all right, I'm against him. He hasn't been instructed to do it by the Minister of the Colonies. In France I expect he'd beat his wife. I've seen a priest, so poor he hasn't a change of trousers, working fifteen hours a day from hut to hut in a cholera epidemic, eating nothing but rice and salt fish, saying his Mass with an old cup—a wooden platter. I don't believe in God and yet I'm for that priest. Why don't you call that colonialism?"

"It *is* colonialism. York says it's often the good administrators who make it hard to change a bad system."

"Anyway, the French are dying every day—that's not a mental concept. They aren't leading these people on with half-lies like your politicians—and ours. I've been in India, Pyle, and I know the harm liberals do. We haven't a liberal party any more—liberalism's infected all the other parties. We are all either liberal conservatives or liberal socialists; we all have a good conscience. I'd rather be an exploiter who fights for what he exploits, and dies with it. Look at the history of Burma. We go and invade the country; the local tribes support us; we are victorious; but like you Americans we weren't colonialists in those days. Oh no, we made peace with the king and we handed him back his province and left our allies to be crucified and sawn in two. They were innocent. They thought we'd stay. But we were liberals and we didn't want a bad conscience."

"That was a long time ago."

"We shall do the same thing here. Encourage them and leave them with a little equipment and a toy industry."

"Toy industry?"

"Your plastic."

"Oh yes, I see."

"I don't know what I'm talking politics for. They don't interest me and I'm a reporter. I'm not engagé."

"Aren't you?" Pyle said.

"For the sake of an argument—to pass this bloody night, that's all. I don't take sides. I'll be still reporting whoever wins."

"If they win, you'll be reporting lies."

"There's usually a way round, and I haven't noticed much regard for truth in our papers either."

I think the fact of our sitting there talking encouraged the two soldiers; perhaps they thought the sound of our white voices—for voices have a colour too: yellow voices sing and black voices gargle, while ours just speak—would give an impression of numbers and keep the Viets away. They picked up their pans and began to eat again, scraping with their chopsticks, eyes watching Pyle and me over the rim of the pan.

"So you think we've lost?"

"That's not the point," I said. "I've no particular desire to see you win. I'd like those two poor buggers there to be happy—that's all. I wish they didn't have to sit in the dark at night, scared."

"You have to fight for liberty."

"I haven't seen any Americans fighting around here. And as for liberty, I don't know what it means. Ask them." I called across the floor in French to them. "La liberté—qu'est-ce que c'est la liberté?" They sucked in the rice and stared back and said nothing.

Pyle said, "Do you want everybody to be made in the same mould? You're arguing for the sake of arguing. You're an intellectual. You stand for the importance of the individual as much as I do—or York."

"Why have we only just discovered it?" I said. "Forty years ago no one talked that way."

"It wasn't threatened then."

"Ours wasn't threatened, oh no, but who cared about the individuality of the man in the paddy field—and who does now? The only man to treat him as a man is the political commissar. He'll sit in his hut and ask his name and listen to his complaints; he'll give up an hour a day to

teaching him—it doesn't matter what, he's being treated like a man, like someone of value. Don't go on in the East with that parrot cry about a threat to the individual soul. Here you'd find yourself on the wrong side—it's they who stand for the individual and we just stand for Private 23987, unit in the global strategy."

"You don't mean half what you are saying," Pyle said uneasily.

"Probably three-quarters. I've been here a long time. You know, it's lucky I'm not engagé; there are things I might be tempted to do—because here in the East—well, I don't like Ike. I like—well, these two. This is their country. What's the time? My watch has stopped."

"It's turned eight-thirty."

"Ten hours and we can move."

"It's going to be quite chilly," Pyle said and shivered. "I never expected that."

"There's water all round. I've got a blanket in the car. That will be enough."

"Is it safe?"

"It's early for the Viets."

"Let me go."

"I'm more used to the dark."

When I stood up, the two soldiers stopped eating. I told them, "Je reviens tout de suite." I dangled my legs over the trapdoor, found the ladder, and went down. It is odd how reassuring conversation is, especially on abstract subjects; it seems to normalize the strangest surroundings. I was no longer scared; it was as though I had left a room and would be returning there to pick up the argument—the watchtower was the rue Catinat, the bar of the Majestic, or even a room off Gordon Square.

I stood below the tower for a minute to get my vision back. There was starlight, but no moonlight. Moonlight reminds me of a mortuary and the cold wash of an unshaded globe over a marble slab, but starlight is alive and never still; it is almost as though someone in those vast spaces is trying to communicate a message of good will, for even the names of the stars are friendly. Venus is any woman we love, the Bears are the bears of childhood, and I suppose the Southern Cross, to those, like my wife, who believe, may be a favourite hymn or a prayer

beside the bed. Once I shivered, as Pyle had done. But the night was hot enough; only the shallow stretch of water on either side gave a kind of icing to the warmth. I started out towards the car, and for a moment when I stood on the road I thought it was no longer there. That shook my confidence, even after I remembered that it had petered out thirty yards away. I couldn't help walking with my shoulders bent; I felt more unobtrusive that way.

I had to unlock the car boot to get the blanket, and the click and squeak startled me in the silence. I didn't relish being the only noise in what must have been a night full of people. With the blanket over my shoulder I lowered the boot more carefully than I had raised it, and then, just as the catch caught, the sky towards Saigon flared with light and the sound of an explosion came rumbling down the road. A bren spat and spat and was quiet again before the rumbling stopped. I thought, Somebody's had it; and very far away heard voices crying with pain or fear or perhaps even triumph. I don't know why, but I had thought all the time of an attack coming from behind, along the road we had passed, and I had a moment's sense of unfairness that the Viet should be there ahead, between us and Saigon. It was as though we had been unconsciously driving towards danger instead of away from it, just as I was now walking in its direction, back towards the tower. I walked because it was less noisy than to run, but my body wanted to run.

At the foot of the ladder I called up to Pyle, "It's me—Fowler." (Even then I couldn't bring myself to use my Christian name to him.) The scene inside the hut had changed. The pans of rice were back on the floor; one man held his rifle on his hip and sat against the wall, staring at Pyle; and Pyle knelt a little away out from the opposite wall with his eyes on the sten gun, which lay between him and the second guard. It was as though he had begun to crawl towards it but had been halted. The second guard's arm was extended towards the gun—no one had fought or even threatened; it was like that child's game when you mustn't be seen to move or you are sent back to base to start again.

"What's going on?" I said.

The two guards looked at me, and Pyle pounced, pulling the sten to his side of the room.

"Is it a game?" I asked.

"I don't trust him with the gun," Pyle said, "if they are coming."

"Ever used a sten?"

"No."

"That's fine. Nor have I. I hope it's loaded—we wouldn't know how to reload."

The guards had quietly accepted the loss of the gun. The one lowered his rifle and laid it across his thighs; the other slumped against the wall and shut his eyes as though, like a child, he believed himself invisible in the dark. Perhaps he was glad to have no more responsibility. Somewhere far away the bren started again—three bursts and then silence. The second guard screwed his eyes closer shut.

"They don't know we can't use it," Pyle said.

"They are supposed to be on our side."

"I thought you didn't have a side."

"Touché," I said. "I wish the Viets knew it."

"What's happening out there?"

I quoted again tomorrow's *Extrême-Orient:* " 'A post fifty kilometres outside Saigon was attacked and temporarily captured last night by Vietminh irregulars.' "

"Do you think it would be safer in the fields?"

"It would be terribly wet."

"You don't seem worried," Pyle said.

"I'm scared stiff—but things are better than they might be. They don't usually attack more than three posts in a night. Our chances have improved."

"What's that?"

It was the sound of a heavy car coming up the road, driving towards Saigon. I went to the rifle slit and looked down, just as a tank went by.

"The patrol," I said. The gun in the turret shifted now to this side, now to that. I wanted to call out to them, but what was the good? They hadn't room on board for two useless civilians. The earth floor shook a little as they passed, and they had gone. I looked at my watch—eight-fifty-one—and waited, straining to read when the light flapped. It was like judging the distance of lightning by the delay before the thunder. It was nearly four minutes before the gun opened

up. Once I thought I detected a bazooka replying; then all was quiet again.

"When they come back," Pyle said, "we could signal them for a lift to the camp."

An explosion set the floor shaking. "If they come back," I said. "That sounded like a mine." When I looked at my watch again it had passed nine-fifteen and the tank had not returned. There had been no more firing.

I sat down beside Pyle and stretched out my legs. "We'd better try to sleep," I said. "There's nothing else we can do."

"I'm not happy about the guards," Pyle said.

"They are all right so long as the Viets don't turn up. Put the sten under your leg for safety." I closed my eyes and tried to imagine my-self somewhere else—sitting up in one of the fourth-class compart-ments the German railways ran before Hitler came to power, in the days when one was young and sat up all night without melancholy, when waking dreams were full of hope and not of fear. This was the hour when Phuong always set about preparing my evening pipes. I wondered whether a letter was waiting for me—I hoped not, for I knew what a letter would contain, and so long as none arrived I could day-dream of the impossible.

"Are you asleep?" Pyle asked.

"No."

"Don't you think we ought to pull up the ladder?"

"I begin to understand why they don't. It's the only way out."

"I wish that tank would come back."

"It won't now."

I tried not to look at my watch except at long intervals, and the in-tervals were never as long as they had seemed. Nine-forty, ten-five, ten-twelve, ten-thirty-two, ten-forty-one.

"You awake?" I said to Pyle.

"Yes."

"What are you thinking about?"

He hesitated. "Phuong," he said.

"Yes?"

"I was just wondering what she was doing."

"I can tell you that. She'll have decided that I'm spending the night at Tanyin—it won't be the first time. She'll be lying on the bed with a joss stick burning to keep away the mosquitoes and she'll be looking at the pictures in an old *Paris-Match*. Like the French, she has a passion for the Royal Family."

He said wistfully, "It must be wonderful to know exactly," and I could imagine his soft dog's eyes in the dark. They ought to have called him Fido, not Alden.

"I don't really know—but it's probably true. There's no good in being jealous when you can't do anything about it. 'No barricado for a belly.' "

"Sometimes I hate the way you talk, Thomas. Do you know how she seems to me? She seems fresh, like a flower."

"Poor flower," I said. "There are a lot of weeds around."

"Where did you meet her?"

"She was dancing at the Grand Monde."

"Dancing!" he exclaimed, as though the idea were painful.

"It's a perfectly respectable profession," I said. "Don't worry."

"You have such an awful lot of experience, Thomas."

"I have an awful lot of years. When you reach my age—"

"I've never had a girl," he said, "not properly. Not what you'd call a real experience."

"A lot of energy with your people seems to go into whistling."

"I've never told anybody else."

"You're young. It's nothing to be ashamed of."

"Have you had a lot of women, Fowler?"

"I don't know what a lot means. Not more than four women have had any importance to me—or me to them. The other forty-odd—one wonders why one does it. A notion of hygiene, of one's social obligations, both mistaken."

"You think they *are* mistaken?"

"I wish I could have those nights back. I'm still in love, Pyle, and I'm a wasting asset. Oh, and there was pride, of course. It takes a long time before we cease to feel proud of being wanted. Though God knows why we should feel it, when we look around and see who is wanted too."

"You don't think there's anything wrong with me, do you, Thomas?"

"No, Pyle."

"It doesn't mean I don't *need* it, Thomas, like everybody else. I'm not—odd."

"Not one of us needs it as much as we say. There's an awful lot of self-hypnosis around. Now I know I need nobody—except Phuong. But that's a thing one learns with time. I could go a year without one restless night if she wasn't there."

"But she *is* there," he said in a voice I could hardly catch.

"One starts promiscuous and ends like one's grandfather, faithful to one woman."

"I suppose it seems pretty naïve to start that way . . ."

"No."

"It's not in the Kinsey Report."

"That's why it's not naïve."

"You know, Thomas, it's pretty good being here, talking to you like this. Somehow it doesn't seem dangerous any more."

"We used to feel that in the blitz," I said, "when a lull came. But they always returned."

"If somebody asked you what your deepest sexual experience had been, what would you say?"

I knew the answer to that. "Lying in bed early one morning and watching a woman in a red dressing gown brush her hair."

"Joe said it was being in bed with a Chink and a Negress at the same time."

"I'd have thought that one up too when I was twenty."

"Joe's fifty."

"I wonder what mental age they gave him in the war."

"Was Phuong the girl in the red dressing gown?"

I wished that he hadn't asked that question.

"No," I said, "that woman came earlier. When I left my wife."

"What happened?"

"I left her too."

"Why?"

Why indeed? "We are fools," I said, "when we love. I was terrified of

losing her. I thought I saw her changing—I don't know if she really was, but I couldn't bear the uncertainty any longer. I ran towards the finish just like a coward runs towards the enemy and wins a medal. I wanted to get death over."

"Death?"

"It was a kind of death. Then I came east."

"And found Phuong?"

"Yes."

"But don't you find the same thing with Phuong?"

"Not the same. You see, the other one loved me. I was afraid of losing love. Now I'm only afraid of losing Phuong." Why had I said that? I wondered. He didn't need encouragement from me.

"But she loves you, doesn't she?"

"Not like that. It isn't in their nature. You'll find that out. It's a cliché to call them children—but there's one thing which is childish. They love you in return for kindness, security, the presents you give them—they hate you for a blow or an injustice. They don't know what it's like—just walking into a room and loving a stranger. For an aging man, Pyle, it's very secure—she won't run away from home so long as the home is happy."

I hadn't meant to hurt him. I only realized I had done it when he said with muffled anger, "She might prefer a greater security or more kindness."

"Perhaps."

"Aren't you afraid of that?"

"Not so much as I was of the other."

"Do you love her at all?"

"Oh yes, Pyle, yes. But that other way I've only loved once."

"In spite of the forty-odd women," he snapped at me.

"I'm sure it's below the Kinsey average. You know, Pyle, women don't want virgins. I'm not sure *we* do, unless we are a pathological type."

"I didn't mean I was a virgin," he said. All my conversations with Pyle seemed to take grotesque directions. Was it because of his sincerity that they so ran off the customary rails? His conversation never took the corners.

"You can have a hundred women and still be a virgin, Pyle. Most of your G.I.'s who were hanged for rape in the war were virgins. We don't have so many in Europe. I'm glad. They do a lot of harm."

"I just don't understand you, Thomas."

"It's not worth explaining. I'm bored with the subject anyway. I've reached the age when sex isn't the problem so much as old age and death. I wake up with these in mind, and not a woman's body. I just don't want to be alone in my last decade. That's all. I wouldn't know what to think about all day long. I'd sooner have a woman in the same room—even one I didn't love. But if Phuong left me, would I have the energy to find another?"

"If that's all she means to you . . ."

"All, Pyle? Wait until you're afraid of living ten years alone with no companion and a nursing home at the end of it. Then you'll start running in any direction, even away from that girl in the red dressing gown, to find someone, anyone, who will last until you are through."

"Why don't you go back to your wife, then?"

"It's not easy to live with someone you've injured."

A sten gun fired a long burst—it couldn't have been more than a mile away. Perhaps a nervous sentry was shooting at shadows; perhaps another attack had begun. I hoped it was an attack—it increased our chances.

"Are you scared, Thomas?"

"Of course I am. With all my instincts. But with my reason I know it's better to die like this. That's why I came east. Death stays with you." I looked at my watch. It had gone eleven. An eight-hour night and then we could relax. I said, "We seem to have talked about pretty nearly everything except God. We'd better leave him to the small hours."

"You don't believe in Him, do you?"

"No."

"Things to me wouldn't make sense without Him."

"They don't make sense to me with him."

"I read a book once—"

I never knew what book Pyle had read. (Presumably it wasn't York Harding or Shakespeare or the anthology of contemporary verse or *The Physiology of Marriage*—perhaps it was *The Triumph of Life*.) A voice

came right into the tower with us; it seemed to speak from the shadows by the trap—a hollow megaphone voice, saying something in Vietnamese.

"We're for it," I said. The two guards listened, their faces turned to the rifle slit, their mouths hanging open.

"What is it?" Pyle said.

Walking to the embrasure was like walking through the voice. I looked quickly out; there was nothing to be seen—I couldn't even distinguish the road—and when I looked back into the room the rifle was pointed, I wasn't sure whether at me or at the slit. But when I moved round the wall the rifle wavered, hesitated, kept me covered; the voice went on saying the same thing over again. I sat down, and the rifle was lowered.

"What's he saying?" Pyle asked.

"I don't know. I expect they've found the car and are telling these chaps to hand us over or else. Better pick up that sten before they make up their minds."

"He'll shoot."

"He's not sure yet. When he is, he'll shoot anyway."

Pyle shifted his leg, and the rifle came up.

"I'll move along the wall," I said. "When his eyes waver get him covered."

Just as I rose, the voice stopped; the silence made me jump. Pyle said sharply, "Drop your rifle!" I had just time to wonder whether the sten was unloaded—I hadn't bothered to look—when the man threw his rifle down.

I crossed the room and picked it up. Then the voice began again— I had the impression that no syllable had changed. Perhaps they used a record. I wondered when the ultimatum would expire.

"What happens next?" Pyle asked, like a schoolboy watching a demonstration in the laboratory; he didn't seem personally concerned.

"Perhaps a bazooka, perhaps a Viet."

Pyle examined his sten. "There doesn't seem to be any mystery about this," he said. "Shall I fire a burst?"

"No, let them hesitate. They'd rather take the post without firing, and it gives us time. We'd better clear out fast."

"They may be waiting at the bottom."

"Yes."

The two men watched us—I write "men," but I doubt whether they had accumulated forty years between them.

"And these?" Pyle asked, and he added with a shocking directness, "Shall I shoot them?" Perhaps he wanted to try the sten.

"They've done nothing."

"They were going to hand us over."

"Why not?" I said. "We've no business here. It's their country." I unloaded the rifle and laid it on the floor.

"Surely you're not leaving that," he said.

"I'm too old to run with a rifle. And this isn't my war. Come on."

It wasn't my war, but I wished those others in the dark knew that as well. I blew the oil lamp out and dangled my legs over the trap, feeling for the ladder. I could hear the guards whispering to each other like crooners in their language like a song. "Make straight ahead," I told Pyle. "Aim for the rice. Remember, there's water—I don't know how deep. Ready?"

"Yes."

"Thanks for the company."

"Always a pleasure," Pyle said.

I heard the guards moving behind us; I wondered if they had knives. The megaphone voice spoke peremptorily, as though offering a last chance. Something shifted softly in the dark below us, but it might have been a rat. I hesitated. "I wish to God I had a drink," I whispered.

"Let's go."

Something was coming up the ladder; I heard nothing, but the ladder shook under my feet.

"What's keeping you?" Pyle said.

I don't know why I thought of it as something, that silent stealthy approach. Only a man could climb a ladder, and yet I couldn't think of it as man like myself—it was as though an animal were moving in to kill, very quietly and certainly, with the remorselessness of another kind of creation. The ladder shook and shook, and I imagined I saw its eyes glaring upwards. Suddenly I could bear it no longer and I jumped and there was nothing there at all but the spongy ground which took

my ankle and twisted it as a hand might have done. I could hear Pyle coming down the ladder; I realized I had been a frightened fool who could not recognize his own trembling, and I had believed I was tough and unimaginative, all that a truthful observer and reporter should be. I got on my feet and nearly fell again with the pain. I started out for the field, dragging one foot after me, and heard Pyle coming behind me. Then the bazooka shell burst on the tower and I was on my face again.

4

"Are you hurt?" Pyle said.

"Something hit my leg. Nothing serious."

"Let's get on," Pyle urged me.

I could just see him, because he seemed to be covered with a fine white dust. Then he simply went out like a picture on the screen when the lamps of the projector fail; only the sound track continued. I got gingerly up onto my good knee and tried to rise without putting any weight on my bad left ankle, and then I was down again, breathless with pain. It wasn't my ankle; something had happened to my left leg. I couldn't worry—pain took away care. I lay very still on the ground, hoping that pain wouldn't find me again; I even held my breath, as one does with toothache. I didn't think about the Viets, who would soon be searching the ruins of the tower; another shell exploded on it—they were making quite sure before they came in. What a lot of money it costs, I thought as the pain receded, to kill a few human beings—you can kill horses so much cheaper. I can't have been fully conscious, for I began to think I had strayed into a knacker's yard which was the terror of my childhood in the small town where I was born. We used to think we heard the horses whinnying with fear and the explosion of the painless killer.

It was some while since the pain had returned, now that I was lying still—and holding my breath; that seemed to me just as important. I wondered quite lucidly whether perhaps I ought to crawl towards the fields. The Viet might not have time to search far. Another patrol would be out by now, trying to contact the crew of the first tank. But I was more afraid of the pain than of the partisans, and I lay still. There was no sound anywhere of Pyle; he must have reached the fields. Then

I heard someone weeping. It came from the direction of the tower, or what had been the tower. It wasn't like a man weeping; it was like a child who is frightened of the dark and yet afraid to scream. I supposed it was one of the two boys—perhaps his companion had been killed. I hoped that the Viets wouldn't cut his throat. One shouldn't fight a war with children, and a little curled body in a ditch came back to mind. I shut my eyes—that helped to keep the pain away too—and waited. A voice called something I didn't understand. I almost felt I could sleep in this darkness and loneliness and absence of pain.

Then I heard Pyle whispering, "Thomas. Thomas." He had learned footcraft quickly; I had not heard him return.

"Go away," I whispered back.

He found me there and lay down flat beside me. "Why didn't you come? Are you hurt?"

"My leg. I think it's broken."

"A bullet?"

"No, no. Log of wood. Stone. Something from the tower. It's not bleeding."

"You've got to make an effort."

"Go away, Pyle. I don't want to; it hurts too much."

"Which leg?"

"Left."

He crept round to my side and hoisted my arm over his shoulder. I wanted to whimper like the boy in the tower, and then I was angry, but it was hard to express anger in a whisper. "God damn you, Pyle, leave me alone. I want to stay."

"You can't."

He was pulling me half onto his shoulder, and the pain was intolerable. "Don't be a bloody hero. I don't want to go."

"You've got to help," he said, "or we're both caught."

"You——"

"Be quiet or they'll hear you."

I was crying with vexation—you couldn't use a stronger word. I hoisted myself against him and let my left leg dangle—we were like awkward contestants in a three-legged race and we wouldn't have stood a chance if, at the moment we set off, a bren had not begun to fire

in quick short bursts somewhere down the road towards the next tower: perhaps a patrol was pushing up or perhaps they were completing their score of three towers destroyed. It covered the noise of our slow and clumsy flight.

I'm not sure whether I was conscious all the time; I think for the last twenty yards Pyle must have almost carried my weight. He said, "Careful here. We're going in." The dry rice rustled around us, and the mud squelched and rose. The water was up to our waists when Pyle stopped. He was panting, and a catch in his breath made him sound like a bullfrog.

"I'm sorry," I said.

"Couldn't leave you," Pyle said.

The first sensation was relief; the water and mud held my leg tenderly and firmly like a bandage, but soon the cold set us chattering. I wondered whether it had passed midnight yet; we might have six hours of this if the Viets didn't find us.

"Can you shift your weight a little?" Pyle said.

"Just for a moment"—and my unreasoning irritation came back; I had no excuse for it but the pain. I hadn't asked to be saved, or to have death so painfully postponed. I thought with nostalgia of my couch on the hard dry ground. I stood like a crane on one leg, trying to relieve Pyle of my weight, and when I moved, the stalks of rice tickled and cut and crackled.

"You saved my life there," I said, and Pyle cleared his throat for the conventional response, "so that I could die here. I prefer dry land."

"Better not talk," Pyle said, as though to an invalid. "Got to save our strength."

"Who the hell asked you to save my life? I came east to be killed. It's like your damned impertinence—"

I staggered in the mud, and Pyle hoisted my arm around his shoulder. "Take it easy," he said.

"You've been seeing war films. We aren't a couple of Marines, and you can't win a war medal."

"Sh-sh." Footsteps could be heard, coming down to the edge of the field; the bren up the road stopped firing, and there was no sound except the footsteps and the slight rustle of the rice when we breathed.

Then the footsteps halted; they seemed only the length of a room away. I felt Pyle's hand on my good side pressing me slowly down; we sank together into the mud very slowly so as to make the least disturbance of the rice. On one knee, by straining my head backwards, I could just keep my mouth out of the water. The pain came back to my leg, and I thought, If I faint here I drown—I had always hated and feared the thought of drowning. Why can't one choose one's death? There was no sound now; perhaps twenty feet away they were waiting for a rustle, a cough, a sneeze. Oh God, I thought, I'm going to sneeze. If only he had left me alone, I would have been responsible only for my own life—not his—and he wanted to live. I pressed my free fingers against my upper lip in that trick we learn when we are children playing at hide-and-seek, but the sneeze lingered, waiting to burst, and silent in the darkness the others waited for the sneeze. It was coming, coming, came . . .

But in the very second that my sneeze broke, the Viets opened with stens, drawing a line of fire through the rice—it swallowed my sneeze with its sharp drilling like a machine punching holes through steel. I took a breath and went under—so instinctively one avoids the loved thing, coquetting with death, like a woman who demands to be raped by her lover. The rice was lashed down over our heads, and the storm passed. We came up for air at the same moment and heard the footsteps going away back towards the tower.

"We've made it," Pyle said, and even in my pain I wondered what we'd made: for me old age, an editor's chair, loneliness; and, as for him, one knows now that he spoke prematurely. Then in the cold we settled down to wait. Along the road to Tanyin a bonfire burst into life; it burned merrily, like a celebration.

"That's my car," I said.

Pyle said, "It's a shame, Thomas. I hate to see waste."

"There must have been just enough petrol in the tank to set it going. Are you as cold as I am, Pyle?"

"I couldn't be colder."

"Suppose we get out and lie flat on the road."

"Let's give them another half-hour."

"The weight's on you."

"I can take it, I'm young." He had meant the claim humorously, but it struck as cold as the mud. I had intended to apologize for the way my pain had spoken, but now it spoke again. "You're young, all right. You can afford to wait, can't you?"

"I don't get you, Thomas."

We had spent what seemed to have been a week of nights together, but he could no more understand me than he could understand French. I said, "You'd have done better to let me be."

"I couldn't have faced Phuong," he said, and the name lay there like a banker's bid. I took it up.

"So it was for her," I said. What made my jealousy more absurd and humiliating was that it had to be expressed in the lowest of whispers— it had no tone, and jealousy likes histrionics. "You think these heroics will get her. How wrong you are. If I were dead you could have had her."

"I didn't mean that," Pyle said. "When you are in love you want to play the game, that's all."

That's true, I thought, but not as he innocently means it. To be in love is to see yourself as someone else sees you, it is to be in love with the falsified and exalted image of yourself. In love we are incapable of honour—the courageous act is no more than playing a part to an audience of two. Perhaps I was no longer in love, but I remembered.

"If it had been you, I'd have left you," I said.

"Oh no, you wouldn't, Thomas." He added with unbearable complacency, "I know you better than you do yourself."

Angrily I tried to move away from him and take my own weight, but the pain came roaring back like a train in a tunnel and I leaned more heavily against him, before I began to sink into the water. He got both his arms round me and held me up, and then inch by inch he began to edge me to the bank and the roadside. When he got me there he lowered me flat in the shallow mud below the bank at the edge of the field, and when the pain retreated, and I opened my eyes and ceased to hold my breath, I could see only the elaborate cipher of the constellations—a foreign cipher which I couldn't read; they were not the stars of home. His face wheeled over me, blotting them out. "I'm going down the road, Thomas, to find a patrol."

"Don't be a fool," I said. "They'll shoot you before they know who you are—if the Viets don't get you."

"It's the only chance. You can't lie in the water for six hours."

"Then lay me in the road."

"It's no good leaving you the sten?" he asked doubtfully.

"Of course it's not. If you are determined to be a hero, at least go slowly through the rice."

"The patrol would pass before I could signal it."

"You don't speak French."

"I shall call out, 'Je suis Frongçais.' Don't worry, Thomas. I'll be very careful."

Before I could reply, he was out of a whisper's range—he was moving as quietly as he knew how, with frequent pauses. I could see him in the light of the burning car, but no shot came; soon he passed beyond the flames, and very soon the silence filled the footprints. Oh yes, he was being careful as he had been careful boating down the river into Phat Diem, with the caution of a hero in a boy's adventure story, proud of his caution like a Scout's badge and quite unaware of the absurdity and improbability of his adventure.

I lay and listened for the shots from the Viet or a Legion patrol, but none came—it would probably take him an hour or even more before he reached a tower, if he ever reached it. I turned my head enough to see what remained of our tower, a heap of mud and bamboo and struts, which seemed to sink lower as the flames of the car sank. There was peace when the pain went—a kind of Armistice Day of the nerves—I wanted to sing. I thought how strange it was that men of my profession would make only two news lines out of all this night—it was just a common or garden night, and I was the only strange thing about it. Then I heard a low crying begin again from what was left of the tower. One of the guards must still be alive.

I thought, Poor devil, if we hadn't broken down outside *his* post, he could have surrendered as they nearly all surrendered, or fled, at the first call from the megaphone. But we were there—two white men—and we had the sten and they didn't dare to move. When we left, it was too late. I was responsible for that voice crying in the dark. I had prided myself on detachment, on not belonging to this war, but those wounds

had been inflicted by me just as though I had used the sten, as Pyle had wanted to do.

I made an effort to get over the bank into the road. I wanted to join him. It was the only thing I could do, to share his pain. But my own personal pain pushed me back. I couldn't hear him any more. I lay still and heard nothing but my own pain beating like a monstrous heart and held my breath and prayed to the God I didn't believe in, "Let me die or faint. Let me die or faint," and then I suppose I fainted and was aware of nothing until I dreamed that my eyelids had frozen together and someone was inserting a chisel to prise them apart, and I wanted to warn them not to damage the eyeballs beneath but couldn't speak, and the chisel bit through and a torch was shining on my face.

"We made it, Thomas," Pyle said. I remember that, but I don't remember what Pyle later described to others: that I waved my hand in the wrong direction and told them there was a man in the tower and they had to see to him. Anyway, I couldn't have made the sentimental assumption that Pyle made. I know myself, and I know the depth of my selfishness. I cannot be at ease (and to be at ease is my chief wish) if someone else is in pain, visibly or audibly or tactually. Sometimes this is mistaken by the innocent for unselfishness, when all I am doing is sacrificing a small good—in this case postponement in attending to my hurt—for the sake of a far greater good, a peace of mind, when I need think only of myself.

They came back to tell me the boy was dead, and I was happy—I didn't even have to suffer much pain after the hypodermic of morphia had bitten my leg.

FROM *THE RUSSIA HOUSE* (1989)

John le Carré (1931–   )

John le Carré reached bestseller prominence with The Spy Who Came
In from the Cold, *a classic instance of the integration of style and substance. The cold war was forty-four years of obliquity, treachery, lies, and
counterlies—the perfect battleground for the le Carré style, which is dark,
ironic, and bristling with aristocratic contempt, a very sharp tool encoun-
tered far more agreeably in literature than in daily life.* The Russia
House *is mature le Carré, and the last, to date, of his cold war novels.*

1

In a broad Moscow street not two hundred yards from the Leningrad
station, on the upper floor of an ornate and hideous hotel built by
Stalin in the style known to Muscovites as Empire During the Plague,
the British Council's first ever audio fair for the teaching of the English language and the spread of British culture was grinding to its ex-
cruciating end. The time was half past five, the summer weather
erratic. After fierce rain showers all day long, a false sunlight was blaz-

ing in the puddles and raising vapour from the pavements. Of the passers-by, the younger ones wore jeans and sneakers, but their elders were still huddled in their warms.

The room the Council had rented was not expensive but neither was it appropriate to the occasion. I have seen it. Not long ago, in Moscow on quite another mission, I tiptoed up the great empty staircase and, with a diplomatic passport in my pocket, stood in the eternal dusk that shrouds old ballrooms when they are asleep. With its plump brown pillars and gilded mirrors, it was better suited to the last hours of a sinking liner than the launch of a great initiative. On the ceiling, snarling Russians in proletarian caps shook their fists at Lenin. Their vigour contrasted unhelpfully with the chipped green racks of sound cassettes along the walls, featuring *Winnie-the-Pooh* and *Advanced Computer English in Three Hours.* The sackcloth sound-booths, locally procured and lacking many of their promised features, had the sadness of deck chairs on a rainy beach. The exhibitors' stands, crammed under the shadow of an overhanging gallery, seemed as blasphemous as betting shops in a tabernacle.

Nevertheless a fair of sorts had taken place. People had come, as Moscow people do, provided they have the documents and status to satisfy the hard-eyed boys in leather jackets at the door. Out of politeness. Out of curiosity. To talk to Westerners. Because it is there. And now on the fifth and final evening the great farewell cocktail party of exhibitors and invited guests was getting into its stride. A handful of the small *nomenklatura* of the Soviet cultural bureaucracy was gathering under the chandelier, the ladies in their beehive hairstyles and flowered frocks designed for slenderer frames, the gentlemen slimmed by the shiny French-tailored suits that signified access to the special clothing stores. Only their British hosts, in despondent shades of grey, observed the monotone of Socialist austerity. The hubbub rose, a brigade of pinafored governesses distributed the curling salami sandwiches and warm white wine. A senior British diplomat who was not quite the Ambassador shook the better hands and said he was delighted.

Only Niki Landau among them had withheld himself from the celebrations. He was stooped over the table in his empty stand, totting up his last orders and checking his dockets against expenses, for it was a

maxim of Landau's never to go out and play until he had wrapped up his day's business.

And in the corner of his eye—an anxious blue blur was all that she amounted to—this Soviet woman he was deliberately ignoring. *Trouble*, he was thinking as he laboured. *Avoid*.

The air of festivity had not communicated itself to Landau, festive by temperament though he was. For one thing, he had a lifelong aversion to British officialdom, ever since his father had been forcibly returned to Poland. The British themselves, he told me later, he would hear no wrong of them. He was one of them by adoption and he had the poker-backed reverence of the convert. But the Foreign Office flunkies were another matter. And the loftier they were, and the more they twitched and smirked and raised their stupid eyebrows at him, the more he hated them and thought about his dad. For another thing, if he had been left to himself, he would never have come to the audio fair in the first place. He'd have been tucked up in Brighton with a nice new little friend he had, called Lydia, in a nice little private hotel he knew for taking little friends.

"Better to keep our powder dry till the Moscow book fair in September," Landau had advised his clients at their headquarters on the Western by-pass. "The Russkies love a book, you see, Bernard, but the audio market scares them and they aren't geared for it. Go in with the book fair, we'll clean up. Go in with the audio fair, we're dead."

But Landau's clients were young and rich and did not believe in death. "Niki boy," said Bernard, walking round behind him and putting a hand on his shoulder, which Landau didn't like, "in the world today, we've got to show the flag. We're patriots, see, Niki? Like you. That's why we're an offshore company. With the *glasnost* today, the Soviet Union, it's the Mount Everest of the recording business. And you're going to put us on the top, Niki. Because if you're not, we'll find somebody who will. Somebody younger, Niki, right? Somebody with the drive and the class."

The drive Landau had still. But the class, as he himself was the first to tell you, the class, forget it. He was a card, that's what he liked to be. A pushy, short-arsed Polish card and proud of it. He was Old Nik the

cheeky chappie of the Eastward-facing reps, capable, he liked to boast, of selling filthy pictures to a Georgian convent or hair tonic to a Roumanian billiard ball. He was Landau the undersized bedroom athlete, who wore raised heels to give his Slav body the English scale he admired, and ritzy suits that whistled "here I am." When Old Nik set up his stand, his travelling colleagues assured our unattributable enquirers, you could hear the tinkle of the handbell on his Polish vendor's barrow.

And little Landau shared the joke with them, he played their game. "Boys, I'm the Pole you wouldn't touch with a barge," he would declare proudly as he ordered up another round. Which was his way of getting them to laugh with him. Instead of at him. And then most likely, to demonstrate his point, he would whip a comb from his top pocket and drop into a crouch. And with the aid of a picture on the wall, or any other polished surface, he'd sweep back his too black hair in preparation for fresh conquest, using both his little hands to coax it into manliness. "Who's that comely one I'm looking at over there in the corner then?" he'd ask, in his godless blend of ghetto Polish and East End cockney. "Hullo there, sweetheart! Why are we suffering all alone tonight?" And once out of five times he'd score, which in Landau's book was an acceptable rate of return, always provided you kept asking.

But this evening Landau wasn't thinking of scoring or even asking. He was thinking that yet again he had worked his heart out all week for a pittance—or, as he put it more graphically to me, a tart's kiss. And that every fair these days, whether it was a book fair or an audio fair or any other kind of fair, took a little more out of him than he liked to admit to himself, just as every woman did. And gave him a fraction too little in return. And that tomorrow's plane back to London couldn't come too soon. And that if this Russian bird in blue didn't stop insinuating herself into his attention when he was trying to close his books and put on his party smile and join the jubilant throng, he would very likely say something to her in her own language that both of them would live to regret.

That she was Russian went without saying. Only a Russian woman would have a plastic perhaps-bag dangling from her arm in readiness

for the chance purchase that is the triumph of everyday life, even if most perhaps-bags were of string. Only a Russian would be so nosy as to stand close enough to check a man's arithmetic. And only a Russian would preface her interruption with one of those fastidious grunts, which in a man always reminded Landau of his father doing up his shoe laces, and in a woman, Harry, bed.

"Excuse me, sir. Are you the gentleman from Abercrombie & Blair?" she asked.

"Not here, dear," said Landau without lifting his head. She had spoken English, so he had spoken English in return, which was the way he played it always.

"Mr. Barley?"

"Not Barley, dear. Landau."

"But this is Mr. Barley's stand."

"This is not Barley's stand. This is my stand. Abercrombie & Blair are next door."

Still without looking up, Landau jabbed his pencil-end to the left, towards the empty stand on the other side of the partition, where a green-and-gold board proclaimed the ancient publishing house of Abercrombie & Blair of Norfolk Street, Strand.

"But that stand is empty. No one is there," the woman objected. "It was empty yesterday also."

"Correct. Right on," Landau retorted in a tone that was final enough for anybody. And he ostentatiously lowered himself further into his account book, waiting for the blue blur to remove itself. Which was rude of him, he knew, and her continuing presence made him feel ruder.

"But where is Scott Blair? Where is the man they call Barley? I must speak to him. It is very urgent."

Landau was by now hating the woman with unreasoning ferocity.

"*Mr.* Scott Blair," he began as he snapped up his head and stared at her full on, "more commonly known to his intimates as Barley, is *awol*, madam. That means absent without leave. His company booked a stand—yes. And Mr. Scott Blair is chairman, president, governor-general and for all I know lifetime dictator of that company. However, he did not occupy his stand—" But here, having caught her eye, he

began to lose his footing. "Listen, dear, I happen to be trying to make a living here, right? I am not making it for Mr. Barley Scott Blair, love him as I may."

Then he stopped, as a chivalrous concern replaced his momentary anger. The woman was trembling. Not only with the hands that held her brown perhaps-bag but also at the neck, for her prim blue dress was finished with a collar of old lace and Landau could see how it shook against her skin and how her skin was actually whiter than the lace. Yet her mouth and jaw were set with determination and her expression commanded him.

"Please, sir, you must be very kind and help me," she said as if there were no choice.

Now Landau prided himself on knowing women. It was another of his irksome boasts but it was not without foundation. "Women, they're my hobby, my life's study and my consuming passion, Harry," he confided to me, and the conviction in his voice was as solemn as a Mason's pledge. He could no longer tell you how many he had had, but he was pleased to say that the figure ran into the hundreds and there was not one of them who had cause to regret the experience. "I play straight, I choose wisely, Harry," he assured me, tapping one side of his nose with his forefinger. "No cut wrists, no broken marriages, no harsh words afterwards." How true this was nobody would ever know, myself included, but there can be no doubt that the instincts that had guided him through his philanderings came rushing to his assistance as he formed his judgments about the woman.

She was earnest. She was intelligent. She was determined. She was scared, even though her dark eyes were lit with humour. And she had that rare quality which Landau in his flowery way liked to call the Class That Only Nature Can Bestow. In other words, she had quality as well as strength. And since in moments of crisis our thoughts do not run consecutively but rather sweep over us in waves of intuition and experience, he sensed all these things at once and was on terms with them by the time she spoke to him again.

"A Soviet friend of mine has written a creative and important work of literature," she said after taking a deep breath. "It is a novel. A great novel. Its message is important for all mankind."

She had dried up.

"A novel," Landau prompted. And then, for no reason he could afterwards think of, "What's its title, dear?"

The strength in her, he decided, came neither from bravado nor insanity but from conviction.

"What's its message then, if it hasn't got a title?"

"It concerns actions before words. It rejects the gradualism of the *perestroika*. It demands action and rejects all cosmetic change."

"Nice," said Landau, impressed.

She spoke like my mother used to, Harry: chin up and straight into your face.

"In spite of *glasnost* and the supposed liberalism of the new guidelines, my friend's novel cannot yet be published in the Soviet Union," she continued. "Mr. Scott Blair has undertaken to publish it with discretion."

"Lady," said Landau kindly, his face now close to hers. "If your friend's novel is published by the great house of Abercrombie & Blair, believe me, you can be assured of total secrecy."

He said this partly as a joke he couldn't resist and partly because his instincts told him to take the stiffness out of their conversation and make it less conspicuous to anybody watching. And whether she understood the joke or not, the woman smiled also, a swift warm smile of self-encouragement that was like a victory over her fears.

"Then, Mr. Landau, if you love peace please take this manuscript with you back to England and give it immediately to Mr. Scott Blair. Only to Mr. Scott Blair. It is a gift of trust."

What happened next happened quickly, a street-corner transaction, willing seller to willing buyer. The first thing Landau did was look behind her, past her shoulder. He did that for his own preservation as well as hers. It was his experience that when the Russkies wanted to get up to a piece of mischief, they always had other people close by. But his end of the assembly room was empty, the area beneath the gallery where the stands were was dark and the party at the centre of the room was by now in full cry. The three boys in leather jackets at the front door were talking stodgily among themselves.

His survey completed, he read the girl's plastic name badge on her

lapel, which was something he would normally have done earlier but
her black-brown eyes had distracted him. Yekaterina Orlova, he read.
And underneath, the word "October," given in both English and Russian, this being the name of one of Moscow's smaller State publishing
houses specialising in translations of Soviet books for export, mainly
to other Socialist countries, which I am afraid condemned it to a certain dowdiness.

Next he told her what to do, or perhaps he was already telling her
by the time he read her badge. Landau was a street kid, up to all the
tricks. The woman might be as brave as six lions and by the look of her
probably was. But she was no conspirator. Therefore he took her un-
hesitatingly into his protection. And in doing so he spoke to her as he
would to any woman who needed his basic counsel, such as where to
find his hotel bedroom or what to tell her hubby when she got home.

"Got it with you then, have you, dear?" he asked, peering down at
the perhaps-bag and smiling like a friend.

"Yes."

"In there, is it?"

"Yes."

"Then give me the whole bag normally," Landau said, talking her
through her act. "That's the way. Now give me a friendly Russian kiss.
The formal sort. Nice. You've brought me an official farewell gift on
the last evening of the fair, you see. Something that will cement
Anglo-Soviet relations and make me overweight on the flight home
unless I dump it in the dustbin at the airport. Very normal transaction.
I must have received half a dozen such gifts today already."

Part of this was spoken while he crouched with his back to her. For,
reaching into the bag, he had already slipped out the brown-paper parcel that was inside it and was dropping it deftly into his briefcase,
which was of the home filing variety, very compendious, with com-
partments that opened in a fan.

"Married, are we, Katya?"

No answer. Maybe she hadn't heard. Or she was too busy watching
him.

"Is it your husband who's written the novel, then?" said Landau,
undeterred by her silence.

"It is dangerous for you," she whispered. "You must believe in what you are doing. Then everything is clear."

As if he had not heard this warning at all, Landau selected, from a pile of samples that he had kept to give away tonight, a four-pack of the Royal Shakespeare Company's specially commissioned reading of *A Midsummer Night's Dream,* which he placed ostentatiously on the table and signed for her on the plastic casing with a felt-tip pen: "From Niki to Katya, Peace," and the date. Then he put the four-pack ceremoniously into the perhaps-bag for her, and gathered the handles of the bag together and pressed them into her hand, because she was becoming lifeless and he was worried she might break down or cease to function. Only then did he give her the reassurance that she seemed to be asking for, while he continued to hold her hand, which was cold, he told me, but nice.

"All of us have got to do something risky now and then, haven't we, dear?" Landau said lightly. "Going to adorn the party, are we?"

"No."

"Like a nice dinner out somewhere?"

"It is not convenient."

"You want me to take you to the door?"

"It doesn't matter."

"I think we've got to smile, dear," he said, still in English as he walked her across the room, chatting to her like the good salesman he had once again become.

Reaching the great landing, he shook her hand. "See you at the book fair, then? September. And thanks for warning me, okay? I'll bear it in mind. Still, the main thing is, we've got a deal. Which is always nice. Right?"

She took his hand and seemed to draw courage from it, for she smiled again and her smile was dazed but grateful, and almost irresistibly warm.

"My friend has made a great gesture," she explained as she pushed back an unruly lock of hair. "Please be sure that Mr. Barley is aware of this."

"I'll tell him. Don't you worry," said Landau jauntily.

He would have liked another smile just for himself, but she had lost

interest in him. She was delving in her bag for her card, which he knew she had forgotten till this moment. "ORLOVA, Yekaterina Borisovna," it read, in Cyrillic one side and Roman the other, again with the name "October" in both renderings. She gave it to him, then walked stiffly down the pompous staircase, head up and one hand on the broad marble balustrade, the other hand trailing the perhaps-bag. The boys in leather jackets watched her all the way down to the hall. And Landau, while he popped the card into his top pocket with the half-dozen others he'd collected in the last two hours, saw them watch her and gave the boys a wink. And the boys after due reflection winked back at him, because this was the new season of openness when a pair of good Russian hips could be acknowledged for what they were, even to a foreigner.

For the fifty minutes of revelry that remained, Niki Landau threw his heart into the party. Sang and danced for a grim-faced Scottish librarian in pearls. Recited a witty political anecdote about Mrs. Thatcher for a pair of pale listeners from the State Copyright Agency, VAAP, till they suddenly emitted wild laughter. Buttered up three ladies from Progress Publishers and, in a series of nimble journeys to his briefcase, presented each with a memento of his stay, for Landau was a natural giver and remembered names and promises, just as he remembered so many other things, with the directness of an unencumbered mind. But all the while he kept the briefcase unobtrusively in view, and even before the guests had left, he was holding it in his spare hand while he made his farewells. And when he boarded the private bus that was waiting to take the reps back to their hotel, he sat with it on his knees while he joined in a tuneful unison of rugby songs, led as usual by Spikey Morgan.

"Ladies present now, boys," Landau warned and, standing up, commanded silence at the passages that he considered too broad. But even when he was playing the great conductor he contrived to keep a firm grip on the briefcase.

At the hotel entrance the usual gaggle of pimps, drug-pushers and currency dealers hung around and, together with their KGB minders, watched the group enter. But Landau saw nothing in their behaviour to concern him, whether over-watchful or over-casual. The

crippled old warrior who guarded the passageway to the lifts demanded as usual to see his hotel pass, but when Landau, who had
already presented him with a hundred Marlboros, asked him accusingly in Russian why he wasn't out flirting with his girlfriend tonight,
he gave a rasping laugh and punched him on the shoulder in good-
fellowship.

"If they're trying to frame me, I thought, they'd better be quick
about it or the trail will be cold, Harry," he told me, taking the part of
the opposition rather than his own. "When you frame, Harry, you've
got to move in fast while the evidence is still planted on the victim," he
explained, as if he had been framing people all his life.

"Bar of the National, nine o'clock then," Spikey Morgan said to him
wearily when they had fought their way out at the fourth floor.

"Could be, could be not, Spikey," Landau replied. "I'm not quite
myself, to be honest."

"Thank God for that," said Spikey through a yawn, and plodded off
into his own dark corridor watched by the evil-eyed floor concierge in
her horsebox.

Reaching his bedroom door Landau braced himself before putting
the key into the lock. They'd do it now, he thought. Here and now
would be the best time to snatch me and the manuscript.

But when he stepped inside, the room was empty and undisturbed
and he felt foolish for having suspected it of being any different. Still
alive, he thought, and set the briefcase on the bed.

Then he pulled the handkerchief-sized curtains as close as they
would go, which was halfway, and hung the useless "Do Not Disturb"
notice on the door, which he then locked. He emptied the pockets of
his suit, including the pocket where he stored incoming business cards,
pulled off his jacket and tie, his metal armbands, finally his shirt. From
the fridge he poured himself half an inch of lemon vodka and took a
sip. Landau was not a drinker really, he explained to me, but when in
Moscow he did like a nice lemon vodka to end his day. Taking his glass
to the bathroom, he stood before the mirror and for a good ten minutes
anxiously examined the roots of his hair for signs of white, touching
out offending spots with the aid of a new formula that was working
wonders. Having completed this labour to his satisfaction, he bound

his skull with an elaborate rubber turban like a bathing cap and show-
ered, while he sang "I am the very model of a modern major-general"
rather well. Then he towelled himself, vigorously for the sake of his
muscle-tone, slipped into a bold flowered bathrobe and marched back
to the bedroom still singing.

And he did these things partly because he always did them and
needed the steadying familiarity of his own routines, but partly also
because he was proud of having thrown caution to the winds for once
and not found twenty-five sound reasons for doing nothing, which
these days he might have done.

She was a lady, she was afraid, she needed help, Harry. When did
Niki Landau ever refuse a lady? And if he was wrong about her, well
then she'd made a crying fool of him and he might as well pack up his
toothbrush and report himself at the front door of the Lubyanka for
five years' study of their excellent graffiti without the option. Because
he'd rather be made a fool of twenty times over than turn away that
woman without a reason. And so saying, if only in his mind, for he was
always alert to the possibility of microphones, Landau drew her parcel
from the briefcase and with a certain shyness set to work untying the
string but not cutting it, just the way he had been taught by his sainted
mother, whose photograph at this moment nestled faithfully in his
wallet. They've got the same glow, he thought in pleasant recognition
as he worried patiently at the knot. It's the Slav skin. It's the Slav eyes,
the smile. Two nice Slav girls together. The only difference was that
Katya hadn't finished up in Treblinka.

The knot finally yielded. Landau coiled up the string and laid it on
the bed. I have to know, you see, dear, he explained to the woman
Yekaterina Borisovna in his mind. I don't want to pry, I'm not the nosy
one, but if I've got to con my way through Moscow customs, I'd better
know what I'm conning them out of, because it helps.

Delicately so as not to tear it, using both hands, Landau parted the
brown paper. He did not see himself as any sort of a hero, or not yet.
What was a danger to a Moscow beauty might not be a danger to him.
He had grown up hard, it was true. The East End of London had been
no rest cure for a ten-year-old Polish immigrant, and Landau had
taken his share of split lips, broken noses, smashed knuckles and

hunger. But if you had asked him now or at any time in the last thirty years what his definition of a hero was, he would have replied without a second's thought that a hero was the first man out of the back door when they started yelling for volunteers.

One thing he did know as he stared at the contents of that brown-paper parcel: he had the buzz on him. Why he had it was something he could sort out later when there weren't better things to do. But if dodgy work needed to be done tonight, Niki Landau was your man. Because when Niki has the buzz, Harry, no one buzzes better, as the girls all know.

The first thing he saw was the envelope. He registered the three notebooks underneath it and saw that the envelope and notebooks were joined with a thick elastic band, the kind he always saved but never found a use for. But it was the envelope that held him because it had her writing on it—a strict copybook kind of writing that confirmed his pure image of her. One square brown envelope, glued rather messily and addressed "Personal for Mr. Bartholomew Scott Blair, urgent."

Slipping it free of the elastic band, Landau held it to the light but it was opaque and revealed no shadow. He explored it with his finger and thumb. One sheet of thin paper inside, two at most. *Mr. Scott Blair has undertaken to publish it with discretion,* he remembered. *Mr. Landau, if you love peace . . . give it immediately to Mr. Scott Blair. Only to Mr. Scott Blair . . . it is a gift of trust.*

She trusts me too, he thought. He turned the envelope over. The back was blank.

And there being only so much that one may learn from a sealed brown envelope, and since Landau drew the line at reading Barley's or anybody else's personal mail, he opened his briefcase again and, having searched the stationery compartment, extracted from it a plain manila envelope of his own, with the words "From the desk of Mr. Nicholas P. Landau" inscribed tastefully on the flap. Then he popped the brown envelope inside the manila one and sealed it. Then he scribbled the name "Barley" on it and filed it in the compartment marked "Social," which contained such oddities as visiting cards that had been pressed on him by strangers and notes of odd commissions he had undertaken

to perform for people—such as the publishing lady who needed refills for her Parker pen or the Ministry of Culture official who wanted a Snoopy T-shirt for his nephew or the lady from October who simply happened to be passing while he was wrapping up his stand.

And Landau did this because with the tradecraft that was instinctive in him, if totally untaught, he knew that his first job was to keep the envelope as far away as possible from the notebooks. If the notebooks were trouble, then he wanted nothing that would link them with the letter. And vice versa. And in this he was entirely right. Our most versatile and erudite trainers, dyed in all the oceans of our Service folklore, would not have told it to him one whit differently.

Only then did he take up the three notebooks and slip off the elastic band while he kept one ear cocked for footfalls in the corridor. Three grubby Russian notebooks, he reflected, selecting the top one and turning it slowly over. Bound in crudely illustrated board, the spine in fraying cloth. Two hundred and twenty-four pages of poor-quality, feint-ruled quarto, if Landau remembered correctly from the days when he peddled stationery, Soviet price around twenty kopeks retail from any good stationer, always provided that the delivery had arrived and that you were standing in the right queue on the right day.

Finally he opened the notebook and stared at the first page.

She's daft, he thought, fighting off his disgust.

She's in the hands of a nutter. Poor kid.

Meaningless scribblings, done by a lunatic with a mapping pen, in India ink at breakneck speed and furious angles. In the margins, sideways, longways. Diagonally across itself like a doctor's writing on the blink. Peppered with stupid exclamation marks and underlinings. Some of it Cyrillic, some English. "The Creator creates creators," he read in English. "To be. Not to be. To counter-be." Followed by a burst of stupid French about the warfare of folly and the folly of warfare, followed by a barbed-wire entanglement. Thank you very much, he thought, and flipped to another page, then another, both so dense with crazy writing you could hardly see the paper. "Having spent seventy years destroying the popular will, we cannot expect it suddenly to rise up and save us," he read. A quote? A night

thought? There was no way to tell. References to writers, Russian, Latin and European. Talk of Nietzsche, Kafka and people he'd never heard of, let alone read. More talk of war, this time in English: "The old declare it, the young fight it, but today the babies and old people fight it too." He turned another page and came on nothing but a round brown stain. He lifted the notebook to his nose and sniffed. Booze, he thought with contempt. Stinks like a brewery. No wonder he's a mate of Barley Blair's. A double page devoted to a series of hysterical proclamations.

OUR GREATEST PROGRESS IS IN THE FIELD OF BACKWARDNESS!
SOVIET PARALYSIS IS THE MOST PROGRESSIVE IN THE WORLD!
OUR BACKWARDNESS IS OUR GREATEST MILITARY SECRET!
IF WE DON'T KNOW OUR OWN INTENTIONS AND OUR OWN CAPACI-
     TIES, HOW CAN WE KNOW YOURS?
THE TRUE ENEMY IS OUR OWN INCOMPETENCE!

And on the next page, a poem, painstakingly copied from Lord knew where:

> He wires in and wires out,
> And leaves the people still in doubt
> Whether the snake that made the track
> Was going south or coming back.

Scrambling to his feet, Landau strode angrily to the window, which gave on to a glum courtyard full of uncollected rubbish.

"A blooming word-artist, Harry. That's what I thought he was. Some long-haired, drug-ridden, self-indulgent genius, and she's gone and thrown herself away on him same as they all do."

She was lucky there was no Moscow telephone directory or he'd have rung her up and told her what she'd got.

To stoke his anger, he took up the second book, licked his fingertip and whisked contemptuously through it page by page, which was how he came upon the drawings. Then everything went blank for him for a moment, like a flash of empty screen in the middle of a film, while he

cursed himself for being an impetuous little Slav instead of a cool calm Englishman. Then he sat down on the bed again, but gently, as if there were someone resting in it, someone he had hurt with his premature condemnations.

For if Landau despised what too often passed for literature, his pleasure in technical matters was unconfined. Even when he didn't follow what he was looking at, he could relish a good page of mathematics all day long. And he knew at one glance, as he had known of the woman Katya, that what he was looking at here was quality. Not your ruled drawing, it was true. Light sketches but all the better for it. Drawn freehand without instruments by somebody who could think with a pencil. Tangents, parabolas, cones. And in between the drawings, businesslike descriptions that architects and engineers use, words like "aimpoint" and "captive carry" and "bias" and "gravity" and "trajectory." "Some in your English, Harry, and some in your Russian."

Though Harry is not my real name.

Yet when he began to compare the lettering of these beautifully written words in the second book with the rambling jungle in the first, he discovered to his astonishment certain unmistakable similarities. So that he had the sensation of looking at a kind of schizophrenic's diary with Dr. Jekyll writing one volume and Mr. Hyde the other.

He looked in the third notebook, which was as orderly and purposeful as the second but arranged like a kind of mathematical log with dates and numbers and formulae, and the word "error" repeating itself frequently, often underlined or lifted with an exclamation mark. Then suddenly Landau stared, and continued staring, and could not remove his eyes from what he was reading. The cosy obscurity of the writer's technical jargon had ended with a bang. So had his philosophical ramblings and elegant annotated drawings. The words came off the page with a blazoned clarity.

"The American strategists can sleep in peace. Their nightmares cannot be realised. The Soviet knight is dying inside his armour. He is a secondary power like you British. He can start a war but cannot continue one and cannot win one. Believe me."

Landau looked no further. A sense of respect, mingled with a strong instinct for self-preservation, advised him that he had disturbed the

tomb enough. Taking up the elastic band, he put the three notebooks together and snapped it back over them. That's it, he thought. From here on I mind my business and do my duty. Which is to take the manuscript to my adopted England and give it immediately to Mr. Bartholomew *alias* Barley Scott Blair.

Barley Blair, he thought in amazement as he opened his wardrobe and hauled out the large aluminum hand-case where he kept his samples. Well, well. We often wondered whether we were nurturing a spy in our midst and now we know.

Landau's calm was absolute, he assured me. The Englishman had once more taken command of the Pole. "If Barley could do it, I could, Harry, that's what I said to myself." And it was what he said to me too, when for a short spell he appointed me his confessor. People do that to me sometimes. They sense the unrealised part of me and talk to it as if it were the reality.

Lifting the case on to the bed he snapped the locks and drew out two audio-visual kits that the Soviet officials had ordered him to remove from his display—one pictorial history of the twentieth century with spoken commentary, which they had arbitrarily ruled to be anti-Soviet, and one handbook of the human body with action photographs and a keep-fit exercise cassette, which, after gazing longingly at the pliant young goddess in the leotard, the officials had decided was pornographic.

The history kit was a glossy affair, built as a coffee table book and containing a quantity of interior pockets for cassettes, parallel texts, progressive vocabulary cards and students' notes. Having emptied the pockets of their contents, Landau offered the notebooks to each in turn but found none large enough. He decided to convert two pockets into one. He fetched a pair of nail scissors from his sponge bag and set to work with steady hands, easing the steel staples out of the centre divide.

Barley Blair, he thought again as he inserted the point of the nail scissors. I should have guessed, if only because you were the one it couldn't possibly be. Mr. Bartholomew Scott Blair, surviving scion of Abercrombie & Blair—spy. The first staple had come loose. He gingerly extracted it. Barley Blair, who couldn't sell hay to a rich horse to

save his dying mother on her birthday, we used to say: spy. He began prising the second staple. Whose principal claim to fame was that two years ago at the Belgrade book fair he had drunk Spikey Morgan under the table on straight vodkas, then played tenor sax with the band so beautifully that even the police were clapping. Spy. Gentleman spy. Well, here's a letter from your lady, as they say in the nursery rhyme.

Landau picked up the notebooks and offered them to the space he had prepared but it was still not big enough. He would have to make one pocket out of three.

Playing the drunk, thought Landau, his mind still on Barley. Playing the fool and fooling us. Burning up the last of your family money, running the old firm deeper into the ground. Oh yes. Except that somehow or another you always managed to find one of those smart City banking houses to bail you out in the nick of time, didn't you? And what about your chess-playing then? *That* should have been a clue, if Landau had only had eyes for it! How does a man who's drunk himself silly beat all comers at chess then, Harry—straight games—if he isn't a trained spy?

The three pockets had become one pocket, the notebooks fitted more or less inside, the printed indication above them still read "Student Notes."

"Notes," Landau explained in his mind to the inquisitive young customs officer at Sheremetyevo airport. "Notes, you see, son, like it says. Student's notes. That's why there's a pocket here for notes. And these notes that you are holding in your hand are the work of an actual student following the course. That's why they're here, son, do you see? They are *demonstration notes.* And the drawings here, they're to do with the—"

With socio-economic patterns, son. With demographic population shifts. With vital statistics that you Russkies can never get enough of, can you? Here, seen one of these? It's called a body book.

Which might or might not save Landau's hide, depending on how smart the boy was, and how much they knew, and how they felt about their wives that day.

But for the long night ahead of him, and for the dawn raid when they kicked the door down and burst in on him with drawn pistols and

shouted, "All right, Landau, give us the notebooks!"—for that happy moment, the kit wouldn't do at all. "Notebooks, Officer? Notebooks? Oh, you mean that bunch of junk some loony Russian beauty pressed on me at the fair tonight. I think you'll probably find them in the rubbish basket, Officer, if the maid hasn't emptied it for once in her life."

For this contingency also, Landau now meticulously set the scene. Removing the notebooks from the pocket of the history kit, he placed them artistically in the wastepaper basket exactly as if he had flung them there in the rage he had felt when he had taken his first look. To keep them company, he tossed in his surplus trade literature and brochures, as well as a couple of useless farewell gifts he had received: the thin volume of yet another Russian poet, a tin-backed blotter. As a final touch, he added a pair of undarned socks that only your rich Westerner throws away.

Once again I must marvel, as later we all did, at Landau's untutored ingenuity.

Landau did not go out and play that night. He endured the familiar imprisonment of his Moscow hotel room. From his window he watched the long dusk turn to darkness and the dim lights of the city reluctantly brighten. He made himself tea in his little travelling kettle and ate a couple of fruit bars from his iron rations. He dwelt gratefully upon the most rewarding of his conquests. He smiled ruefully at others. He braced himself for pain and solitude and summoned up his hard childhood to help him. He went through the contents of his wallet and his briefcase and his pockets and took out everything that was particularly private to him which he would not wish to answer for across a bare table—a hot letter a little friend sent him years ago that could still revive his appetites, membership of a certain video-by-mail club that he belonged to. His first instinct was to "burn them like in the movies" but he was restrained by the sight of the smoke detectors in the ceiling, though he'd have laid any money they didn't work.

So he found a paper bag and, having torn up everything very small, he put the pieces in the bag, dropped the bag out of the window and saw it join the rubbish in the courtyard. Then he lay on the bed and watched the dark go by. Sometimes he felt brave, sometimes he was so

scared that he had to drive his fingernails into his palms to hold himself together. Once he turned on the television set, hoping for nubile girl gymnasts, which he liked. But instead he got the Emperor himself telling his bemused children for the umpteenth time that the old order had no clothes. And when Spikey Morgan, half drunk at best, telephoned from the bar of the National, Landau kept him on the line for company till old Spikey fell asleep.

Only once, at his lowest point, did it cross Landau's mind to present himself at the British Embassy and seek the assistance of the diplomatic bag. His momentary weakness angered him. "Those flunkies?" he asked himself in scorn. "The ones who sent my dad back to Poland? I wouldn't trust them with a picture postcard of the Eiffel Tower, Harry."

Besides, that wasn't what she had asked him to do.

In the morning he dressed himself for his own execution, in his best suit, with the photograph of his mother inside his shirt.

And that is how I see Niki Landau still, whenever I dip into his file, or receive him for what we call a six-monthly top-up, which is when he likes to relive his hour of glory before signing yet another declaration of the Official Secrets Act. I see him stepping jauntily into the Moscow street with the metal suitcase in his hand, not knowing from Adam what's in it, but determined to risk his brave little neck for it anyway.

How he sees me, if he ever thinks of me, I dare not wonder. Hannah, whom I loved but failed, would have no doubt at all. "As another of those Englishmen with hope in their faces and none in their hearts," she would say, flushing with anger. For I am afraid she says whatever comes to her these days. Much of her old forbearance is gone.

2

The whole of Whitehall was agreed that no story should ever begin that way again. Indoctrinated ministers were furious about it. They set up a frightfully secret committee of enquiry to find out what went wrong, hear witnesses, name names, spare no blushes, point fingers, close gaps, prevent a recurrence, appoint me Chairman and draft a report. What

conclusions our committee reached, if any, remains the loftiest secret of them all, particularly from those of us who sat on it. For the function of such committees, as we all well knew, is to talk earnestly until the dust has settled, and then ourselves return to dust. Which, like a disgruntled Cheshire cat, our committee duly did, leaving nothing behind us but our frightfully secret frown, a meaningless interim working paper, and a bunch of secret annexes in the Treasury archives.

It began, in the less sparing language of Ned and his colleagues at the Russia House, with an imperial cock-up, between the hours of five and eight-thirty on a warm Sunday evening, when one Nicholas P. Landau, travelling salesman and taxpayer in good standing, if of Polish origin, with nothing recorded against, presented himself at the doors of no fewer than four separate Whitehall ministries to plead an urgent interview with an officer of the British Intelligence Branch, as he was pleased to call it, only to be ridiculed, fobbed off and in one instance physically manhandled. Though whether the two temporary doormen at the Defence Ministry went so far as to grab Landau by the collar and the seat of his pants, as he maintained they did, and frogmarch him to the door, or whether they merely assisted him back into the street, to use *their* words, is a point on which we were unable to achieve a consensus.

But why, our committee asked sternly, did the two doormen feel obliged to provide this assistance in the first place?

Mr. Landau refused to let us look inside his briefcase, sir. Yes, he offered to let us take charge of the briefcase while he waited, provided he kept charge of the key, sir. But that wasn't regulations. And yes, he shook it in our faces, patted it for us, tossed it about in his hands, apparently in order to demonstrate that there was nothing in it that any of us needed to be afraid of. But that wasn't regulations either. And when we tried with a minimum of force to relieve him of the said briefcase, this *gentleman*—as Landau in their testimony had belatedly become—resisted our efforts, sir, and shouted loudly in a foreign accent, causing a disturbance.

But what did he shout? we asked, distressed by the notion of anybody shouting in Whitehall on a Sunday.

Well, sir, so far as we were able to make him out, him in his emo-

tional state, he shouted that this briefcase of his contained highly secret papers, sir. Which had been entrusted to him by a Russian, sir, in Moscow.

And him a rampageous little Pole, sir, they might have added. On a hot cricketing Sunday in London, sir, and us watching the replay of the Pakistanis against Botham in the back room.

Even at the Foreign Office, that freezing hearth of official British hospitality, where the despairing Landau presented himself as a last resort and with the greatest of reluctance, it was only by dint of high entreaty and some honest-to-God Slav tears that he fought his way to the rarefied ear of the Honourable Palmer Wellow, author of a discerning monograph on Liszt.

And if Landau had not used a new tactic, probably the Slav tears would not have helped. Because this time he placed the briefcase open on the counter so that the doorman, who was young but sceptical, could crane his pomaded head to the recently installed armoured glass and scowl down into it with his indolent eyes, and see for himself that it was only a bunch of dirty old notebooks in there and a brown envelope, not bombs.

"Come-back-Monday-ten-to-five," the doorman said through the wonderfully new electric speaker, as if announcing a Welsh railway station, and slumped back into the darkness of his box.

The gate stood ajar. Landau looked at the young man, and looked past him at the great portico built a hundred years earlier to daunt the unruly princes of the Raj. And the next thing anyone knew, he had picked up his briefcase and, defeating all the seemingly impenetrable defences set up to prevent exactly such an onslaught, was pelting hell-for-leather with it—"like a bloomin' Springbok, sir"—across the hallowed courtyard up the steps into the enormous hall. And he was in luck. Palmer Wellow, whatever else he was, belonged to the appeasement side of the Foreign Office. And it was Palmer's day on.

"Hullo, *hullo*," Palmer murmured as he descended the great steps and beheld the disordered figure of Landau panting between two stout guards. "Well you *are* in a muck. My name's Wellow. I'm a resident clerk here." He held his left fist to his shoulder as if he hated dogs. But his right hand was extended in greeting.

"I don't want a clerk," said Landau. "I want a high officer or nothing."

"Well, a clerk is *fairly* high," Palmer modestly assured him. "I expect you're put off by the language."

It was only right to record—and our committee did—that nobody could fault Palmer Wellow's performance thus far. He was droll but he was effective. He put no polished foot wrong. He led Landau to an interviewing room and sat him down, all attention. He ordered a cup of tea for him with sugar for his shock, and offered him a digestive biscuit. With a costly fountain pen given him by a friend, he wrote down Landau's name and address and those of the companies that hired his services. He wrote down the number of Landau's British passport and his date and place of birth, 1930 in Warsaw. He insisted with disarming truthfulness that he had no knowledge of intelligence matters, but undertook to pass on Landau's material to the "competent people," who would no doubt give it whatever attention it deserved. And because Landau once again insisted on it, he improvised a receipt for him on a sheet of Foreign Office blue draft, signed it and had the janitor add a date-and-time stamp. He told him that if there was anything further the authorities wished to discuss they would very probably get in touch with him, perhaps by means of the telephone.

Only then did Landau hesitatingly pass his scruffy package across the table and watch with lingering regret as Palmer's languid hand enfolded it.

"But why don't you simply give it to Mr. Scott Blair?" Palmer asked after he had studied the name on the envelope.

"I tried, for Christ's sake!" Landau burst out in fresh exasperation. "I told you. I rang him everywhere. I've rung him till I'm blue in the face, I tell you. He's not at his home, he's not at work, he's not at his club, he's not at anywhere," Landau protested, his English grammar slipping in despair. "From the airport I tried. All right, it's a Saturday."

"But it's Sunday," Palmer objected with a forgiving smile.

"So it was a Saturday yesterday, wasn't it! I try his firm. I get an electronic howl. I look in the phone book. There's one in Hammersmith. Not his initials but Scott Blair. I get an angry lady, tells me to go to hell. There's a rep I know, Archie Parr, does the West Country for him. I ask

Archie: 'Archie, for Christ's sake, how do I get hold of Barley in a hurry?' 'He's skedaddled, Niki. Done one of his bunks. Hasn't been seen in the shop for weeks.' Enquiries, I try. London, the Home Counties. Not listed, not a Bartholomew. Well he wouldn't be, would he, not if he's a—"

"Not if he's a what?" said Palmer, intrigued.

"Look, he's vanished, right? He's vanished before. There could be reasons why he vanishes. Reasons that you don't know of because you're not meant to. Lives are at stake, could be. Not only his either. It's top urgent, she told me. And top secret. Now get on with it. Please."

The same evening, there being not much doing on the world front apart from a dreary crisis in the Gulf and a squalid television scandal about soldiers and money in Washington, Palmer took himself off to a rather good party in Montpelier Square that was being thrown by a group of his year from Cambridge—bachelors like himself, but fun. An account of this occasion, too, reached our committee's ears.

"Have any of you heard of a Somebody Scott Blair, by the by?" Wellow asked them at a late hour when his memory of Landau happened to have been revived by some bars of Chopin he was playing on the piano. "Wasn't there a Scott Blair who was up with us or something?" he asked again when he failed to get through the noise.

"Couple of years ahead of us. Trinity," came a fogged reply from across the room. "Read History. Jazz fiend. Wanted to blow his saxophone for a living. Old man wouldn't wear it. Barley Blair. Pissed as a rat from daybreak."

Palmer Wellow played a thunderous chord that stunned the garrulous company to silence. "I said, is he a poisonous spy?" he enunciated.

"The father? He's dead."

"The son, ass. Barley."

Like someone stepping from behind a curtain, his informant emerged from the crowd of young and less young men and stood before him, glass in hand. And Palmer to his pleasure recognised him as a dear chum from Trinity a hundred years ago.

"I really don't know whether Barley's a poisonous spy or not, I'm afraid," said Palmer's chum, with an asperity habitual to him, as the

background babel rose to its former roar. "He's certainly a failure, if that's a qualification."

His curiosity whetted still further, Palmer returned to his spacious rooms at the Foreign Office and to Landau's envelope and notebooks, which he had entrusted to the janitor for safekeeping. And it is at this point that his actions, in the words of our interim working paper, took an unhelpful course. Or in the harsher words of Ned and his colleagues in the Russia House, this was where, in any civilised country, P. Wellow would have been strung by his thumbs from a high point in the city and left there in peace to reflect upon his attainments.

For what Palmer did was have a nice time with the notebooks. For two nights and one and a half days. Because he found them so amusing. He did not open the buff envelope—which was by now marked in Landau's handwriting "Extremely Private for the attention of Mr. B. Scott Blair or a top member of the Intelligence"—because like Landau he was of a school that felt it unbecoming to read other people's mail. In any case, it was glued at both ends, and Palmer was not a man to grapple with physical obstacles. But the notebook—with its crazed aphorisms and quotations, its exhaustive loathing of politicians and soldiery, its scatter-shot references to Pushkin the pure Renaissance man and to Kleist the pure suicide—held him fascinated.

He felt little sense of urgency, none of responsibility. He was a diplomat, not a Friend, as the spies were called. And Friends in Palmer's zoology were people without the intellectual horsepower to be what Palmer was. Indeed it was his outspoken resentment that the orthodox Foreign Office to which he belonged resembled more and more a cover organisation for the Friends' disgraceful activities. For Palmer too was a man of impressive erudition, if of a random kind. He had read Arabic and taken a First in Modern History. He had added Russian and Sanskrit in his spare time. He had everything but mathematics and common sense, which explains why he passed over the dreary pages of algebraic formulae, equations and diagrams that made up the other two notebooks, and in contrast to the writer's philosophical ramblings had a boringly disciplined appearance. And which also explains—though the committee had difficulty accepting such an explanation—why Palmer chose to ignore the Standing Order to Resi-

dent Clerks Relating to Defectors and Offers of Intelligence, whether solicited or otherwise, and to do his own thing.

"He makes the most frantic connections right across the board, Tig," he told a rather senior colleague in Research Department on the Tuesday, having decided that it was finally time to share his acquisition. "You simply must read him."

"But how do we know it's a he, Palms?"

Palmer just felt it, Tig. The vibes.

Palmer's senior colleague glanced at the first notebook, then at the second, then sat down and stared at the third. Then he looked at the drawings in the second book. Then his professional self took over in the emergency.

"I think I'd get this lot across to them fairly sharpish if I were you, Palms," he said. But on second thoughts he got it across to them himself, very sharpish indeed, having first telephoned Ned on the green line and told him to stand by.

Upon which, two days late, hell broke loose. At four o'clock on the Wednesday morning the lights on the top floor of Ned's stubby brick out-station in Victoria known as the Russia House were still burning brightly as the first bemused meeting of what later became the Bluebird team drew to a close. Five hours after that, having sat out two more meetings in the Service's headquarters in a grand new high-rise block on the Embankment, Ned was back at his desk, the files gathering around him as giddily as if the girls in Registry had decided to erect a street barricade.

"God may move in a mysterious way," Ned was heard to remark to his redheaded assistant, Brock, in a lull between deliveries, "but it's nothing to the way He picks his joes."

A joe in the parlance is a live source, and a live source in sane English is a spy. Was Ned referring to Landau when he spoke of joes? To Katya? To the unchristened writer of the notebooks? Or was his mind already fixed upon the vaporous outlines of that great British gentleman spy, Mr. Bartholomew Scott Blair? Brock did not know or care. He came from Glasgow but of Lithuanian parents, and abstract concepts made him angry.

FROM *ASHENDEN* (1928)

W. Somerset Maugham (1874–1965)

At the age of forty-one, during the First World War, William Somer-
set Maugham was recruited to the British secret service and, like the hero
of Ashenden, *served in Switzerland. According to John le Carré,*
Maugham was "the first person to write about espionage in a mood of dis-
enchantment and almost prosaic reality." Ashenden is also said to be the
spiritual father to the spies of Graham Greene, Eric Ambler, and, eventu-
ally, to le Carré's Alec Leamas and George Smiley. Some of the original
stories in Ashenden *are said to have been burned by Maugham when his*
friend Winston Churchill suggested that they violated the Official Secrets
Act. Maugham, prominent as a British dramatist and novelist, did not
again attempt an espionage novel.

I
R.

It was not till the beginning of September that Ashenden, a writer by
profession, who had been abroad at the outbreak of the war, managed

to get back to England. He chanced soon after his arrival to go to a party and was there introduced to a middle-aged Colonel whose name he did not catch. He had some talk with him. As he was about to leave this officer came up to him and asked:

"I say, I wonder if you'd mind coming to see me. I'd rather like to have a chat with you."

"Certainly," said Ashenden. "Whenever you like."

"What about to-morrow at eleven?"

"All right."

"I'll just write down my address. Have you a card on you?"

Ashenden gave him one and on this the Colonel scribbled in pencil the name of a street and the number of a house. When Ashenden walked along next morning to keep his appointment he found himself in a street of rather vulgar red-brick houses in a part of London that had once been fashionable, but was now fallen in the esteem of the house-hunter who wanted a good address. On the house at which Ashenden had been asked to call there was a board up to announce that it was for sale, the shutters were closed and there was no sign that anyone lived in it. He rang the bell and the door was opened by a non-commissioned officer so promptly that he was startled. He was not asked his business, but led immediately into a long room at the back, once evidently a dining-room, the florid decoration of which looked oddly out of keeping with the office furniture, shabby and sparse, that was in it. It gave Ashenden the impression of a room in which the brokers had taken possession. The Colonel, who was known in the Intelligence Department, as Ashenden later discovered, by the letter R., rose when he came in and shook hands with him. He was a man somewhat above the middle height, lean, with a yellow, deeply-lined face, thin grey hair and a toothbrush moustache. The thing immediately noticeable about him was the closeness with which his blue eyes were set. He only just escaped a squint. They were hard and cruel eyes, and very wary; and they gave him a cunning, shifty look. Here was a man that you could neither like nor trust at first sight. His manner was pleasant and cordial.

He asked Ashenden a good many questions and then, without fur-

ther to-do, suggested that he had particular qualifications for the secret service. Ashenden was acquainted with several European languages and his profession was excellent cover; on the pretext that he was writing a book he could without attracting attention visit any neutral country. It was while they were discussing this point that R. said:

"You know you ought to get material that would be very useful to you in your work."

"I shouldn't mind that," said Ashenden.

"I'll tell you an incident that occurred only the other day and I can vouch for its truth. I thought at the time it would make a damned good story. One of the French ministers went down to Nice to recover from a cold and he had some very important documents with him that he kept in a dispatch-case. They were very important indeed. Well, a day or two after he arrived he picked up a yellow-haired lady at some restaurant or other where there was dancing, and he got very friendly with her. To cut a long story short he took her back to his hotel—of course it was a very imprudent thing to do—and when he came to himself in the morning the lady and the dispatch-case had disappeared. They had one or two drinks up in his room and his theory is that when his back was turned the woman slipped a drug into his glass."

R. finished and looked at Ashenden with a gleam in his close-set eyes.

"Dramatic, isn't it?" he asked.

"Do you mean to say that happened the other day?"

"The week before last."

"Impossible," cried Ashenden. "Why, we've been putting that incident on the stage for sixty years, we've written it in a thousand novels. Do you mean to say that life has only just caught up with us?"

R. was a trifle disconcerted.

"Well, if necessary, I could give you names and dates, and believe me, the Allies have been put to no end of trouble by the loss of the documents that the dispatch-case contained."

"Well, sir, if you can't do better than that in the secret service," sighed Ashenden, "I'm afraid that as a source of inspiration to the

writer of fiction, it's a washout. We really *can't* write that story much longer."

It did not take them long to settle things and when Ashenden rose to go he had already made careful note of his instructions. He was to start for Geneva next day. The last words that R. said to him, with a casualness that made them impressive, were:

"There's just one thing I think you ought to know before you take on this job. And don't forget it. If you do well you'll get no thanks and if you get into trouble you'll get no help. Does that suit you?"

"Perfectly."

"Then I'll wish you good-afternoon."

II
A DOMICILIARY VISIT

Ashenden was on his way back to Geneva. The night was stormy and the wind blew cold from the mountains, but the stodgy little steamer plodded sturdily through the choppy waters of the lake. A scudding rain, just turning into sleet, swept the deck in angry gusts, like a nagging woman who cannot leave a subject alone. Ashenden had been to France in order to write and dispatch a report. A day or two before, about five in the afternoon, an Indian agent of his had come to see him in his rooms; it was only by a lucky chance that he was in, for he had no appointment with him, and the agent's instructions were to come to the hotel only in a case of urgent importance. He told Ashenden that a Bengali in the German service had recently come from Berlin with a black cane trunk in which were a number of documents interesting to the British Government. At that time the Central Powers were doing their best to foment such an agitation in India as would make it necessary for Great Britain to keep their troops in the country and perhaps send others from France. It had been found possible to get the Bengali arrested in Berne on a charge that would keep him out of harm's way for a while, but the black cane trunk could not be found. Ashenden's agent was a very brave and very clever fellow and he mixed freely with such of his countrymen as were disaffected to the interests of Great

Britain. He had just discovered that the Bengali before going to Berne had, for greater safety, left the trunk in the cloak-room at Zürich Station, and now that he was in jail, awaiting trial, was unable to get the *bulletin* by which it might be obtained into the hands of any of his confederates. It was a matter of great urgency for the German Intelligence Department to secure the contents of the trunk without delay, and since it was impossible for them to get hold of it by the ordinary official means, they had decided to break into the station that very night and steal it. It was a bold and ingenious scheme and Ashenden felt a pleasant exhilaration (for a great deal of his work was uncommonly dull) when he heard of it. He recognized the dashing and unscrupulous touch of the head of the German secret service at Berne. But the burglary was arranged for two o'clock on the following morning and there was not a moment to lose. He could trust neither the telegraph nor the telephone to communicate with the British officer at Berne, and since the Indian agent could not go, (he was taking his life in his hands by coming to see Ashenden and if he were noticed leaving his room it might easily be that he would be found one day floating in the lake with a knife-thrust in his back,) there was nothing for it but to go himself.

There was a train to Berne that he could just catch and he put on his hat and coat as he ran downstairs. He jumped into a cab. Four hours later he rang the bell of the headquarters of the Intelligence Department. His name was known there but to one person, and it was for him that Ashenden asked. A tall tired-looking man, whom he had not met before, came out and without a word led him into an office. Ashenden told him his errand. The tall man looked at his watch.

"It's too late for us to do anything ourselves. We couldn't possibly get to Zürich in time."

He reflected.

"We'll put the Swiss authorities on the job. They can telephone, and when your friends attempt their little burglary, I have no doubt they'll find the station well-guarded. Anyhow you had better get back to Geneva."

He shook hands with Ashenden and showed him out. Ashenden was

well aware that he would never know what happened then. Being no more than a tiny rivet in a vast and complicated machine, he never had the advantage of seeing a completed action. He was concerned with the beginning or the end of it, perhaps, or with some incident in the middle, but what his own doings led to he had seldom a chance of discovering. It was as unsatisfactory as those modern novels that give you a number of unrelated episodes and expect you by piecing them together to construct in your mind a connected narrative.

Notwithstanding his fur coat and his muffler, Ashenden was chilled to the bone. It was warm in the saloon and there were good lights to read by, but he thought it better not to sit there in case some habitual traveller, recognizing him, wondered why he made these constant journeys between Geneva in Switzerland and Thonon in France; and so, making the best of what shelter could be found, he passed the tedious time in the darkness of the deck. He looked in the direction of Geneva, but could see no lights, and the sleet, turning into snow, prevented him from recognizing the landmarks. Lake Leman, on fine days so trim and pretty, artificial like a piece of water in a French garden, in this tempestuous weather was as secret and as menacing as the sea. He made up his mind that, on getting back to his hotel, he would have a fire lit in his sitting-room, a hot bath and dinner comfortably by the fireside in pyjamas and a dressing-gown. The prospect of spending an evening by himself with his pipe and a book was so agreeable that it made the misery of that journey across the lake positively worth while. Two sailors tramped past him heavily, their heads bent down to save themselves from the sleet that blew in their faces, and one of them shouted to him: *nous arrivons;* they went to the side and withdrew a bar to allow passage for the gangway, and looking again Ashenden through the howling darkness saw mistily the lights of the quay. A welcome sight. In two or three minutes the steamer was made fast and Ashenden joined himself to the little knot of passengers, muffled to the eyes, that waited to step ashore. Though he made the journey so often—it was his duty to cross the lake into France once a week to deliver his reports and to receive instructions—he had always a faint sense of trepidation when he stood among the crowd at the gangway and waited to land. There was nothing on his passport to show that he had been in

France; the steamer went round the lake touching French soil at two places, but going from Switzerland to Switzerland, so that his journey might have been to Vevey or to Lausanne; but he could never be sure that the secret police had not taken note of him, and if he had been followed and seen to land in France, the fact that there was no stamp on his passport would be difficult to explain. Of course he had his story ready, but he well knew that it was not a very convincing one, and though it might be impossible for the Swiss authorities to prove that he was anything but a casual traveller he might nevertheless spend two or three days in jail, which would be uncomfortable, and then be firmly conducted to the frontier, which would be mortifying. The Swiss knew well that their country was the scene of all manner of intrigues; agents of the secret service, spies, revolutionaries and agitators infested the hotels of the principal towns and, jealous of their neutrality, they were determined to prevent conduct that might embroil them with any of the belligerent powers.

There were as usual two police officers on the quay to watch the passengers disembark and Ashenden, walking past them with as unconcerned an air as he could assume, was relieved when he had got safely by. The darkness swallowed him up and he stepped out briskly for his hotel. The wild weather with a scornful gesture had swept all the neatness from the trim promenade. The shops were closed and Ashenden passed only an occasional pedestrian who sidled along, scrunched up, as though he fled from the blind wrath of the unknown. You had a feeling in that black and bitter night that civilization, ashamed of its artificiality, cowered before the fury of elemental things. It was hail now that blew in Ashenden's face and the pavement was wet and slippery so that he had to walk with caution. The hotel faced the lake. When he reached it and a page-boy opened the door for him, he entered the hall with a flurry of wind that sent the papers on the porter's desk flying into the air. Ashenden was dazzled by the light. He stopped to ask the porter if there were letters for him. There was nothing, and he was about to get into the lift when the porter told him that two gentlemen were waiting in his room to see him. Ashenden had no friends in Geneva.

"Oh?" he answered, not a little surprised. "Who are they?"

He had taken care to get on friendly terms with the porter and his tips for trifling services had been generous. The porter gave a discreet smile.

"There is no harm in telling you. I think they are members of the police."

"What do they want?" asked Ashenden.

"They did not say. They asked me where you were, and I told them you had gone for a walk. They said they would wait till you came back."

"How long have they been there?"

"An hour."

Ashenden's heart sank, but he took care not to let his face betray his concern.

"I'll go up and see them," he said. The liftman stood aside to let him step into the lift, but Ashenden shook his head. "I'm so cold," he said, "I'll walk up."

He wished to give himself a moment to think, but as he ascended the three flights slowly his feet were like lead. There could be small doubt why two police officers were so bent upon seeing him. He felt on a sudden dreadfully tired. He did not feel he could cope with a multitude of questions. And if he were arrested as a secret agent he must spend at least the night in a cell. He longed more than ever for a hot bath and a pleasant dinner by his fireside. He had half a mind to turn tail and walk out of the hotel, leaving everything behind him; he had his passport in his pocket and he knew by heart the hours at which trains started for the frontier: before the Swiss authorities had made up their minds what to do he would be in safety. But he continued to trudge upstairs. He did not like the notion of abandoning his job so easily, he had been sent to Geneva, knowing the risks, to do work of a certain kind, and it seemed to him that he had better go through with it. Of course it would not be very nice to spend two years in a Swiss prison, but the chance of this was, like assassination to kings, one of the inconveniences of his profession. He reached the landing of the third floor and walked to his room. Ashenden had in him, it seems, a strain of flippancy (on account of which, indeed, the critics had often reproached him) and as he stood for a moment outside the door his

predicament appeared to him on a sudden rather droll. His spirits went up and he determined to brazen the thing out. It was with a genuine smile on his lips that he turned the handle and entering the room faced his visitors.

"Good evening, gentlemen," said he.

The room was brightly lit, for all the lights were on, and a fire burned in the hearth. The air was grey with smoke, since the strangers, finding it long to wait for him, had been smoking strong and inexpensive cigars. They sat in their great-coats and bowler-hats as though they had only just that moment come in; but the ashes in the little tray on the table would alone have suggested that they had been long enough there to make themselves familiar with their surroundings. They were two powerful men, with black moustaches, on the stout side, heavily built, and they reminded Ashenden of Fafner and Fasolt, the giants in the Rhinegold; their clumsy boots, the massive way they sat in their chairs and the ponderous alertness of their expression, made it obvious that they were members of the detective force. Ashenden gave his room an enveloping glance. He was a neat creature and saw at once that his things, though not in disorder, were not as he had left them. He guessed that an examination had been made of his effects. That did not disturb him, for he kept in his room no document that would compromise him; his code he had learned by heart and destroyed before leaving England, and such communications as reached him from Germany were handed to him by third parties and transmitted without delay to the proper places. There was nothing he need fear in a search, but the impression that it had been made confirmed his suspicion that he had been denounced to the authorities as a secret agent.

"What can I do for you, gentlemen?" he asked affably. "It's warm in here, wouldn't you like to take off your coats—and hats?"

It faintly irritated him that they should sit there with their hats on.

"We're only staying a minute," said one of them. "We were passing and as the *concierge* said you would be in at once, we thought we would wait."

He did not remove his hat. Ashenden unwrapped his scarf and disembarrassed himself of his heavy coat.

"Won't you have a cigar?" he asked, offering the box to the two detectives in turn.

"I don't mind if I do," said the first, Fafner, taking one, upon which the second, Fasolt, helped himself without a word, even of thanks.

The name on the box appeared to have a singular effect on their manners, for both now took off their hats.

"You must have had a very disagreeable walk in this bad weather," said Fafner, as he bit half an inch off the end of his cigar and spat it in the fire-place.

Now it was Ashenden's principle (a good one in life as well as in the Intelligence Department) always to tell as much of the truth as he conveniently could; so he answered as follows:

"What do you take me for? I wouldn't go out in such weather if I could help it. I had to go to Vevey to-day to see an invalid friend and I came back by boat. It was bitter on the lake."

"We come from the police," said Fafner casually.

Ashenden thought they must consider him a perfect idiot if they imagined he had not long discovered that, but it was not a piece of information to which it was discreet to reply with a pleasantry.

"Oh, really," he said.

"Have you your passport on you?"

"Yes. In these war-times I think a foreigner is wise always to keep his passport on him."

"Very wise."

Ashenden handed the man the nice new passport that gave no information about his movements other than that he had come from London three months before and had since then crossed no frontier. The detective looked at it carefully and passed it on to his colleague.

"It appears to be all in order," he said.

Ashenden, standing in front of the fire to warm himself, a cigarette between his lips, made no reply. He watched the detectives warily, but with an expression, he flattered himself, of amiable unconcern. Fasolt handed back the passport to Fafner, who tapped it reflectively with a thick forefinger.

"The chief of police told us to come here," he said, and Ashenden

was conscious that both of them now looked at him with attention, "to make a few enquiries of you."

Ashenden knew that when you have nothing apposite to say it is better to hold your tongue; and when a man has made a remark that calls to his mind for an answer, he is apt to find silence a trifle disconcerting. Ashenden waited for the detective to proceed. He was not quite sure, but it seemed to him that he hesitated.

"It appears that there have been a good many complaints lately of the noise that people make when they come out of the Casino late at night. We wish to know if you personally have been troubled by the disturbance. It is evident that as your rooms look on the lake and the revellers pass your windows, if the noise is serious, you must have heard it."

For an instant Ashenden was dumbfounded. What balderdash was this the detective was talking to him (boom, boom, he heard the big drum as the giant lumbered on the scene), and why on earth should the chief of police send to him to find out if his beauty sleep had been disturbed by vociferous gamblers? It looked very like a trap. But nothing is so foolish as to ascribe profundity to what on the surface is merely inept; it is a pitfall into which many an ingenuous reviewer has fallen headlong: Ashenden had a confident belief in the stupidity of the human animal, which in the course of his life had stood him in good stead. It flashed across him that if the detective asked him such a question it was because he had no shadow of proof that he was engaged in any illegal practice. It was clear that he had been denounced, but no evidence had been offered, and the search of his rooms had been fruitless. But what a silly excuse was this to make for a visit and what a poverty of invention it showed! Ashenden immediately thought of three reasons the detectives might have given for seeking an interview with him and he wished that he were on terms sufficiently familiar with them to make the suggestions. This was really an insult to the intelligence. These men were even stupider than he thought; but Ashenden had always a soft corner in his heart for the stupid and now he looked upon them with a feeling of unexpected kindliness. He would have liked to pat them gently. But he answered the question with gravity.

"To tell you the truth, I am a very sound sleeper (the result doubtless of a pure heart and an easy conscience), and I have never heard a thing."

Ashenden looked at them for the faint smile that he thought his remark deserved, but their countenances remained stolid. Ashenden, as well as an agent of the British Government, was a humorist, and he stifled the beginnings of a sigh. He assumed a slightly imposing air and adopted a more serious tone.

"But even if I had been awakened by noisy people I should not dream of complaining. At a time when there is so much trouble, misery and unhappiness in the world, I cannot but think it very wrong to disturb the amusement of persons who are lucky enough to be able to amuse themselves."

"*En effet*," said the detective. "But the fact remains that people have been disturbed and the chief of police thought the matter should be enquired into."

His colleague, who had hitherto preserved a silence that was positively sphinx-like, now broke it.

"I notice by your passport that you are an author, *monsieur*," he said.

Ashenden in reaction from his previous perturbation was feeling exceedingly debonair and he answered with good humour.

"It is true. It is a profession full of tribulation, but it has now and then its compensations."

"*La gloire*," said Fafner politely.

"Or shall we say notoriety?" hazarded Ashenden.

"And what are you doing in Geneva?"

The question was put so pleasantly that Ashenden felt it behooved him to be on his guard. A police officer amiable is more dangerous to the wise than a police officer aggressive.

"I am writing a play," said Ashenden.

He waved his hand to the papers on his table. Four eyes followed his gesture. A casual glance told him that the detectives had looked and taken note of his manuscripts.

"And why should you write a play here rather than in your own country?"

Ashenden smiled upon them with even more affability than before,

since this was a question for which he had long been prepared, and it was a relief to give the answer. He was curious to see how it would go down.

"*Mais, monsieur,* there is the war. My country is in a turmoil, it would be impossible to sit there quietly and write a play."

"Is it a comedy or a tragedy?"

"Oh, a comedy, and a light one at that," replied Ashenden. "The artist needs peace and quietness. How do you expect him to preserve that detachment of spirit that is demanded by creative work unless he can have perfect tranquillity? Switzerland has the good fortune to be neutral, and it seemed to me that in Geneva I should find the very surroundings I wanted."

Fafner nodded slightly to Fasolt, but whether to indicate that he thought Ashenden an imbecile or whether in sympathy with his desire for a safe retreat from a turbulent world, Ashenden had no means of knowing. Anyhow the detective evidently came to the conclusion that he could learn nothing more from talking to Ashenden, for his remarks grew now desultory and in a few minutes he rose to go.

When Ashenden, having warmly shaken their hands, closed the door behind the pair he heaved a great sigh of relief. He turned on the water for his bath, as hot as he thought he could possibly bear it, and as he undressed reflected comfortably over his escape.

The day before, an incident had occurred that had left him on his guard. There was in his service a Swiss, known in the Intelligence Department as Bernard, who had recently come from Germany, and Ashenden had instructed him to go to a certain café desiring to see him, at a certain time. Since he had not seen him before, so that there might be no mistake he had informed him through an intermediary what question himself would ask and what reply he was to give. He chose the luncheon hour for the meeting, since then the café was unlikely to be crowded, and it chanced that on entering he saw but one man of about the age he knew Bernard to be. He was by himself and going up to him Ashenden casually put to him the pre-arranged question. The pre-arranged answer was given, and sitting down beside him, Ashenden ordered himself a Dubonnet. The spy was a stocky little fellow, shabbily dressed, with a bullet-shaped head, close-cropped, fair,

with shifty blue eyes and a sallow skin. He did not inspire confidence, and but that Ashenden knew by experience how hard it was to find men willing to go into Germany he would have been surprised that his predecessor had engaged him. He was a German-Swiss and spoke French with a strong accent. He immediately asked for his wages and these Ashenden passed over to him in an envelope. They were in Swiss francs. He gave a general account of his stay in Germany and answered Ashenden's careful questions. He was by calling a waiter and had found a job in a restaurant near one of the Rhine bridges, which gave him good opportunity to get the information that was required of him. His reasons for coming to Switzerland for a few days were plausible and there could apparently be no difficulty in his crossing the frontier on his return. Ashenden expressed his satisfaction with his behaviour, gave him his orders and was prepared to finish the interview.

"Very good," said Bernard. "But before I go back to Germany I want two thousand francs."

"Do you?"

"Yes, and I want them now, before you leave this café. It's a sum I have to pay, and I've got to have it."

"I'm afraid I can't give it to you."

A scowl made the man's face even more unpleasant to look at than it was before.

"You've got to."

"What makes you think that?"

The spy leaned forward and, not raising his voice, but speaking so that only Ashenden could hear, burst out angrily.

"Do you think I'm going on risking my life for that beggarly sum you give me? Not ten days ago a man was caught at Mainz and shot. Was that one of your men?"

"We haven't got anyone at Mainz," said Ashenden, carelessly, and for all he knew it was true. He had been puzzled not to receive his usual communications from that place and Bernard's information might afford the explanation. "You knew exactly what you were to get when you took on the job, and if you weren't satisfied you needn't have taken it. I have no authority to give you a penny more."

"Do you see what I've got here?" said Bernard.

He took a small revolver out of his pocket and fingered it significantly.

"What are you going to do with it? Pawn it?"

With an angry shrug of the shoulders he put it back in his pocket. Ashenden reflected that had he known anything of the technique of the theatre Bernard would have been aware that it was useless to make a gesture that had no ulterior meaning.

"You refuse to give me the money?"

"Certainly."

The spy's manner, which at first had been obsequious, was now somewhat truculent, but he kept his head and never for a moment raised his voice. Ashenden could see that Bernard, however big a ruffian, was a reliable agent, and he made up his mind to suggest to R. that his salary should be raised. The scene diverted him. A little way off two fat citizens of Geneva, with black beards, were playing dominoes, and on the other side a young man with spectacles was with great rapidity writing sheet after sheet of an immensely long letter. A Swiss family (who knows, perhaps Robinson by name), consisting of a father and mother and four children, were sitting round a table making the best of two small cups of coffee. The *caissière* behind the counter, an imposing brunette with a large bust encased in black silk, was reading the local paper. The surroundings made the melodramatic scene in which Ashenden was engaged perfectly grotesque. His own play seemed to him much more real.

Bernard smiled. His smile was not engaging.

"Do you know that I have only to go to the police and tell them about you to have you arrested? Do you know what a Swiss prison is like?"

"No, I've often wondered lately. Do you?"

"Yes, and you wouldn't much like it."

One of the things that had bothered Ashenden was the possibility that he would be arrested before he finished his play. He disliked the notion of leaving it half done for an indefinite period. He did not know whether he would be treated as a political prisoner or as a common criminal and he had a mind to ask Bernard whether in the latter case (the only one Bernard was likely to know anything about) he would be

allowed writing materials. He was afraid Bernard would think the inquiry an attempt to laugh at him. But he was feeling comparatively at ease and was able to answer Bernard's threat without heat.

"You could of course get me sentenced to two years' imprisonment."

"At least."

"No, that is the maximum, I understand, and I think it is quite enough. I won't conceal from you that I should find it extremely disagreeable. But not nearly so disagreeable as you would."

"What could you do?"

"Oh, we'd get you somehow. And after all, the war won't last for ever. You are a waiter, you want your freedom of action. I promise you that if I get into any trouble, you will never be admitted into any of the allied countries for the rest of your life. I can't help thinking it would cramp your style."

Bernard did not reply, but looked down sulkily at the marble-topped table. Ashenden thought this was the moment to pay for the drinks and go.

"Think it over, Bernard," he said. "If you want to go back to your job, you have your instructions, and your usual wages shall be paid through the usual channels."

The spy shrugged his shoulders, and Ashenden, though not knowing in the least what was the result of their conversation, felt that it behoved him to walk out with dignity. He did so.

And now as he carefully put one foot into the bath, wondering if he could bear it, he asked himself what Bernard had in the end decided on. The water was just not scalding and he gradually let himself down into it. On the whole it seemed to him that the spy had thought it would be as well to go straight, and the source of his denunciation must be looked for elsewhere. Perhaps in the hotel itself. Ashenden lay back, and as his body grew used to the heat of the water gave a sigh of satisfaction.

"Really," he reflected, "there are moments in life when all this to-do that has led from the primeval slime to myself seems almost worth while."

Ashenden could not but think he was lucky to have wriggled out of

the fix he had found himself in that afternoon. Had he been arrested and in due course sentenced R., shrugging his shoulders, would merely have called him a damned fool and set about looking for someone to take his place. Already Ashenden knew his chief well enough to be aware that when he had told him that if he got into trouble he need look for no help he meant exactly what he said. . . .

IV
THE HAIRLESS MEXICAN

"Do you like macaroni?" said R.

"What do you mean by macaroni?" answered Ashenden. "It is like asking me if I like poetry. I like Keats and Wordsworth and Verlaine and Goethe. When you say macaroni, do you mean *spaghetti, tagliatelli, rigatoni, vermicelli, fettucini, tufali, farfalli,* or just macaroni?"

"Macaroni," replied R., a man of few words.

"I like all simple things, boiled eggs, oysters and caviare, *truite au bleu,* grilled salmon, roast lamb (the saddle by preference), cold grouse, treacle tart and rice pudding. But of all simple things the only one I can eat day in and day out, not only without disgust but with the eagerness of an appetite unimpaired by excess, is macaroni."

"I am glad of that because I want you to go down to Italy."

Ashenden had come from Geneva to meet R. at Lyons and having got there before him had spent the afternoon wandering about the dull, busy and prosaic streets of that thriving city. They were sitting now in a restaurant on the *place* to which Ashenden had taken R. on his arrival because it was reputed to give you the best food in that part of France. But since in so crowded a resort (for the Lyonese like a good dinner) you never knew what inquisitive ears were pricked up to catch any useful piece of information that might fall from your lips, they had contented themselves with talking of indifferent things. They had reached the end of an admirable repast.

"Have another glass of brandy?" said R.

"No, thank you," answered Ashenden, who was of an abstemious turn.

"One should do what one can to mitigate the rigours of war," remarked R. as he took the bottle and poured out a glass for himself and another for Ashenden.

Ashenden, thinking it would be affectation to protest, let the gesture pass, but felt bound to remonstrate with his chief on the unseemly manner in which he held the bottle.

"In my youth I was always taught that you should take a woman by the waist and a bottle by the neck," he murmured.

"I am glad you told me. I shall continue to hold a bottle by the waist and give women a wide berth."

Ashenden did not know what to reply to this and so remained silent. He sipped his brandy and R. called for his bill. It was true that he was an important person, with power to make or mar quite a large number of his fellows, and his opinions were listened to by those who held in their hands the fate of empires; but he could never face the business of tipping a waiter without an embarrassment that was obvious in his demeanour. He was tortured by the fear of making a fool of himself by giving too much or of exciting the waiter's icy scorn by giving too little. When the bill came he passed some hundred-franc notes over to Ashenden and said:

"Pay him, will you? I can never understand French figures."

The groom brought them their hats and coats.

"Would you like to go back to the hotel?" asked Ashenden.

"We might as well."

It was early in the year, but the weather had suddenly turned warm, and they walked with their coats over their arms. Ashenden knowing that R. liked a sitting-room had engaged one for him and to this, when they reached the hotel, they went. The hotel was old-fashioned and the sitting-room was vast. It was furnished with a heavy mahogany suite upholstered in green velvet and the chairs were set primly round a large table. On the walls, covered with a dingy paper, were large steel engravings of the battles of Napoleon, and from the ceiling hung an enormous chandelier once used for gas, but now fitted with electric bulbs. It flooded the cheerless room with a cold, hard light.

"This is very nice," said R., as they went in.

"Not exactly cosy," suggested Ashenden.

"No, but it looks as though it were the best room in the place. It all looks very *good* to me."

He drew one of the green velvet chairs away from the table and, sitting down, lit a cigar. He loosened his belt and unbuttoned his tunic.

"I always thought I liked a cheroot better than anything," he said, "but since the war I've taken quite a fancy to Havanas. Oh, well, I suppose it can't last for ever." The corners of his mouth flickered with the beginning of a smile. "It's an ill wind that blows nobody any good."

Ashenden took two chairs, one to sit on and one for his feet, and when R. saw him he said: "That's not a bad idea," and swinging another chair out from the table with a sigh of relief put his boots on it.

"What room is that next door?" he asked.

"That's your bedroom."

"And on the other side?"

"A banqueting hall."

R. got up and strolled slowly about the room and when he passed the windows, as though in idle curiosity, peeped through the heavy rep curtains that covered them, and then returning to his chair once more comfortably put his feet up.

"It's just as well not to take any more risk than one need," he said.

He looked at Ashenden reflectively. There was a slight smile on his thin lips, but the pale eyes, too closely set together, remained cold and steely. R.'s stare would have been embarrassing if Ashenden had not been used to it. He knew that R. was considering how he would broach the subject that he had in mind. The silence must have lasted for two or three minutes.

"I'm expecting a fellow to come and see me to-night," he said at last. "His train gets in about ten." He gave his wrist-watch a glance. "He's known as the Hairless Mexican."

"Why?"

"Because he's hairless and because he's a Mexican."

"The explanation seems perfectly satisfactory," said Ashenden.

"He'll tell you all about himself. He talks nineteen to the dozen. He was on his uppers when I came across him. It appears that he was mixed up in some revolution in Mexico and had to get out with nothing but the clothes he stood up in. They were rather the worse for wear

when I found him. If you want to please him you call him General. He claims to have been a general in Huerta's army, at least I think it was Huerta; anyhow he says that if things had gone right he would be minister of war now and no end of a big bug. I've found him very useful. Not a bad chap. The only thing I really have against him is that he will use scent."

"And where do I come in?" asked Ashenden.

"He's going down to Italy. I've got rather a ticklish job for him to do and I want you to stand by. I'm not keen on trusting him with a lot of money. He's a gambler and he's a bit too fond of the girls. I suppose you came from Geneva on your Ashenden passport."

"Yes."

"I've got another for you, a diplomatic one, by the way, in the name of Somerville with visas for France and Italy. I think you and he had better travel together. He's an amusing cove when he gets going, and I think you ought to get to know one another."

"What is the job?"

"I haven't yet quite made up my mind how much it's desirable for you to know about it."

Ashenden did not reply. They eyed one another in a detached manner, as though they were strangers who sat together in a railway carriage and each wondered who and what the other was.

"In your place I'd leave the General to do most of the talking. I wouldn't tell him more about yourself than you find absolutely necessary. He won't ask you any questions, I can promise you that, I think he's by way of being a gentleman after his own fashion."

"By the way, what is his real name?"

"I always call him Manuel, I don't know that he likes it very much, his name is Manuel Carmona."

"I gather by what you have not said that he's an unmitigated scoundrel."

R. smiled with his pale blue eyes.

"I don't know that I'd go quite so far as that. He hasn't had the advantages of a public-school education. His ideas of playing the game are not quite the same as yours or mine. I don't know that I'd leave a gold cigarette-case about when he was in the neighbourhood, but if he

lost money to you at poker and had pinched your cigarette case he would immediately pawn it to pay you. If he had half a chance he'd seduce your wife, but if you were up against it he'd share his last crust with you. The tears will run down his face when he hears Gounod's 'Ave Maria' on the gramophone, but if you insult his dignity he'll shoot you like a dog. It appears that in Mexico it's an insult to get between a man and his drink and he told me himself that once when a Dutchman who didn't know passed between him and the bar he whipped out his revolver and shot him dead."

"Did nothing happen to him?"

"No, it appears that he belongs to one of the best families. The matter was hushed up and it was announced in the papers that the Dutchman had committed suicide. He did practically. I don't believe the Hairless Mexican has a great respect for human life."

Ashenden who had been looking intently at R. started a little and he watched more carefully than ever his chief's tired, lined and yellow face. He knew that he did not make this remark for nothing.

"Of course a lot of nonsense is talked about the value of human life. You might just as well say that the counters you use at poker have an intrinsic value, their value is what you like to make it; for a general giving battle men are merely counters and he's a fool if he allows himself for sentimental reasons to look upon them as human beings."

"But, you see, they're counters that feel and think and if they believe they're being squandered they are quite capable of refusing to be used any more."

"Anyhow that's neither here nor there. We've had information that a man called Constantine Andreadi is on his way from Constantinople with certain documents that we want to get hold of. He's a Greek. He's an agent of Enver Pasha and Enver has great confidence in him. He's given him verbal messages that are too secret and too important to be put on paper. He's sailing from the Piræus, on a boat called the Ithaca, and will land at Brindisi on his way to Rome. He's to deliver his dispatches at the German embassy and impart what he has to say personally to the ambassador."

"I see."

At this time Italy was still neutral; the Central Powers were strain-

ing every nerve to keep her so; the Allies were doing what they could to induce her to declare war on their side.

"We don't want to get into any trouble with the Italian authorities, it might be fatal, but we've got to prevent Andreadi from getting to Rome."

"At any cost?" asked Ashenden.

"Money's no object," answered R., his lips twisting into a sardonic smile.

"What do you propose to do?"

"I don't think you need bother your head about that."

"I have a fertile imagination," said Ashenden.

"I want you to go down to Naples with the Hairless Mexican. He's very keen on getting back to Cuba. It appears that his friends are organizing a show and he wants to be as near at hand as possible so that he can hop over to Mexico when things are ripe. He needs cash. I've brought money down with me, in American dollars, and I shall give it to you to-night. You'd better carry it on your person."

"Is it much?"

"It's a good deal, but I thought it would be easier for you if it wasn't bulky, so I've got it in thousand dollar notes. You will give the Hairless Mexican the notes in return for the documents that Andreadi is bringing."

A question sprang to Ashenden's lips, but he did not ask it. He asked another instead.

"Does this fellow understand what he has to do?"

"Perfectly."

There was a knock at the door. It opened and the Hairless Mexican stood before them.

"I have arrived. Good-evening, Colonel. I am enchanted to see you."

R. got up.

"Had a nice journey, Manuel? This is Mr. Somerville who's going to Naples with you. General Carmona."

"Pleased to meet you, sir."

He shook Ashenden's hand with such force that he winced.

"Your hands are like iron, General," he murmured.

The Mexican gave them a glance.

"I had them manicured this morning. I do not think they were very well done. I like my nails much more highly polished."

They were cut to a point, stained bright red, and to Ashenden's mind shone like mirrors. Though it was not cold the General wore a fur-coat with an astrakhan collar and with his every movement a wave of perfume was wafted to your nose.

"Take off your coat, General, and have a cigar," said R.

The Hairless Mexican was a tall man, and though thinnish gave you the impression of being very powerful; he was smartly dressed in a blue serge suit, with a silk handkerchief neatly tucked in the breast pocket of his coat, and he wore a gold bracelet on his wrist. His features were good, but a little larger than life-size, and his eyes were brown and lustrous. He was quite hairless. His yellow skin had the smoothness of a woman's and he had no eyebrows nor eyelashes; he wore a pale brown wig, rather long, and the locks were arranged in artistic disorder. This and the unwrinkled sallow face, combined with his dandified dress, gave him an appearance that was at first glance a trifle horrifying. He was repulsive and ridiculous, but you could not take your eyes from him. There was a sinister fascination in his strangeness.

He sat down and hitched up his trousers so that they should not bag at the knee.

"Well, Manuel, have you been breaking any hearts to-day?" said R. with his sardonic joviality.

The General turned to Ashenden.

"Our good friend, the Colonel, envies me my successes with the fair sex. I tell him he can have just as many as I if he will only listen to me. Confidence, that is all you need. If you never fear a rebuff you will never have one."

"Nonsense, Manuel, one has to have your way with the girls. There's something about you that they can't resist."

The Hairless Mexican laughed with a self-satisfaction that he did not try to disguise. He spoke English very well, with a Spanish accent, but with an American intonation.

"But since you ask me, Colonel, I don't mind telling you that I got

into conversation on the train with a little woman who was coming to Lyons to see her mother-in-law. She was not very young and she was thinner than I like a woman to be, but she was possible, and she helped me to pass an agreeable hour."

"Well, let's get to business," said R.

"I am at your service, Colonel." He gave Ashenden a glance. "Is Mr. Somerville a military man?"

"No," said R., "he's an author."

"It takes all sorts to make a world, as you say. I am happy to make your acquaintance, Mr. Somerville. I can tell you many stories that will interest you; I am sure that we shall get on well together. You have a sympathetic air. I am very sensitive to that. To tell you the truth I am nothing but a bundle of nerves and if I am with a person who is antipathetic to me I go all to pieces."

"I hope we shall have a pleasant journey," said Ashenden.

"When does our friend arrive at Brindisi?" asked the Mexican, turning to R.

"He sails from the Piræus in the Ithaca on the fourteenth. It's probably some old tub, but you'd better get down to Brindisi in good time."

"I agree with you."

R. got up and with his hands in his pockets sat on the edge of the table. In his rather shabby uniform, his tunic unbuttoned, he looked a slovenly creature beside the neat and well-dressed Mexican.

"Mr. Somerville knows practically nothing of the errand on which you are going and I do not desire you to tell him anything. I think you had much better keep your own counsel. He is instructed to give you the funds you need for your work, but your actions are your own affair. If you need his advice of course you can ask for it."

"I seldom ask other people's advice and never take it."

"And should you make a mess of things I trust you to keep Mr. Somerville out of it. He must on no account be compromised."

"I am a man of honour, Colonel," answered the Hairless Mexican with dignity, "and I would sooner let myself be cut in a thousand pieces than betray my friends."

"That is what I have already told Mr. Somerville. On the other hand if everything pans out O. K. Mr. Somerville is instructed to give you

the sum we agreed on in return for the papers I spoke to you about. In what manner you get them is no business of his."

"That goes without saying. There is only one thing I wish to make quite plain; Mr. Somerville understands of course that I have not accepted the mission with which you have entrusted me on account of the money?"

"Quite," replied R., gravely, looking him straight in the eyes.

"I am with the Allies body and soul, I cannot forgive the Germans for outraging the neutrality of Belgium, and if I accept the money that you have offered me it is because I am first and foremost a patriot. I can trust Mr. Somerville implicitly, I suppose?"

R. nodded. The Mexican turned to Ashenden.

"An expedition is being arranged to free my unhappy country from the tyrants that exploit and ruin it and every penny that I receive will go on guns and cartridges. For myself I have no need of money; I am a soldier and I can live on a crust and a few olives. There are only three occupations that befit a gentleman, war, cards and women; it costs nothing to sling a rifle over your shoulder and take to the mountains—and that is real warfare, not this manœuvring of battalions and firing of great guns—women love me for myself, and I generally win at cards."

Ashenden found the flamboyance of this strange creature, with his scented handkerchief and his gold bracelet, very much to his taste. This was far from being just the man in the street (whose tyranny we rail at but in the end submit to) and to the amateur of the baroque in human nature he was a rarity to be considered with delight. He was a purple patch on two legs. Notwithstanding his wig and his hairless big face he had undoubtedly an air; he was absurd, but he did not give you the impression that he was a man to be trifled with. His self-complacency was magnificent.

"Where is your kit, Manuel?" asked R.

It was possible that a frown for an instant darkened the Mexican's brow at the abrupt question that seemed a little contemptuously to brush to one side his eloquent statement, but he gave no other sign of displeasure. Ashenden suspected that he thought the Colonel a barbarian insensitive to the finer emotions.

"I left it at the station."

"Mr. Somerville has a diplomatic passport so that he can get it through with his own things at the frontier without examination if you like."

"I have very little, a few suits and some linen, but perhaps it would be as well if Mr. Somerville would take charge of it. I bought half a dozen suits of silk pyjamas before I left Paris."

"And what about you?" asked R., turning to Ashenden.

"I've only got one bag. It's in my room."

"You'd better have it taken to the station while there's someone about. Your train goes at one ten."

"Oh?"

This was the first Ashenden had heard that they were to start that night.

"I think you'd better get down to Naples as soon as possible."

"Very well."

R. got up.

"I'm going to bed. I don't know what you fellows want to do."

"I shall take a walk about Lyons," said the Hairless Mexican. "I am interested in life. Lend me a hundred francs, Colonel, will you? I have no change on me."

R. took out his pocket-book and gave the General the note he asked for. Then to Ashenden:

"What are you going to do? Wait here?"

"No," said Ashenden, "I shall go to the station and read."

"You'd both of you better have a whisky and soda before you go, hadn't you? What about it, Manuel?"

"It is very kind of you, but I never drink anything but champagne and brandy."

"Mixed?" asked R. drily.

"Not necessarily," returned the other with gravity.

R. ordered brandy and soda and when it came, whereas he and Ashenden helped themselves to both, the Hairless Mexican poured himself out three parts of a tumbler of neat brandy and swallowed it in two noisy gulps. He rose to his feet and put on his coat with the astrakhan collar, seized in one hand his bold black hat and, with the ges-

ture of a romantic actor giving up the girl he loved to one more worthy of her, held out the other to R.

"Well, Colonel, I will bid you goodnight and pleasant dreams. I do not expect that we shall meet again so soon."

"Don't make a hash of things, Manuel, and if you do keep your mouth shut."

"They tell me that in one of your colleges where the sons of gentlemen are trained to become naval officers it is written in letters of gold: there is no such word as impossible in the British Navy. I do not know the meaning of the word failure."

"It has a good many synonyms," retorted R.

"I will meet you at the station, Mr. Somerville," said the Hairless Mexican, and with a flourish left them.

R. looked at Ashenden with that little smile of his that always made his face look so dangerously shrewd.

"Well, what d'you think of him?"

"You've got me beat," said Ashenden. "Is he a mountebank? He seems as vain as a peacock. And with that frightful appearance can he really be the lady's man he pretends? What makes you think you can trust him?"

R. gave a low chuckle and he washed his thin, old hands with imaginary soap.

"I thought you'd like him. He's quite a character, isn't he? I think we can trust him." R.'s eyes suddenly grew opaque. "I don't believe it would pay him to double-cross us." He paused for a moment. "Anyhow we've got to risk it. I'll give you the tickets and the money and then you can take yourself off; I'm all in and I want to go to bed."

Ten minutes later Ashenden set out for the station with his bag on a porter's shoulder.

Having nearly two hours to wait he made himself comfortable in the waiting-room. The light was good and he read a novel. When the time drew near for the arrival of the train from Paris that was to take them direct to Rome and the Hairless Mexican did not appear Ashenden, beginning to grow a trifle anxious, went out on the platform to look for him. Ashenden suffered from that distressing malady known as train fever: an hour before his train was due he began to have appre-

hensions lest he should miss it; he was impatient with the porters who would never bring his luggage down from his room in time and he could not understand why the hotel bus cut it so fine; a block in the street would drive him to frenzy and the languid movements of the station porters infuriate him. The whole world seemed in a horrid plot to delay him; people got in his way as he passed through the barriers; others, a long string of them, were at the ticket-office getting tickets for other trains than his and they counted their change with exasperating care; his luggage took an interminable time to register; and then if he was travelling with friends they would go to buy newspapers, or would take a walk along the platform and he was certain they would be left behind, they would stop to talk to a casual stranger or suddenly be seized with a desire to telephone and disappear at a run. In fact the universe conspired to make him miss every train he wanted to take and he was not happy unless he was settled in his corner, his things on the rack above him, with a good half hour to spare. Sometimes by arriving at the station too soon he had caught an earlier train than the one he had meant to, but that was nerve-racking and caused him all the anguish of very nearly missing it.

The Rome express was signalled and there was no sign of the Hairless Mexican, it came in and he was not to be seen. Ashenden became more and more harassed. He walked quickly up and down the platform, looked in all the waiting-rooms, went to the *consigne* where the luggage was left; he could not find him. There were no sleeping-cars, but a number of people got out and he took two seats in a first-class carriage. He stood at the door, looking up and down the platform and up at the clock; it was useless to go if his travelling companion did not turn up and Ashenden made up his mind to take his things out of the carriage as the porter cried *en voiture;* but, by George! he would give the brute hell when he found him. There were three minutes more, then two minutes, then one; at that late hour there were few persons about and all who were travelling had taken their seats. Then he saw the Hairless Mexican, followed by two porters with his luggage and accompanied by a man in a bowler-hat, walk leisurely on to the platform. He caught sight of Ashenden and waved to him.

"Ah, my dear fellow, there you are, I wondered what had become of you."

"Good God, man, hurry up or we shall miss the train."

"I never miss a train. Have you got good seats? The *chef de gare* has gone for the night; this is his assistant."

The man in the bowler-hat took it off when Ashenden nodded to him.

"But this is an ordinary carriage. I am afraid I could not travel in that." He turned to the station-master's assistant with an affable smile. "You must do better for me than that, *mon cher.*"

"*Certainement, mon général,* I will put you into a *salon-lit.* Of course."

The assistant station-master led them along the train and put them in an empty compartment where there were two beds. The Mexican eyed it with satisfaction and watched the porters arrange the luggage.

"That will do very well. I am much obliged to you." He held out his hand to the man in the bowler-hat. "I shall not forget you and next time I see the Minister I will tell him with what civility you have treated me."

"You are too good, General. I shall be very grateful."

A whistle was blown and the train started.

"This is better than an ordinary first-class carriage, I think, Mr. Somerville," said the Mexican. "A good traveller should learn how to make the best of things."

But Ashenden was still extremely cross.

"I don't know why the devil you wanted to cut it so fine. We should have looked a pair of damned fools if we'd missed the train."

"My dear fellow, there was never the smallest chance of that. When I arrived I told the station-master that I was General Carmona, Commander-in-Chief of the Mexican Army, and that I had to stop off in Lyons for a few hours to hold a conference with the British Field-Marshal. I asked him to hold the train for me if I was delayed and suggested that my government might see its way to conferring an order on him. I have been to Lyons before, I like the girls here; they have not the *chic* of the Parisians, but they have something, there is no denying that they have something. Will you have a mouthful of brandy before you go to sleep?"

"No, thank you," said Ashenden morosely.

"I always drink a glass before going to bed, it settles the nerves."

He looked in his suit-case and without difficulty found a bottle. He put it to his lips and had a long drink, wiped his mouth with the back of his hand and lit a cigarette. Then he took off his boots and lay down. Ashenden dimmed the light.

"I have never yet made up my mind," said the Hairless Mexican reflectively, "whether it is pleasanter to go to sleep with the kisses of a beautiful woman on your mouth or with a cigarette between your lips. Have you ever been to Mexico? I will tell you about Mexico to-morrow. Goodnight."

Presently Ashenden heard from his steady breathing that he was asleep and in a little while himself dozed off. Presently he woke. The Mexican, deep in slumber, lay motionless; he had taken off his fur coat and was using it as a blanket; he still wore his wig. Suddenly there was a jolt and the train with a noisy grinding of brakes stopped; in the twinkling of an eye, before Ashenden could realize that anything had happened, the Mexican was on his feet with his hand to his hip.

"What is it?" he cried.

"Nothing. Probably only a signal against us."

The Mexican sat down heavily on his bed. Ashenden turned on the light.

"You wake quickly for such a sound sleeper," he said.

"You have to in my profession."

Ashenden would have liked to ask him whether this was murder, conspiracy or commanding armies, but was not sure that it would be discreet. The General opened his bag and took out the bottle.

"Will you have a nip?" he asked. "There is nothing like it when you wake suddenly in the night."

When Ashenden refused he put the bottle once more to his lips and poured a considerable quantity of liquor down his throat. He sighed and lit a cigarette. Although Ashenden had seen him now drink nearly a bottle of brandy and it was probable that he had had a good deal more when he was going about the town he was cer-

tainly quite sober. Neither in his manner nor in his speech was there any indication that he had drunk during the evening anything but lemonade.

The train started and soon Ashenden again fell asleep. When he awoke it was morning and turning round lazily he saw that the Mexican was awake too. He was smoking a cigarette. The floor by his side was strewn with burnt-out butts and the air was thick and grey. He had begged Ashenden not to insist on opening a window, for he said the night air was dangerous.

"I did not get up, because I was afraid of waking you. Will you do your toilet first or shall I?"

"I'm in no hurry," said Ashenden.

"I am an old campaigner, it will not take me long. Do you wash your teeth every day?"

"Yes," said Ashenden.

"So do I. It is a habit I learned in New York. I always think that a fine set of teeth are an adornment to a man."

There was a wash-basin in the compartment and the General scrubbed his teeth, with gurglings and garglings, energetically. Then he got a bottle of eau-de-cologne from his bag, poured some of it on a towel and rubbed it over his face and hands. He took a comb and carefully arranged his wig; either it had not moved in the night or else he had set it straight before Ashenden awoke. He got another bottle out of his bag, with a spray attached to it, and squeezing a bulb covered his shirt and coat with a fine cloud of scent, did the same to his handkerchief, and then with a beaming face, like a man who has done his duty by the world and is well pleased, turned to Ashenden and said:

"Now I am ready to brave the day. I will leave my things for you, you need not be afraid of the eau-de-cologne, it is the best you can get in Paris."

"Thank you very much," said Ashenden. "All I want is soap and water."

"Water? I never use water except when I have a bath. Nothing can be worse for the skin."

When they approached the frontier, Ashenden, remembering the

General's instructive gesture when he was suddenly awakened in the night, said to him:

"If you've got a revolver on you I think you'd better give it to me. With my diplomatic passport they're not likely to search me, but they might take it into their heads to go through you and we don't want to have any bothers."

"It is hardly a weapon, it is only a toy," returned the Mexican, taking out of his hip-pocket a fully loaded revolver of formidable dimensions. "I do not like parting with it even for an hour, it gives me the feeling that I am not fully dressed. But you are quite right, we do not want to take any risks; I will give you my knife as well. I would always rather use a knife than a revolver; I think it is a more elegant weapon."

"I daresay it is only a matter of habit," answered Ashenden. "Perhaps you are more at home with a knife."

"Anyone can pull a trigger, but it needs a man to use a knife."

To Ashenden it looked as though it were in a single movement that he tore open his waistcoat and from his belt snatched and opened a long knife of murderous aspect. He handed it to Ashenden with a pleased smile on his large, ugly and naked face.

"There's a pretty piece of work for you, Mr. Somerville. I've never seen a better bit of steel in my life, it takes an edge like a razor and it's strong; you can cut a cigarette-paper with it and you can hew down an oak. There is nothing to get out of order and when it is closed it might be the knife a schoolboy uses to cut notches in his desk."

He shut it with a click and Ashenden put it along with the revolver in his pocket.

"Have you anything else?"

"My hands," replied the Mexican with arrogance, "but those I daresay the custom officials will not make trouble about."

Ashenden remembered the iron grip he had given him when they shook hands and slightly shuddered. They were large and long and smooth; there was not a hair on them or on the wrists, and with the pointed, rosy, manicured nails there was really something sinister about them. . . .

VI
THE GREEK

Ashenden arrived in Naples and having taken a room at the hotel, wrote its number on a sheet of paper in block letters and posted it to the Hairless Mexican. He went to the British Consulate where R. had arranged to send any instructions he might have for him and found that they knew about him and everything was in order. Then he put aside these matters and made up his mind to amuse himself. Here in the South the spring was well advanced and in the busy streets the sun was hot. Ashenden knew Naples pretty well. The Piazza di San Ferdinando, with its bustle, the Piazza del Plebiscito, with its handsome church, stirred in his heart pleasant recollections. The Strada di Chiaia was as noisy as ever. He stood at corners and looked up the narrow alleys that climbed the hill precipitously, those alleys of high houses with the washing set out to dry on lines across the street like pennants flying to mark a feast-day; and he sauntered along the shore, looking at the burnished sea with Capri faintly outlined against the day, till he came to Posilippo where there was an old, rambling and bedraggled *palazzo* in which in his youth he had spent many a romantic hour. He observed the curious little pain with which the memories of the past wrung his heart-strings. Then he took a fly drawn by a small and scraggy pony and rattled back over the stones to the *Galleria* where he sat in the cool and drank an *americano* and looked at the people who loitered there, talking, for ever talking with vivacious gestures, and, exercising his fancy, sought from their appearance to divine their reality.

For three days Ashenden led the idle life that fitted so well the fantastical, untidy and genial city. He did nothing from morning till night but wander at random, looking, not with the eye of the tourist who seeks for what ought to be seen, nor with the eye of the writer who looks for his own, (seeing in a sunset a melodious phrase or in a face the inkling of a character,) but with that of the tramp to whom whatever happens is absolute. He went to the museum to look at the statue of Agrippina the Younger, which he had particular reasons for remembering with affection, and took the opportunity to see once

more the Titian and the Brueghel in the picture gallery. But he always came back to the church of Santa Chiara. Its grace, its gaiety, the airy persiflage with which it seemed to treat religion and at the back of this its sensual emotion; its extravagance, its elegance of line; to Ashenden it seemed to express, as it were in one absurd and grandiloquent metaphor, the sunny, dusty, lovely city and its bustling inhabitants. It said that life was charming and sad; it's a pity one hadn't any money, but money wasn't everything, and anyway why bother when we are here to-day and gone to-morrow, and it was all very exciting and amusing, and after all we must make the best of things: *facciamo una piccola combinazione.*

But on the fourth morning when Ashenden, having just stepped out of his bath, was trying to dry himself on a towel that absorbed no moisture, his door was quickly opened and a man slipped into his room.

"What d'you want?" cried Ashenden.

"It's all right. Don't you know me?"

"Good Lord, it's the Mexican. What have you done to yourself?"

He had changed his wig and wore now a black one, close cropped, that fitted on his head like a cap. It entirely altered the look of him and though this was still odd enough, it was quite different from that which he had borne before. He wore a shabby grey suit.

"I can only stop a minute. He's getting shaved."

Ashenden felt his cheeks suddenly redden.

"You found him then?"

"That wasn't difficult. He was the only Greek passenger on the ship. I went on board when she got in and asked for a friend who had sailed from the Piræus. I said I had come to meet a Mr. George Diogenidis. I pretended to be much puzzled at his not coming and I got into conversation with Andreadi. He's travelling under a false name. He calls himself Lombardos. I followed him when he landed and do you know the first thing he did? He went into a barber's and had his beard shaved. What do you think of that?"

"Nothing. Anyone might have his beard shaved."

"That is not what I think. He wanted to change his appearance. Oh, he's cunning. I admire the Germans, they leave nothing to chance, he's got his whole story pat, but I'll tell you that in a minute."

"By the way, you've changed your appearance too."

"Ah yes, this is a wig I'm wearing; it makes a difference, doesn't it?"

"I should never have known you."

"One has to take precautions. We are bosom friends. We had to spend the day in Brindisi and he cannot speak Italian. He was glad to have me help him and we travelled up together. I have brought him to this hotel. He says he is going to Rome to-morrow, but I shall not let him out of my sight; I do not want him to give me the slip. He says that he wants to see Naples and I have offered to show him everything there is to see."

"Why isn't he going to Rome to-day?"

"That is part of the story. He pretends he is a Greek business man who has made money during the war. He says he was the owner of two coasting steamers and has just sold them. Now he means to go to Paris and have his fling. He says he has wanted to go to Paris all his life and at last has the chance. He is close. I tried to get him to talk. I told him I was a Spaniard and had been to Brindisi to arrange communications with Turkey about war material. He listened to me and I saw he was interested, but he told me nothing and of course I did not think it wise to press him. He has the papers on his person."

"How do you know?"

"He is not anxious about his grip, but he feels every now and then round his middle, they're either in a belt or in the lining of his vest."

"Why the devil did you bring him to this hotel?"

"I thought it would be more convenient. We may want to search his luggage."

"Are you staying here too?"

"No, I am not such a fool as that, I told him I was going to Rome by the night train and would not take a room. But I must go, I promised to meet him outside the barber's in fifteen minutes."

"All right."

"Where shall I find you to-night if I want you?"

Ashenden for an instant eyed the Hairless Mexican, then with a slight frown looked away.

"I shall spend the evening in my room."

"Very well. Will you just see that there's nobody in the passage."

Ashenden opened the door and looked out. He saw no one. The hotel in point of fact at that season was nearly empty. There were few foreigners in Naples and trade was bad.

"It's all right," said Ashenden.

The Hairless Mexican walked boldly out. Ashenden closed the door behind him. He shaved and slowly dressed. The sun was shining as brightly as usual on the square and the people who passed, the shabby little carriages with their scrawny horses, had the same air as before, but they did not any longer fill Ashenden with gaiety. He was not comfortable. He went out and called as was his habit at the Consulate to ask if there was a telegram for him. Nothing. Then he went to Cook's and looked out the trains to Rome: there was one soon after midnight and another at five in the morning. He wished he could catch the first. He did not know what were the Mexican's plans; if he really wanted to get to Cuba he would do well to make his way to Spain, and, glancing at the notices in the office, Ashenden saw that next day there was a ship sailing from Naples to Barcelona.

Ashenden was bored with Naples. The glare in the streets tired his eyes, the dust was intolerable, the noise was deafening. He went to the *Galleria* and had a drink. In the afternoon he went to a cinema. Then, going back to his hotel, he told the clerk that since he was starting so early in the morning he preferred to pay his bill at once, and he took his luggage to the station, leaving in his room only a dispatch-case in which were the printed part of his code and a book or two. He dined. Then returning to the hotel, he sat down to wait for the Hairless Mexican. He could not conceal from himself the fact that he was exceedingly nervous. He began to read, but the book was tiresome, and he tried another: his attention wandered and he glanced at his watch. It was desperately early; he took up his book again, making up his mind that he would not look at his watch till he had read thirty pages, but though he ran his eyes conscientiously down one page after another he could not tell more than vaguely what it was he read. He looked at the time again. Good God, it was only half-past ten. He wondered where the Hairless Mexican was, and what he was doing; he was afraid he would make a mess of things. It was

a horrible business. Then it struck him that he had better shut the window and draw the curtains. He smoked innumerable cigarettes. He looked at his watch and it was a quarter past eleven. A thought struck him and his heart began to beat against his chest; out of curiosity he counted his pulse and was surprised to find that it was normal. Though it was a warm night and the room was stuffy his hands and feet were icy. What a nuisance it was, he reflected irritably, to have an imagination that conjured up pictures of things that you didn't in the least want to see! From his standpoint as a writer he had often considered murder and his mind went to that fearful description of one in *Crime and Punishment.* He did not want to think of this topic, but it forced itself upon him; his book dropped to his knees and staring at the wall in front of him (it had a brown wall-paper with a pattern of dingy roses) he asked himself how, if one had to, one would commit a murder in Naples. Of course there was the Villa, the great leafy garden facing the bay in which stood the aquarium; that was deserted at night and very dark; things happened there that did not bear the light of day and prudent persons after dusk avoided its sinister paths. Beyond Posilippo the road was very solitary and there were byways that led up the hill in which by night you would never meet a soul, but how would you induce a man who had any nerves to go there? You might suggest a row in the bay, but the boatman who hired the boat would see you; it was doubtful indeed if he would let you go on the water alone; there were disreputable hotels down by the harbour where no questions were asked of persons who arrived late at night without luggage; but here again the waiter who showed you your room had the chance of a good look at you and you had on entering to sign an elaborate questionnaire.

Ashenden looked once more at the time. He was very tired. He sat now not even trying to read, his mind a blank.

Then the door opened softly and he sprang to his feet. His flesh crept. The Hairless Mexican stood before him.

"Did I startle you?" he asked smiling. "I thought you would prefer me not to knock."

"Did anyone see you come in?"

"I was let in by the night-watchman; he was asleep when I rang and didn't even look at me. I'm sorry I'm so late, but I had to change."

The Hairless Mexican wore now the clothes he had travelled down in and his fair wig. It was extraordinary how different he looked. He was bigger and more flamboyant; the very shape of his face was altered. His eyes were shining and he seemed in excellent spirits. He gave Ashenden a glance.

"How white you are, my friend! Surely you're not nervous?"

"Have you got the documents?"

"No. He hadn't got them on him. This is all he had."

He put down on the table a bulky pocket-book and a passport.

"I don't want them," said Ashenden quickly. "Take them."

With a shrug of the shoulders the Hairless Mexican put the things back in his pocket.

"What was in his belt? You said he kept feeling round his middle."

"Only money. I've looked through the pocket-book. It contains nothing but private letters and photographs of women. He must have locked the documents in his grip before coming out with me this evening."

"Damn," said Ashenden.

"I've got the key of his room. We'd better go and look through his luggage."

Ashenden felt a sensation of sickness in the pit of his stomach. He hesitated. The Mexican smiled not unkindly.

"There's no risk, *amigo*," he said, as though he were reassuring a small boy, "but if you don't feel happy, I'll go alone."

"No, I'll come with you," said Ashenden.

"There's no one awake in the hotel and Mr. Andreadi won't disturb us. Take off your shoes if you like."

Ashenden did not answer. He frowned because he noticed that his hands were slightly trembling. He unlaced his shoes and slipped them off. The Mexican did the same.

"You'd better go first," he said. "Turn to the left and go straight along the corridor. It's number thirty-eight."

Ashenden opened the door and stepped out. The passage was dimly lit. It exasperated him to feel so nervous when he could not but be

aware that his companion was perfectly at ease. When they reached the door the Hairless Mexican inserted the key, turned the lock and went in. He switched on the light. Ashenden followed him and closed the door. He noticed that the shutters were shut.

"Now we're all right. We can take our time."

He took a bunch of keys out of his pocket, tried one or two and at last hit upon the right one. The suitcase was filled with clothes.

"Cheap clothes," said the Mexican contemptuously as he took them out. "My own principle is that it's always cheaper in the end to buy the best. After all one is a gentleman or one isn't a gentleman."

"Are you obliged to talk?" asked Ashenden.

"A spice of danger affects people in different ways. It only excites me, but it puts you in a bad temper, *amigo*."

"You see I'm scared and you're not," replied Ashenden with candour.

"It's merely a matter of nerves."

Meanwhile he felt the clothes, rapidly but with care, as he took them out. There were no papers of any sort in the suit-case. Then he took out his knife and slit the lining. It was a cheap piece and the lining was gummed to the material of which the suit-case was made. There was no possibility of anything being concealed in it.

"They're not here. They must be hidden in the room."

"Are you sure he didn't deposit them in some office? At one of the consulates for example?"

"He was never out of my sight for a moment except when he was getting shaved."

The Hairless Mexican opened the drawers and the cupboard. There was no carpet on the floor. He looked under the bed, in it, and under the mattress. His dark eyes shot up and down the room, looking for a hiding-place, and Ashenden felt that nothing escaped him.

"Perhaps he left them in charge of the clerk downstairs?"

"I should have known it. And he wouldn't dare. They're not here. I can't understand it."

He looked about the room irresolutely. He frowned in the attempt to guess at a solution of the mystery.

"Let's get out of here," said Ashenden.

"In a minute."

The Mexican went down on his knees, quickly and neatly folded the clothes, and packed them up again. He locked the bag and stood up. Then, putting out the light, he slowly opened the door and looked out. He beckoned to Ashenden and slipped into the passage. When Ashenden had followed him he stopped and locked the door, put the key in his pocket and walked with Ashenden to his room. When they were inside it and the bolt drawn Ashenden wiped his clammy hands and his forehead.

"Thank God, we're out of that!"

"There wasn't really the smallest danger. But what are we to do now? The Colonel will be angry that the papers haven't been found."

"I'm taking the five o'clock train to Rome. I shall wire for instructions there."

"Very well, I will come with you."

"I should have thought it would suit you better to get out of the country more quickly. There's a boat to-morrow that goes to Barcelona. Why don't you take that and if necessary I can come to see you there?"

The Hairless Mexican gave a little smile.

"I see that you are anxious to be rid of me. Well, I won't thwart a wish that your inexperience in these matters excuses. I will go to Barcelona. I have a visa for Spain."

Ashenden looked at his watch. It was a little after two. He had nearly three hours to wait. His companion comfortably rolled himself a cigarette.

"What do you say to a little supper?" he asked. "I'm as hungry as a wolf."

The thought of food sickened Ashenden, but he was terribly thirsty. He did not want to go out with the Hairless Mexican, but neither did he want to stay in that hotel by himself.

"Where could one go at this hour?"

"Come along with me. I'll find you a place."

Ashenden put on his hat and took his dispatch-case in his hand. They went downstairs. In the hall the porter was sleeping soundly on a mattress on the floor. As they passed the desk, walking softly in order

not to wake him, Ashenden noticed in the pigeon-hole belonging to his room a letter. He took it out and saw that it was addressed to him. They tiptoed out of the hotel and shut the door behind them. Then they walked quickly away. Stopping after a hundred yards or so under a lamp-post Ashenden took the letter out of his pocket and read it; it came from the Consulate and said: *The enclosed telegram arrived to-night and in case it is urgent I am sending it round to your hotel by messenger.* It had apparently been left some time before midnight while Ashenden was sitting in his room. He opened the telegram and saw that it was in code.

"Well, it'll have to wait," he said, putting it back in his pocket.

The Hairless Mexican walked as though he knew his way through the deserted streets and Ashenden walked by his side. At last they came to a tavern in a blind alley, noisome and evil, and this the Mexican entered.

"It's not the Ritz," he said, "but at this hour of the night it's only in a place like this that we stand a chance of getting something to eat."

Ashenden found himself in a long sordid room at one end of which a wizened young man sat at a piano; there were tables standing out from the wall on each side and against them benches. A number of persons, men and women, were sitting about. They were drinking beer and wine. The women were old, painted, and hideous; and their harsh gaiety was at once noisy and lifeless. When Ashenden and the Hairless Mexican came in they all stared and when they sat down at one of the tables Ashenden looked away in order not to meet the leering eyes, just ready to break into a smile, that sought his insinuatingly. The wizened pianist strummed a tune and several couples got up and began to dance. Since there were not enough men to go round some of the women danced together. The General ordered two plates of spaghetti and a bottle of Capri wine. When the wine was brought he drank a glassful greedily and then waiting for the *pasta* eyed the women who were sitting at the other tables.

"Do you dance?" he asked Ashenden. "I'm going to ask one of these girls to have a turn with me."

He got up and Ashenden watched him go up to one who had at

least flashing eyes and white teeth to recommend her; she rose and he put his arm round her. He danced well. Ashenden saw him begin talking; the woman laughed and presently the look of indifference with which she had accepted his offer changed to one of interest. Soon they were chatting gaily. The dance came to an end and putting her back at her table he returned to Ashenden and drank another glass of wine.

"What do you think of my girl?" he asked. "Not bad, is she? It does one good to dance. Why don't you ask one of them? This is a nice place, is it not? You can always trust me to find anything like this. I have an instinct."

The pianist started again. The woman looked at the Hairless Mexican and when with his thumb he pointed to the floor she jumped up with alacrity. He buttoned up his coat, arched his back and standing up by the side of the table waited for her to come to him. He swung her off, talking, smiling, and already he was on familiar terms with everyone in the room. In fluent Italian, with his Spanish accent, he exchanged badinage with one and the other. They laughed at his sallies. Then the waiter brought two heaped platefuls of macaroni and when the Mexican saw them he stopped dancing without ceremony and allowing his partner to get back to her table as she chose hurried to his meal.

"I'm ravenous," he said. "And yet I ate a good dinner. Where did you dine? You're going to eat some macaroni, aren't you?"

"I have no appetite," said Ashenden.

But he began to eat and to his surprise found that he was hungry. The Hairless Mexican ate with huge mouthfuls, enjoying himself vastly; his eyes shone and he was loquacious. The woman he had danced with had in that short time told him all about herself and he repeated now to Ashenden what she had said. He stuffed huge pieces of bread into his mouth. He ordered another bottle of wine.

"Wine?" he cried scornfully. "Wine is not a drink, only champagne; it does not even quench your thirst. Well, *amigo*, are you feeling better?"

"I'm bound to say I am," smiled Ashenden.

"Practice, that is all you want, practice."

He stretched out his hand to pat Ashenden on the arm.

"What's that?" cried Ashenden with a start. "What's that stain on your cuff?"

The Hairless Mexican gave his sleeve a glance.

"That? Nothing. It's only blood. I had a little accident and cut myself."

Ashenden was silent. His eyes sought the clock that hung over the door.

"Are you anxious about your train? Let me have one more dance and then I'll accompany you to the station."

The Mexican got up and with his sublime self-assurance seized in his arms the woman who sat nearest to him and danced away with her. Ashenden watched him moodily. He was a monstrous, terrible figure with that blond wig and his hairless face, but he moved with a matchless grace; his feet were small and seemed to hold the ground like the pads of a cat or a tiger; his rhythm was wonderful and you could not but see that the bedizened creature he danced with was intoxicated by his gestures. There was music in his toes and in the long arms that held her so firmly, and there was music in those long legs that seemed to move strangely from the hips. Sinister and grotesque though he was, there was in him now a feline elegance, even something of beauty, and you felt a secret, shameful fascination. To Ashenden he suggested one of those sculptures of the pre-Aztec hewers of stone, in which there is barbarism and vitality, something terrible and cruel, and yet withal a brooding and significant loveliness. All the same he would gladly have left him to finish the night by himself in that sordid dance-hall, but he knew that he must have a business conversation with him. He did not look forward to it without misgiving. He had been instructed to give Manuel Carmona certain sums in return for certain documents. Well, the documents were not forthcoming, and as for the rest—Ashenden knew nothing about that; it was no business of his. The Hairless Mexican waved gaily as he passed him.

"I will come the moment the music stops. Pay the bill and then I shall be ready."

Ashenden wished he could have seen into his mind. He could not

even make a guess at its workings. Then the Mexican, with his scented handkerchief wiping the sweat from his brow, came back.

"Have you had a good time, General?" Ashenden asked him.

"I always have a good time. Poor white trash, but what do I care? I like to feel the body of a woman in my arms and see her eyes grow languid and her lips part as her desire for me melts the marrow in her bones like butter in the sun. Poor white trash, but women."

They sallied forth. The Mexican proposed that they should walk and in that quarter, at that hour, there would have been little chance of finding a cab; but the sky was starry. It was a summer night and the air was still. The silence walked beside them like the ghost of a dead man. When they neared the station the houses seemed on a sudden to take on a greyer, more rigid line, and you felt that the dawn was at hand. A little shiver trembled through the night. It was a moment of apprehension and the soul for an instant was anxious; it was as though, inherited down the years in their countless millions, it felt a witless fear that perhaps another day would not break. But they entered the station and the night once more enwrapped them. One or two porters lolled about like stage-hands after the curtain has rung down and the scene is struck. Two soldiers in dim uniforms stood motionless.

The waiting-room was empty, but Ashenden and the Hairless Mexican went to sit in the most retired part of it.

"I still have an hour before my train goes. I'll just see what this cable's about."

He took it out of his pocket and from the dispatch-case got his code. He was not then using a very elaborate one. It was in two parts, one contained in a slim book and the other, given him on a sheet of paper and destroyed by him before he left allied territory, committed to memory. Ashenden put on his spectacles and set to work. The Hairless Mexican sat in a corner of the seat, rolling himself cigarettes and smoking; he sat there placidly, taking no notice of what Ashenden did, and enjoyed his well-earned repose. Ashenden deciphered the groups of numbers one by one and as he got it out jotted down each word on a piece of paper. His method was to abstract his mind from the sense till he had finished, since he had discovered that if you took notice of the words as they came along you often jumped to a conclusion and

sometimes were led into error. So he translated quite mechanically, without paying attention to the words as he wrote them one after the other. When at last he had done he read the complete message. It ran as follows:

Constantine Andreadi has been detained by illness at Piræus. He will be unable to sail. Return Geneva and await instructions.

At first Ashenden could not understand. He read it again. He shook from head to foot. Then, for once robbed of his self-possession, he blurted out, in a hoarse, agitated and furious whisper:

"You bloody fool, you've killed the wrong man."

From *The Tears of Autumn* (1974)

Charles McCarry (1930–   )

Charles McCarry spent twenty-five years as a CIA officer in Europe, and his novels, featuring the American intelligence officer Paul Christopher, bear the authenticity of his experience. McCarry should be considered one of the most sophisticated writers working at the height of the espionage genre. The Tears of Autumn *is a reflection on the Kennedy assassination, viewed in the light of the coup d'état that overthrew Ngo Dinh Diem, the president of South Vietnam, in 1963.*

One

Paul Christopher had been loved by two women who could not understand why he had stopped writing poetry. Cathy, his wife, imagined that some earlier girl had poisoned his gift. She became hysterical in bed, believing that she could draw the secret out of his body and into her own, as venom is sucked from a snakebite. Christopher did not try to tell her the truth; she had no right to know it and could not have understood it. Cathy wanted nothing except a poem about herself. She

wanted to watch their lovemaking in a sonnet. Christopher could not write it. She punished him with lovers and went back to America.

Now his new girl had found, in a flea market on the Ponte Sisto, the book of verses he had published fifteen years earlier, before he became a spy. Christopher read her letter in the Bangkok airport; her headlong sentences, covering the crisp airmail sheet, were like a photograph of her face. She made him smile. His flight was called over the loud-speaker in Thai; he waited for the English announcement before he moved toward the door, so that no one who might be watching him should guess that he understood the local language. His girl was wait-ing in Rome, changed by her discovery that he had once been able to describe what he felt.

Christopher walked across the scorched tarmac into the cool Ameri-can airplane. He didn't smile at the stewardess; his teeth were black with the charcoal he had chewed to cure his diarrhea. He had been traveling down the coast of Asia for three weeks, and he had spent the last night of his journey in Bangkok with a man he knew was going to die. The man was a Vietnamese named Luong. He thought Christo-pher's name was Crawford.

They had met in the evening, when it was cool enough to remain outside, and walked together along the river while Luong delivered his report. Later, at a restaurant, the two of them ate Thai food, drank champagne, and talked in French about the future. Just before dawn, Christopher gave his agent money to pay for the girl, quiet and smooth as a child, who sat down beside Luong and placed her small hand in his lap. Luong smiled, closed his eyes, and ran his fingertips over the flowered material of the girl's dress and onto the skin of her neck. "No difference, silk and silk," he said. "Can you loan me some *baht*?" Christopher handed Luong two dirty Thai bank notes. Luong, his face reddened by drink, started to leave with the girl, then came back to Christopher. "Is it true that these girls will dance on your spine before making love?" he asked. Christopher nodded and gave him another hundred-*baht* note.

Christopher paid the bartender and left. He walked through the city with its smell of waste: dead vegetation, open drains, untreated diseases of the skin. The people who slept in the streets were awaken-

ing as the sun, coming up on the flat horizon, flashed into the city like light through the lens of a camera. A leper, opening his eyes and seeing a white man, showed Christopher his sores. Christopher gave him a coin and walked on.

When he reached the river, he hired a boatman to take him to the floating market. He had three hours to kill before going to the airport. It was cooler on the river, and he was just another white man among dozens who had risen early to be paddled past the grinning naked boys standing in the roiled waters and the market boats filled with odorless flowers and lovely fruits that had no taste. He bought some limes and shared them with the boatman.

The night before, in the toilet of a bar, Luong had put his thumbprint on a receipt for the money Christopher brought to him, his monthly stipend. While Luong cleaned the ink off his thumb with whiskey from the glass he had carried with him into the toilet, Christopher showed him the envelope. It was filled with Swiss francs, new blue hundred-franc notes. "I'd better keep this till morning," Christopher said. Luong, who always ended the night with a girl, nodded. They agreed on a plan for a meeting in the morning, checking their watches to be sure that they showed the same time.

Now, as Luong slept, Christopher took the envelope out of his coat pocket. He put the stamp pad inside with the money, sealed it, and dropped it over the side of the boat. The white envelope twisted in the moving brown water of the Chao Phraya and disappeared.

Christopher smiled at his own gesture. It was not likely that Luong would understand the message. He trusted Christopher. Luong knew, of course, that agents were sometimes sacrificed, but he did not consider himself an agent. He did things for Christopher and Christopher did things for him: though Christopher was white and Luong was brown, they had the same beliefs. "This money," he asked once, "it's good money, from people like us?" Christopher replied, "Yes." Luong was a subtle man, but Christopher, throwing ten thousand francs in secret funds into a tropical river, did not really believe that the Vietnamese would understand that the loss of the money meant the loss of Christopher's protection. It was more likely that he'd think there had been a mistake, that Christopher would come back, as he had always done. Luong would go back to Saigon and die.

Christopher was in no danger. If the secret police in Saigon interrogated Luong before they killed him, he would speak about a blond American named Crawford who believed in social justice and spoke unaccented French. Christopher had what no American is supposed to have, an ear for languages. He registered everything he heard, sense and tone, so that he understood even Oriental languages he had never studied after hearing them spoken for a few days. This trick was the fossil of his talent for poetry.

———

"Luong can vomit all over the floor about you," said Wolkowicz, the man from the station in Saigon. "The Vietnamese are never going to believe that an American can speak French the way you do. They'll figure some Frenchman has been passing himself off to Luong as an American, and we'll be off the hook."

"At Luong's expense. There's no reason to let him be arrested. You know they don't have any evidence he's tied up with the VC. He's not."

Wolkowicz put bread in his mouth and softened it with a sip of wine so he could chew it. Wolkowicz was self-conscious about his false teeth, but not for any cosmetic reason: his own teeth had been pulled by a Japanese interrogator in Burma during the Second World War, and there was a belief in the profession that a man who had been tortured, and stood up under it, could not afterward be trusted. He would know too well what to expect.

"Since when do facts make any difference?" Wolkowicz asked. "There's nothing you can do about this, Christopher."

"Luong is in Bangkok, waiting to meet me. I can tell him to stay there."

"What good would that do? Nhu told us he was going to grab Luong because he wanted to see if we'd warn him. If we do, Nhu will know we've been running Luong. We don't need that. We have enough trouble with the bastard without giving him proof that Luong and that noisy little political party of his have an American case officer."

"They'll kill him," Christopher said.

"They'll kill him in Bangkok if they have to. We can't salvage him without blowing you and the whole political operation. One agent isn't worth it."

"Do me a favor, will you? Call him by his name. He's not an ab-

straction. He's five feet six inches tall, twenty-nine years old, married, three children, a university graduate. For three years he's done everything he's been asked to do. We got him into this."

"All right, so he's flesh and blood," Wolkowicz said. "He proved that when he struck out in Vientiane last month."

"He's not supposed to be an FI operator. He's paid to act, not to steal information. Luong was not the only one who couldn't find out what Do Minh Kha was doing in Vientiane in September."

"Action is what I wanted from Luong. He's supposed to be a boyhood chum of Do's. He should have walked in on him, like I suggested."

"Barney, Do would have shot him. He's a chief of section of the North Vietnamese intelligence service. Do you think he doesn't know who Luong works for?"

"I don't know what Do knows," Wolkowicz said. "I know Luong struck out on me."

"Luong reported what he saw—Do and the girl, constantly together for three days. At least he brought you back photographs."

"With no identification of the girl. Very useful."

Wolkowicz called for the check. They were sitting at a table at the Cercle Sportif. "Do you notice anything unusual about the girl in the white bikini?" he asked.

Christopher looked at a French girl who had just pulled herself out of the pool. She was wringing the water out of her long bleached hair, and her body curved like a dancer's. "No," he said.

"She has no navel. Look again."

It was true. The girl's belly was smooth except for a thin white surgical scar that ran through her tan into the waist of her bathing suit.

"She had an umbilical hernia," said Wolkowicz, "so she asked them to remove it when she had a cesarean. The clever Vietnamese just removed her belly button altogether."

The waiter went away with the signed chit.

"Christopher," said Wolkowicz, "you're a conscientious officer, everybody knows that. But Luong is not your child. He's an agent. Go to Bangkok. Meet him. Give him his pay. Wipe his eyes. But leave well enough alone."

"You mean let Nhu have him."

"Nhu may not live forever," said Wolkowicz.

———

On the airplane in Bangkok, a stewardess handed Christopher a hot towel. Stewardesses disliked him. He had no sexual thoughts about them; combed and odorless, in their uniforms, they seemed as artificial as airline food and drink. He had been in nine countries in twenty days, flying in and out of climates and time zones, changing languages and his name at each landing. His appetites and his emotions were suspended.

The jet turned over the city. Sunlight flashed on a pagoda that quivered on the brown plain like a column of crystal; Christopher knew that the pagoda was faced with broken blue china saucers, smashed in the hold of an English sailing ship by a storm a century before. He stood up when the seat-belt warning went out and removed his jacket. The jacket was wool because he was flying into a cold climate, and it was clammy with sweat. It was the last day of October, 1963, and it would be chilly in Paris, where he was going to make his report.

Christopher organized his mind, sorting out what he had learned and what he had done in the past twenty days. When he closed his eyes, he saw the girl who had no navel beside the pool in Saigon, the brown girl he had bought in Bangkok for Luong, and finally the girl in Rome who was waiting with his book of poems to make love to him.

> Desire is not a thing that stops with death,
> but joins the corpse and fetus breath to breath. . . .

Christopher remembered what he had written well enough, but not so well as he remembered what had made him write. His grandfather's death had given him his first poem, eight quatrains in Tennyson's voice. The old man, lying in a hospital with the tubes removed from his arms so that he might die in his own time, thought that he was in a railroad station; as he ran for his train he met his friends, and they were young again: "Mae Foster! Your cheeks are as red as the rose! . . . Caroline! You're wearing the white dress I always loved!" Christopher's last poem was written in his own voice after he slept with a girl whose

brother, who trusted Christopher as Luong did, had died for nothing. She sobbed all through the act.

After the girl had gone to sleep, Christopher wrote a sonnet and left it beside her; rhyme and meter came as easily to him as the technique of sex, and had as little to do with love. This happened in Geneva, on a night when snow had fallen, so that the gray city under its winter clouds gave off a little light. Christopher, as he stepped off the curb, was nearly hit by a car. The incident did not frighten him. It interrupted his behavior, as a slight electric shock will cause a schizophrenic to cross over in the mind from one personality to another. He saw what his poems had become: another part of his cover, a way of beautifying what he did. He went back to the bedroom of the sleeping girl and burned what he had written. She found the ashes when she woke, and knowing what they were because Christopher had written her other poems, considered them more romantic than the sonnet.

———

"Do you wish to sleep?" the stewardess asked.

"No," said Christopher. "Give me a large whiskey."

2

Christopher walked out of the Aérogare des Invalides, under the bare elms along the Seine. Autumn chill, smelling of wet pavement and the river, went through his clothes and dried the sweat on his spine. He walked across the Pont Alexandre-III, where he had once kissed his wife and tasted the orange she had eaten. The winged horses on the roof of the Grand Palais were black against the electric glow above the city. "The French do have the courage of their vulgarity," Cathy had said when, as a bride, she had first seen the colossal bronze animals trying to fly away with the ugliest building in France.

There were two policemen on the bridge. Each carried a submachine gun under his cape. Christopher walked by them and waited until he was in the shadows at the other end of the bridge before checking again to see that he was not being followed. Christopher knew Paris better than any city in America. He had learned to speak French in Paris, had written his book of poems and discovered how to take girls to bed there, but he no longer loved it. More, even, than most

places in the world, Paris was a city where his nationality was deplored and his profession was despised; he could not stay there long without being watched.

Near the Madeleine, Christopher went into a café, bought a *jeton,* and called his case officer. When Tom Webster answered, Christopher heard the click of the poor equipment the French used to tap Webster's telephone. The volume of their speech faded and increased as the recording machine in the vault under the Invalides pulled power out of the line.

"Tom? Calisher here."

They spoke in English because Webster did not understand French easily; he was slightly deaf, and he had learned Arabic as a young officer. The effort, Webster said, had been so great that it had destroyed his capacity to learn any other foreign tongue.

"I'm staying with Margaret tonight," Christopher said.

"Then you've got better things to do than come over for a drink," Webster said.

Christopher smiled. Webster's tone of voice told him that he was proud of this quick-witted reply; he thought it made the conversation sound natural. Webster paused, sorting out with an almost audible effort the simple code they used on the telephone.

"Let's have lunch," he said at last. "Tomorrow, one o'clock at the Taillevent. I know you like the lobster there."

"Fine," Christopher said, and hung up. By the time he had climbed the stairs and ordered a beer at the bar, he had overcome the smile Webster's voice had brought to his lips. Webster was not very good at telephone codes. After seven years, he knew that any name beginning with a *C* was Christopher's telephone name. He was able to remember that "Margaret" was the euphemism for the safe house in the rue Bonaparte to which Christopher carried a key. It was the time-and-place formula that confused him. Christopher had spent many hours waiting alone in expensive restaurants like a disconsolate social climber because Webster was never sure whether to add or subtract seven hours from the time stated over the telephone for a meeting. Lunch at the Taillevent at one o'clock meant dinner at Webster's apartment at eight o'clock.

In other ways, Webster was a skillful professional. When he was still in his twenties, he had saved a kingdom in the Near East by penetrating a revolutionary organization and turning it against itself, so that the terrorists murdered each other instead of their monarch. The king he saved was still his friend. Like all good intelligence officers, Webster knew how to form friendships and use the friends he made. No human action surprised him or touched his emotions.

Webster and Christopher needed to make no allowances for one another. They lived in a world where all personal secrets were known. They had been investigated before they were employed; everything that could be remembered and repeated about them was on file, the truth along with the gossip and the lies. Gossip and lies were valuable: much can be understood about a man by the untruths that are told about him. Once a year, on the anniversary of their employment, they submitted to a lie detector test. The machine measured their breathing, the sweat on their palms, their blood pressure and pulse, and it knew whether they had stolen money from the government, submitted to homosexual advances, been doubled by the opposition, committed adultery. The test was called the "flutter." They would ask of a new man, "Has he been fluttered?" If the answer was no, the man was told nothing, not even the true name of his case officer.

To Webster, the flutter was the ordeal of brotherhood. He believed that those who went through it were cold in their minds, trained to observe and report but never to judge. They looked for flaws in men and were never surprised to find them: the polygraph had taught them that guilt can be read on human skin with a meter—that they knew what all men were.

They had no politics. They had no morals, except among themselves. They lied to everyone except their government, even to their children and the women they entered, about their purposes and their work. Yet they cared about nothing but the truth. They would corrupt men, suborn women, steal, remove governments to obtain the truth, cleansed of rationalization and every other modifer. To one another, they spoke only the truth. Their friendships were deeper than marriage. They needed each other's trust as other men needed love.

Webster recited these things to Christopher when he was far gone in drink. They were true enough. Webster, a phlegmatic man, had tears in his eyes; he had lost a young American in Accra. The boy had been shot by members of the Ghanaian service, who thought murder was the way in which secret agents dealt with their enemies. "What that kid really liked about this life is what we all like," Christopher said. "It's like living in a book for boys." Webster was outraged; he leaped at Christopher. "But he died! How many have you seen die? I can name them for you." Christopher gave his old friend another drink. "No need; I remember," he said. "But, Tom, be honest. If it had been you those black amateurs shot, what would have been your last thought?" Webster shook his head to clear the whiskey from his voice: "I'd laugh. It would be such a goddamn joke of a death." Christopher lifted his glass. "Absent friends," he said.

Webster was short and muscular. He had once held the shot-put record at Yale. He wore the clothes he had had in college, fifteen years before, and shoes he had inherited from his father that were a half size too small for him. Though he was homely and had no luck with women, he was amused by Christopher's good looks and the way girls came to him. "I'm the portrait you keep in your attic," he told Christopher. "Each time you sin, I get another wart."

Christopher, finishing his beer, remembered this and laughed aloud as in his mind he saw Webster as clearly as in life. The bartender took his glass and didn't ask if he wanted another drink.

———

In the safe house, an apartment on the sixth floor of an old building behind the Ecole des Beaux-Arts, Christopher ate the food that had been left in the refrigerator for him, took a shower, and sat down at a portable typewriter. He worked steadily on his report until he heard the morning traffic moving on the quais along the Seine. He wrote nothing about Luong, except to include the receipt for the money he had thrown into the river. He burned his notes and the typewriter ribbon and flushed the ashes down the toilet.

Then, placing the typed report inside the pillowcase, he went to bed and slept for twelve hours. He dreamed that his wife, standing

with the light behind her in a room in Madrid where he had slept with another girl, told him that she had given birth; even asleep, his mind knew that he had no child, and he ended the dream.

3

Tom Webster's apartment in the avenue Hoche had once belonged to a member of the Bonapartean nobility. Its salon preserved the taste of the marquis and his descendants. Caryatids with broken noses stood at the corners of the ceiling; rosy women picnicked on the grassy banks of a painted brook that flowed along the wainscoting.

"Tom makes fun of the decor," said Sybille, his wife. "But really, in his heart of hearts, he thinks it's *très luxe*."

"There's no need for all that before the other guests come," Webster said. "Paul knows that the chief decoration in all our houses is my scrotum, which you nailed to the wall years and years ago, Sybille."

"Does Paul know that?" Sybille asked. "But then he's trained to notice everything, isn't he? Paul, Tom is always so glad to see you. He tells me in bed that you're absolutely the best in the whole company. In *bed*—what is the significance of that, do you suppose?"

Sybille Webster was a quick woman who liked to pretend that she was married to a slow man. Her fine face was more beautiful in photographs than in life. There were pictures of her in every room, and these were an embarrassment to her; she cleared away the frames when she invited strangers into the house. Webster married her thinking that he would want sex with no one else for the rest of his life, and he still gazed through his glasses at his wife as if she were, at all times, whirling about the room in a ballet costume. It was he who had taken the photographs.

Christopher took the drink Sybille had made for him and kissed her on the cheek. He handed his report to Webster. "Read the first two contact reports, if you have a minute," he said. "You may want to send something tonight."

"Why are you so good at the work, Paul?" asked Sybille. "Do you know?"

"People trust him," Webster said.

"Do they? Wouldn't you think that word would get around?"

"Oh, I think it has, Sybille," Christopher said. "You notice that Tom never leaves us alone."

"He's been that way ever since he started to flag," Sybille said. "That was, oh, the fourth day of our honeymoon. He took me to New York—the Astor Hotel. I was just a simple virgin from Tidewater Virginia. So many memories. Tom used to go to the Astor when he was a soldier and meet interesting people in the bar."

Sybille, sitting on the arm of Christopher's chair with her legs crossed, pointed a finger at Webster, who never gave any sign that he heard the things she had said about him.

Webster tapped the report. "This is hotter than a firecracker," he said. "Do you think Diem and Nhu are really in touch with the North?"

"Why not? They sure as hell don't trust Washington anymore."

"What was Nhu like at the party?"

"Polite. I didn't ask him to his face what he was planning. Wolkowicz didn't like that."

"Screw Wolkowicz. All he wants to do is clean out wastebaskets."

"Well, he's expected to know everything that happens in Vietnam," Christopher said. "He doesn't see any sense in the things I do, running people like Luong. It upsets the police liaison. In a way, he's being logical. What good is building democratic institutions to Wolkowicz? Diem and Nhu don't like it, and they know who's doing it."

"What about Luong?" Webster asked. He drained his glass and held it out to Sybille to be refilled.

"Nhu is going to pick him up and kill him. They'll torture him a little first for appearances' sake."

Webster stared at Christopher for a second, then took off his glasses and rubbed his eyes. "Did you warn him off?"

"I was instructed not to," Christopher said.

Webster put his glasses back on his nose and resumed reading.

Sybille brought them another drink. "It surely is difficult for me not to overhear some of the things you two say to each other," she said. "Paul, do you want to play tennis with me tomorrow?"

"I'm going to Rome tonight."

Sybille raised her hands in protest. "But dinner!" she cried.

Christopher told her that his plane didn't leave until two in the

morning, and Sybille went on with what she wanted to say as if he had not spoken to her. He wondered how Webster had found a way to propose to her; Sybille sometimes answered questions a day or a week after they had been asked.

"You don't know what a coup you're going to witness," she said. "Tom has invited Dennis Foley, the President's *right-hand man*. And I remember that Harry McKinney is out of town, so I asked his lovely wife, Peggy, who thinks *she's* the counselor to the embassy instead of her husband. Peggy thought that about herself even when we were at Sweet Briar together. It's going to be a treat, Paul."

Webster put Christopher's report into his briefcase and locked it. "Foley's brother and I used to put the shot together," he said. "The brother's all right. I don't know this one."

"You've been to lots of meetings with him all week," Sybille said. "The entire embassy has been meeting with him. Foley came to Paris to tell de Gaulle who's really running the world. President Kennedy thought he ought to know—only de Gaulle won't give Foley an appointment. Wonderful JFK! Oh, that man is so sexy. He squeezed this little hand when he was here with the First Lady and I said, 'I, too, think you're absolutely irresistible, Mr. President.'"

"What did he say to you, Sybille?"

"He said, 'How nice to see you,' and sort of flung me down the reception line toward Jackie. Then she said the same thing and flung me again. They shake hands like a couple of black belts."

Webster grasped Sybille's chin. "Sybille," he said, "let's not have any of this Southern-belle chatter when Foley gets here. He doesn't know you."

"Oh, we're all going to be very respectful, Tom. I do think this administration has raised the whole tone of American life. Why, Peggy McKinney has been reading Proust in the original French and learning the names of all those new African countries. She says the people of Zimbabwe want rice and respect. I always thought they wanted money."

"Sybille, how about making this your last martini?" Webster said.

"I have to do something while you and Paul talk about betrayal and torture."

"We don't enjoy it," Webster said.

"Oh," said Sybille, "I think it makes you happy enough."

4

Dennis Foley, arriving with Peggy McKinney, did not have the air of a man who expected to have a good time. He nodded to Sybille and to Christopher when he was introduced, but did not offer to shake hands. Foley was a bony man who had played basketball in college, and he had still the manner, self-aware and faintly contemptuous, of the athlete. He had a habit of touching his own body as he talked, running a hand over the waves of stiff black hair on the back of his head, unstrapping his large gold watch and massaging his wrist. His eyes, pale blue with tiny irises, looked beyond the person with whom he was conversing. His face, which changed color rather than expression when he was pleased or annoyed by something that was said to him, was roughened by acne scars. Foley wore a two-button suit with a tin PT-109 clasp on a Sulka tie. Like President Kennedy, he drank daiquiris without sugar and smoked long, thin cigars. He had been talking to Peggy McKinney when he arrived, and he moved her across the vast room, away from the others, to continue the conversation. As Sybille and Christopher watched, Peggy lit Foley's cigar for him with a table lighter.

"Observe his gestures, listen to his voice," Sybille said. "He's turning into a JFK. All these New Frontier people are like that, have you noticed? It must be some royal virus. The closer you are to the throne, the worse the infection. Poor Peggy McKinney—see how she's trying to get everything just right? Way over here in Paris, all she can do is read Proust and take up touch football. She plays left end in the Bois de Boulogne every Sunday."

Across the room, Foley nodded brusquely, as if Peggy had told him everything he was interested in hearing. He brought his empty glass to Sybille.

"This is quite a place," Foley said. "How did you find it?"

"Oh, the French have this idea that Americans will rent *anything*," Sybille replied.

Foley's glance ran like an adder's tongue over Sybille's face and body, and a corner of his mouth lifted, as if he were rejecting a sexual

invitation. "I'll bet you're the wittiest woman in Paris," he said. "I'd like some soda water. Just plain, with an ice cube."

Sybille took his glass and went to the bar. Foley turned to Christopher. "Webster tells me you're just back from Saigon," he said.

"Yes."

"I understand you talked to Diem and his brother."

"I saw them at a reception Nhu gave. It was more a matter of overhearing what they said to others."

Foley took the glass Sybille handed to him and turned his back on her. "I've read some of your stuff in the magazine," he said. "I had a feeling you were holding back. Don't you write everything you know?"

"Usually. I don't write what I don't know."

"Look, let's cut the crap. I've got eyes—you work with Webster."

"Do I?"

"I can confirm it in thirty seconds if I have to. You're fresh from Saigon. You seem to circulate at pretty high levels out there. I'd like to hear your reactions. If they're worth it, I'll pass them on to the boss when I see him tomorrow."

The others overheard. Webster fell silent and put a cold pipe between his teeth. Peggy McKinney's face, as smooth as an ingenue's, was suddenly alight with curiosity; though she saw his name listed in the front of a great magazine and read his articles, she had never believed Christopher's cover story.

"The Americans are talking to themselves," Christopher said. "The Vietnamese say that the U.S. is working up to a coup to remove the Ngos."

"We know that the ruling family, and Nhu and his wife especially, are rabidly anti-American. What about that?"

Christopher shrugged.

"You think the U.S. government can work with a man like Diem?" Foley asked.

"Maybe not. He wants to stop the war and get us out of there. His brother is talking to the North. They have relatives in Hanoi, and Ho and Diem know each other from the old days."

"That's beautiful. Do you think we can countenance their talking to Ho Chi Minh behind our backs?"

Webster had begun to move across the room toward Foley and Christopher. Foley moved a step closer to Christopher, as if to prevent anyone stepping between them.

"They asked for our help," he said. "We've committed our power. You suggest that we stand by, tolerate corruption and wink at what amounts to Fascism, and let the whole project go down the drain?"

"I don't know that it would make much difference, except in terms of American domestic politics."

Foley's face had gone red. He tapped Christopher's chest with a blunt forefinger.

"The freedom of a people is involved," he said, "and that's all that's involved. If you think we're holding on in Vietnam because we're afraid of losing the next election, you don't know a hell of a lot about John F. Kennedy or the men around him."

"I've got no answer to that, Mr. Foley."

Webster put a hand on Foley's arm. "Sybille says dinner is ready," he said.

Foley continued to stare into Christopher's face. "What do you suggest we do out there?" he asked. "Nothing?"

"Sometimes," Christopher answered, "that's the best thing to do."

"Well, buddy, that's not the style any longer."

Foley put his glass into Webster's hand and strode into the dining room with Sybille and Peggy McKinney trailing after him.

5

At dinner, Foley's mood improved. He entertained Sybille on his right and Peggy McKinney on his left with stories about the President.

"There are dogs and kids, great books and great paintings and good music all over the White House," he said. "It's human again, the way it must have been under Franklin Roosevelt. If I want to see the boss, I just go in. You know you'll come out of there with a decision. The door is wide open on the world. He's likely to pick up the phone and call some little twirt way down the ladder in the Labor Department. Imagine, you're forty and gray-faced, wearing a suit from Robert Hall, and for fifteen years you haven't even been able to get an office with a window. Then—*ring* and 'Mr. Snodgrass, this is the President. What the

hell are you doing about migrant workers today?' It stirs up the tired blood." Foley looked around the table at the smiles of his listeners.

"The bureaucracy can use a little of that, believe me," said Peggy McKinney. "God, how we've needed to bring brains and style back into the government. The embassy just *crackles* with ideas and energy. *De l'audace, et encore de l'audace*—that's what the foreign policy of a great nation should be."

"Christopher was just telling me the opposite," Foley said.

"Oh? Well, so many of Tom's friends have to be cautious."

"What do you mean by that?" Sybille asked, with her elbow on the table and her wineglass held against her cheek.

"Oh, Sybille, come along now. We all know about Tom's friends," Peggy McKinney said. "Is it true," she asked Foley, "that the President putts when he thinks? I mean, does he really get out his putter and knock golf balls around the Oval Office? I think that's so lovely, do say it's true. I just devour all this gossipy stuff. You really don't have to humor me."

"I don't mind. I've just spent a week listening to Couve de Murville. Believe me, you're a welcome change," Foley said. "Yes, the boss putts occasionally. He'll do it at the damnedest times. The other day a couple of us came in with a recommendation. It was serious stuff. A decision had to be made—the kind of decision that would drive me, for instance, into agony. But his mind is like crystal. He's right on top of everything. He knew the situation—*felt* it, if you will, better than any of us. We gave him some new information. He absorbed it. We gave him the options. He didn't say a word at first. He got up, grabbed his putter, lined up a shot, and tapped it across the rug. We all watched the ball roll. Somehow—this will sound corny, but it's true—we all suddenly saw that golf ball as the symbol of the fate of a nation. Not a very big nation, not our nation, but a nation. The ball ran straight into the cup. 'Okay,' said the boss. 'Go.' There's never been another like him."

Sybille turned to Christopher. "Paul has just seen a president out in Vietnam," she said. "A *little* president. Do tell, Paul."

"Oh," said Peggy. "Diem or Ziem, or whatever his name is. Horrid man."

"I'm interested," Foley said.

"There's not much to tell," Christopher said. "I stood by while he talked to somebody else. Or, rather, listened. The other man was an American."

"Who's that?" Foley asked.

"Carson Wendell. He's a Republican from California."

"I know about him," Foley said. "What poison is he spreading?"

"I don't think you want to hear it, Mr. Foley."

"Now I do," Foley said.

"You may not like this," Christopher said. "Wendell hates you people. He said Kennedy ran a dishonest, dishonorable campaign in 1960—lying about a missile gap that didn't exist and inventing a USIA report that was supposed to show American prestige abroad was at an all-time low."

"Losers have to have some excuse," Foley said. "What else?"

"Wendell told Nhu that Kennedy wasn't elected President—Nixon was. He claimed there's evidence that votes were stolen in Illinois and a couple of other states where there was a small difference in the popular vote. The Democrats are in the White House by fraud, according to Wendell. He was very circumstantial, citing numbers and precincts to Nhu."

Peggy McKinney beat her fist on Sybille's tablecloth. "I've never heard such slander," she cried. "That man's passport ought to be taken away from him! I mean, *Christ.* . . ."

Foley unwrapped a cigar. "What did Nhu say to all that?" he asked.

"Nothing. I had a feeling he'd heard it all before."

Peggy McKinney opened her mouth to speak. Foley laid a hand on her arm. "People like Wendell and Nhu don't count," he said. "Power counts—and the right people are in power. I think we'll stay in power for quite a while." He grinned for the first time all evening, and sipped his wine. "In fact, if I can use one of the Republicans' more famous phrases, I think Mr. Nixon can look forward to at least twenty years of treason."

"Wit is back in the White House," said Peggy McKinney with tears of laughter in her eyes. "Let's drink to that."

6

Sybille led her guests into the salon for coffee. Peggy McKinney stood with Foley, her feet placed at right angles like a model's. She wore a pink Chanel suit, pearls, and a half-dozen golden bracelets on her right wrist. With her thin, nervous body and her bold features, she might have been taken for a Frenchwoman who had affairs. That, she told Foley, was the impression she had cultivated until the last election; the Kennedys had made her want to be an American again.

Tom Webster had said nothing during dinner. The evening had been spoiled for him by outsiders. Christopher operated all the time on hostile ground; in every country but his own he was a criminal. Outsiders, who did not know how fast betrayal traveled, could do him harm, perhaps even kill him, by knowing his name and speaking it at a cocktail party. Tonight Webster had entrusted Christopher's identity to two people who had no right to know it. He put his hand on Christopher's shoulder and began to speak.

He never got the words out. The doorbell rang and Webster went to answer it, closing the door behind him so that no other stranger could catch a glimpse of Christopher. The others went on talking; Christopher heard Webster speaking English in the hall.

When he came back, he held a perforated embassy envelope in his hand. He opened it and read the cable it contained.

"Wonderful," Webster said in a flat tone. "There's been a coup d'etat in Saigon. Some generals have seized power. The Saigon station says the coup has succeeded."

"What about Diem and Nhu?" Foley asked. He took the long white cable out of Webster's hand and read it. Peggy McKinney, not cleared to read secret traffic, stepped back discreetly; she gazed at Foley and her eyes danced.

"No one knows," Webster said. "The ambassador talked to Diem and offered him asylum, but he didn't accept."

"He's a dead man," Christopher said.

Foley handed the cable back to Webster. His face was expressionless.

Christopher watched Sybille put her coffee cup down, very gently, on the table. She sat in a corner of the sofa and looked out the window. Christopher, remembering the anecdote about the golf ball that sym-

bolized a nation, stared at Foley, but the presidential assistant did not glance his way.

Tom Webster went to answer the ringing telephone. When he returned his hair was disheveled. "Diem is dead," he said. "So is Nhu. They were shot by a young officer in the back of an M-113 armored personnel carrier."

"American aid," said Peggy McKinney.

Foley let out a long breath through his nose and made a chopping gesture, as if to drive home a point.

Peggy McKinney, flushed and smiling, took five small running steps toward the middle of the room. Planting her sharp heels in the carpet, legs apart, she said, "All together, folks—three cheers!"

Lifting her thin arm, bracelets jangling, she cried, "Hip, hip, hooray!" She repeated the cheer three times. No one joined in.

Sybille put a fist to her mouth; Tom Webster fumbled for a pocket comb and ran it through his hair.

"Paul," Peggy cried, pointing a long finger. "Did you do this? I'll bet you did, you sly spy—you were just out there in your false mustache."

"No," Christopher said. "I didn't do it and I don't know who did. I hope it really was the Vietnamese."

"Oh, come *on*," Peggy said.

"Peggy, I'm going to tell you once more. I didn't know anything about this, and I want that to be clear to you. Don't give me credit for murder, if you don't mind."

"Murder?" said Peggy. *"Surgery."*

"Jesus Christ," Sybille said. "Excuse me." She left the room.

"Did I say something?" Peggy asked, touching Foley's sleeve. "You'd think Sybille would be a little tougher, considering Tom's line of work."

"I guess Sybille's got the idea that assassination is foul work," Christopher said.

"Well, she can shed tears for both of us," Peggy said. "What happened tonight—what's the date? November 1, 1963—may show the world that the United States is going to take the initiative for change. God knows they need to wake up to the reality of power in this world."

"You think assassination is the way to wake them up?"

"Oh, Paul, come on—a petty Asiatic dictator and a secret-police chief."

Christopher said, "Well, I have a plane to catch."

Peggy shook hands with him. Foley stayed where he was, across the room, looking Christopher up and down as if he wanted to remember every detail of his appearance.

In the hall, Webster helped Christopher into his raincoat. "There's one thing about this," he said. "Luong should be all right."

"Maybe," Christopher said. "I don't think they'd have had time to take him with them."

Sybille came into the hall on tiptoe. She put her arms around Christopher. "Sorry I fled, love," she said. "I've reached the age where everything reminds me of something that happened in the past. Wherever we go, it's corpse after corpse. God, how I hate death and politics."

———

Christopher walked up the shallow hill to the Etoile and found a taxi. The streets shone with rain. No one else was out walking. His mouth was dry with the metallic aftertaste of wine. He closed his eyes and tried to hear the whine of the taxi's tires: he did not want to use any of his senses. In his mind, as if it were a clear photograph projected on a screen, he saw Molly's face, framed in russet hair and filled with belief. He had a sexual thought, his first in three weeks: it was a memory of the sun on her skin.

Two

They were in Molly's bed when she asked him about his poems. She lay on an elbow, her lips a little swollen, a strip of yellow sunlight running through her hair and across her cheek.

"Why didn't you ever tell me about your poetry?" Molly asked. " 'How odd,' I thought, when I saw the traditional slim volume, all covered with coffee stains, lying in a barrow on the Ponte Sisto. 'Here's a chap with my lover's name who writes poetry.' Then I read them, and it was your voice, you infamous wretch."

"I think I'd like dinner at Dal Bolognese tonight," Christopher said.

"Ah, things of the flesh and things of the spirit. Such an odd combination in an American. I want to know what you were like when you wrote those verses."

"Young."

"What was she like, the girl in the sonnets?"

"Oh, Molly—that was fifteen years ago. I invented her."

"Were you the man of her dreams?"

"She didn't like me at all, and when the book was published she liked me even less. She said people would think she wasn't a virgin."

"But you loved her."

"I was crazy about her."

"What was her name? Tell."

"Shirley."

"Shirley? Jesus—didn't *that* discourage you?"

"All right, what was the name of your first love?"

"Paul Christopher," Molly said. "That much is true. But now I find he has deceived me with a bird named Shirley. Paul, those poems are so good. I'm bloody jealous. Why don't you write like that now, instead of doing journalism?"

"I've lost the touch."

"Why didn't you tell me?"

"Because it didn't matter."

"It matters. What else haven't you told me?"

"Quite a lot, Molly."

"I've often thought so. Paul, I wish you'd *talk*."

"I talk all the time. We agree that Red China should be in the United Nations. I ask you about Australia and your girlhood in the outback. I explore your reasons for hating kangaroos. I praise your body."

Molly kissed him and raised his hand to her breast. "Yes, all that, but you never go deep. I dream about you, I see you in your past, I see you in Kuala Lumpur and in the Congo when you're away. But you never *speak*—you're making me invent you, as you invented that girl."

"What do you want to know?"

"What is the worst wound you have ever suffered?"

"Ah, Molly—I'm bulletproof."

"You're covered with scars. Please tell me, Paul. I'll not ask you another question, ever."

Christopher sat up in bed, moving his body away from Molly's, and pulled the sheet over both of them. "All right," he said. "Cathy could not bear to be alone. Her life, our marriage, took place in bed. She was a hungry lover, not graceful as you are. She needed sex, she'd scream and wail. Once we were thrown out of a hotel in Spain—they thought we were using whips. I knew she slept with men when I was away. I had no rule about it—it was her body, she could use it as she wished. She thought that showed a lack of love. She'd never believe I could feel sexual jealousy."

"I believe it," Molly said.

———

Cathy had not been content to let their marriage die. She set out to kill it. Christopher realized soon after he met her that he had never been so aroused by a female; his desire for her showed him a part of his nature he had not known to exist; he was seized by a biological force that had nothing to do with the mind, and he was driven to have her as, he supposed, a father would be seized by the instinct to kill the man who attacked his child. Cathy was a lovely girl with elongated gray eyes like a cat's, perfect teeth, a straight nose, a lithe, frank body. She had been sent to college, and then to Europe to study languages and art, but she did nothing. She had superstitions, but no ideas; she had learned to play the piano and talk and wear clothes. She was beautiful and wanted to be nothing else. "What do you want?" Christopher asked her as they walked along a beach in Spain. "Not what other girls want—I'm not domestic. No children, no career. I want, Paul, a perfect union with a man."

Cathy believed that she was different from all other human beings. Christopher was the first man in whom she had confided; she thought he was more like her in mind and soul than anyone else could be. When at last they went to bed, she was rapturous. But her passion was all she had. She had no skill as a lover and could not learn.

After a time she sensed that this was the trouble. Cathy wanted to satisfy Christopher. He wanted to reassure her. They made love constantly, in bed, in the car. She would meet him at the airport naked

under a raincoat, and removed the coat as they drove home, pulling the wheel so that he would turn into the ruins at Ostia Antica, where they would lie behind the broken stones of an old wall, shuddering on the cold earth in a rainfall. Because she was an American and his wife, he told her about his work—the nature of his profession, not its details. She thought that he kept more from her than official secrets—that he could not forget some other woman whose name he wouldn't reveal. She begged him to write about her. "You won't give me what you *are*," she said. "That's all I want."

Christopher loved to look at her. He bought her jewels and clothes and read to her. After a time, they lived in public as much as possible. They went to bullfights in Madrid, to the theater in London, they had restaurants they always went to and favorite drinks. Cathy loved to eat wild boar at Da Mario in the Via della Vite, she liked to sit up late on the sidewalk at Doney's, drinking Negronis.

When Christopher was away, she would ride through Rome on summer nights in his convertible with the top down. Finally, while he was in Africa, she met an Italian actor. After Christopher came back, she kept up the affair. She found other lovers. She went back to the actor. She would come home to Christopher, still wet, and want to make love. Christopher knew the Italian—he took Dexedrine and it made him violent. He was a Maoist who hated America; Cathy, who looked like a girl in an American film, was something he wanted to spoil.

Finally Cathy decided to break off with the actor. She had left some things at his apartment, dresses, jewelry, books. When she arrived, in the afternoon, she found him waiting with a dozen of his friends, all Italian except for a couple of Scandinavian girls. They were drinking *spumante*. The actor pulled Cathy into the apartment and threw her into the center of the living room. He had arranged the furniture so that the chairs were all around the walls, like a theater in the round. While his friends watched, the actor beat her with his fists. He punched her breasts, smashed her face. It went on for a long time—her nose and the bones in her cheeks were broken, some of her teeth were knocked out.

Cathy went downstairs to a coffee bar and called Christopher.

When he got to her, her face was a mass of blood. Her hair was soaked with blood. She had vomited on her clothes. She wore only one shoe. Christopher took her to the hospital. The car was open. "Put up the top," she kept saying, "put up the top."

———

"I see," Molly said.

"Do you? Outside the hospital, I kissed her mouth. She was blinded by blood. I was enough like her by then that I would have pulled off her clothes right there, but they came out with a stretcher."

2

That evening, seated at Doney's while the crowd drifted by on the Via Veneto, they read the papers. Christopher saw, for the first time, photographs of the dead bodies of the Ngo brothers. Diem's corpse was closer to the camera, and a broad streak of blood ran from the wound in his temple over his cheek.

"What happens to your piece on Diem now?" Molly asked.

"I don't know. I cabled the magazine. They may want a fix, or they may not run it. They wanted something unflattering, but that may not seem appropriate to them now."

"You saw him?"

"Only for a few minutes. It's odd, you know, but no one knows anything about him, really. He was sealed up in his family, never talked to strangers. All the stuff about him in the papers was science fiction."

Piero Cremona, wearing a perfectly pressed tan suit and a silk scarf around his neck, came out of the crowd, lifting his hand in greeting.

"The famous American correspondent is back from—where was it this time, Paul?"

Christopher shook hands. "How's the world's best-dressed Communist?" he said.

Cremona ran the fingernails of both hands down the breast of his jacket, making the silk whistle. "The true revolutionary blends into his environment," Cremona said. "In the jungles of Vietnam, I would wear the branches of trees. Here, this is my camouflage."

Cremona wrote political articles for *L'Unità*, the Communist newspaper. He signed his pieces with the *nom de guerre* he had used as a partisan; everyone but the police had forgotten the name Cremona was

born with. Christopher avoided American reporters, and Americans generally, in Rome, but he had got to know a lot of Italians when he was learning the language. He never reported on them or carried out any intelligence activities in Italy; it was his rule never to operate in the country where he lived.

Cremona sat down with Christopher and Molly. He tapped the newspaper photograph of the dead Vietnamese. "The imperialist eagle devours its young, eh?" he said.

"Is that the line this week, Piero?"

"It's the obvious truth, Paul. Read my piece tomorrow. Brilliant. I've just come from the typewriter."

"Why is it so obvious? *Corriere della Sera* says the trigger was pulled by a South Vietnamese lieutenant."

"Yes, and the junta in Saigon says Diem and Nhu committed suicide," Cremona said. "Everyone knew it was going to happen—you have a man of action in the White House now. I predicted it weeks ago. A handful of dollars, a head full of bullets. Madame Nhu, when she was here last month, predicted it."

"Well, if you're right, it ought to be a very good thing for the revolution."

"The best, dear Paul, the best. Ah, you capitalist-imperialists are so adept at fulfilling the predictions of Lenin. You are eager for your own doom. Up to now, you've been growing in Indochina like a caged tiger. Now you must bleed, Paul. There will be chaos—generals cannot run a government in a civil war. Their army has always been a joke, now their country will be a joke. The U.S. Marines will land—they must. You're committed now to playing a bad hand."

"Last time I saw you, you were telling me that Diem and Nhu were a couple of Nazis."

"They were—but they were no joke," Cremona said. "Well, I must leave you. Molly, why does a beautiful girl like you consort with this running dog of Wall Street?"

"Our relationship is not political," Molly said.

—

They had made love all afternoon. While Christopher took a shower, Molly wrote five hundred words on Italian fashions for the Australian weekly she represented in Rome. Christopher found her at the type-

writer, naked, with her glasses slipping down her nose and a yellow pencil clenched in her teeth, when he came out of the bathroom.

"Tripe," she mumbled. Molly wanted to live the life she thought he led, interviewing foreign ministers and film directors for a great American magazine. She kept all his articles, and would have typed them if he let her. Christopher did not want a secretary or a wife. He had hired Molly as an assistant two years before, to have someone in his office while he was away. It was important to his cover that someone answer the telephone and collect the mail. He kept nothing in the office, or anywhere else, that would connect him to his work as an agent. Molly could discover nothing.

Molly, who talked so beautifully, wrote badly, and she had never had an editor who knew enough about English to punish her for it. She asked too many questions when she interviewed; she had not learned to let her sources talk and betray themselves. Mostly she did stories about Italians, who liked the flat accent she used to speak their language, and tried to seduce her. She had beautiful legs and a soft way of smiling that made men want her.

Christopher had realized that he wanted her to stay with him after they had gone to bed for the first time. They had eaten lunch together on the first warm day of the year in the Piazza Novaona. Molly had tied a scarf under her chin, and her bright hair was hidden. When Christopher spoke to her she searched his face, as though for some hint that he was mocking her. She spoke English with a public school accent, but when she talked Italian to the waiter her Australian intonations were audible.

She wore a gray sweater and a pleated skirt like a schoolgirl, and Christopher thought she was ashamed of her clothes, as she was ashamed of her Australian accent. He wanted to ask why she flinched when he talked to her; he thought she must be having a bad love affair. Her eyes were flecked with copper, and when she peeled a mandarine he saw that she had lovely, skillful hands.

Out of mischief, because she was so shy, he said, "Would you like to make love?" Molly replied, touching the corner of her mouth with a napkin, "Yes, I think I would."

Webster knew that Christopher slept with Molly. He sent her name

in for a background investigation without mentioning that she was Christopher's mistress. "Do you want to read the file?" Webster asked when it came back from Canberra. "No," Christopher said. "She seems to be okay," Webster said. "If you have to live with a foreigner, an Australian is as clean as you can do." They did not live together; Molly kept her own small apartment. She didn't like the bed at his place, where Cathy had slept.

———

They walked to the restaurant through the Borghese Gardens. Molly did not hold his arm; she never touched him in public. Streetlights glowed in the branches of the trees. They paused on the Pincio and looked out over the dark city.

"We're too late for sunset," Molly said.

After dinner, they drank coffee in the Piazza del Popolo. "Rome does smell of coffee in the winter," Molly said. "Have you ever mentioned that to me?"

She grinned at him. Christopher loved the scent of Rome, a mixture of dust and cooking and bitter coffee. When he had drunk enough wine, he described the aroma of the city to Molly, and they tried to separate the odors.

Molly had caught him in the middle of a thought. He didn't want to leave her, but she mistook what she saw in his face.

"You don't much like being loved, do you?" Molly said.

Christopher stopped himself from touching her. "I'm going to the States next week," he said.

"For how long?"

"A week, ten days."

"Will you be coming back to Rome, or going on?"

"To Rome. Maybe we can go somewhere together."

Molly read his face again. "We're already here," she said.

3

David Patchen came to the safe house in Q Street at three o'clock in the morning. He was white with fatigue, and the glass of scotch Christopher gave him trembled in his hand. He drank it and poured another before he spoke.

"Dennis Foley wants your balls for breakfast," he said.

As a seventeen-year-old Marine on Okinawa, Patchen had been wounded by grenade fragments. The left side of his face was paralyzed. He walked with a limp. One of his eyes had been frozen open and he had learned not to blink the other; he wore a black eye patch when he slept. Patchen had no gestures. He was so still, like a hunting animal lying on the branch of a tree, that people would cough in nervous relief when finally he moved, and they saw that he limped.

Christopher was Patchen's only friend. They met in a naval hospital in the last days of the war and played chess together. While Patchen was still in a wheelchair, they were mustered with a handful of other wounded men to be decorated by a visiting admiral. Afterward, as Christopher pushed Patchen along a path planted with oleanders, Patchen unpinned the Silver Star from his bathrobe and threw it into the bushes. Both men were younger sons who had grown up in families in which an older brother was the preferred child. They were contemptuous of human beings who needed admiration.

Later, they had been roommates at Harvard. Another Harvard man, a few years older, took them to dinner at Locke-Ober's in the spring of their senior year. He ordered Pouilly-Fumé with the oysters and Médoc with the roast lamb, and afterward, in his room at the Parker House, recruited them for intelligence work. Neither man hesitated; they understood that what the recruiter was offering them was a lifetime of inviolable privacy.

Because people who had seen him remembered his wounds, Patchen remained in Washington. He was a natural administrator; he absorbed written material at a glance and never forgot anything. He knew the names and pseudonyms, the photographs and the operative weakness of every agent controlled by Americans everywhere in the world. Patchen never met any of them, and none of them knew he existed, but he designed their lives, forming them into a global sub-society that had become what it was, and remained so, at his pleasure. His hair turned gray when he was thirty, possibly from the pain of his wounds. At thirty-five he was outranked by only four men in the American intelligence community.

Christopher had gone into the field almost at once. It was thought

that his book of poems gave him reality and an excuse to go anywhere. He began to write magazine articles after the brief notoriety of his poems dissipated.

They met once or twice a year in Washington. Patchen's wife was gone, like Cathy Christopher. Patchen and Christopher saw changes in one another, but the changes were physical. Their minds were as they had always been. They believed in intellect as a force in the world and understood that it could be used only in secret. They knew, because they had spent their lives doing it, that it was possible to break open the human experience and find the dry truth hidden at its center. Their work had taught them that the truth, once discovered, was usually of little use: men denied what they had done, forgot what they had believed, and made the same mistakes over and over again. Patchen and Christopher were valuable because they had learned how to predict and use the mistakes of others.

"Foley ordered me to destroy any report you'd filed on that theory of Carson Wendell's about the 1960 election," Patchen said. "I told him there was no report."

"Did he believe that?"

"Of course not. He's got the idea we run a gossip mill. You may have to write something, so he can burn it in his ashtray."

Christopher smiled.

"He wanted you fired," Patchen said. "The Director put a hand-written note in your file explaining that you were responding to a direct request for information and had no political motive."

"Does Foley believe that?"

"How could he? He lives on loyalty to one man, the President. He's had no experience with cold-hearted bastards like you. No one but us can see that information is just information. Foley thinks you're an enemy if you don't agree with everything the President does, one hundred percent."

"So now everyone agrees with assassination?"

Patchen lifted his bad leg, using both hands, and crossed it over the other one. "Foley thought you were being emotional," he said. "I could kick Tom Webster's ass for bringing you two together."

"That doesn't answer the question."

Patchen hesitated. It was not like Christopher to ask for information he didn't need to have.

"The outfit had nothing to do with what happened to Diem and Nhu," he said.

"Foley didn't seem very surprised at the news."

"I can't explain Foley, or what he does," Patchen said.

Patchen opened his briefcase with a snap; he had had enough of this subject. He handed Christopher a newspaper clipping, the obituary of an Asian political figure who had died the week before of a heart attack.

"Did you see this? It isn't often that an agent dies of natural causes."

Christopher read the obituary. It said that the Asian would be remembered by history for three things: his autobiography, which made the world aware of the struggle of a whole people through the description of the author's own life; the Manifesto of 1955, which had influenced political thought and action throughout the Third World; and the statesman's success in driving Communists out of the political life of his country.

"Not even a chuckle?" Patchen asked.

Christopher shook his head. It was a convention that agents, even after they were dead, were called by their code names, never by their own. The Asian's pseudonym had been "Ripsaw."

"How much of Ripsaw's autobiography actually happened in his life?" Patchen asked.

"Most of the anecdotes were true as he told them to me. I just put in the parts where he had deep, deep thoughts. The Manifesto of 1955 I wrote on a plane, going down from Japan. It was the universal text— I'd done things like it before for some of the Africans. There just happened to be a guy from the *Times* incountry when Ripsaw issued it, so it got publicity."

"Don't you think it's funny, the way the *Times* is always reporting on you, and it doesn't know you exist?"

"That's what newspapers are for."

"Yes, to explain the real world."

"There is no real world, David."

Patchen smiled at the irony. He took back the clipping and closed

his briefcase. He sat for a long moment with his good eye closed and a hand over the other one, sipping from his glass of whiskey. He took his hand away from his face and stared at Christopher.

"I've been thinking about you," he said. "I got out your file and read it; you've been through a lot in twelve years. You're losing your humor, Paul. I've seen it happen to others who stay in the field too long, do too much."

"Seen what happen?"

"Professional fatigue. I believe, in the case of Christians, it's called religious melancholy. Do you play with the thought of getting out? I know you like to be with this girl Molly."

"Sometimes I play with the thought. I'm tired of the travel, and once or twice a year I meet someone I'd rather not lie to."

"Molly wouldn't be enough for you, you know, any more than poetry was, or your wife. You say there's no real world, but if there is one, it consists of you and maybe a dozen other operators like you on both sides. You ought to be intoxicated."

"Maybe I am."

"No. Your agents are intoxicated. Foley is intoxicated. That's why you don't like him—you know how easily you could use him if he was a foreigner."

"Well, I'm going back out. I have to meet Spendthrift in Léopoldville later this week, and after that I want to see what's left of the network in Vietnam."

"Who knows?" Patchen said. "You may find the atmosphere improved in Saigon. The embassy's traffic is full of bounce and optimism."

"I'll bet. Do you think the Foleys have any idea of what's going to happen to them out there?"

Patchen stood up. When he spoke, he turned the dead side of his face toward Christopher. "They're a funny bunch," he said. "They're bright. They believe in action, and at first that seemed refreshing. But they're almost totally innocent. They have about as much experience as you and I had when we were recruited, and there's no way to season them. They got into the White House and opened the safe, and the power they discovered took their breath away. *'Christ, let's use it!'* Power

really does corrupt. They think they can do anything they like, to any-one in the world, and there'll be no consequences."

"But there always are."

"*You* know that," Patchen said. "For those who never smell the corpse, there's no way of knowing."

FROM *THE SCARLET PIMPERNEL* (1905)

Baroness Orczy (1865–1947)

Baroness Orczy was born into the Hungarian nobility in 1865, to a family forced by peasant uprisings to flee its estates, first to Budapest, then, as titled émigrés, to Brussels, Paris, and eventually, when she was fifteen, to London. The Scarlet Pimpernel *is the story of the triumph of adventurous, brave aristocrats over the revolutionary secret police of the Robespierre (Stalinist) period of the French revolution. In our selection, Chauvelin is the French secret agent; Marguerite, Lady Blakeney, is the wife of Sir Percy Blakeney, in clandestine life known as "the Scarlet Pimpernel."*

The Scarlet Pimpernel, "a device drawn in red—a little star-shaped flower," was used in the novel as the sign, in fact the signature, of the secret organization formed to save the lives of French aristocrats.

CHAPTER X
IN THE OPERA BOX

It was one of the gala nights at Covent Garden Theatre, the first of the autumn season in this memorable year of grace 1792.

The house was packed, both in the smart orchestra boxes and the pit, as well as in the more plebeian balconies and galleries above. Glück's *Orpheus* made a strong appeal to the more intellectual portions of the house, whilst the fashionable women, the gaily-dressed and brilliant throng, spoke to the eye of those who cared but little for this "latest importation from Germany."

Selina Storace had been duly applauded after her grand *aria* by her numerous admirers; Benjamin Incledon, the acknowledged favourite of the ladies, had received special gracious recognition from the royal box; and now the curtain came down after the glorious finale to the second act, and the audience, which had hung spell-bound on the magic strains of the great maestro, seemed collectively to breathe a long sigh of satisfaction, previous to letting loose its hundreds of waggish and frivolous tongues.

In the smart orchestra boxes many well-known faces were to be seen. Mr. Pitt, overweighted with cares of state, was finding brief relaxation in to-night's musical treat; the Prince of Wales, jovial, rotund, somewhat coarse and commonplace in appearance, moved about from box to box, spending brief quarters of an hour with those of his more intimate friends.

In Lord Grenville's box, too, a curious, interesting personality attracted everyone's attention; a thin, small figure with shrewd, sarcastic face and deep-set eyes, attentive to the music, keenly critical of the audience, dressed in immaculate black, with dark hair free from any powder. Lord Grenville—Foreign Secretary of State—paid him marked, though frigid deference.

Here and there, dotted about among distinctly English types of beauty, one or two foreign faces stood out in marked contrast: the haughty aristocratic cast of countenance of the many French royalist *émigrés* who, persecuted by the relentless, revolutionary faction of their country, had found a peaceful refuge in England. On these faces sorrow and care were deeply writ; the women especially paid but little heed, either to the music or to the brilliant audience; no doubt their thoughts were far away with husband, brother, son maybe, still in peril, or lately succumbed to a cruel fate.

Among these the Comtesse de Tournay de Basserive, but lately ar-

rived from France, was a most conspicuous figure: dressed in deep, heavy black silk, with only a white lace kerchief to relieve the aspect of mourning about her person, she sat beside Lady Portarles, who was vainly trying by witty sallies and somewhat broad jokes, to bring a smile to the Comtesse's sad mouth. Behind her sat little Suzanne and the Vicomte, both silent and somewhat shy among so many strangers. Suzanne's eyes seemed wistful; when she first entered the crowded house, she had looked eagerly all around, scanned every face, scrutinised every box. Evidently the one face she wished to see was not there, for she settled herself down quietly behind her mother, listened apathetically to the music, and took no further interest in the audience itself.

"Ah, Lord Grenville," said Lady Portarles, as following a discreet knock, the clever, interesting head of the Secretary of State appeared in the doorway of the box, "you could not arrive more *à propos*. Here is Madame la Comtesse de Tournay positively dying to hear the latest news from France."

The distinguished diplomatist had come forward and was shaking hands with the ladies.

"Alas!" he said sadly, "it is of the very worst. The massacres continue; Paris literally reeks with blood; and the guillotine claims a hundred victims a day."

Pale and tearful, the Comtesse was leaning back in her chair, listening horror-struck to this brief and graphic account of what went on in her own misguided country.

"Ah, monsieur!" she said in broken English, "it is dreadful to hear all that—and my poor husband still in that awful country. It is terrible for me to be sitting here, in a theatre, all safe and in peace, whilst he is in such peril."

"Lud, Madame!" said honest, bluff Lady Portarles, "your sitting in a convent won't make your husband safe, and you have your children to consider: they are too young to be dosed with anxiety and premature mourning."

The Comtesse smiled through her tears at the vehemence of her friend. Lady Portarles, whose voice and manner would not have misfitted a jockey, had a heart of gold, and hid the most genuine sympathy

and most gentle kindliness, beneath the somewhat coarse manners affected by some ladies at that time.

"Besides which, Madame," added Lord Grenville, "did you not tell me yesterday that the League of the Scarlet Pimpernel had pledged their honour to bring M. le Comte safely across the Channel?"

"Ah, yes!" replied the Comtesse, "and that is my only hope. I saw Lord Hastings yesterday . . . he reassured me again."

"Then I am sure you need have no fear. What the league have sworn, that they surely will accomplish. Ah!" added the old diplomatist with a sigh, "if I were but a few years younger . . ."

"La, man!" interrupted honest Lady Portarles, "you are still young enough to turn your back on that French scarecrow that sits enthroned in your box to-night."

"I wish I could . . . but your ladyship must remember that in serving our country we must put prejudices aside. M. Chauvelin is the accredited agent of his Government . . ."

"Odd's fish, man!" she retorted, "you don't call those bloodthirsty ruffians over there a government, do you?"

"It has not been thought advisable as yet," said the Minister, guardedly, "for England to break off diplomatic relations with France, and we cannot therefore refuse to receive with courtesy the agent she wishes to send to us."

"Diplomatic relations be demmed, my lord! That sly little fox over there is nothing but a spy, I'll warrant, and you'll find—an I'm much mistaken, that he'll concern himself little with diplomacy, beyond trying to do mischief to royalist refugees—to our heroic Scarlet Pimpernel and to the members of that brave little league."

"I am sure," said the Comtesse, pursing up her thin lips, "that if this Chauvelin wishes to do us mischief, he will find a faithful ally in Lady Blakeney."

"Bless the woman!" ejaculated Lady Portarles, "did ever anyone see such perversity? My Lord Grenville, you have the gift of the gab, will you please explain to Madame la Comtesse that she is acting like a fool. In your position here in England, Madame," she added, turning a wrathful and resolute face towards the Comtesse, "you cannot afford to put on the hoity-toity airs you French aristocrats are so fond of.

Lady Blakeney may or may not be in sympathy with those Ruffians in France; she may or may not have had anything to do with the arrest and condemnation of St. Cyr, or whatever the man's name is, but she is the leader of fashion in this country; Sir Percy Blakeney has more money than any half-dozen other men put together, he is hand and glove with royalty, and your trying to snub Lady Blakeney will not harm her, but will make you look a fool. Isn't that so, my lord?"

But what Lord Grenville thought of this matter, or to what reflections this homely tirade of Lady Portarles led the Comtesse de Tournay, remained unspoken, for the curtain had just risen on the third act of *Orpheus,* and admonishments to silence came from every part of the house.

Lord Grenville took a hasty farewell of the ladies and slipped back into his box, where M. Chauvelin had sat all through this *entr'acte,* with his eternal snuff-box in his hand, and with his keen pale eyes intently fixed upon a box opposite to him, where, with much frou-frou of silken skirts, much laughter and general stir of curiosity amongst the audience, Marguerite Blakeney had just entered, accompanied by her husband, and looking divinely pretty beneath the wealth of her golden, reddish curls, slightly besprinkled with powder, and tied back at the nape of her graceful neck with a gigantic black bow. Always dressed in the very latest vagary of fashion, Marguerite alone among the ladies that night had discarded the cross-over fichu and broad-lapelled overdress, which had been in fashion for the last two or three years. She wore the short-waisted classical-shaped gown, which so soon was to become the approved mode in every country in Europe. It suited her graceful, regal figure to perfection, composed as it was of shimmering stuff which seemed a mass of rich gold embroidery.

As she entered, she leant for a moment out of the box, taking stock of all those present whom she knew. Many bowed to her as she did so, and from the royal box there came also a quick and gracious salute.

Chauvelin watched her intently all through the commencement of the third act, as she sat enthralled with the music, her exquisite little hand toying with a small jewelled fan, her regal head, her throat, arms and neck covered with magnificent diamonds and rare gems, the gift of the adoring husband who sprawled leisurely by her side.

Marguerite was passionately fond of music. *Orpheus* charmed her to-night. The very joy of living was writ plainly upon the sweet young face, it sparkled out of the merry blue eyes and lit up the smile that lurked around the lips. She was after all but five-and-twenty, in the hey day of youth, the darling of a brilliant throng, adored, *fêted*, petted, cherished. Two days ago the *Day Dream* had returned from Calais, bringing her news that her idolised brother had safely landed, that he thought of her, and would be prudent for her sake.

What wonder for the moment, and listening to Glück's impassioned strains, that she forgot her disillusionments, forgot her vanished love-dreams, forgot even the lazy, good-humoured nonentity who had made up for his lack of spiritual attainments by lavishing worldly advantages upon her.

He had stayed beside her in the box just as long as convention de-manded, making way for His Royal Highness, and for the host of ad-mirers who in a continued procession came to pay homage to the queen of fashion. Sir Percy had strolled away, to talk to more congenial friends probably. Marguerite did not even wonder whither he had gone—she cared so little; she had had a little court round her, com-posed of the *jeunesse dorée* of London, and had just dismissed them all, wishing to be alone with Glück for a brief while.

A discreet knock at the door roused her from her enjoyment.

"Come in," she said with some impatience, without turning to look at the intruder.

Chauvelin, waiting for his opportunity, noted that she was alone, and now, without pausing for that impatient "Come in," he quietly slipped into the box, and the next moment was standing behind Mar-guerite's chair.

"A word with you, citoyenne," he said quietly.

Marguerite turned quickly, in alarm, which was not altogether feigned.

"Lud, man! you frightened me," she said with a forced little laugh, "your presence is entirely inopportune. I want to listen to Glück, and have no mind for talking."

"But this is my only opportunity," he said, as quietly, and without waiting for permission, he drew a chair close behind her—so close that

he could whisper in her ear, without disturbing the audience, and without being seen, in the dark background of the box. "This is my only opportunity," he repeated, as she vouchsafed him no reply, "Lady Blakeney is always so surrounded, so *fêted* by her court, that a mere old friend has but very little chance."

"Faith, man!" she said impatiently, "you must seek for another opportunity then. I am going to Lord Grenville's ball to-night after the opera. So are you, probably. I'll give you five minutes then. . . ."

"Three minutes in the privacy of this box are quite sufficient for me," he rejoined placidly, "and I think that you will be wise to listen to me, Citoyenne St. Just."

Marguerite instinctively shivered. Chauvelin had not raised his voice above a whisper; he was now quietly taking a pinch of snuff, yet there was something in his attitude, something in those pale, foxy eyes, which seemed to freeze the blood in her veins, as would the sight of some deadly hitherto unguessed peril.

"Is that a threat, citoyen?" she asked at last.

"Nay, fair lady," he said gallantly, "only an arrow shot into the air."

He paused a moment, like a cat which sees a mouse running heedlessly by, ready to spring, yet waiting with that feline sense of enjoyment of mischief about to be done. Then he said quietly—

"Your brother, St. Just, is in peril."

Not a muscle moved in the beautiful face before him. He could only see it in profile, for Marguerite seemed to be watching the stage intently, but Chauvelin was a keen observer; he noticed the sudden rigidity of the eyes, the hardening of the mouth, the sharp, almost paralysed tension of the beautiful, graceful figure.

"Lud, then," she said, with affected merriment, "since 'tis one of your imaginary plots, you'd best go back to your own seat and leave me to enjoy the music."

And with her hand she began to beat time nervously against the cushion of the box. Selina Storace was singing the "Che faro" to an audience that hung spellbound upon the prima donna's lips. Chauvelin did not move from his seat; he quietly watched that tiny nervous hand, the only indication that his shaft had indeed struck home.

"Well?" she said suddenly and irrelevantly, and with the same feigned unconcern.

"Well, citoyenne?" he rejoined placidly.

"About my brother?"

"I have news of him for you which, I think, will interest you, but first let me explain. . . . May I?"

The question was unnecessary. He felt, though Marguerite still held her head steadily averted from him, that her every nerve was strained to hear what he had to say.

"The other day, citoyenne," he said, "I asked for your help. . . . France needed it, and I thought I could rely on you, but you gave me your answer. . . . Since then the exigencies of my own affairs and your own social duties have kept us apart . . . although many things have happened. . . ."

"To the point, I pray you, citoyen," she said lightly; "the music is entrancing, and the audience will get impatient of your talk."

"One moment, citoyenne. The day on which I had the honor of meeting you at Dover, and less than an hour after I had your final answer, I obtained possession of some papers, which revealed another of those subtle schemes for the escape of a batch of French aristocrats—that traitor de Tournay amongst others—all organized by that arch-meddler, the Scarlet Pimpernel. Some of the threads, too, of this mysterious organization have come into my hands, but not all, and I want you—nay! you *must* help me to gather them together."

Marguerite seemed to have listened to him with marked impatience; she now shrugged her shoulders and said gaily—

"Bah! man. Have I not already told you that I care nought about your schemes or about the Scarlet Pimpernel. And had you not spoken about my brother . . ."

"A little patience, I entreat, citoyenne," he continued imperturbably. "Two gentlemen, Lord Antony Dewhurst and Sir Andrew Ffoulkes were at 'The Fisherman's Rest' at Dover that same night."

"I know. I saw them there."

"They were already known to my spies as members of that accursed league. It was Sir Andrew Ffoulkes who escorted the Comtesse de Tournay and her children across the Channel. When the two young

men were alone, my spies forced their way into the coffee-room of the inn, gagged and pinioned the two gallants, seized their papers, and brought them to me."

In a moment she had guessed the danger. Papers? . . . Had Armand been imprudent? . . . The very thought struck her with nameless terror. Still she would not let this man see that she feared; she laughed gaily and lightly.

"Faith! and your impudence passes belief," she said merrily. "Robbery and violence!—in England!—in a crowded inn! Your men might have been caught in the act!"

"What if they had? They are children of France, and have been trained by your humble servant. Had they been caught they would have gone to jail, or even to the gallows, without a word of protest or indiscretion; at any rate it was well worth the risk. A crowded inn is safer for these little operations than you think, and my men have experience."

"Well? And those papers?" she asked carelessly.

"Unfortunately, though they have given me cognisance of certain names . . . certain movements . . . enough, I think, to thwart their projected *coup* for the moment, it would only be for the moment, and still leaves me in ignorance of the identity of the Scarlet Pimpernel."

"La! my friend," she said, with the same assumed flippancy of manner, "then you are where you were before, aren't you? and you can let me enjoy the last strophe of the *aria*. Faith!" she added, ostentatiously smothering an imaginary yawn, "had you not spoken about my brother . . ."

"I am coming to him now, citoyenne. Among the papers there was a letter to Sir Andrew Ffoulkes, written by your brother, St. Just."

"Well? And?"

"That letter shows him to be not only in sympathy with the enemies of France, but actually a helper, if not a member, of the League of the Scarlet Pimpernel."

The blow had been struck at last. All along, Marguerite had been expecting it; she would not show fear, she was determined to seem unconcerned, flippant even. She wished, when the shock came, to be prepared for it, to have all her wits about her—those wits which had been nicknamed the keenest in Europe. Even now she did not flinch. She

knew that Chauvelin had spoken the truth; the man was too earnest, too blindly devoted to the misguided cause he had at heart, too proud of his countrymen, of those makers of revolutions, to stoop to low, purposeless falsehoods.

That letter of Armand's—foolish, imprudent Armand—was in Chauvelin's hands. Marguerite knew that as if she had seen the letter with her own eyes; and Chauvelin would hold that letter for purposes of his own, until it suited him to destroy it or to make use of it against Armand. All that she knew, and yet she continued to laugh more gaily, more loudly than she had done before.

"La, man!" she said, speaking over her shoulder and looking him full and squarely in the face, "did I not say it was some imaginary plot.... Armand in league with that enigmatic Scarlet Pimpernel!... Armand busy helping those French aristocrats whom he despises!... Faith, the tale does infinite credit to your imagination!"

"Let me make my point clear, citoyenne," said Chauvelin, with the same unruffled calm, "I must assure you that St. Just is compromised beyond the slightest hope of pardon."

Inside the orchestra box all was silent for a moment or two. Marguerite sat, straight upright, rigid and inert, trying to think, trying to face the situation, to realise what had best be done.

In the house Storace had finished the *aria,* and was even now bowing in her classic garb, but in approved eighteenth-century fashion, to the enthusiastic audience, who cheered her to the echo.

"Chauvelin," said Marguerite Blakeney at last, quietly, and without that touch of bravado which had characterised her attitude all along, "Chauvelin, my friend, shall we try to understand one another. It seems that my wits have become rusty by contact with this damp climate. Now, tell me, you are very anxious to discover the identity of the Scarlet Pimpernel, isn't that so?"

"France's most bitter enemy, citoyenne . . . all the more dangerous, as he works in the dark."

"All the more noble, you mean.... Well!—and you would now force me to do some spying work for you in exchange for my brother Armand's safety?—Is that it?"

"Fie! two very ugly words, fair lady," protested Chauvelin, urbanely.

"There can be no question of force, and the service which I would ask of you, in the name of France, could never be called by the shocking name of spying."

"At any rate, that is what it is called over here," she said drily. "That is your intention, is it not?"

"My intention is, that you yourself win a free pardon for Armand St. Just by doing me a small service."

"What is it?"

"Only watch for me to-night, Citoyenne St. Just," he said eagerly. "Listen: among the papers which were found about the person of Sir Andrew Ffoulkes there was a tiny note. See!" he added, taking a tiny scrap of paper from his pocket-book and handing it to her.

It was the same scrap of paper which, four days ago, the two young men had been in the act of reading, at the very moment when they were attacked by Chauvelin's minions. Marguerite took it mechanically and stooped to read it. There were only two lines, written in a distorted, evidently disguised, handwriting; she read them half aloud—

" 'Remember we must not meet more often than is strictly necessary. You have all instructions for the 2nd. If you wish to speak to me again, I shall be at G.'s ball.' "

"What does it mean?" she asked.

"Look again, citoyenne, and you will understand."

"There is a device here in the corner, a small red flower . . ."

"Yes."

"The Scarlet Pimpernel," she said eagerly, "and G.'s ball means Grenville's ball. . . . He will be at my Lord Grenville's ball to-night."

"That is how I interpret the note, citoyenne," concluded Chauvelin, blandly. "Lord Antony Dewhurst and Sir Andrew Ffoulkes, after they were pinioned and searched by my spies, were carried by my orders to a lonely house on the Dover Road, which I had rented for the purpose: there they remained close prisoners until this morning. But having found this tiny scrap of paper, my intention was that they should be in London, in time to attend my Lord Grenville's ball. You see, do you not? that they must have a great deal to say to their chief . . . and thus they will have an opportunity of speaking to him to-night, just as he

directed them to do. Therefore, this morning, those two young gallants found every bar and bolt open in that lonely house on the Dover Road, their jailers disappeared, and two good horses standing ready saddled and tethered in the yard. I have not seen them yet, but I think we may safely conclude that they did not draw rein until they reached London. Now you see how simple it all is, citoyenne!"

"It does seem simple, doesn't it?" she said, with a final bitter attempt at flippancy, "when you want to kill a chicken . . . you take hold of it . . . then you wring its neck . . . it's only the chicken who does not find it quite so simple. Now you hold a knife at my throat, and a hostage for my obedience. . . . You find it simple. . . . I don't."

"Nay, citoyenne, I offer you a chance of saving the brother you love from the consequences of his own folly."

Marguerite's face softened, her eyes at last grew moist, as she murmured, half to herself:

"The only being in the world who has loved me truly and constantly. . . . But what do you want me to do, Chauvelin?" she said, with a world of despair in her tear-choked voice. "In my present position, it is well-nigh impossible!"

"Nay, citoyenne," he said drily and relentlessly, not heeding that despairing, childlike appeal, which might have melted a heart of stone, "as Lady Blakeney, no one suspects you, and with your help to-night I may—who knows?—succeed in finally establishing the identity of the Scarlet Pimpernel. . . . You are going to the ball anon. . . . Watch for me there, citoyenne, watch and listen. . . . You can tell me if you hear a chance word or whisper. . . . You can note everyone to whom Sir Andrew Ffoulkes or Lord Antony Dewhurst will speak. You are absolutely beyond suspicion now. The Scarlet Pimpernel will be at Lord Grenville's ball to-night. Find out who he is, and I will pledge the word of France that your brother shall be safe."

Chauvelin was putting the knife to her throat. Marguerite felt herself entangled in one of those webs, from which she could hope for no escape. A precious hostage was being held for her obedience: for she knew that this man would never make an empty threat. No doubt Armand was already signalled to the Committee of Public Safety as one of the "suspect"; he would not be allowed to leave France again,

and would be ruthlessly struck, if she refused to obey Chauvelin. For a moment—woman-like—she still hoped to temporise. She held out her hand to this man, whom she now feared and hated.

"If I promise to help you in this matter, Chauvelin," she said pleasantly, "will you give me that letter of St. Just's?"

"If you render me useful assistance to-night, citoyenne," he replied with a sarcastic smile, "I will give you that letter . . . to-morrow."

"You do not trust me?"

"I trust you absolutely, dear lady, but St. Just's life is forfeit to his country . . . it rests with you to redeem it."

"I may be powerless to help you," she pleaded, "were I ever so willing."

"That would be terrible indeed," he said quietly, "for you . . . and for St. Just."

Marguerite shuddered. She felt that from this man she could expect no mercy. All-powerful, he held the beloved life in the hollow of his hand. She knew him too well not to know that, if he failed in gaining his own ends, he would be pitiless.

She felt cold in spite of the oppressive air of the opera-house. The heart-appealing strains of the music seemed to reach her, as from a distant land. She drew her costly lace scarf up around her shoulders, and sat silently watching the brilliant scene, as if in a dream.

For a moment her thoughts wandered away from the loved one who was in danger, to that other man who also had a claim on her confidence and her affection. She felt lonely, frightened for Armand's sake; she longed to seek comfort and advice from someone who would know how to help and console. Sir Percy Blakeney had loved her once; he was her husband; why should she stand alone through this terrible ordeal? He had very little brains, it is true, but he had plenty of muscle: surely, if she provided the thought, and he the manly energy and pluck, together they could outwit the astute diplomatist, and save the hostage from his vengeful hands, without imperilling the life of the noble leader of that gallant little band of heroes. Sir Percy knew St. Just well—he seemed attached to him—she was sure that he could help.

Chauvelin was taking no further heed of her. He had said his cruel "Either—or—" and left her to decide. He, in his turn now, appeared to

be absorbed in the soul-stirring melodies of *Orpheus*, and was beating time to the music with his sharp, ferret-like head.

A discreet rap at the door roused Marguerite from her thoughts. It was Sir Percy Blakeney, tall, sleepy, good-humoured, and wearing that half-shy, half-inane smile, which just now seemed to irritate her every nerve.

"Er . . . your chair is outside . . . m'dear," he said, with his most exasperating drawl, "I suppose you will want to go to that demme ball. . . . Excuse me—er—Monsieur Chauvelin—I had not observed you. . . ."

He extended two slender, white fingers toward Chauvelin, who had risen when Sir Percy entered the box.

"Are you coming, m'dear?"

"Hush! Sh! Sh!" came in angry remonstrance from different parts of the house.

"Demmed impudence," commented Sir Percy with a good-natured smile.

Marguerite sighed impatiently. Her last hope seemed suddenly to have vanished away. She wrapped her cloak round her and without looking at her husband:

"I am ready to go," she said, taking his arm. At the door of the box she turned and looked straight at Chauvelin, who, with his *chapeau-bras* under his arm, and a curious smile round his thin lips, was preparing to follow the strangely ill-assorted couple.

"It is only *au revoir*, Chauvelin," she said pleasantly, "we shall meet at my Lord Grenville's ball, anon."

And in her eyes the astute Frenchman read, no doubt, something which caused him profound satisfaction, for, with a sarcastic smile, he took a delicate pinch of snuff, then, having dusted his dainty lace jabot, he rubbed his thin, bony hands contentedly together.

Chapter XI
Lord Grenville's Ball

The historic ball given by the then Secretary of State for Foreign Affairs—Lord Grenville—was the most brilliant function of the year.

Though the autumn season had only just begun, everybody who was anybody had contrived to be in London in time to be present there, and to shine at this ball, to the best of his or her respective ability.

His Royal Highness the Prince of Wales had promised to be present. He was coming on presently from the opera. Lord Grenville himself had listened to the two first acts of *Orpheus,* before preparing to receive his guests. At ten o'clock—an unusually late hour in those days—the grand rooms of the Foreign Office, exquisitely decorated with exotic palms and flowers, were filled to overflowing. One room had been set apart for dancing, and the dainty strains of the minuet made a soft accompaniment to the gay chatter, the merry laughter of the numerous and brilliant company.

In a smaller chamber, facing the top of the fine stairway, the distinguished host stood ready to receive his guests. Distinguished men, beautiful women, notabilities from every European country had already filed past him, had exchanged the elaborate bows and curtsies with him, which the extravagant fashion of the time demanded, and then, laughing and talking, had dispersed in the ball, reception, and card rooms beyond.

Not far from Lord Grenville's elbow, leaning against one of the console tables, Chauvelin, in his irreproachable black costume, was taking a quiet survey of the brilliant throng. He noted that Sir Percy and Lady Blakeney had not yet arrived, and his keen, pale eyes glanced quickly towards the door every time a new-comer appeared.

He stood somewhat isolated: the envoy of the Revolutionary Government of France was not likely to be very popular in England, at a time when the news of the awful September massacres, and of the Reign of Terror and Anarchy, had just begun to filtrate across the Channel.

In his official capacity he had been received courteously by his English colleagues: Mr. Pitt had shaken him by the hand; Lord Grenville had entertained him more than once; but the more intimate circles of London society ignored him altogether; the women openly turned their backs upon him; the men who held no official position refused to shake his hand.

But Chauvelin was not the man to trouble himself about these social amenities, which he called mere incidents in his diplomatic career. He was blindly enthusiastic for the revolutionary cause, he despised all social inequalities, and he had a burning love for his own country: these three sentiments made him supremely indifferent to the snubs he received in this fog-ridden, loyalist, old-fashioned England.

But, above all, Chauvelin had a purpose at heart. He firmly believed that the French aristocrat was the most bitter enemy of France; he would have wished to see every one of them annihilated: he was one of those who, during this awful Reign of Terror, had been the first to utter the historic and ferocious desire "that aristocrats might have but one head between them, so that it might be cut off with a single stroke of the guillotine." And thus he looked upon every French aristocrat, who had succeeded in escaping from France, as so much prey of which the guillotine had been unwarrantably cheated. There is no doubt that those royalist *émigrés*, once they had managed to cross the frontier, did their very best to stir up foreign indignation against France. Plots without end were hatched in England, in Belgium, in Holland, to try and induce some great power to send troops into revolutionary Paris, to free King Louis, and to summarily hang the bloodthirsty leaders of that monster republic.

Small wonder, therefore, that the romantic and mysterious personality of the Scarlet Pimpernel was a source of bitter hatred to Chauvelin. He and the few young jackanapes under his command, well furnished with money, armed with boundless daring, and acute cunning, had succeeded in rescuing hundreds of aristocrats from France. Nine-tenths of the *émigrés*, who were *fêted* at the English court, owed their safety to that man and to his league.

Chauvelin had sworn to his colleagues in Paris that he would discover the identity of that meddlesome Englishman, entice him over to France, and then . . . Chauvelin drew a deep breath of satisfaction at the very thought of seeing that enigmatic head falling under the knife of the guillotine, as easily as that of any other man.

Suddenly there was a great stir on the handsome staircase, all conversation stopped for a moment as the major-domo's voice outside announced,—

"His Royal Highness the Prince of Wales and suite, Sir Percy Blakeney, Lady Blakeney."

Lord Grenville went quickly to the door to receive his exalted guest.

The Prince of Wales, dressed in a magnificent court suit of salmon-coloured velvet richly embroidered with gold, entered with Marguerite Blakeney on his arm; and on his left Sir Percy, in gorgeous shimmering cream satin, cut in the extravagant "Incroyable" style, his fair hair free from powder, priceless lace at his neck and wrists, and the flat *chapeau-bras* under his arm.

After the few conventional words of deferential greeting, Lord Grenville said to his royal guest,—

"Will your Highness permit me to introduce M. Chauvelin, the accredited agent of the French Government?"

Chauvelin, immediately the Prince entered, had stepped forward, expecting this introduction. He bowed very low, whilst the Prince returned his salute with a curt nod of the head.

"Monsieur," said His Royal Highness coldly, "we will try to forget the government that sent you, and look upon you merely as our guest—a private gentleman from France. As such you are welcome, Monsieur."

"Monseigneur," rejoined Chauvelin, bowing once again. "Madame," he added, bowing ceremoniously before Marguerite.

"Ah! my little Chauvelin!" she said with unconcerned gaiety, and extending her tiny hand to him. "Monsieur and I are old friends, your Royal Highness."

"Ah, then," said the Prince, this time very graciously, "you are doubly welcome, Monsieur."

"There is someone else I would crave permission to present to your Royal Highness," here interposed Lord Grenville.

"Ah! who is it?" asked the Prince.

"Madame la Comtesse de Tournay de Basserive and her family, who have but recently come from France."

"By all means!—They are among the lucky ones then!"

Lord Grenville turned in search of the Comtesse, who sat at the further end of the room.

"Lud love me!" whispered his Royal Highness to Marguerite, as

soon as he had caught sight of the rigid figure of the old lady; "Lud love me! she looks very virtuous and very melancholy."

"Faith, your Royal Highness," she rejoined with a smile, "virtue is like precious odours, most fragrant when it is crushed."

"Virtue, alas!" sighed the Prince, "is mostly unbecoming to your charming sex, Madame."

"Madame la Comtesse de Tournay de Basserive," said Lord Grenville, introducing the lady.

"This is a pleasure, Madame; my royal father, as you know, is ever glad to welcome those of your compatriots whom France has driven from her shores."

"Your Royal Highness is ever gracious," replied the Comtesse with becoming dignity. Then, indicating her daughter, who stood timidly by her side: "My daughter Suzanne, Monseigneur," she said.

"Ah! charming!—charming!" said the Prince, "and now allow me, Comtesse, to introduce to you, Lady Blakeney, who honours us with her friendship. You and she will have much to say to one another, I vow. Every compatriot of Lady Blakeney's is doubly welcome for her sake . . . her friends are our friends . . . her enemies, the enemies of England."

Marguerite's blue eyes had twinkled with merriment at this gracious speech from her exalted friend. The Comtesse de Tournay, who lately had so flagrantly insulted her, was here receiving a public lesson, at which Marguerite could not help but rejoice. But the Comtesse, for whom respect of royalty amounted almost to a religion, was too well-schooled in courtly etiquette to show the slightest sign of embarrassment, as the two ladies curtsied ceremoniously to one another.

"His Royal Highness is ever gracious, Madame," said Marguerite, demurely, and with a wealth of mischief in her twinkling blue eyes, "but here there is no need for his kind mediation. . . . Your amiable reception of me at our last meeting still dwells pleasantly in my memory."

"We poor exiles, Madame," rejoined the Comtesse, frigidly, "show our gratitude to England by devotion to the wishes of Monseigneur."

"Madame!" said Marguerite, with another ceremonious curtsey.

"Madame," responded the Comtesse with equal dignity.

The Prince in the meanwhile was saying a few gracious words to the young Vicomte.

"I am happy to know you, Monsieur le Vicomte," he said. "I knew your father well when he was ambassador in London."

"Ah, Monseigneur!" replied the Vicomte, "I was a leetle boy then . . . and now I owe the honour of this meeting to our protector, the Scarlet Pimpernel."

"Hush!" said the Prince, earnestly and quickly, as he indicated Chauvelin, who had stood a little on one side throughout the whole of this little scene, watching Marguerite and the Comtesse with an amused, sarcastic little smile around his thin lips.

"Nay, Monseigneur," he said now, as if in direct response to the Prince's challenge, "pray do not check this gentleman's display of gratitude; the name of that interesting red flower is well known to me—and to France."

The Prince looked at him keenly for a moment or two.

"Faith, then, Monsieur," he said, "perhaps you know more about our national hero than we do ourselves . . . perchance you know who he is. . . . See!" he added, turning to the groups round the room, "the ladies hang upon your lips . . . you would render yourself popular among the fair sex if you were to gratify their curiosity."

"Ah, Monseigneur," said Chauvelin, significantly, "rumour has it in France that your Highness could—an you would—give the truest account of that enigmatical wayside flower."

He looked quickly and keenly at Marguerite as he spoke; but she betrayed no emotion, and her eyes met his quite fearlessly.

"Nay, man," replied the Prince, "my lips are sealed! and the members of the league jealously guard the secret of their chief . . . so his fair adorers have to be content with worshipping a shadow. Here in England, Monsieur," he added, with wonderful charm and dignity, "we but name the Scarlet Pimpernel, and every fair cheek is suffused with a blush of enthusiasm. None have seen him save his faithful lieutenants. We know not if he be tall or short, fair or dark, handsome or ill-formed; but we know that he is the bravest gentleman in all the world, and we all feel a little proud, Monsieur, when we remember that he is an Englishman."

"Ah, Monsieur Chauvelin," added Marguerite, looking almost with

defiance across at the placid, sphinx-like face of the Frenchman, "His Royal Highness should add that we ladies think of him as of a hero of old . . . we worship him . . . we wear his badge . . . we tremble for him when he is in danger, and exult with him in the hour of his victory."

Chauvelin did no more than bow placidly both to the Prince and to Marguerite; he felt that both speeches were intended—each in their way—to convey contempt or defiance. The pleasure-loving, idle Prince he despised: the beautiful woman, who in her golden hair wore a spray of small red flowers composed of rubies and diamonds—her he held in the hollow of his hand: he could afford to remain silent and to wait events.

A long, jovial, inane laugh broke the sudden silence which had fallen over everyone.

"And we poor husbands," came in slow, affected accents from gorgeous Sir Percy, "we have to stand by . . . while they worship a demmed shadow."

Everyone laughed—the Prince more loudly than anyone. The tension of subdued excitement was relieved, and the next moment everyone was laughing and chatting merrily as the gay crowd broke up and dispersed in the adjoining rooms.

CHAPTER XII
THE SCRAP OF PAPER

Marguerite suffered intensely. Though she laughed and chatted, though she was more admired, more surrounded, more *fêted* than any woman there, she felt like one condemned to death, living her last day upon this earth.

Her nerves were in a state of painful tension, which had increased a hundredfold during that brief hour which she had spent in her husband's company, between the opera and the ball. The short ray of hope—that she might find in this good-natured, lazy individual a valuable friend and adviser—had vanished as quickly as it had come, the moment she found herself alone with him. The same feeling of good-humoured contempt which one feels for an animal or a faithful ser-

vant, made her turn away with a smile from the man who should have been her moral support in this heart-rending crisis through which she was passing: who should have been her cool-headed adviser, when feminine sympathy and sentiment tossed her hither and thither, between her love for her brother, who was far away and in mortal peril, and horror of the awful service which Chauvelin had exacted from her, in exchange for Armand's safety.

There he stood, the moral support, the cool-headed adviser, surrounded by a crowd of brainless, empty-headed young fops, who were even now repeating from mouth to mouth, and with every sign of the keenest enjoyment, a doggerel quatrain which he had just given forth.

Everywhere the absurd, silly words met her: people seemed to have little else to speak about, even the Prince had asked her, with a laugh, whether she appreciated her husband's latest poetic efforts.

"All done in the tying of a cravat," Sir Percy had declared to his clique of admirers.

> "We seek him here, we seek him there,
> Those Frenchies seek him everywhere.
> Is he in heaven?—Is he in hell?
> That demmed, elusive Pimpernel?"

Sir Percy's *bon mot* had gone the round of the brilliant reception-rooms. The Prince was enchanted. He vowed that life without Blakeney would be but a dreary desert. Then, taking him by the arm, had led him to the card-room, and engaged him in a long game of hazard.

Sir Percy, whose chief interest in most social gatherings seemed to centre round the card-table, usually allowed his wife to flirt, dance, to amuse or bore herself as much as she liked. And to-night, having delivered himself of his *bon mot,* he had left Marguerite surrounded by a crowd of admirers of all ages, all anxious and willing to help her to forget that somewhere in the spacious reception rooms, there was a long, lazy being who had been fool enough to suppose that the cleverest woman in Europe would settle down to the prosaic bonds of English matrimony.

Her still overwrought nerves, her excitement and agitation, lent

beautiful Marguerite Blakeney much additional charm: escorted by a veritable bevy of men of all ages and of most nationalities, she called forth many exclamations of admiration from everyone as she passed.

She would not allow herself any more time to think. Her early, somewhat Bohemian training had made her something of a fatalist. She felt that events would shape themselves, that the directing of them was not in her hands. From Chauvelin she knew that she could expect no mercy. He had set a price upon Armand's head, and left it to her to pay or not, as she chose.

Later on in the evening she caught sight of Sir Andrew Ffoulkes and Lord Antony Dewhurst, who seemingly had just arrived. She noticed at once that Sir Andrew immediately made for little Suzanne de Tournay, and that the two young people soon managed to isolate themselves in one of the deep embrasures of the mullioned windows, there to carry on a long conversation, which seemed very earnest and very pleasant on both sides.

Both the young men looked a little haggard and anxious, but otherwise they were irreproachably dressed, and there was not the slightest sign, about their courtly demeanour, of the terrible catastrophe, which they must have felt hovering round them and round their chief.

That the League of the Scarlet Pimpernel had no intention of abandoning its cause, she had gathered through little Suzanne herself, who spoke openly of the assurance she and her mother had had that the Comte de Tournay would be rescued from France by the league, within the next few days. Vaguely she began to wonder, as she looked at the brilliant and fashionable crowd in the gaily-lighted ball-room, which of these worldly men round her was the mysterious "Scarlet Pimpernel," who held the threads of such daring plots, and the fate of valuable lives in his hands.

A burning curiosity seized her to know him: although for months she had heard of him and had accepted his anonymity, as everyone else in society had done; but now she longed to know—quite impersonally, quite apart from Armand, and oh! quite apart from Chauvelin—only for her own sake, for the sake of the enthusiastic admiration she had always bestowed on his bravery and cunning.

He was at the ball, of course, somewhere, since Sir Andrew Ffoulkes and Lord Antony Dewhurst were here, evidently expecting to meet their chief—and perhaps to get a fresh *mot d'ordre* from him.

Marguerite looked round at everyone, at the aristocratic high-typed Norman faces, the squarely-built, fair-haired Saxon, the more gentle, humorous caste of the Celt, wondering which of these betrayed the power, the energy, the cunning which had imposed its will and its leadership upon a number of high-born English gentlemen, among whom rumour asserted was His Royal Highness himself.

Sir Andrew Ffoulkes? Surely not, with his gentle blue eyes, which were looking so tenderly and longingly after little Suzanne, who was being led away from the pleasant *tête-à-tête* by her stern mother. Marguerite watched him across the room, as he finally turned away with a sigh, and seemed to stand, aimless and lonely, now that Suzanne's dainty little figure had disappeared in the crowd.

She watched him as he strolled towards the doorway, which led to a small boudoir beyond, then paused and leaned against the framework of it, looking still anxiously all round him.

Marguerite contrived for the moment to evade her present attentive cavalier, and she skirted the fashionable crowd, drawing nearer to the doorway, against which Sir Andrew was leaning. Why she wished to get closer to him, she could not have said: perhaps she was impelled by an all-powerful fatality, which so often seems to rule the destinies of men.

Suddenly she stopped: her very heart seemed to stand still, her eyes, large and excited, flashed for a moment towards that doorway, then as quickly were turned away again. Sir Andrew Ffoulkes was still in the same listless position by the door, but Marguerite had distinctly seen that Lord Hastings—a young buck, a friend of her husband's and one of the Prince's set—had, as he quickly brushed past him, slipped something into his hand.

For one moment longer—oh! it was the merest flash—Marguerite paused: the next she had, with admirably played unconcern, resumed her walk across the room—but this time more quickly towards that doorway whence Sir Andrew had now disappeared.

All this, from the moment that Marguerite had caught sight of Sir Andrew leaning against the doorway, until she followed him into the

little boudoir beyond, had occurred in less than a minute. Fate is usually swift when she deals a blow.

Now Lady Blakeney had suddenly ceased to exist. It was Marguerite St. Just who was there only: Marguerite St. Just who had passed her childhood, her early youth, in the protecting arms of her brother Armand. She had forgotten everything else—her rank, her dignity, her secret enthusiasms—everything save that Armand stood in peril of his life, and that there, not twenty feet away from her, in the small boudoir which was quite deserted, in the very hands of Sir Andrew Ffoulkes, might be the talisman which would save her brother's life.

Barely another thirty seconds had elapsed between the moment when Lord Hastings slipped the mysterious "something" into Sir Andrew's hand, and the one when she, in her turn, reached the deserted boudoir. Sir Andrew was standing with his back to her and close to a table upon which stood a massive silver candelabra. A slip of paper was in his hand, and he was in the very act of perusing its contents.

Unperceived, her soft clinging robe making not the slightest sound upon the heavy carpet, not daring to breathe until she had accomplished her purpose, Marguerite slipped close behind him. . . . At that moment he looked round and saw her; she uttered a groan, passed her hand across her forehead, and murmured faintly:

"The heat in the room was terrible . . . I felt so faint . . . Ah! . . ."

She tottered almost as if she would fall, and Sir Andrew, quickly recovering himself, and crumpling in his hand the tiny note he had been reading, was only, apparently, just in time to support her.

"You are ill, Lady Blakeney?" he asked with much concern. "Let me . . ."

"No, no, nothing—" she interrupted quickly. "A chair—quick."

She sank into a chair close to the table, and throwing back her head, closed her eyes.

"There!" she murmured, still faintly; "the giddiness is passing off. . . . Do not heed me, Sir Andrew; I assure you I already feel better."

At moments like these there is no doubt—and psychologists actually assert it—that there is in us a sense which has absolutely nothing to do with the other five: it is not that we see, it is not that we hear or touch, yet we seem to do all three at once. Marguerite sat there with her eyes apparently closed. Sir Andrew was immediately behind her,

and on her right was the table with the five-armed candelabra upon it. Before her mental vision there was absolutely nothing but Armand's face. Armand, whose life was in the most imminent danger, and who seemed to be looking at her from a background upon which were dimly painted the seething crowd of Paris, the bare walls of the Tribunal of Public Safety, with Foucquier-Tinville, the Public Prosecutor, demanding Armand's life in the name of the people of France, and the lurid guillotine with its stained knife waiting for another victim . . . Armand! . . .

For one moment there was dead silence in the little boudoir. Beyond, from the brilliant ball-room, the sweet notes of the gavotte, the frou-frou of rich dresses, the talk and laughter of a large and merry crowd, came as a strange, weird accompaniment to the drama which was being enacted here.

Sir Andrew had not uttered another word. Then it was that that extra sense became potent in Marguerite Blakeney. She could not see, for her eyes were closed, she could not hear, for the noise from the ball-room drowned the soft rustle of that momentous scrap of paper; nevertheless she knew—as if she had both seen and heard—that Sir Andrew was even now holding the paper to the flame of one of the candles.

At the exact moment that it began to catch fire, she opened her eyes, raised her hand and, with two dainty fingers, had taken the burning scrap of paper from the young man's hand. Then she blew out the flame, and held the paper to her nostril with perfect unconcern.

"How thoughtful of you, Sir Andrew," she said gaily, "surely 'twas your grandmother who taught you that the smell of burnt paper was a sovereign remedy against giddiness."

She sighed with satisfaction, holding the paper tightly between her jewelled fingers; that talisman which perhaps would save her brother Armand's life. Sir Andrew was staring at her, too dazed for the moment to realise what had actually happened; he had been taken so completely by surprise, that he seemed quite unable to grasp the fact that the slip of paper, which she held in her dainty hand, was one perhaps on which the life of his comrade might depend.

Marguerite burst into a long, merry peal of laughter.

"Why do you stare at me like that?" she said playfully. "I assure you

I feel much better; your remedy has proved most effectual. This room is most delightfully cool," she added, with the same perfect composure, "and the sound of the gavotte from the ball-room is fascinating and soothing."

She was prattling on in the most unconcerned and pleasant way, whilst Sir Andrew, in an agony of mind, was racking his brains as to the quickest method he could employ to get that bit of paper out of that beautiful woman's hand. Instinctively, vague and tumultuous thoughts rushed through his mind: he suddenly remembered her nationality, and worst of all, recollected that horrible tale anent the Marquis de St. Cyr, which in England no one had credited for the sake of Sir Percy, as well as for her own.

"What? Still dreaming and staring?" she said, with a merry laugh, "you are most ungallant, Sir Andrew; and now I come to think of it, you seemed more startled than pleased when you saw me just now. I do believe, after all, that it was not concern for my health, nor yet a remedy taught you by your grandmother that caused you to burn this tiny scrap of paper. . . . I vow it must have been your lady love's last cruel epistle you were trying to destroy. Now confess!" she added, playfully holding up the scrap of paper, "does this contain her final *congé*, or a last appeal to kiss and make friends?"

"Whichever it is, Lady Blakeney," said Sir Andrew, who was gradually recovering his self-possession, "this little note is undoubtedly mine, and . . ."

Not caring whether his action was one that would be styled ill-bred towards a lady, the young man had made a bold dash for the note; but Marguerite's thoughts flew quicker than his own; her actions, under pressure of this intense excitement, were swifter and more sure. She was tall and strong; she took a quick step backwards and knocked over the small Sheraton table which was already top-heavy, and which fell down with a crash, together with the massive candelabra upon it.

She gave a quick cry of alarm:

"The candles, Sir Andrew—quick!"

There was not much damage done; one or two of the candles had blown out as the candelabra fell; others had merely sent some grease upon the valuable carpet; one had ignited the paper shade

over it. Sir Andrew quickly and dexterously put out the flames and replaced the candelabra upon the table; but this had taken him a few seconds to do, and those seconds had been all that Marguerite needed to cast a quick glance at the paper, and to note its contents— a dozen words in the same distorted handwriting she had seen before, and bearing the same device—a star-shaped flower drawn in red ink.

When Sir Andrew once more looked at her, he only saw on her face alarm at the untoward accident and relief at its happy issue; whilst the tiny and momentous note had apparently fluttered to the ground. Eagerly the young man picked it up, and his face looked much relieved, as his fingers closed tightly over it.

"For shame, Sir Andrew," she said, shaking her head with a playful sigh, "making havoc in the heart of some impressionable duchess, whilst conquering the affections of my sweet little Suzanne. Well, well! I do believe it was Cupid himself who stood by you, and threatened the entire Foreign Office with destruction by fire, just on purpose to make me drop love's message, before it had been polluted by my indiscreet eyes. To think that, a moment longer, and I might have known the secrets of an erring duchess."

"You will forgive me, Lady Blakeney," said Sir Andrew, now as calm as she was herself, "if I resume the interesting occupation which you had interrupted?"

"By all means, Sir Andrew! How should I venture to thwart the love-god again? Perhaps he would mete out some terrible chastisement against my presumption. Burn your love-token, by all means!"

Sir Andrew had already twisted the paper into a long spill, and was once again holding it to the flame of the candle, which had remained alight. He did not notice the strange smile on the face of his fair *vis-à-vis,* so intent was he on the work of destruction; perhaps, had he done so, the look of relief would have faded from his face. He watched the fateful note, as it curled under the flame. Soon the last fragment fell on the floor, and he placed his heel upon the ashes.

"And now, Sir Andrew," said Marguerite Blakeney, with the pretty nonchalance peculiar to herself, and with the most winning of smiles, "will you venture to excite the jealousy of your fair lady by asking me to dance the minuet?"

From *The Moon Is Down* (1942)

John Steinbeck (1902–1968)

John Steinbeck, who was born in California, was, like Gorky, a passionate humanist, and a true poet of the underdog—poor farmers, Mexican Americans, migrant workers, people at the margin of the American dream. The Moon Is Down, *a World War II novel of fascist oppression that virtually sings with anger, was written to be a sort of* Everyman *of occupation and resistance. The setting is probably Norway, though the situation—involving small-town leaders and their people—was common across occupied Europe during World War II, and the novel was written when the outcome of the war was very much in doubt. Steinbeck was awarded the Nobel Prize for Literature in 1962.*

CHAPTER SEVEN

In the dark, clear night a white, half-withered moon brought little light. The wind was dry and singing over the snow, a quiet wind that blew steadily, evenly from the cold point of the Pole. Over the land the snow lay very deep and dry as sand. The houses snuggled down in the

hollows of banked snow, and their windows were dark and shuttered against the cold, and only a little smoke rose from the banked fires.

In the town the footpaths were frozen hard and packed hard. And the streets were silent, too, except when the miserable, cold patrol came by. The houses were dark against the night, and a little lingering warmth remained in the houses against the morning. Near the mine entrance the guards watched the sky and trained their instruments on the sky and turned their listening-instruments against the sky, for it was a clear night for bombing. On nights like this the feathered steel spindles came whistling down and roared to splinters. The land would be visible from the sky tonight, even though the moon seemed to throw little light.

Down toward one end of the village, among the small houses, a dog complained about the cold and the loneliness. He raised his nose to his god and gave a long and fulsome account of the state of the world as it applied to him. He was a practiced singer with a full bell throat and great versatility of range and control. The six men of the patrol slogging dejectedly up and down the streets heard the singing of the dog, and one of the muffled soldiers said, "Seems to me he's getting worse every night. I suppose we ought to shoot him."

And another answered, "Why? Let him howl. He sounds good to me. I used to have a dog at home that howled. I never could break him. Yellow dog. I don't mind the howl. They took my dog when they took the others," he said factually, in a dull voice.

And the corporal said, "Couldn't have dogs eating up food that was needed."

"Oh, I'm not complaining. I know it was necessary. I can't plan the way the leaders do. It seems funny to me, though, that some people here have dogs, and they don't have even as much food as we have. They're pretty gaunt, though, dogs and people."

"They're fools," said the corporal. "That's why they lost so quickly. They can't plan the way we can."

"I wonder if we'll have dogs again after it's over," said the soldier. "I suppose we could get them from America or some place and start the breeds again. What kind of dogs do you suppose they have in America?"

"I don't know," said the corporal. "Probably dogs as crazy as every-

thing else they have." And he went on, "Maybe dogs are no good, any-way. It might be just as well if we never bothered with them, except for police work."

"It might be," said the soldier. "I've heard the Leader doesn't like dogs. I've heard they make him itch and sneeze."

"You hear all kinds of things," the corporal said. "Listen!" The patrol stopped and from a great distance came the bee hum of planes.

"There they come," the corporal said. "Well, there aren't any lights. It's been two weeks, hasn't it, since they came before?"

"Twelve days," said the soldier.

The guards at the mine heard the high drone of the planes. "They're flying high," a sergeant said. And Captain Loft tilted his head back so that he could see under the rim of his helmet. "I judge over 20,000 feet," he said. "Maybe they're going on over."

"Aren't very many." The sergeant listened. "I don't think there are more than three of them. Shall I call the battery?"

"Just see they're alert, and then call Colonel Lanser—no, don't call him. Maybe they aren't coming here. They're nearly over and they haven't started to dive yet."

"Sounds to me like they're circling. I don't think there are more than two," the sergeant said.

In their beds the people heard the planes and they squirmed deep into their featherbeds and listened. In the palace of the Mayor the little sound awakened Colonel Lanser, and he turned over on his back and looked at the dark ceiling with wide-open eyes, and he held his breath to listen better and then his heart beat so that he could not hear as well as he could when he was breathing. Mayor Orden heard the planes in his sleep and they made a dream for him and he moved and whispered in his sleep.

High in the air the two bombers circled, mud-colored planes. They cut their throttles and soared, circling. And from the belly of each one tiny little objects dropped, hundreds of them, one after another. They plummeted a few feet and then little parachutes opened and drifted small packages silently and slowly downward toward the earth, and the planes raised their throttles and gained altitude, and then cut their throttles and circled again, and more of the little objects plummeted

down, and then the planes turned and flew back in the direction from which they had come.

The tiny parachutes floated like thistledown and the breeze spread them out and distributed them as seeds on the ends of thistledown are distributed. They drifted so slowly and landed so gently that sometimes the ten-inch packages of dynamite stood upright in the snow, and the little parachutes folded gently down around them. They looked black against the snow. They landed in the white fields and among the woods of the hills and they landed in trees and hung down from the branches. Some of them landed on the housetops of the little town, some in the small front yards, and one landed and stood upright in the snow crown on top of the head of the village statue of St. Albert the Missionary.

One of the little parachutes came down in the street ahead of the patrol and the sergeant said, "Careful! It's a time bomb."

"It ain't big enough," a soldier said.

"Well, don't go near it." The sergeant had his flashlight out and he turned it on the object, a little parachute no bigger than a hand-kerchief, colored light blue, and hanging from it a package wrapped in blue paper.

"Now don't anybody touch it," the sergeant said. "Harry, you go down to the mine and get the captain. We'll keep an eye on this damn thing."

The late dawn came and the people moving out of their houses in the country saw the spots of blue against the snow. They went to them and picked them up. They unwrapped the paper and read the printed words. They saw the gift and suddenly each finder grew furtive, and he concealed the long tube under his coat and went to some secret place and hid the tube.

And word got to the children about the gift and they combed the countryside in a terrible Easter egg hunt, and when some lucky child saw the blue color, he rushed to the prize and opened it and then he hid the tube and told his parents about it. There were some people who were frightened, who turned the tubes over to the military, but they were not very many. And the soldiers scurried about the town in another Easter egg hunt, but they were not so good at it as the children were.

In the drawing-room of the palace of the Mayor the dining-table remained with the chairs about as it had been placed the day Alex Morden was shot. The room had not the grace it had when it was still the palace of the Mayor. The walls, bare of standing chairs, looked very blank. The table with a few papers scattered about on it made the room look like a business office. The clock on the mantel struck nine. It was a dark day now, overcast with clouds, for the dawn had brought the heavy snow clouds.

Annie came out of the Mayor's room; she swooped by the table and glanced at the papers that lay there. Captain Loft came in. He stopped in the doorway, seeing Annie.

"What are you doing here?" he demanded.

And Annie said sullenly, "Yes, sir."

"I said, what are you doing here?"

"I thought to clean up, sir."

"Let things alone, and go along."

And Annie said, "Yes, sir," and she waited until he was clear of the door, and she scuttled out.

Captain Loft turned back through the doorway and he said, "All right, bring it in." A soldier came through the door behind him, his rifle hung over his shoulder by a strap, and in his arms he held a number of the blue packages, and from the ends of the packages there dangled the little strings and pieces of blue cloth.

Loft said, "Put them on the table." The soldier gingerly laid the packages down. "Now go upstairs and report to Colonel Lanser that I'm here with the—things," and the soldier wheeled about and left the room.

Loft went to the table and picked up one of the packages, and his face wore a look of distaste. He held up the little blue cloth parachute, held it above his head and dropped it, and the cloth opened and the package floated to the floor. He picked up the package again and examined it.

Now Colonel Lanser came quickly into the room, followed by Major Hunter. Hunter was carrying a square of yellow paper in his hand. Lanser said, "Good morning, Captain," and he went to the head of the table and sat down. For a moment he looked at the little pile of

tubes, and then he picked one up and held it in his hand. "Sit down, Hunter," he said. "Have you examined these?"

Hunter pulled out a chair and sat down. He looked at the yellow paper in his hand. "Not very carefully," he said. "There are three breaks in the railroad all within ten miles."

"Well, take a look at them and see what you think," Lanser said.

Hunter reached for a tube and stripped off the outer covering, and inside was a small package next to the tube. Hunter took out a knife and cut into the tube. Captain Loft looked over his shoulder. Then Hunter smelled the cut and rubbed his fingers together, and he said, "It's silly. It's commercial dynamite. I don't know what per cent of nitro-glycerin until I test it." He looked at the end. "It has a regular dynamite cap, fulminate of mercury, and a fuse—about a minute, I suppose." He tossed the tube back onto the table. "It's very cheap and very simple," he said.

The colonel looked at Loft. "How many do you think were dropped?"

"I don't know, sir," said Loft. "We picked up about fifty of them, and about ninety parachutes they came in. For some reason the people leave the parachutes when they take the tubes, and then there are probably a lot we haven't found yet."

Lanser waved his hand. "It doesn't really matter," he said. "They can drop as many as they want. We can't stop it, and we can't use it against them, either. They haven't conquered anybody."

Loft said fiercely, "We can beat them off the face of the earth!"

Hunter was prying the copper cap out of the top of one of the sticks, and Lanser said, "Yes—we can do that. Have you looked at this wrapper, Hunter?"

"Not yet, I haven't had time."

"It's kind of devilish, this thing," said Colonel Lanser. "The wrapper is blue, so that it's easy to see. Unwrap the outer paper and here"— he picked up the small package—"here is a piece of chocolate. Everybody will be looking for it. I'll bet our own soldiers steal the chocolate. Why, the kids will be looking for them, like Easter eggs."

A soldier came in and laid a square of yellow paper in front of the colonel and retired, and Lanser glanced at it and laughed harshly. "Here's something for you, Hunter. Two more breaks in your line."

Hunter looked up from the copper cap he was examining, and he asked, "How general is this? Did they drop them everywhere?"

Lanser was puzzled. "Now, that's the funny thing. I've talked to the capital. This is the only place they've dropped them."

"What do you make of that?" Hunter asked.

"Well, it's hard to say. I think this is a test place. I suppose if it works here they'll use it all over, and if it doesn't work here they won't bother."

"What are you going to do?" Hunter asked.

"The capital orders me to stamp this out so ruthlessly that they won't drop it any place else."

Hunter said plaintively, "How am I going to mend five breaks in the railroad? I haven't rails right now for five breaks."

"You'll have to rip out some of the old sidings, I guess," said Lanser.

Hunter said, "That'll make a hell of a roadbed."

"Well, anyway, it will make a roadbed."

Major Hunter tossed the tube he had torn apart onto the pile, and Loft broke in, "We must stop this thing at once, sir. We must arrest and punish people who pick these things up, before they use them. We have to get busy so these people won't think we are weak."

Lanser was smiling at him, and he said, "Take it easy, Captain. Let's see what we have first, and then we'll think of remedies."

He took a new package from the pile and unwrapped it. He took the little piece of chocolate, tasted it, and he said, "This is a devilish thing. It's good chocolate, too. I can't even resist it myself. The prize in the grab-bag." Then he picked up the dynamite. "What do you think of this really, Hunter?"

"What I told you. It's very cheap and very effective for small jobs, dynamite with a cap and a one-minute fuse. It's good if you know how to use it. It's no good if you don't."

Lanser studied the print on the inside of the wrapper. "Have you read this?"

"Glanced at it," said Hunter.

"Well, I have read it, and I want you to listen to it carefully," said Lanser. He read from the paper, " 'To the unconquered people: Hide this. Do not expose yourself. You will need this later. It is a present

from your friends to you and from you to the invader of your country. Do not try to do large things with it.' " He began to skip through the bill. "Now here, 'rails in the country.' And, 'work at night.' And, 'tie up transportation.' Now here, 'Instructions: rails. Place stick under rail close to the joint, and tight against a tie. Pack mud or hard-beaten snow around it so that it is firm. When the fuse is lighted you have a slow count of sixty before it explodes.' "

He looked up at Hunter and Hunter said simply, "It works." Lanser looked back at his paper and he skipped through. " 'Bridges: Weaken, do not destroy.' And here, 'transmission poles,' and here, 'culverts, trucks.' " He laid the blue handbill down. "Well, there it is."

Loft said angrily, "We must do something! There must be a way to control this. What does headquarters say?"

Lanser pursed his lips and his fingers played with one of the tubes. "I could have told you what they'd say before they said it. I have the orders. 'Set booby traps and poison the chocolate.' " He paused for a moment and then he said, "Hunter, I'm a good, loyal man, but sometimes when I hear the brilliant ideas of headquarters, I wish I were a civilian, an old, crippled civilian. They always think they are dealing with stupid people. I don't say that this is a measure of their intelligence, do I?"

Hunter looked amused. "Do you?"

Lanser said sharply, "No, I don't. But what will happen? One man will pick up one of these and get blown to bits by our booby trap. One kid will eat chocolate and die of strychnine poisoning. And then?" He looked down at his hands. "They will poke them with poles, or lasso them, before they touch them. They will try the chocolate on the cat. Goddamn it, Major, these are intelligent people. Stupid traps won't catch them twice."

Loft cleared his throat. "Sir, this is defeatist talk," he said. "We must do something. Why do you suppose it was only dropped here, sir?"

And Lanser said, "For one of two reasons: either this town was picked at random or else there is communication between this town and the outside. We know that some of the young men have got away."

Loft repeated dully, "We must do something, sir."

Now Lanser turned on him. "Loft, I think I'll recommend you for the General Staff. You want to get to work before you even know what

the problem is. This is a new kind of conquest. Always before, it was possible to disarm a people and keep them in ignorance. Now they listen to their radios and we can't stop them. We can't even find their radios."

A soldier looked in through the doorway. "Mr. Corell to see you, sir."

Lanser replied, "Tell him to wait." He continued to talk to Loft. "They read the handbills; weapons drop from the sky for them. Now it's dynamite, Captain. Pretty soon it may be grenades, and then poison."

Loft said anxiously, "They haven't dropped poison yet."

"No, but they will. Can you think what will happen to the morale of our men or even to you if the people had some of those little game darts, you know, those silly little things you throw at a target, the points coated perhaps with cyanide, silent, deadly little things that you couldn't hear coming, that would pierce the uniform and make no noise? And what if our men knew that arsenic was about? Would you or they drink or eat comfortably?"

Hunter said dryly, "Are you writing the enemy's campaign, Colonel?"

"No, I'm trying to anticipate it."

Loft said, "Sir, we sit here talking when we should be searching for this dynamite. If there is organization among these people, we have to find it, we have to stamp it out."

"Yes," said Lanser, "we have to stamp it out, ferociously, I suppose. You take a detail, Loft. Get Prackle to take one. I wish we had more junior officers. Tonder's getting killed didn't help us a bit. Why couldn't he let women alone?"

Loft said, "I don't like the way Lieutenant Prackle is acting, sir."

"What's he doing?"

"He isn't doing anything, but he's jumpy and he's gloomy."

"Yes," Lanser said, "I know. It's a thing I've talked about so much. You know," he said, "I might be a major-general if I hadn't talked about it so much. We trained our young men for victory and you've got to admit they're glorious in victory, but they don't quite know how to act in defeat. We told them they were brighter and braver than other young men. It was a kind of shock to them to find out that they aren't a bit braver or brighter than other young men."

Loft said harshly, "What do you mean by defeat? We are not defeated."

And Lanser looked coldly up at him for a long moment and did not speak, and finally Loft's eyes wavered, and he said, "Sir."

"Thank you," said Lanser.

"You don't demand it of the others, sir."

"They don't think about it, so it isn't an insult. When you leave it out, it's insulting."

"Yes, sir," said Loft.

"Go on, now, try to keep Prackle in hand. Start your search. I don't want any shooting unless there's an overt act, do you understand?"

"Yes, sir," said Loft, and he saluted formally and went out of the room.

Hunter regarded Colonel Lanser amusedly. "Weren't you rough on him?"

"I had to be. He's frightened. I know his kind. He has to be disciplined when he's afraid or he'll go to pieces. He relies on discipline the way other men rely on sympathy. I suppose you'd better get to your rails. You might as well expect that tonight is the time when they'll really blow them, though."

Hunter stood up and he said, "Yes. I suppose the orders are coming in from the capital?"

"Yes."

"Are they——"

"You know what they are," Lanser interrupted. "You know what they'd have to be. Take the leaders, shoot the leaders, take hostages, shoot the hostages, take more hostages, shoot them"—his voice had risen but now it sank almost to a whisper—"and the hatred growing and the hurt between us deeper and deeper."

Hunter hesitated. "Have they condemned any from the list of names?" and he motioned slightly toward the Mayor's bedroom.

Lanser shook his head. "No, not yet. They are just arrested so far."

Hunter said quietly, "Colonel, do you want me to recommend— maybe you're overtired, Colonel? Could I—you know—could I report that you're overtired?"

For a moment Lanser covered his eyes with his hand, and then his shoulders straightened and his face grew hard. "I'm not a civilian,

Hunter. We're short enough of officers already. You know that. Get to your work, Major. I have to see Corell."

Hunter smiled. He went to the door and opened it, and he said out of the door, "Yes, he's here," and over his shoulder he said to Lanser, "It's Prackle. He wants to see you."

"Send him in," said Lanser.

Prackle came in, his face sullen, belligerent. "Colonel Lanser, sir, I wish to——"

"Sit down," said Lanser. "Sit down and rest a moment. Be a good soldier, Lieutenant."

The stiffness went out of Prackle quickly. He sat down beside the table and rested his elbows on it. "I wish——"

And Lanser said, "Don't talk for a moment. I know what it is. You didn't think it would be this way, did you? You thought it would be rather nice."

"They hate us," Prackle said. "They hate us so much."

Lanser smiled. "I wonder if I know what it is. It takes young men to make good soldiers, and young men need young women, is that it?"

"Yes, that's it."

"Well," Lanser said kindly, "does she hate you?"

Prackle looked at him in amazement. "I don't know, sir. Sometimes I think she's only sorry."

"And you're pretty miserable?"

"I don't like it here, sir."

"No, you thought it would be fun, didn't you? Lieutenant Tonder went to pieces and then he went out and they got a knife in him. I could send you home. Do you want to be sent home, knowing we need you here?"

Prackle said uneasily, "No, sir, I don't."

"Good. Now I'll tell you, and I hope you'll understand it. You're not a man any more. You are a soldier. Your comfort is of no importance and, Lieutenant, your life isn't of much importance. If you live, you will have memories. That's about all you will have. Meanwhile you must take orders and carry them out. Most of the orders will be unpleasant, but that's not your business. I will not lie to you, Lieutenant. They should have trained you for this, and not for flower-strewn

streets. They should have built your soul with truth, not led it along with lies." His voice grew hard. "But you took the job, Lieutenant. Will you stay with it or quit it? We can't take care of your soul."

Prackle stood up. "Thank you, sir."

"And the girl," Lanser continued, "the girl, Lieutenant, you may rape her, or protect her, or marry her—that is of no importance so long as you shoot her when it is ordered."

Prackle said wearily, "Yes, sir, thank you, sir."

"I assure you it is better to know. I assure you of that. It is better to know. Go now, Lieutenant, and if Corell is still waiting, send him in." And he watched Lieutenant Prackle out of the doorway.

When Mr. Corell came in, he was a changed man. His left arm was in a cast, and he was no longer the jovial, friendly, smiling Corell. His face was sharp and bitter, and his eyes squinted down like little dead pig's eyes.

"I should have come before, Colonel," he said, "but your lack of co-operation made me hesitant."

Lanser said, "You were waiting for a reply to your report, I remember."

"I was waiting for much more than that. You refused me a position of authority. You said I was valueless. You did not realize that I was in this town long before you were. You left the Mayor in his office, contrary to my advice."

Lanser said, "Without him here we might have had more disorder than we have."

"That is a matter of opinion," Corell said. "This man is a leader of a rebellious people."

"Nonsense," said Lanser; "he's just a simple man."

With his good hand Corell took a black notebook from his right pocket and opened it with his fingers. "You forgot, Colonel, that I had my sources, that I had been here a long time before you. I have to report to you that Mayor Orden has been in constant contact with every happening in this community. On the night when Lieutenant Tonder was murdered, he was in the house where the murder was committed. When the girl escaped to the hills, she stayed with one of his relatives. I traced her there, but she was gone. Whenever men have

escaped, Orden has known about it and has helped them. And I even strongly suspect that he is somewhere in the picture of these little parachutes."

Lanser said eagerly, "But you can't prove it."

"No," Corell said, "I can't prove it. The first thing I know; the last I only suspect. Perhaps now you will be willing to listen to me."

Lanser said quietly, "What do you suggest?"

"These suggestions, Colonel, are a little stronger than suggestions. Orden must now be a hostage and his life must depend on the peacefulness of this community. His life must depend on the lighting of one single fuse on one single stick of dynamite."

He reached into his pocket again and brought out a little folding book, and he flipped it open and laid it in front of the colonel. "This, sir, was the answer to my report from headquarters. You will notice that it gives me certain authority."

Lanser looked at the little book and he spoke quietly. "You really did go over my head, didn't you?" He looked up at Corell with frank dislike in his eyes. "I heard you'd been injured. How did it happen?"

Corell said, "On the night when your lieutenant was murdered I was waylaid. The patrol saved me. Some of the townsmen escaped in my boat that night. Now, Colonel, must I express more strongly than I have that Mayor Orden must be held hostage?"

Lanser said, "He is here, he hasn't escaped. How can we hold him more hostage than we are?"

Suddenly in the distance there was a sound of an explosion, and both men looked around in the direction from which it came. Corell said, "There it is, Colonel, and you know perfectly well that if this experiment succeeds there will be dynamite in every invaded country."

Lanser repeated quietly, "What do you suggest?"

"Just what I have said. Orden must be held against rebellion."

"And if they rebel and we shoot Orden?"

"Then that little doctor is next; although he holds no position, he's next in authority in the town."

"But he holds no office."

"He has the confidence of the people."

"And when we shoot him, what then?"

"Then we have authority. Then rebellion will be broken. When we have killed the leaders, the rebellion will be broken."

Lanser asked quizzically, "Do you really think so?"

"It must be so."

Lanser shook his head slowly and then he called, "Sentry!" The door opened and a soldier appeared in the doorway. "Sergeant," said Lanser, "I have placed Mayor Orden under arrest, and I have placed Doctor Winter under arrest. You will see to it that Orden is guarded and you will bring Winter here immediately."

The sentry said, "Yes, sir."

Lanser looked up at Corell and he said, "You know, I hope you know what you're doing. I do hope you know what you're doing."

CHAPTER EIGHT

In the little town the news ran quickly. It was communicated by whispers in doorways, by quick, meaningful looks—"The Mayor's been arrested"—and through the town a little quiet jubilance ran, a fierce little jubilance, and people talked quietly together and went apart, and people going in to buy food leaned close to the clerks for a moment and a word passed between them.

The people went into the country, into the woods, searching for dynamite. And children playing in the snow found the dynamite, and by now even the children had their instructions. They opened the packages and ate the chocolate, and then they buried the dynamite in the snow and told their parents where it was.

Far out in the country a man picked up a tube and read the instructions and he said to himself, "I wonder if this works." He stood the tube up in the snow and lighted the fuse, and he ran back from it and counted, but his count was fast. It was sixty-eight before the dynamite exploded. He said, "It does work," and he went hurriedly about looking for more tubes.

Almost as though at a signal the people went into their houses and the doors were closed, the streets were quiet. At the mine the soldiers carefully searched every miner who went into the shaft, searched and

researched, and the soldiers were nervous and rough and they spoke harshly to the miners. The miners looked coldly at them, and behind their eyes was a little fierce jubilation.

In the drawing-room of the palace of the Mayor the table had been cleaned up, and a soldier stood guard at Mayor Orden's bedroom door. Annie was on her knees in front of the coal grate, putting little pieces of coal on the fire. She looked up at the sentry standing in front of Mayor Orden's door and she said truculently, "Well, what are you going to do to him?" The soldier did not answer.

The outside door opened and another soldier came in, holding Doctor Winter by the arm. He closed the door behind Doctor Winter and stood against the door inside the room. Doctor Winter said, "Hello, Annie, how's His Excellency?"

And Annie pointed at the bedroom and said, "He's in there."

"He isn't ill?" Doctor Winter said.

"No, he didn't seem to be," said Annie. "I'll see if I can tell him you're here." She went to the sentry and spoke imperiously. "Tell His Excellency that Doctor Winter is here, do you hear me?"

The sentry did not answer and did not move, but behind him the door opened and Mayor Orden stood in the doorway. He ignored the sentry and brushed past him and stepped into the room. For a moment the sentry considered taking him back, and then he returned to his place beside the door. Orden said, "Thank you, Annie. Don't go too far away, will you? I might need you."

Annie said, "No, sir, I won't. Is Madame all right?"

"She's doing her hair. Do you want to see her, Annie?"

"Yes, sir," said Annie, and she brushed past the sentry, too, and went into the bedroom and shut the door.

Orden said, "Is there something you want, Doctor?"

Winter grinned sardonically and pointed over his shoulder to his guard. "Well, I guess I'm under arrest. My friend here brought me."

Orden said, "I suppose it was bound to come. What will they do now, I wonder?" And the two men looked at each other for a long time and each one knew what the other one was thinking.

And then Orden continued as though he had been talking. "You know, I couldn't stop it if I wanted to."

"I know," said Winter, "but they don't know." And he went on with

a thought he had been having. "A time-minded people," he said, "and the time is nearly up. They think that just because they have only one leader and one head, we are all like that. They know that ten heads lopped off will destroy them, but we are a free people; we have as many heads as we have people, and in a time of need leaders pop up among us like mushrooms."

Orden put his hand on Winter's shoulder and he said, "Thank you. I knew it, but it's good to hear you say it. The little people won't go under, will they?" He searched Winter's face anxiously.

And the doctor reassured him, "Why, no, they won't. As a matter of fact, they will grow stronger with outside help."

The room was silent for a moment. The sentry shifted his position a little and his rifle clinked on a button.

Orden said, "I can talk to you, Doctor, and I probably won't be able to talk again. There are little shameful things in my mind." He coughed and glanced at the rigid soldier, but the soldier gave no sign of having heard. "I have been thinking of my own death. If they follow the usual course, they must kill me, and then they must kill you." And when Winter was silent, he said, "Mustn't they?"

"Yes, I guess so." Winter walked to one of the gilt chairs, and as he was about to sit down he noticed that its tapestry was torn, and he petted the seat with his fingers as though that would mend it. And he sat down gently because it was torn.

And Orden went on, "You know, I'm afraid, I have been thinking of ways to escape, to get out of it. I have been thinking of running away. I have been thinking of pleading for my life, and it makes me ashamed."

And Winter, looking up, said, "But you haven't done it."

"No, I haven't."

"And you won't do it."

Orden hesitated. "No, I won't. But I have thought of it."

And Winter said, gently, "How do you know everyone doesn't think of it? How do you know I haven't thought of it?"

"I wonder why they arrested you, too," Orden said. "I guess they will have to kill you, too."

"I guess so," said Winter. He rolled his thumbs and watched them tumble over and over.

"You know so." Orden was silent for a moment and then he said,

"You know, Doctor, I am a little man and this is a little town, but there must be a spark in little men that can burst into flame. I am afraid, I am terribly afraid, and I thought of all the things I might do to save my own life, and then that went away, and sometimes now I feel a kind of exultation, as though I were bigger and better than I am, and do you know what I have been thinking, Doctor?" He smiled, remembering. "Do you remember in school, in the *Apology*? Do you remember Socrates says, 'Someone will say, "And are you not ashamed, Socrates, of a course of life which is likely to bring you to an untimely end?" To him I may fairly answer, "There you are mistaken: a man who is good for anything ought not to calculate the chance of living or dying; he ought only to consider whether he is doing right or wrong." ' " Orden paused, trying to remember.

Doctor Winter sat tensely forward now, and he went on with it, " 'Acting the part of a good man or of a bad.' I don't think you have it quite right. You never were a good scholar. You were wrong in the denunciation, too."

Orden chuckled. "Do you remember that?"

"Yes," said Winter, eagerly, "I remember it well. You forgot a line or a word. It was graduation, and you were so excited you forgot to tuck in your shirt-tail and your shirt-tail was out. You wondered why they laughed."

Orden smiled to himself, and his hand went secretly behind him and patrolled for a loose shirt-tail. "I was Socrates," he said, "and I denounced the School Board. How I denounced them! I bellowed it, and I could see them grow red."

Winter said, "They were holding their breaths to keep from laughing. Your shirt-tail was out."

Mayor Orden laughed. "How long ago? Forty years."

"Forty-six."

The sentry by the bedroom door moved quietly over to the sentry by the outside door. They spoke softly out of the corners of their mouths like children whispering in school. "How long you been on duty?"

"All night. Can't hardly keep my eyes open."

"Me too. Hear from your wife on the boat yesterday?"

"Yes! She said say hello to you. Said she heard you was wounded. She don't write much."

"Tell her I'm all right."

"Sure—when I write."

The Mayor raised his head and looked at the ceiling and he muttered, "Um—um—um. I wonder if I can remember—how does it go?"

And Winter prompted him, " 'And now, O men——' "

And Orden said softly, " 'And now, O men who have condemned me——' "

Colonel Lanser came quietly into the room; the sentries stiffened. Hearing the words, the colonel stopped and listened.

Orden looked at the ceiling, lost in trying to remember the old words. " 'And now, O men who have condemned me,' " he said, " 'I would fain prophesy to you—for I am about to die—and—in the hour of death—men are gifted with prophetic power. And I—prophesy to you who are my murderers—that immediately after my—my death——' "

And Winter stood up, saying, "Departure."

Orden looked at him. "What?"

And Winter said, "The word is 'departure,' not 'death.' You made the same mistake before. You made that mistake forty-six years ago."

"No, it is death. It is death." Orden looked around and saw Colonel Lanser watching him. He asked, "Isn't it 'death'?"

Colonel Lanser said, " 'Departure.' It is 'immediately after my departure.' "

Doctor Winter insisted, "You see, that's two against one. 'Departure' is the word. It is the same mistake you made before."

Then Orden looked straight ahead and his eyes were in his memory, seeing nothing outward. And he went on, " 'I prophesy to you who are my murderers that immediately after my—departure punishment far heavier than you have inflicted on me will surely await you.' "

Winter nodded encouragingly, and Colonel Lanser nodded, and they seemed to be trying to help him to remember. And Orden went on, " 'Me you have killed because you wanted to escape the accuser, and not to give an account of your lives—!' "

Lieutenant Prackle entered excitedly, crying, "Colonel Lanser!"

Colonel Lanser said, "Shh——" and he held out his hand to restrain him.

And Orden went on softly, " 'But that will not be as you suppose; far otherwise.' " His voice grew stronger. " 'For I say that there will be more accusers of you than there are now' "—he made a little gesture with his hand, a speech-making gesture—" 'accusers whom hitherto I have restrained; and as they are younger they will be more inconsiderate with you, and you will be more offended at them.' " He frowned, trying to remember.

And Lieutenant Prackle said, "Colonel Lanser, we have found some men with dynamite."

And Lanser said, "Hush."

Orden continued. " 'If you think that by killing men you can prevent someone from censuring your evil lives, you are mistaken.' " He frowned and thought and he looked at the ceiling, and he smiled embarrassedly and he said, "That's all I can remember. It is gone away from me."

And Doctor Winter said, "It's very good after forty-six years, and you weren't very good at it forty-six years ago."

Lieutenant Prackle broke in, "The men have dynamite, Colonel Lanser."

"Did you arrest them?"

"Yes, sir. Captain Loft and——"

Lanser said, "Tell Captain Loft to guard them." He recaptured himself and he advanced into the room and he said, "Orden, these things must stop."

And the Mayor smiled helplessly at him. "They cannot stop, sir."

Colonel Lanser said harshly, "I arrested you as a hostage for the good behavior of your people. Those are my orders."

"But that won't stop it," Orden said simply. "You don't understand. When I have become a hindrance to the people, they will do without me."

Lanser said, "Tell me truly what you think. If the people know you will be shot if they light another fuse, what will they do?"

The Mayor looked helplessly at Doctor Winter. And then the bedroom door opened and Madame came out, carrying the Mayor's chain of office in her hand. She said, "You forgot this."

Orden said, "What? Oh, yes," and he stooped his head and Madame slipped the chain of office over his head, and he said, "Thank you, dear."

Madame complained, "You always forget it. You forget it all the time."

The Mayor looked at the end of the chain he held in his hand—the gold medallion with the insignia of his office carved on it. Lanser pressed him. "What will they do?"

"I don't know," said the Mayor. "I think they will light the fuse."

"Suppose you ask them not to?"

Winter said, "Colonel, this morning I saw a little boy building a snow man, while three grown soldiers watched to see that he did not caricature your leader. He made a pretty good likeness, too, before they destroyed it."

Lanser ignored the doctor. "Suppose you ask them not to?" he repeated.

Orden seemed half asleep; his eyes were drooped, and he tried to think. He said, "I am not a very brave man, sir. I think they will light it, anyway." He struggled with his speech. "I hope they will, but if I ask them not to, they will be sorry."

Madame said, "What is this all about?"

"Be quiet a moment, dear," the Mayor said.

"But you think they will light it?" Lanser insisted.

The Mayor spoke proudly. "Yes, they will light it. I have no choice of living or dying, you see, sir, but—I do have a choice of how I do it. If I tell them not to fight, they will be sorry, but they will fight. If I tell them to fight, they will be glad, and I who am not a very brave man will have made them a little braver." He smiled apologetically. "You see, it is an easy thing to do, since the end for me is the same."

Lanser said, "If you say yes, we can tell them you said no. We can tell them you begged for your life."

And Winter broke in angrily, "They would know. You do not keep secrets. One of your men got out of hand one night and he said the flies had conquered the flypaper, and now the whole nation knows his words. They have made a song of it. The flies have conquered the flypaper. You do not keep secrets, Colonel."

From the direction of the mine a whistle tooted shrilly. And a quick gust of wind sifted dry snow against the windows.

Orden fingered his gold medallion. He said quietly, "You see, sir, nothing can change it. You will be destroyed and driven out." His voice was very soft. "The people don't like to be conquered, sir, and so they will not be. Free men cannot start a war, but once it is started, they can fight on in defeat. Herd men, followers of a leader, cannot do that, and so it is always the herd men who win battles and the free men who win wars. You will find that is so, sir."

Lanser was erect and stiff. "My orders are clear. Eleven o'clock was the deadline. I have taken hostages. If there is violence, the hostages will be executed."

And Doctor Winter said to the colonel, "Will you carry out the orders, knowing they will fail?"

Lanser's face was tight. "I will carry out my orders no matter what they are, but I do think, sir, a proclamation from you might save many lives."

Madame broke in plaintively, "I wish you would tell me what all this nonsense is."

"It is nonsense, dear."

"But they can't arrest the Mayor," she explained to him.

Orden smiled at her. "No," he said, "they can't arrest the Mayor. The Mayor is an idea conceived by free men. It will escape arrest."

From the distance there was a sound of an explosion. And the echo of it rolled to the hills and back again. The whistle at the coal mine tooted a shrill, sharp warning. Orden stood very tensely for a moment and then he smiled. A second explosion roared—nearer this time and heavier—and its echo rolled back from the mountains. Orden looked at his watch and then he took his watch and chain and put them in Doctor Winter's hand. "How did it go about the flies?" he asked.

"The flies have conquered the flypaper," Winter said.

Orden called, "Annie!" The bedroom door opened instantly and the Mayor said, "Were you listening?"

"Yes, sir." Annie was embarrassed.

And now an explosion roared near by and there was a sound of splintering wood and breaking glass, and the door behind the sentries puffed open. And Orden said, "Annie, I want you to stay with Madame

as long as she needs you. Don't leave her alone." He put his arm around Madame and he kissed her on the forehead and then he moved slowly toward the door where Lieutenant Prackle stood. In the doorway he turned back to Doctor Winter. "Crito, I owe a cock to Asclepius," he said tenderly. "Will you remember to pay the debt?"

Winter closed his eyes for a moment before he answered, "The debt shall be paid."

Orden chuckled then. "I remembered that one. I didn't forget that one." He put his hand on Prackle's arm, and the lieutenant flinched away from him.

And Winter nodded slowly. "Yes, you remembered. The debt shall be paid."

FROM *THE BIRDS FALL DOWN* (1966)

Rebecca West (1892–1983)

Dame Rebecca West was known primarily as a brilliant journalist; she is perhaps now best known for her magnificent Black Lamb and Grey Falcon, *an inquiry, in the form of a travel book, into the heart and soul of Yugoslavia in 1937. In her novel* The Birds Fall Down, *it is "the very beginning of the twentieth century"—the first Russian revolution, in 1905, is on the horizon, as Count Nikolai Diakonov, former minister of justice under the czar, now an émigré living in Paris, and his grand-daughter, Laura Rowan, eighteen, are going by train to Diakonov's seaside villa on the coast of Normandy. In their compartment on the train, they are confronted by the revolutionary, Chubinov.*

IV

. . . He had spoken in Russian. But he was not one of the Russians she knew. She had not met him in Paris or in London. Slowly she said, "Good morning, Monsieur," taking a good look at him, and was still sure that she had never seen him before. He was middle-sized, lean

and pale, with unkempt hair and meagre beard and moustache, all mouse-brown, and grey eyes behind spectacles. He would have passed unnoticed if it had not been that he was very badly dressed. His great-coat looked like a dressing-gown, for it was made of an odd fawn-and-blue striped material and too loosely cut, and it was worn carelessly, the belt twisted, the collar half up, half down. He looked Russian, she would have known he was that, even if he had never opened his mouth. . . .

". . . Well, Nikolai Nikolaievitch, if you will not help me, I'll have to give you the whole story. Tell me, does the name of Gorin mean anything to you?"

"It does indeed," said Nikolai. "I've never been able to forget a disreputable connection between you and him. When you were still at Moscow University and had just begun breaking your father's heart by joining the Union of Social Revolutionaries, you started a seditious journal named *The Morning Star.* In its first number, which I am pleased to say I contrived should be the last, you published an article calling for the assassination of the Tsar. The only sympathetic response you received was from a man named Gorin, who was then an engineering student at the polytechnic in Karlsruhe in Germany, and played a prominent part in a Union of Expatriate Social Revolutionaries which had been started by the Russian students there, God forgive them."

"That's the man," sighed Chubinov. "But did you ever meet him?"

"No. I never even saw him. He came to Moscow shortly after he wrote to you, but we didn't arrest him. We hardly troubled to watch him. It was ascertained that he was of no importance."

"Of no importance?" repeated Chubinov, raising his eyebrows.

"Quite negligible. He was one of the older men in the movement, older than you, much older than you, and in such poor health that he was always retiring to somewhere in the South to a certain sanatorium."

"Now, why do you say that?"

"As to his age, we had his birth certificate. He was born in Baku. I don't know why I remember that, but I do. As for the sanatorium, it regularly reported his admission and his discharge. He was visited there by the police on one or two occasions."

Chubinov said, "No. At some point your men went wrong. Gorin

wrote to me about my call for the assassination of the Tsar, yes. But none of the rest fits." His manner was dispassionate, professional, brooding, and Nikolai answered in the same tone. "There could very well be a confusion. Gorin is a common name, and one lazy official, or one lazy morning indulged in by an active man could substitute your Gorin for my Gorin on the records for ever. Do what one can, such things will happen."

"Mm," agreed Chubinov, reflectively, and again they were policemen. ("Sergeant, there's a pane here that's been taken out and put back recently." "Yes, but not last night. There's three kids in the house, see if one of them hasn't sent a ball through the window a week or so ago.") Chubinov went on, "I'd better tell you about my Gorin, the one who quite certainly wrote to me about my article. He's no older than I am. He was born in Lyskovo in the Gordnensko province. I've never known him to be ill till recently, and I doubt if even now he's gone to a sanatorium. He's a man of nondescript but pleasing appearance, so indeterminate that I don't know why it pleases. He is," he said hesitantly, "a wonderful man. Tell me, didn't any of your men who spied on the students at Karlsruhe, didn't any of them tell you that Gorin was a wonderful man?"

"They reported his height, the colour of his hair and beard and his eyes, and his treachery and blasphemies," said Nikolai. "Nothing else would be in their line of business. We are not composing fairy-tales like your lot."

"Well, Gorin, my Gorin, is a wonderful man. An old professor at Karlsruhe who was a German but was on our side said to me, 'It's a pity that future generations will know nothing of your friend. He can have no future for he's spending himself on the present. Nobody can meet him without becoming a better man, without being purged of all trivial or base thought, all crude instincts. He can never achieve a great historical act or a scientific discovery or a work of art, because all his force is expended on his elevated personal life. Be happy,' he told me, 'for your friend is bestowing on you what would have enabled him to write another *Hamlet* or add a third part of *Faust.*' "

"German professors gush like young ladies but are not so pretty," said Nikolai.

"The years have not made this praise of my friend seem anything but literally true. Not that Gorin ever gives any proof of outstanding intellectual gift. Of course he knows where he is with the philosophic fathers of our Party, with Kant and Hegel. He's against Marx and for Mikhailovsky, he's always ready to demonstrate lucidly and without heat that the existence of our movement refutes Marxist dogma, for it's born of the intelligentsia and the people, and couldn't be termed a class movement. He's warned us often that we must listen to Nietzsche's call for a transvaluation of values but must close our eyes to his hatred of the state."

"You speak of names that will be forgotten in twenty years' time," said Nikolai. "Except, of course, Kant and Hegel. But you have misread them. They prove our case, not yours."

"Yes, they can be read both ways," said Chubinov dryly, and again changed his pair of spectacles for the other. "But one way is wrong and one is right. Ours is the right way. But all that isn't really Gorin's field. He's never been attached to the theoretical branch of the Party. He was an organizer of our practical activities."

"You mean he's a damned murderer," said Nikolai.

"I was about to say that his field was friendship. One would be sitting in the dark in some wretched lodging in a strange town, afraid to light the lamp because some comrade had been arrested, some plan aborted, and there would be footsteps on the rickety stairs, one's heart would sink, there would be the five reassuring taps on the door, the handle would turn, the unknown would enter and annul the blackness with the spark of a match, would bring out a little dark-lantern and through the half-light there would show the face of Gorin, smiling. And then, with so little demand for thanks, he would set down on the table a loaf and some sausage and a bottle of vodka and perhaps a precious revolutionary book, and it would be as if there were no such thing as despair."

"The only one of you who had the sense to think that you might need a dark-lantern, the only one who knew where and how and when to buy bread and sausage and vodka," said Nikolai. "There was no reason, was there, why you shouldn't have had all these things by you? It is an extraordinary thing that suddenly village idiots have become

enormously prolific, and their spawn has all joined the intelligentsia. Well, while the men and women who truly love the people were training as schoolteachers and building hospitals and going to schools of agriculture, you were sitting in garrets—either before you had done mischief or after you had done it—sustained by your infernal Gorin who might have added a third part to *Faust,* though even the second was too many, all feeling like little lambs."

"Oh, Gorin was certainly no lamb," said Chubinov. "He was a wolf. He has in his time slain many. And always, from the beginning, with your help."

Nikolai looked at him with hooded eyes.

"Did you never wonder how one of our members presented himself at the Ministry of the Interior in the guise of the aide-de-camp of the Grand Duke Serge, and was shown straight into the presence of General Sipyagin? It was because Sipyagin had received a letter that very morning, forged in your handwriting, on your private note-paper, sealed with your seal, and making an allusion to a funny story he had told you when he had dined with you at your house a week before. The letter told Sipyagin that the Grand Duke Serge was sending him a newly appointed aide-de-camp who would not know the routine and should be shown straight into the Ministerial office. Gorin arranged all that for us."

"I've only your word for it," said Nikolai.

"Better take it," said Chubinov. "For that story, and for much else. A railway worker and a schoolteacher both went one day to see the Governor of Ufa. Neither had had any opportunity to learn his habits. But they climbed over a wall and went straight to a secluded corner in the cathedral garden where he went every day to sit and recite the day's prayers. And he had told you this was his custom in a letter you had received a fortnight before. So Gorin had told us."

Nikolai covered his mouth with a trembling hand.

"And that letter displeased you, for the Governor was a worldly man, and you suspected that when he did this at noon he was trying to curry favour with you and your devout kind. That was what you wrote in your diary. Gorin read it."

"God forgive me for my lack of charity," said Nikolai. "You do not

hurt me as much as you hope by telling me that I am betrayed. I am a Christian and I know it must be so. Judas exists for all of us. That he touched Christ with his foul hand means that he touches every member of the human race with his eternally polluted finger, at all moments in time, in the past, in the present, in the future."

"If I pester you for the name which Judas has assumed for you and for me at this particular moment of time," said Chubinov, "it must by your showing be the will of God that I should pester you."

"Leave me alone," said Nikolai. "Give me a moment that I may pray for forgiveness for my lack of charity towards that poor man who was slaughtered by your assassins as he sat with God in a book upon his knee—"

"Grandfather, Grandfather," said Laura, "what are you saying? Do you mean that these people killed the Governor?"

"Yes, indeed, and Sipyagin also was shot through the heart," said Nikolai. "But my lack of charity, how unseeing, how insolent it was. If a man is brought to God by hopes of advancement, and the Governor of Ufa was a man with few social advantages and must have been much tempted that way, nevertheless he is brought to God and is sacred."

Her spine stiffened, she sat up and stared at Chubinov with the total fury of a cat. She said to him, "You're mixed up with all these murders?"

"They were not murders but surgical operations designed to cure the cancer which devours our Russia," he answered. She hissed with hatred. She could not bear to think of a man with such meagre hair, such weak eyes, being responsible for the stopping of life. But he ignored her, asking Nikolai, "Don't you really want to know the identity of the man who has made use of you to remove those objects of your loyalty, Dubassoff, Plehve, the Grand Duke Serge—"

"Oh, God," exclaimed Nikolai, "were you, the son of my friend, a party to all those crimes?"

"Why, so were you," said Chubinov.

The old man winced. She put her arms about him. "Why do we have to bother with this awful man?" she asked. He said, "Leave me alone, Sofia, Tania, Laura. I have to find out whether I have been negligent." She had not the slightest idea what to do. This was possibly be-

cause she was only half-Russian. She had an idea that her grandmother or her mother would have found some means, which would perhaps have been a gesture rather than anything said, of persuading Nikolai to stop talking to this horrible man who owned he was as wicked as Jack the Ripper or Charles Peace. Perhaps they would have thrown themselves kneeling at his feet. But if she had done that she would simply have looked silly. It was open to her of course to go along the corridor and get the attendant to put Chubinov out of the carriage, but she did not dare to leave him alone with her grandfather, for he probably had a revolver on him. Perhaps she could get the Frenchwomen to watch for that while she went and got the attendant, they looked as if they might have a talent for screaming. She turned to them and was checked by the repugnance on their faces. She remembered that nannies and schoolmistresses were always saying that people who behaved oddly made themselves unpopular. The truth seemed to be sharper than that. Also, if she got the attendant, her grandfather would probably say he wanted to go on talking to Chubinov, that he was a friend. She kept her arms ineffectually on the great mass of his body while he and Chubinov talked about people with Russian names in the policemanly way.

"Yes," said Nikolai, thoughtfully. "I did know someone called Pravdine. And, yes, I have a vague impression that he had some connection with the Ministry of Justice. I can even remember what he looked like. He was a small man, a very small man. And now I speak of him, I can see him quite distinctly, holding his little daughter by the hand, a little girl who looked like a doll, who had golden curls and blue eyes and cheeks like painted wax. There was a toy trumpet swinging from her little hand. But I had hardly anything to do with him. He can't have told your Gorin anything about me of importance."

"I'm of that opinion also," said Chubinov. "I think Gorin lied when he said his informant was Pravdine. There. I have said it. I think Gorin lied."

"Yes," Nikolai went on, "now I see Pravdine very clearly. He's standing in the entrance of his apartment with this little girl by his side, this child who looked like a French doll. She was wearing a fine muslin dress which spread out like the lampshades ladies have in their

boudoirs, and she carried this toy trumpet. Behind him was an open door, opening on a gaslit room, and I can just see the tips of the branches of a Christmas tree, and I hear the sounds of children's voices. I can't imagine why I should have been present on such an occasion at this man's home, for he was a person of no importance. Ah, yes, now it comes back to me, Pravdine was the man we used to call the fifth cow in the Ministry of Justice. But you wouldn't understand that."

"Indeed I do," said Chubinov. "I've known the story ever since I was a child. When your father inherited your grandfather's St. Petersburg palace he invited my grandfather to go over it with him, and they found five cows kept in stalls on the roof, with a serf from the estate living with his wife and children in a hut beside them. That was usual enough, of course. But only four of the cows belonged to the family, the fifth was an intruder whose milk was sold in the street by a Kalmuck who was living in another hut on the roof and could give no account of how he came to be there. The serf had found him there when he was sent up from the estate. And always at my home, as I think at yours, we spoke of the unidentifiable person, the guest at the party whom nobody knows, the speaker at the conference whose name is not on the agenda, as 'the fifth cow.' "

"Oh, Vassili Iulievitch," breathed Nikolai, "how pleasant it is to talk of what there was between your father and me, your family and mine. You smiled like an innocent man when you told me that story. For a minute it seemed as if nothing had gone wrong, with any of us, with Russia. Ah, well, the fifth cow. The fifth cow. But of course I know why we called Pravdine that. He had a room in the short corridor leading from the main one to my office—"

"Then Gorin's story might be true?" Chubinov asked eagerly.

"Not possibly. The room was very small. At one time the cleaners had kept their pails and brooms there, and it was no place for any official, but we had to find somewhere to put poor Pravdine, who kept office hours but had almost nothing to do. You see, this was a case of impulsive royal generosity. The Empress Mother had visited some town in the provinces and had been touched by the plight of the widow of an official who had been struck by lightning in a storm which struck the city at the moment of her arrival. The official was of quite a

humble rank and his family were left with no means, and therefore the Empress arranged for the woman's son, who was Pravdine, to be appointed to a post in the Ministry of Justice which she herself had just insisted on being created because she had formed an erroneous impression that there was no school for the staff's children in a prison she had inspected on the Polish border, and had concluded, as erroneously, there were no schools for the children of prison staffs anywhere in Russia. The whole story was consonant with the Empress Mother's unique personality."

"You know what the Tsar and Tsarina call her in private?" asked Chubinov, smiling. "*'L'Irascible.'*"

"You know that too," said Nikolai and fell silent for a moment. "Well, there Pravdine lived in his little cupboard, sometimes ordering a blackboard or some exercise-books. But I never spoke to him except once, when I went to his Christmas party at his apartment, because his wife's sister had married a priest of whom my wife thought well. I don't see how the poor man could possibly have told you anything about me, even if he had wanted to, and I don't believe he would want to."

"I'm sure that's so," said Chubinov. "This is, as you say, a case of A bringing valid information about B and saying falsely that it comes from C. Now let's get on to the next stage in the story. For years we accepted that Pravdine was our informant on you. Then when you went for your trip to Paris, which we knew, long before you did, was to be your permanent exile, we were distressed. We were, you see, specially anxious to go on studying the serial story of the Tsar's perfidy which you were writing in your diary without knowing it. Also, we wanted to know whether you and your associates went on being baffled by the mystery of who it was in your entourage who had betrayed you over the attack on the two Grand Dukes at Kiev and the one on the Tsar at Reval. Then, also, and perhaps most important for those of us who bear the responsibility for the terrorist branch of the revolutionary movement, there was another mystery which had to be solved. I'll talk of that later. But for the meantime, you'll see the situation. It was important that we should find someone to spy on you in Paris as Pravdine had spied on you in St. Petersburg. Yes, yes, I realize now Pravdine

wasn't the man, but we then thought that he was. But we never imagined we'd find anybody who could get his foot inside your door in Paris
for weeks, or months, or even years. Just think how difficult it was
bound to be, with the Russian Secret Police having its own office in
Paris to deal with expatriates."

"Well, those fellows don't do much," said Nikolai. "They all get cor-
rupted by the West. The ideal would be for all Russians to live and die
in Russia, seeing only their own kind and maintaining their own system. It's only you accursed expatriates which make us break our rule
in the case of the police."

"Oh, those fellows keep their claws. You're wrong if you think they
give our people much rope. Well, it seemed to us a remarkable example of Gorin's efficiency that almost at once he found someone in Paris
who would be able to report to us just as regularly as we thought Pravdine had done. But that's what's so wonderful about Gorin. He seems
so gentle and, as it were, so bemused, turning from one object of kindness to another, not knowing whom to comfort first, and then there's a
specific task to be done, and all of a sudden he changes into somebody
else—he might be one of those great industrialists, those railway mag-
nates, those capitalist monsters whom Count Witte is always trying to
let loose on our country for the exploitation of our wretched people.
Well, Gorin sprang into action now. In no time he found us a man who
could tell us from moment to moment what you are doing. A man
named Porfirio Ilyitch Berr." He repeated the name softly. "Porfirio
Ilyitch Berr."

"You ought to be in a lunatic asylum," said Nikolai Nikolaievitch.
"You and all your friends. First my diaries are being read and my most
intimate secrets revealed by a man named Pravdine who in fact sat in
a housemaid's cupboard all day ordering blackboards and spoke with
me, so far as I can remember, once in my life and then to wish me a
happy Christmas, and never set foot in my office. Now I'm having my
soul put under the Röntgen rays by a man I've never seen or heard of,
Porfirio Ilyitch Berr. You're all mad."

"You're wrong when you say you don't know Berr," said Chubinov,
looking for the first time rather disagreeable, sly and harsh. "It's the
world you live in that makes you think you don't. That world where

everything good and noble and enduring is annulled by the system, the monstrous, murderous system that subordinates everything to the aim of putting the few over the many. You know Berr. You even derive, because not all your heart is callused by power, the most exquisite pleasure from his company."

"Mad," said Nikolai, "raving mad, the lot of you."

"But all that I'll explain later. First, before I can make that explanation, I must express to you that we are two halves of a whole. We're in the same plight as you. We have our Judas."

"Oh, I know who he is," said Nikolai.

"You know?" cried Chubinov. "Then tell me, tell me!"

"Berr," said Nikolai, "old Berr," and chuckled into his beard.

"You're impossible. For God's sake do not be light-minded, as all you reactionaries always are, and answer me one question seriously. The names of Vesnin, Patopenko, and Komissaroff mean to you what they mean to me. They mean a man who was shot, and two men who are slowly dying in the most northerly penal settlement of Siberia. Oh, the cruelty of Tsarist authority, which sends the political idealist into the Arctic cold. How did you come to arrest these three men?"

"That's an official secret," said Nikolai, "so I'll not discuss it."

"You must tell me if you want to live."

"I wouldn't buy my life by the betrayal of any official secret."

"Imbecile old man," shouted Chubinov, "will you risk your personal safety to keep the secrets of the Tsar, when he has treated you far worse than my grandfather or yours would have treated one of their serfs?"

"The answer is, yes. I will do nothing to help the enemies of the Tsar, even to save my life, or the life of any one of my family. There are men who are called to serve God by conformity and I'm one of them. I've always known that. At certain times in my life I've greatly longed to drink and to gamble, I've been hungry for the enormous pleasure in the loss of my senses and in gaining or in losing large sums for no reason. But I've always foreseen that these things would give me no lasting happiness, that my part was to be a pillar and that a pillar must never even sway. Go on telling your story if you like. But I can't believe it'll mean anything to me. You and I were created in different dreams of God."

"There you're mistaken. We're the children of the same dream. Listen. We revolutionaries have, as you know, had many successes in the last few years, but many failures also. We've inflicted the sentence of death on a far greater number of social criminals than have ever been brought to justice before in the same period, but at the same time we've lost more and more of our men to your forces of reaction. Of these Vesnin, Patopenko, and Komissaroff were the most important. They'd all the qualities that would have made them leaders of our organization, particularly Vesnin. But there were many others, and we find the circumstances under which you arrested them incomprehensible. There was always a great knowledge of the workings of our organization behind all these arrests, but they weren't the arrests one would have expected any man who had that knowledge to make. Before each of our great achievements—"

"You mean assassinations."

"Of course. Before each of them, and after them, the police became very active and rounded up a number of terrorists, but never the men and women really engaged in the current conspiracy. Vesnin, however, was arrested just after he had killed the Commandant of St. Petersburg"—Laura drew in her breath with a hiss again—"and Patopenko and Komissaroff when they were just about to execute another important plan, but they were exceptions. Most of the arrested revolutionaries had either struck their last blows some time before or were subordinates not yet ripe for terrorist action. Now, Nikolai Nikolaievitch, what would you make of that?"

"Why, what you do, I expect," answered Nikolai slowly. "That on our side we weren't receiving the information which we'd really have liked, which would have enabled us to uproot the terrorist organization there and then. We were being given just enough to let us cripple the revolutionary movement and prevent it from realizing its full potential. Awkward for us. Awkward for you, too. You lost your leaders of five or ten years ahead, and the survivors are left in a state of mutual distrust, without the old hands to steady them."

They grumbled on. They talked about a lot of people. In Russian conversations there always seemed a crowd of faceless personalities doing violent things. It seemed that many of them lived very uncomfortable lives. Men were told to go from St. Petersburg to Kharkov and

choose their own day and their own route and keep the choice a secret. That, apparently, was insisted on by this man Gorin. Then the traveller arrived at noon and sat about in a dark corner of the station with the story of a further journey ready on his lips if he were questioned, and waited till the afternoon to go into the town, because by then the police were less vigilant. Then he'd be crossing the station square and as he went by the line of drojkis two of the lean horses would paw the ground and jangle their harness, fretted by the two men standing in wait between them, two policemen, who stepped forward with the right interrogations, the proper incredulities. In some room at the headquarters of the Secret Police a voice had said, "Don't try to take him at the station, inside or at the exits. Many of the workers are on his side and they'll warn every solitary traveller if you're about. But you'll find him making his way across the square at about four o'clock in the afternoon." Yet the traveller had never said to himself, "At four o'clock I'll go across the square into the town." He'd just gone there when he felt like it. Some of them had been able to tell the organization that afterwards.

Nikolai said, "Someone knew that if one sits on a station bench from noon one's back feels as if it were breaking just about four o'clock, and stretching one's legs doesn't do any good. Just as someone on your side knows that when my lot have to raid a café where your miserable pack meet to plan their villainies, it's nervous work, as your lot have their revolvers and their bombs and no mercy in their hearts, and the inspector's nerve will break at a particular hour and he'll hustle out his men to get the thing over. And when they get to the café they find no soul there who isn't a blessed saint."

Chubinov said, "But it remains to be learned how they know the day."

"Yes. Or the place."

Both sighed. Then they talked of more men with Russian names that had to be heard several times before they could be clearly grasped. How could Nikolai be content to absorb his attention in this ugly male world when his women called for his interest, his pity! Only a little time ago, when Sofia lifted her small strong ringed hands to pat a hunter's neck and rub his muzzle, it had been on a parity of health; and

at night she had stood upright within her satin gowns, unbowed by the weight of her jewels, while now she was a shrunken mummy, dead except for her courage which was kept alive by her fear. And Tania, she needed pity too. When she used to stand by the window of her bedroom, her elbows supported on the sash and her cheek pressed against the glass, scanning the gardens to see if the double peonies with the heavy scent were open, the corner house to see if the South African diamond people who had bought it had moved in yet, the summer-house to see if the old colonel who lived next door and had been so ill was sitting there with his nurse, she had had the air of an inquisitive child happily dispelling the boredom of the nursery; now she looked as if she were hanging face backwards on a cross, as if you would only have had to turn her round to see tears on her cheeks, bitten lips. How could Nikolai free himself from the thought of these two women who needed his help and listen to this chit-chat about murderers who should only be hanged!

Chubinov was saying, in the unctuous tones of a medical missionary lecturing to the upper fifth: "In order that the secret should be kept, we didn't disperse at the end of the meeting, we stayed together in the café until there was time for them to have executed the plan and got away. That was Gorin's idea. 'Just so that there can be no Judas work,' he said. He and I sat down together and played a game of chess. I can see him now, pausing in play and putting down his queen, to say to me in his gentle way that we must avoid all bitterness in thinking of the traitor amongst us, for it might be that he was one of the older members of the Party and had perhaps been deranged by many years of imprisonment. And then I tried to go on with the game, but kept on making the stupidest mistakes. And Gorin laughed and said, 'You're like me, all the Party members are as your own children and when they are in danger it is as if one had sent into battle the real fruit of one's loins.' But then Lydia Sture came into the café, weaving her way among the tables like a drunken woman, and she bent over our chessboard and whispered that Patopenko and Komissaroff had been arrested even as they left their lodgings with their bombs. For a long time we three were silent and stared at the chessmen as if the way the game was set out would give us a clue to the mystery which was engulfing us."

"Very touching," said Nikolai. "Particularly as Patopenko and Komissaroff's arrest meant that they weren't able to murder the Chief Military Prosecutor. I can't cry over your story, Vassili Iulievitch."

"And you won't tell me how those three arrests were made? Then I'll have to tell you how it is our paths have crossed again."

"The most talkative man I ever heard of was Goethe," answered Nikolai. "Dear God, why should I be called upon to be another Eckermann? Particularly as you're no Goethe so far as quality rather than quantity is concerned."

The train was slowing down, and the two Frenchwomen were collecting their bags. "Where are we?" asked Chubinov, staring about him. "I forget what line we are on."

"It's Amiens," said Laura.

"A town I've never liked," said Nikolai. "A blasphemy is committed here. In the cathedral there is a Byzantine Christ which should not be in a heretical place of worship. But one can't do anything about it. I once tried. The Bishop was most unreasonable."

Chubinov politely helped the Frenchwomen get their luggage out into the corridor and got them a porter by gesticulating from the window. Then they sat in silence while the hubbub of the station boiled around them. But as soon as the train started again Chubinov said, "It's the *Rurik*."

"The *Rurik*, the cruiser we're having built in Glasgow? Do you mean to say that your infamous company of assassins have got to work there too?"

"As you probably know, the ship is so far advanced that the skeleton crew has been sent over to get their hand in so that when the full crew comes to take her to the Baltic they can be taught quickly the ways of the new ship. Among the skeleton crew are several members of our Party. More of us will come out with the full crew."

"Everywhere, everywhere," muttered Nikolai. "When I told them so, they wouldn't believe me. They said it was only students and the intelligentsia, but I knew better. Plague doesn't select its victims."

"These sailors and some of the Admiralty staff have informed our committee that all arrangements have been made for a ceremonial review by the Tsar on the ship's arrival at a Baltic port. These sailors and officials were eager to use the opportunity to assassinate the tyrant."

"This appetite for death, it's amazing," said Nikolai. "The whole of our social structure is being liberalized, people are being taught to read and write as never before, they are less hungry, they've less reason for social vengeance than ever before, and all they think of is killing."

"But they thought it unwise that one of their own number should be made responsible for the deed, for it was certain that some agents of the Secret Police had been planted among the crew and would keep a continuous watch on the men who had shown signs of revolutionary sympathies as the time of the naval review drew near."

He said this, Laura thought, as if he regarded this police action as unsporting, like shooting a fox.

"Therefore the sailors begged our committee to send to Glasgow some of our members who were properly trained in terrorist methods, so that arrangements could be made to smuggle aboard one or two activists at the proper time, who could be kept in some safe corner until the North Sea was crossed on the homeward journey." His eyes became glazed and he went into an account of the plans the committee had made to prevent detection. It was as boring as a card-game. "... So we've been sending small groups to Glasgow, never less than two or more than four, to travel on false passports to Paris or Berlin or Brussels, where our local branches gave them a new set of false passports, made out in names they had invented, till then unknown even to the travellers themselves, and instructions from the Glasgow sailors as to the place and time of the meetings, couched in a code unknown to the French or German or Belgian members who transmitted them, though it had been imparted to all the delegates before they left Russia. There was also a lapse of time left between the delegates' departure, first from Russia and then from whatever Western centres they used, and their arrival in Glasgow, so that nobody knew exactly till the last moment when they would get there—"

"Such an ingenious plan that I'll give you a hundred to one that there's a member of yours sitting at this very moment in a bathing-machine at Ostend wondering how he got there and what he should do next," said Nikolai, "and I'll lay another bet that you get a lot of your delegates cutting off with the travelling expenses." He laughed hugely, vulgarly, with his mouth open, like a peasant. " 'Ah, poor Ivan Ivanovitch, he must have been arrested by the wicked police.' And

where Ivan Ivanovitch really is I wouldn't like to say in front of my granddaughter."

"Nothing of that sort has ever happened," snapped Chubinov. "At least, only once or twice."

"Forgive me, Vassili Iulievitch," said Nikolai. "For what you've spent your life doing, you're a sensitive man." But Chubinov was bitter as he said, "What has gone wrong is quite different, and it went wrong in your apartment in the Avenue Kléber." ...

VI

"I've told you," said Chubinov, "that Gorin has been ill of late years, though it's not true that he's ever been in a sanatorium. I was one of the first to realize that at last his vitality had snapped under the strain of constant warfare for the rights of the people, austerity, and rough travelling. About eighteen months ago, while you were still in office, the police suddenly threw a dragnet over the larger towns and made innumerable arrests. At once our organization warned its members to leave their homes and lodgings till the storm was over, to sleep here and there in hotels not ordinarily used by the movement, to keep away from friends and write no letters, and to give up frequenting our usual cafés. I myself took refuge in a cottage on a sympathizer's estate thirty miles out in the country, but I was called back to the city to dismantle one of our printing-presses, as the police had been making some inquiries about a man with the same name as the landlord of the little workshop where it had been set up. I went to that workshop, packed the parts of the press under the floorboards, brushed shavings all over them, and saw to all the other little precautions one has to take in such circumstances, locked up, and went out into the street, and the first thing I saw was Gorin, the head of our Battle Organization, driving by in an open cab, wearing that little air of peace which he carries about with him as his own private angelic world. I couldn't believe my eyes.

"He didn't see me. But as soon as the bad time was passed and we revolutionaries could safely meet again, he sent for me and without knowing it, provided an explanation for this curious event. He told me

that he'd had a most disquieting experience. For several days and nights he'd worked without cease, getting this suspected man out to Scandinavia on the Finland route, getting that unsuspected woman home to her family in the Urals because she was a chatterbox, snatching an hour's sleep when he could, and forgetting all about food and drink. Suddenly he had a brainstorm. He'd no recollection of what he did or where he was for a period of about twenty-four hours, and suddenly he found himself sitting in a night-club in the Nova Derevnia, with two police agents at the next table staring at him. When he got out into the street he nearly fainted. 'What am I to do?' he asked, smiling that very sweet smile I knew very well, which meant that he wanted to soothe me but at the same time warn me of a danger, 'if I become a peril to you all?'

"When I told him that I'd seen him driving through the streets of Petersburg in an open cab during that terrible period, he was shocked. He hadn't the slightest recollection of doing any such thing. Then he admitted to me that for some time past he'd been hiding from us that he was not well. He'd been suffering from attacks of dizziness, lapses of memory, and headaches. At once he consented to go to a doctor. I don't think he would have done this for his own sake, but he realized he'd become a danger to his comrades. Well, there were some visits to a couple of specialists, and the verdict came, that he must live, at any rate for a time, in a milder climate. The doctors recommended the isle of Capri, but Gorin insisted on going to Lausanne, though it was not nearly so suitable for his condition, because there he could establish relations with the Swiss universities and carry on collaboration with our French and Italian members.

"We haven't had to say good-bye to him. Every now and then, when he feels better, he returns to us and though there's now another head of the Battle Organization—I expect you know all about him . . . yes, I mean 'Hilarion'—he always defers to Gorin, and we accept his advice and the admirable material he brings us. About a month ago he was with us again in Petersburg, and he arranged that I should go to England, to take some manuscripts of pamphlets to be printed at a Russian press we have working in a district of London called Camden Town. There's an English wine merchant who's enthusiastic for our

cause and not only gives us money but lets us use his name and his warehouse as a cover for our work. I tell you we are going to win, we are going to take over the world. Well, to my delight Gorin told me that he wished me to break my journey to England by a detour to Lausanne, so that I could stay with him and receive some last instructions. I went there ten days ago, and stayed for five days.

"I haven't had such a happy time for many years. Gorin doesn't live in Lausanne, nor even very near it, but in a pretty lakeside village on the outskirts of Montreux, where there's an Italianate villa on a little island in the middle of a harbour, so that one has the illusion of living on a stage set for an opera. Gorin's lodgings are in a *pension* with a fine view of the lake and the harbour, and it's more than comfortable, it's even luxurious. His sitting-room is really beautiful, it opens on a marble balcony covered with wisteria. I was filled with nostalgia, it was so like the places I used to go to with my parents when I was a boy and even until I was a young man, before I had seen the light and taken to the way of suffering. For though my father was not rich like yours, Nikolai Nikolaievitch, who owned a villa in Corfu, I seem to remember—and there was one at Nice, wasn't there—still we had our holidays abroad at beautiful hotels, at the Schweizerhof in Lucerne, at the Grand in Rome, at Danieli's in Venice. It was surprising to find Gorin in such quarters, for he came from a poor family, he hadn't the habit of going to such places, and he's never taken a moment's thought for his own comfort. Of course there was an explanation. Though the proprietress looked precisely like any other proprietress of an expensive *pension,* a stout woman with a military expression and pompous yet obsequious manners, she was a sympathizer and she gave Gorin special terms. I was very pleased to hear this, for it removed the scruples I would otherwise have felt at returning to a way of life I had promised myself to abandon for ever.

"What filled my happiness to the brim was the arrival, the day after my own, of three comrades from Moscow, Korolenko, Primar, and Damatov. They're all younger than I am, much younger, and of each I'd thought at one time or another, 'How I wish there was more leisure in my life, so that I could make this young man my friend.' Korolenko had just graduated as a doctor, and I remember that when I heard that

I reflected happily, 'How fortunate, if there is any young wife among my kin who is going to have a child, any old man who is finding it difficult to leave the world, here's someone who will be the rock they can cling to,' though of course I now have no kin, they will have nothing to do with me. Primar was the son of a timber merchant who had renounced a rich inheritance and never thought of it again, plunging himself into poverty and danger as into a carnival ball. He had a wave of fair hair which curled forward across his head, like the crest of a macaw, which somehow aroused one's tenderness. And Damatov was the most charming of them all. He was one of those who are born to make a mock of our aristocracy, for he looked like a prince, he might have been Hamlet, but he was the son of a rich fishmonger in a town two hundred miles north of Kharkov on the river Selm. You know how such people used to pile up the roubles before there were railways, when they fetched the fish up in ice from the Sea of Azov. It happened that his father was one of those whom the tours of the State Theatre Company make stage-struck, and he'd bred his son to be the same. So Damatov had come up to Petersburg to work at the State Theatre, and had soon become a stage-designer, and then a dramatist. But simply to be with him was to attend a better play than he would ever write, indeed it was like crossing the footlights and changing into a character in a drama written by Shakespeare or by Schiller.

"Now I had leisure to know them, and to know them well, better than it might seem I could, in such a short time. You can't think what Gorin adds to any meeting by the quality of his friendship. He turns his face from one friend to another, and his smile says, 'Not one person here but is wonderful.' This is not empty benevolence, not the unfocused beam which shines from the bland faces of so many holy personages in pictures, for he opens his friends' minds like jewel-boxes and brings the enclosed treasures out into the light. It turned out Korolenko could play the piano like a master, that Primar's supple mind had a talent for mathematics, and when he talked of a problem it was like watching the faultless tumbling of a child acrobat at a fair. Damatov made up poetry, not the elegant odes and tragic laments one would have expected, but funny little poems, about such things as a fat lady taking a fat little pug-dog for a walk by the lakeside, not at all vulgar,

not at all cruel, indeed kind and good-natured. What added to our happiness was that all this talk and laughter and music never seemed too much for Gorin. He had evidently recovered from his illness to a degree quite wonderful in a middle-aged man who had suffered years of privation and strain. He even insisted on going on a long walk with us up in the mountains, and though he did things we knew his doctors wouldn't have allowed, he really seemed afterwards to have done himself no damage. He actually took a swim in a lake up in the mountains.

"The three young men left in the afternoon of the fourth day, and I wasn't invited to go with Gorin to the station to see them off. I found this natural enough. It had crossed my mind that this must be another team on its way to a *Rurik* conference in Glasgow, and it would have been contrary to our security plans for anyone to see what train they'd boarded. When Gorin came back he asked me to go for a stroll by the harbour, and we got there just at the time when, one by one, the lamps went up on the mast-heads of the little lake-going craft, and the windows of the Italianate villa on the island began to glow a beautiful rose-colour—they must have had red curtains. I can never see lights coming on in summer twilight without emotion. When I was a little boy the sight always made me cry, not because I wasn't happy, for I was a happy child—as you know, ours was a happy home—but because I used to feel that my happiness would not last. My mother would be trailing her long flounced skirt round the croquet lawn, still playing though it was too dark to see the balls except when they rolled into the bright panels cast on the grass by the lit rooms in the house, simply because her nature, which was like a child's, couldn't bear to admit that the little pleasure of the game was coming to an end; and then I used to weep because, though I really was a child and she wasn't, I was so much less childish that I could see farther than she did, to a day when she'd be unable to finish the game, not because the twilight had fallen but because she would be neither in the dark garden nor in any of the rooms, lit or unlit, of the house. My throat would swell with love for this precious figure, which would not always be there, and I felt a return of that emotion when I walked by the little harbour with my dear friend in the dusk. This made me think of you, Nikolai Nikolaievitch. Such recollections always make me think of you, you were such a commanding figure in my childhood. To cover my emotion, I said to

Gorin, 'What of the Diakonov situation?' and he answered, 'Well, you have seen the material I've been forwarding. Valuable as it is, it's very painful reading, and it's not easy to collect either, for Berr is nothing like so amenable and comradely as Pravdine.'

"Yes, yes, I know, it is not necessary for you to protest, Nikolai Nikolaievitch, I am just telling you what Gorin said. He went on to tell me that this man, Porfirio Ilyitch Berr, had been employed at the Ministry of Justice, but in middle life had inherited some money and had come to France with his wife to live with a niece, who had married the proprietor of a small restaurant near Les Halles in Paris. Berr was apparently an unamiable character, so unamiable that Gorin expressed surprise that you, Nikolai Nikolaievitch, should have engaged him to act as a sort of clerk and account-keeper to come to your house every day for an hour or two. But Gorin supposed it had something to do with his qualifications as a book-keeper, which were high. It wasn't so, then? Well, that tells us nothing about Gorin's honesty. For he explained that he was only vaguely informed regarding Berr, whom he had dealt with always through an intermediary, who said that Berr must never be approached by anybody but himself, because his niece's husband was fiercely opposed to his political views and might even denounce Berr to the police if he had any idea of Berr's role as a member of the revolutionary movement. Gorin said that at any rate he believed the stories of Berr's unamiability, for an agent of his had once followed Berr from your house, and found him most unprepossessing. We then talked of you, Nikolai Nikolaievitch, with great respect and a sense of shame. We both wished we were not obliged to set spies on you, we wished we were not obliged to eavesdrop on the Tsar's attempts to degrade you. But we have assumed responsibility for the future of Russia, and that involves us in much guilt which we must accept for the sake of the people. We were so unhappy about it that we fell silent, and simply sat together, watching the strange whitish radiance which the night casts on the waters and the sparkling lights in the towns on the other side of the lake. I felt that if I could have given my life for you I would have offered it up gladly. When we rose to go home Gorin laid his hand on my shoulder and said, 'I know well that much that is best in you comes from Nikolai Nikolaievitch.'

"I left Montreux the next morning, and after a day at our centre in

Lille I got to London the next evening and was met at Victoria by two English comrades. I was still so happy at having been with Gorin that I had walked the whole length of the platform before I realized that they were utterly overcome by misery. They laid their fingers across their lips to tell me that the cause of their distress could be safely discussed only in some private place, and they took me in a cab to a room in a dark and dingy place called Pimlico, very Gothic, which was no surprise to me, for I know my Dickens. Locking the door, they asked me if I had known that Primar, Korolenko, and Damatov had been intending to come to London. I stared at them in embarrassment. I hadn't known it, but I'd guessed it, and I was very sure that there were very good reasons why they shouldn't be told. However, they informed me that that morning a woman named Nadya Sarin had arrived from Paris with a story that these three comrades had been arrested there on the eve of their departure for London. They themselves had known that a team was to arrive on its way to Glasgow, but they hadn't known how many men were coming, or who they were, or when they would come, and they were not certain that she was not mistaken or, perhaps, a lying police agent.

"When I cast my mind back I remembered that an actress called Nadya had been Damatov's mistress at one time, and that they had parted because she had a brother much younger than herself who was still at the gymnasium, and several incidents had suggested that her love-affair was leading the authorities to regard the boy with suspicion. I remembered also hearing that as her French was unusually good she had joined a Parisian company of players then in Petersburg and had returned with them to France. So I told the English comrades that in all probability the woman was who she said she was and that her story was true, and I asked them to take me to her at once. We then got into another cab, and went to another part of London called Notting Hill. She had been taken in by one of our members who ran a lodging-house and we found her lying in bed, surrounded by comrades, in a room which looked across a wide railway-cutting, a positive chasm, with many tracks running along the bottom. The aspect was not un-picturesque, for on the opposite cliff of the chasm stood a line of tall houses, neo-classical in design, which were reflecting an orange sunset

from their stucco façades. London is very exotic. All these places like Camden Town and Pimlico and Notting Hill have a wild majesty.

"But it was a pity the poor woman hadn't been found other quarters, for every time a train ran through the cutting she buried her head in the pillows and screamed. Also, the room was too full of people who seemed to be taking pleasure in witnessing her agitation, and even going to some pains to outdo it. There was one person I marked with special disapproval, a tall young man with straight yellow hair and broad shoulders who was striding up and down with a glass in his hand, making exaggerated gestures of despair. In consternation I asked the comrades who had brought me to this place what sort of story we were all going to tell if the police broke in, but they assured me that this was most unlikely. It filled me with joy that an admittedly great power should be so much more liberal than Russia, but I also saw that it must be difficult to run a revolutionary movement if one cannot tell the comrades that if they make too much noise they may attract the attention of the police. It was some time before I could make myself heard and really get down to questioning the actress, who was of a refined and elevated type, pale and slender, with an oval face and long black hair. She could have sat to an artist for a picture called 'Melancholy' or 'Autumn.'

"She told me that she and Damatov had never ceased to be sincerely devoted, and that she had been overjoyed when he had called on her at her lodgings in Paris, which were somewhere near the Bridge of Passy, about one o'clock two days before. He had told her that he had come to acquire the rights of a French play which the Petersburg State Theatre wished to perform, and that he had two friends with him, named Primar and Korolenko, who would call for him later. The other two came about five, and as it was a very fine evening they decided to go for a walk. The actress went with them, though she had to leave them before long, as she was acting that night. When they were outside on the pavement, Korolenko, who knew Paris better than his friends, said, 'Here, this way,' and they made their way up the Avenue Kléber. They went the whole length of the avenue, right up to the Étoile, and there the actress said good-bye to them, and took a cab to her theatre. She had imagined that she would be seeing Damatov before very long,

for he had promised to be at her lodgings when she returned from her performance, and to stay with her till he had to go to the station in the morning.

"She stayed awake all night, but Damatov never came to her. In this London room, she beat the people away from her bedside with a gesture so that she could whisper in my ear, and she told me that as the hours had passed she had grown terrified, she found herself praying that he might have changed since their separation, into the sort of man capable of insulting a woman. In the morning she was at a loss to know what to do. Though he had told her he would have to leave Paris that morning, he hadn't said where he was going, so she couldn't go to any station and see whether he was leaving. But she hadn't believed for one moment his story about buying the rights of a play, she had known he hadn't expected her to believe it, that he was telling it as part of his terrorist drill. So, in the end, she went to consult a Russian medical student living in a hotel not far from hers, and when he heard what had happened he took her to an old revolutionary who was having a late breakfast in a near-by café. He had known Korolenko, he was sure too that there would be a terrorist reason for the presence of these particular three young men in Paris; and, thinking it over, he thought it probable that if Korolenko had taken his party up the Avenue Kléber it was with the intention of ending up at the Café Viborg in the Avenue de la Grande Armée, which is much frequented by our people. They hailed a taxi and went straight there, and had to look no farther. The proprietor told them that Korolenko and two young men unknown to him had come into the café early on the previous evening, and a quarter of an hour later half a dozen police agents had driven up in a van and taken them away.

"On hearing this, the actress assumed that her friend was doomed either to death or to many years of imprisonment, and, as you know, Nikolai Nikolaievitch, she would be right. The older man took her back to her lodgings and went to see somebody, but she didn't know who it was. He came back after an hour and helped her pack her baggage and put her in the afternoon train for London, giving her the address of some London members, and telling her that he would telegraph them and they would meet her at Victoria. He said she was

not to mind leaving Paris so suddenly and embarrassing her employers, for she must be removed from the sphere of the French police and the Russian Secret Police operating in Paris. She said that, as for that, she didn't care, she only wanted to die. But then she was told that the three young men might have been going to London, and that their interception might mean danger to members of our movement there, and the brave woman had consented to make the journey. So there she was, in this London room, full of chattering and gesticulating people who seemed far more theatrical than she was, and she looked up at me and said that she had accomplished her mission, and she lived now only to find out whether Damatov was alive or dead. She said it very quietly. One would not have thought that an actress could speak with such little resonance. It was as if her voice had been taken out of her throat and beaten and put back. I did not doubt what she thought she would do if she found out that he was dead.

"I had to do my duty, I had to inquire into all the circumstances as if I were a police officer. She had fallen back on the pillows and I made them give her some brandy, and then I asked her if she had had any impression during her walk through Paris with the three young men that they had been watched. No. Not exactly. But that there had been one little incident which she had noticed with distaste and could not forget, though she thought it impossible that it could have any bearing on what had happened. As they were drawing near the end of their walk and the Arc de Triomphe was well in sight, Korolenko's cigarette went out, and Primar stopped to give him a light but found his match-box empty and called out to Damatov, who turned back and gave them his. While the three men were halted, the actress strolled slowly on, came to a stop, and stood smiling around her at nothing, as she put it, because it was all so delightful. Suddenly she realized that she had been smiling at something, or rather at someone. She had come to a standstill a few yards away from the doorway of one of the larger houses on the avenue, which was wide open, showing the vaulted entry to the courtyard. Unconsciously she had been smiling into the shadows of the entry, just where a man was standing. She couldn't see him very well. There was a blank space of wall between the left-hand leaf of the door which had been folded back, and the entrance to the concierge's

lodge; and this man was in the thickest of the shadow. He wore spectacles, and he was holding a pair of gloves in front of his mouth and chin. She wouldn't venture to say he was doing that to hide his face. It was something people did when they were sunk in thought. She could really see nothing of him except that he was of medium size, and she could not have sworn to anything about him. Yet she had a nagging impression that when she first caught sight of him he had already been staring out at her with the intensest interest.

"For an instant she was terrified, and thought of running back to the three young men and saying to them, 'There's a man here watching us.' But then the man in the shadows made a gesture of unmistakable meaning. It was as if he said to her, 'Just wait for a minute, my dear, you're just what I fancy, I'm coming out, or will you come in?' She forgot everything in her indignation, and just then Damatov and the others caught up with her. The man in the entry shrugged his shoulders and spread out his hands in a pantomime of dismay, spun around on his heel, and withdrew into the courtyard. Damatov just saw the tail-end of the movement, and said with not very great anger, 'What's this going on? If I'd the time I'd stop and give that Don Juan a black eye.' That was how it had seemed to him, and how it had seemed to her, and she had some experience, for since she had come to Paris many men had spoken to her on the street. She still thought that might have been all that happened, for the gesture of invitation had been so truly vulgar, so deeply nasty in its lecherous bourgeois way, that it couldn't have been feigned, except by a really great character actor. Yet she had to admit that when she first saw the man he seemed to be watching her with an intensity beyond that, and a selective intensity, which would not have been satisfied by the sight of anybody but herself and her companions.

"When I heard this I couldn't speak. I was sure that the man in the entry had been our scourge, our Judas, our false brother, the traitor who could betray the secrets he had never been told, because his experience was our experience, his past our past, his present our present. Of course he hadn't had to follow his quarry. The actress had told us with some wonder how the old revolutionary had known from the mere fact that Korolenko had led the party up the Avenue Kléber that

he meant to take them to the Café Viborg, but I had drawn the very same conclusion myself. 'Ah,' I'd said to myself, 'he was going to take them up to see old Alaner at the Café Viborg.' No doubt our traitor had told Korolenko to take them there. Then he'd only to stand in a doorway at the Avenue Kléber, which was right on the route they were bound to take, to make sure that his victims were on the way to the place where, as soon as he had time to make the necessary telephone call, the police would pick them up. Our traitor had the knowledge for that, and also the abominable intelligence to throw off the scent a woman whose sensitiveness had detected him, by an insulting trick which depended on her being virtuous.

"I asked the actress, 'Can you give us any idea of the whereabouts of the house? Was it on the right or the left of the Avenue? Was it as far up as the Rue Dumont-d'Urville just off the Avenue des Portugais?' But she interrupted me by saying, 'I can do better than that. I remember the number.' It seemed that as she turned away in disgust from the door the small enamel number-plate on the wall had caught her eye, and she had noted the figures because they were three more than the year of the century in which she had been born. Perhaps because I was so tired by my long journey, and because I was so overcome with grief over the capture of these three young men, with whom I had been so recently, I passed at this moment into a state of light-mindedness. I didn't listen to the number as she said it. I sat there, smiling, almost openly laughing, because it struck me as so ridiculously characteristic of an actress to remember a number because it was three more than the year in which she was born. Any of us might say, 'Why, '68 or '69, or whatever it might be, that's the year I was born,' but to say, ''71, that's three more than the year I was born,' that takes the theatrical temperament, the innocent egotism of the player.

"Then I suddenly heard the young man with the straight yellow hair, of whom I've already spoken, exclaim, 'Why, that's the number of the house where the Minister of Justice who was disgraced, the Count Diakonov, has an apartment. And it explains the whole thing. For there's a Tsarist spy working in that household.' I asked stupidly, 'How should you, an Englishman, know that?' He answered, 'What do you mean? I'm not English, I'm Russian. You should know that, aren't we

talking Russian now? Very few Englishmen know any Russian and when they speak it you'd take it for Double Dutch. I'm a student at Oxford. I'm here only because my father's one of the secretaries at our Embassy in Paris. It's from my father's papers that I know there's a Tsarist spy working in Diakonov's household.' I thought he was talking nonsense. A revolutionary spy, but not a Tsarist spy. What an extraordinary idea, I told myself, and wondered how the confusion could have arisen; and I said coldly, 'What grounds can you have for saying that?' as I have often said before, when we older ones have had occasion to keep our younger comrades from spreading false rumours.

"The young man said with what I realized afterwards was great good nature, considering my tone, 'I go home for my holidays to stay with my father in Paris. He knows nothing of my revolutionary sympathies and I see what I can see for the good of the cause. I can tell you for certain that there is a Tsarist spy in Diakonov's household who sends to our Embassy in Paris the fullest reports of all his doings, and who photographs all his diaries and his letters. His diaries are pitiful, and show the Tsar in the worst light, and as they are all sent back to Petersburg, the old man is in great danger. The Tsar is eagerly looking for some excuse to recall him to Russia and lay some trumped-up charge against him, and then discredit him thoroughly by never bringing him to trial and abandoning the proceedings on the pretence of showing him mercy. It's easy to see that my father, who is an honourable though unenlightened man, hates the whole business, which is indeed repulsive. There was one letter from Baron Roller, written from Vichy, in which he refused to come and see old Diakonov, though they'd been friends since childhood, because the Tsar had forbidden it, and that disgusted my father so much that when he read it he tore the copy across, and it had to go on its way to the Tsar, with a note from the secretary saying there'd been an accident. My father's often quite bitter these days, and I'm sure it's about this.'

"I sat there, asking the actress questions which I knew didn't matter, while it sank in: the knowledge that the Tsarist authorities were receiving precisely the same documents which were being regularly transmitted to us by our agent, Porfirio Ilyitch Berr. But when I tried to visualize a Tsarist spy and a revolutionary spy working side by side in

your apartment I couldn't believe it. We know, of course, how many rooms there are in your apartment and how many servants you have. You've greatly reduced your household. It could be said that you live more like a French or an English aristocrat than a Russian one. It seems most unlikely that in your comparatively modest household there should be two men, both having access to your papers and both taking advantage of their opportunities to remove those papers and photograph them surreptitiously, who didn't sooner or later become aware of each other. But I knew Berr's reports by heart, and I was sure he'd never expressed any suspicion that there was a police spy working beside him in your study. I could draw only one conclusion. There were not two spies in your household, but one. The spy who was working for us was also working for the police. It was he who had stood in the entry and looked out at Korolenko and Primar and Damatov; and if he knew enough to betray them, then he was the Judas who had long persecuted us. I remembered too the unpleasant impression Berr had made on the few people who had seen him. I said to the diplomat's son, 'Have you no idea who supplies your father with Diakonov's papers?' and he answered, 'I don't know the man's name, he's always referred to by a number, which I've forgotten. But he's an agent who has worked for the police over a number of years, and again and again he has given them most valuable information.'"

———

"Laura," said Nikolai.

"Grandfather?"

"You're biting your nails," he said icily. "It's an ill-bred trick. You have the good fortune to inherit the long, narrow hands of our family, do not spoil them."

"Yes, Grandfather," she said, tears standing in her eyes. He should not have said that in front of a stranger.

———

"As I've said," continued Chubinov, "there was no further doubt in my mind. I was sure that at last we'd uncovered the trail of our Judas, and that we knew his name. I had to keep my thoughts to myself. There might be some traitors in that very room. I stood up and said that I could do nothing, I must return to Paris and confer with the head of

the organization there, to the end of finding out what charges the police had brought against Primar and Korolenko and Damatov, and of warning our other centres that a traitor was at work. I also told them that I would try to get in touch with Gorin, and the mention of his name instantly tranquillized everybody. I bent over the actress and kissed her hand, and she looked up at me with her great eyes and told me that if Damatov were to die she would not wait a single day before following him into the Absolute. She said this with perfect sincerity, but also in perfect style, with that same utterly heart-breaking lack of resonance, and I knew that she would not fulfil this prediction, but would live to enjoy much happiness and success. There was nothing unpleasant about this realization, on the contrary, it was as agreeable as looking forward to spring in the middle of winter. I smiled down at her and kissed her hand again, and then asked the comrades who had met me in the station to take me somewhere where I could send a telegram, and said my good-byes.

"We had to walk quite a long way, and then take a bus, and then go a journey by underground railway, to the General Post Office, which was the only place from which I could send a telegram at that hour. It was dark now, and the city was fascinating and terrifying in its exoticism. The streets round the General Post Office were empty, except for a large number of cats. It all might have been a fantasy drawn by Gustave Doré. I sent a telegram to the deputy head of our Battle Organization in Paris, whom I can now dare to name to you as a man called Stankovitch, who would, I was certain, know all that was to be known about the investigation of Berr, asking him to meet me at the station when I arrived in Paris the next afternoon. Then, finding that it was not so very late, I asked my companions to take me to look at St. Paul's Cathedral, as I remembered from a passage in the correspondence of either Herzen or Marx that it was not far away. The two Englishmen seemed surprised by the request but agreed. I stood with them in the street looking up at the dark mass of the superb building against the starlit sky, but when I turned to them to compliment them on their national possession and ask them if they didn't consider it wonderful that Wren had never seen a dome until he built one for himself, I found they were looking not at the cathedral but at me. One

of them said, 'You know a lot about all this, don't you?' I said that I knew no more than he and his friends. They said, 'Well, when we asked you if you had known that Primar and Korolenko and Damatov were coming to London, you said you hadn't, but it seemed to us you weren't entirely surprised to hear that they'd meant to. And why were you smiling? You smiled twice when that woman was telling her story. What's funny about all this?' I could not tell them that I had smiled at the actress remembering a number because it was three more than the year she was born, or because I thought she would not take poison if Damatov were to die. They were good men, but they wouldn't have understood. They took me back to my room in Pimlico, and arrived next morning to take me to Victoria as if they were police agents seeing a criminal out of town. I found myself resenting this for reasons which made me ashamed. It is hard to overcome the disadvantages of one's birth. I was angry because one of the men who doubted me was an old soldier from the ranks, the other a tailor.

"When I arrived at the Gare du Nord, Stankovitch was waiting for me. We went to a bar, and ordered a meal, and I left him in order to telephone to Gorin at the *pension* near Montreux. But he wasn't there. The proprietress answered me and told me that he'd gone to Paris to see his doctor. This disquieted me and I asked anxiously about his health, but she answered with such indifference that, remembering she was a sympathizer, I concluded that she was probably repeating an untruth which Gorin had told her to give strangers. I rang off and tried to find him at the hotel he always stayed at in Paris, the Hôtel de Guipuzcoa et de Racine, it's a little place between the Hôtel de Ville and the Tour Saint-Jacques. But he wasn't there either. My heart sank. I then went back to Stankovitch and the meal we had ordered, and while we ate I spoke of the disappearance of the three young men and found that he knew all about that and the dispatch of Nadya Sarin to London, so I went on to question him about Berr. He answered reticently. Gorin, he said, had always impressed on him that Berr was to be handled with kid gloves, he might at any moment throw up his job as an informer. 'Is he really so disagreeable?' I asked. 'I don't know that firsthand, I've never spoken to him, but Gorin's had him thoroughly investigated, and all the reports say so. Apparently he strides along with the

most arrogant expression on his face, and he's unkind to his wife, leaves her trotting after him, hardly able to catch up, and never seems to speak to her. But it's not merely a question of his disposition. What's to be feared is that he may get into difficulties with his niece's husband, who's a reactionary and who, if he found any of us hanging about, might denounce him and us.' I found myself wondering if Gorin had not, since his illness, lost something of his genius. Surely this tale that no revolutionary must speak to an informer on account of his family was the very yarn which would be spun by a police spy who didn't want his master to know that he was doing business with both sides.

" 'So you're quite satisfied,' I asked, 'that Berr is loyal to us?' 'Yes, quite satisfied,' he said. 'He's a very isolated man. He makes no contacts at all except with the Diakonov household, and nobody goes there now except the blind and the halt and the lame who are pensioners of the Countess's charity. There's nobody else at all,' he said, 'except a man named Kamensky, who worked for Diakonov when he was Minister of Justice and is of no importance at all. Gorin was interested in him at first, and three times set a comrade outside the Diakonov apartment to see if perhaps he was someone we'd known in Russia under a different name, and twice he didn't turn up, but the third time he did. I forget who saw him, but anyway he was nobody; and Gorin put me to search Kamensky's room at his hotel, the San Marino, near the Hôtel de Ville, and that told us everything we needed to learn. It's a funny thing, he's an engineer, and apparently quite a good one, and one would expect him to be enlightened, but he ought to have been a monk. There were several icons and shelves of religious books and a very full diary, full of pious vapourings. He's evidently a thorough nincompoop and he spends much of his time toadying to the Countess Diakonova, who is a bigoted and reactionary woman.' I must beg your pardon for that, Nikolai Nikolaievitch. 'Anyway,' Stankovitch went on, 'Berr keeps us fully posted about all Kamensky's doings, and they add up to exactly nothing. But don't worry about Berr. He's completely reliable. We've tested him again and again.'

"It was on the tip of my tongue to tell him what I had heard from the diplomat's son in London. But then it suddenly struck me that if Stankovitch spoke so well of Berr he was probably a traitor himself. It

struck me that my world was terribly uncertain. I had been seen off from Victoria by men who thought I was a traitor, though I was loyal, and here I had landed at the Gare du Nord to be met by a man whom I had thought was loyal but who was probably a traitor. And I could not get in touch with Gorin. 'Where does Berr live?' I asked, quite without subtlety. I try to follow technique but I am apt to get flustered. That is one of the reasons why I admire Gorin, who is never at fault. 'There's no harm in my telling you that,' said Stankovitch, 'for strangely enough he's in the telephone book. He lives in a block of flats in one of the newer working-class suburbs to the north-east of Paris, one of those places built on the English model, with gardens round them. He really must be a very disagreeable man. Apparently his wife runs about like mad all day, working for him, but Gorin says that in fine weather he's apt to spend the whole day idling in a queer sort of hut, a summer-house affair, in a patch of his own he has in the vegetable patches which are part of the estate. I'll tell you something. I think Gorin has kept a pretty close watch on this man Berr, in case we have to take disciplinary action against him some day.'

"When Stankovitch said that, I saw my duty clear before me. I'd been wrong to doubt Gorin's efficiency. He'd long suspected what I had just found out. Had he been available I'd have asked him what the next step should be, but he wasn't and I didn't think he would be for some time. He wasn't in Lausanne and he wasn't in Paris, and I suspected that either he had gone back to Russia on one of his periodic trips or had gone to London or Glasgow to look into the *Rurik* situation. So there was no help for it. I myself would have to kill Berr. This wasn't easy for me. Not in any sense. I love humanity, therefore I can't wish to shed human blood. I also have insufficient preparation for the performance of such a deed. It isn't that I can't shoot, you know I can. But as I've told you, though I'm associated with the terrorist group within our organization, it's only as a theoretician and an archivist. I don't know how to set about such things.

"But I hadn't the slightest doubt that that was my duty. Berr is a traitor to our movement, who had just betrayed Korolenko, Primar, and Damatov, and God knows how many of our comrades before that. As for the future, I didn't believe that Berr could yet know of our plan to

take over the *Rurik* and use it as a stage for the supremely desirable purge, the extirpation of the Tsar, but in view of his known resourcefulness I was afraid that once he had the three young men's papers in his hands, he might report to his superiors some deductions which would lead them fairly near to the truth. I also wished, for once, to take some of the guilt from the shoulders of my beloved friend Gorin. Not that I thought the guilt of eliminating Berr was heavy, if, indeed, it existed at all. I would probably pay for Berr's life with my own. I believe in Kant's Law of Nature and it follows that I have a right to kill only if I am willing to give my own life in expiation. I am aware that there are philosophical difficulties in this position, but I think I could justify it, though perhaps this is not the most suitable time and place for such a discussion.

"Also I was drawn to this deed because it centred round you, Nikolai Nikolaievitch. For many years I've had dreams which I always felt were important, though I didn't know what they meant, and they were inherently absurd. In these dreams I see something familiar, something rooted in my infancy and my childhood, mixed up with things quite unrelated to them. You remember that little lake in front of my father's country house—it wasn't a lake, really, just a large pond. In the middle of it was an island covered with birch trees, and coarse yellow grasses, an island which is round, quite round, as if it were drawn with compasses. Well, I dream that someone has set down on that little island a merry-go-round, the kind you see at fairs, with swing-boats like dragons painted scarlet and gold, or I dream of our conservatory, and it's got a printing-press set down among all the delicate stove-plants my mother loved to cultivate, and that's funny too, the press is rose-pink. Now I'm having a waking dream of that kind. There you are, whom I've known all my life, my father's dearest friend, who far more than my father was the image of the man I hoped to be, for you were stronger than he was. You taught me to shoot, game-birds and red deer and the wild boar, because you were a better shot than my father, and though you are not a patient man you were more patient with my sickliness, too. I can still shoot, you know. Every now and then I take out my revolver again and go to a range and practise, because—that's what I pretend to myself—it's the most useful small arm for our movement.

But it's also because you always said that good revolver shots were very rare, and I was one of them. Now I'm going to use my revolver to protect you, the giant. I'm protecting you from your Judas. I know that it's absurd to think of me protecting you, but that's what I'm doing."

———

"For God's sake," said Nikolai, wiping the sweat from his brow, "did you kill this poor devil, Berr?"

"Wait, wait," said Chubinov.

"Or did another of you hyenas get him? But probably not. Since so far as I can remember the man never existed."

"You'll wish that it were so. I had to take the train to get to Berr's home, and I found myself in one of those very ugly suburbs of Paris where the town suddenly stops, leaving a raw selvage which isn't Paris and isn't countryside. There's a jumble of factories and small houses and tenements along the high road, and then a large new factory. Just beyond it a track leaves the high road and runs a couple of hundred yards up a hill to two blocks of tenements, which, I learned at the station, had been put up for the workers in the new factory. They're the kind of hideous buildings which capitalists think fit for the dispossessed. I realized how unpleasant a character Berr must have, for he must be a materialist, or he would not be a Tsarist spy, yet he is indifferent to material beauty, or he would not live in such a drab place. I followed the track, which ends in a big square pavement, with some flower beds set into it, extending all round the two blocks. I identified the block in which Berr lived, according to the address in the telephone book. The track started again on the other side of the square and led up a slope covered with vegetable gardens divided into allotments. There were several benches on this paved square, and I sat down on one facing the door from which Berr must come out.

"I opened a newspaper and pretended to read it, but I had no real need to keep up this pretence, for there was nobody about except some children playing together in a sandpit on the edge of the square, near an open washhouse where their mothers were working. So I was able to look about me, and I soon saw the hut in which I would have to confront the traitor Berr. There were many bits of home-made carpentering standing among the vegetable plots, but they were all simply

tool-sheds. This one alone looked as if it had been made by a builder and planned as a summer-house, with a wide casement-window. I recognized the peculiar character of Berr in the perversity with which the window had been set on the side which had no view but looked back at the two hideous tenements. It was troublesome that it was not far away from them, but I counted on being able to induce him to take a walk with me, and I had a silencer on my revolver.

"I wondered how long I'd have to wait. But the morning, which had been cloudy, suddenly cleared, and as soon as the sun was shining the Berrs came out of the block opposite me and made their way to the hut. They answered exactly to the descriptions I had been given. Berr had an arrogant appearance which was peculiarly objectionable because he was so mediocre that he should have felt obliged to be humble. His pride was generalized, it even made him walk stiffly and slowly, but it had not given him the geniality which sometimes accompanies self-satisfaction. His expression was like barbed wire. As for his wife, she was the very prototype of the bullied wife. She was a stout, short woman with a round face and flat nose, like millions of our Russian peasant women, and she had about her a goodness that can often be remarked in her kind. She had to hurry, hurry, hurry to keep up with her striding, scowling husband. When they came to the iron gate into the vegetable gardens she ran ahead and opened the heavy catch for him with a willingness which could only be described as pretty. But he stood back and let her do it, without a flicker of gratitude on his pompous face. She was talking all the time and he did not answer, and this was very touching, for it was clear that she was talking sensibly, she wasn't babbling, and she was speaking playfully and kindly. I could imagine she was using all those endearing diminutives in which our language is so rich. I thought Berr must have a heart of stone to remain mute and unsmiling.

"I watched them go up the slope, keeping to a strip of grass that ran beside the vegetable plots. Her arm had been in his, but as might have been expected he soon disengaged it and fell a pace behind her. For that coldness, however, he showed some remorse, for he put out his hand and rested his finger-tips on her shoulder, in a way which would have seemed inexpressive enough in an ordinary person, but which no

doubt counted almost as a caress from him. When they got to the hut he stood aside while she opened the door, flung wide the windows, and shook some cushions out into the sunlight. He did not offer to help her, but when she had finished he went in and sat down. She made as if she were at once going to return to the tenements, but before she'd gone a few steps she looked down on the ground, halted, dropped awkwardly on her knees, picked a sprig of some plant, held it to her nose, then struggled to her feet again, flapping her arms like a hen, and went back to the hut and handed the sprig to him. My heart began to beat very fast. I wished I was not under the necessity of bringing pain to this excellent creature.

"There was now no reason why I shouldn't carry out my plan. But my legs refused to raise me from the bench, and I began to wonder whether my whole life was not a pretence and an evasion, whether I had not adopted intellectual pursuits simply to cover up an inaptitude for action. But I turned my mind back to Kant and Hegel and received their benediction. Fitting my hand round the revolver in my pocket, I went through the iron gate. I found myself walking more and more slowly as I drew nearer the hut. I decided I wouldn't try to get Berr to take a walk with me, I would satisfy myself of his guilt in the hut and shoot him down there, and take my chance of being caught. If fate was against me, so much better for the Law of Nature. But when I came to the hut and looked through the window I did not see the man I had come to find. True, there was a man in there, sitting in a cushioned chair and holding a sprig of green leaves to his nostrils, but he looked as humble and patient as a saint on an icon. And he took no more notice of me than if he were a saint on an icon. Though I had come as close to the hut as I could without treading on the flowers growing round the walls, and though I was darkening his window, he did not raise his head.

"I gripped the window-sill and leaned right into the room. Immediately the man's expression changed, and he assumed again his air of arrogance. He lifted his head and asked, in French, 'Is someone there?' He was looking straight at me, but not at my face, at a point somewhere below my collarbone. I remained quite still, and after some seconds his proud mask melted, he again appeared gentle and abstracted,

though he continued to stare in my direction. I was incredulous and leaned farther into the hut. I took my revolver out of my pocket and then, without releasing the safety catch, I pointed it straight at him. Knitting his brows doubtfully, summoning back part of his insolence, he asked again, 'Is someone there?' And then I knew that he was not our spy, he was not a Tsarist spy, and that if a million men told me so, they would all be perjurers. For he was blind."

PERMISSION CREDITS

ABOUT THE EDITOR

ALAN FURST is widely recognized as the master of the historical spy novel. He is the author of *Night Soldiers, Dark Star, The Polish Officer, The World at Night, Red Gold, Kingdom of Shadows,* and *Blood of Victory.* Born in New York, he has lived for long periods in France, especially Paris. He now lives on Long Island, New York.

A Note on the Type

The principal text of this Modern Library edition
was set in a digitized version of Janson, a typeface that
dates from about 1690 and was cut by Nicholas Kis,
a Hungarian working in Amsterdam. The original matrices have
survived and are held by the Stempel foundry in Germany.
Hermann Zapf redesigned some of the weights and sizes for
Stempel, basing his revisions on the original design.